Praise for Charles Kenney's
The Son of John Devlin

"GRITTY AND BELIEVABLE . . . Kenney deftly deals with police corruption and the blue wall of silence."
—*San Francisco Examiner*

"[A] STIRRING POLICE THRILLER . . . [Kenney] asks all the tough questions about what makes good cops go bad, and he draws poignant studies of the weak ones, the cruel ones, and the ones who turn into bitter old men."
—*The New York Times Book Review*

"A TOUGH-GUY TALE THAT ALSO SUCCEEDS AS A TEARJERKER . . . Kenney has joined the small fraternity of crime writers whose insights into the underside of their cities are as profound as their command of character."
—*Boston Herald*

"A GIFTED NOVELIST . . . What drives this story is its accomplished portrait of a child struggling with the betrayal of parental suicide, and a most persuasive rendering of the power of faith."
—*The New York Post*

Also by the Author

CODE OF VENGEANCE
THE SON OF JOHN DEVLIN

THE LAST MAN

CHARLES KENNEY

BALLANTINE BOOKS • NEW YORK

Published by The Ballantine Publishing Group
Copyright © 2001 by Charles Kenney

www.ballantinebooks.com

ISBN 0-345-44180-X

Manufactured in the United States of America

First Hardcover Edition: June 2001
First Mass Market Edition: December 2002

10   9   8   7   6   5   4   3   2   1

1

When Gerta Wahljak glanced across the waiting room and saw Friedrich Schillinghaussen she felt a sudden pressure in her chest, a ferocious pressure that made her feel as though she had been stricken with another heart attack. When she saw Schillinghaussen, she clutched the arms of her chair, grasping them so tightly her knuckles turned white. She drew back instinctively, recoiling from him. Gerta Wahljak was seventy-eight years old, and when the color drained from her face and her eyes widened, her companion, a young woman named Amy Scott, glanced at her and thought, for the briefest moment, that she was on the verge of death. Amy Scott, a licensed practical nurse who worked for the Wahljaks, reached out in alarm and placed her hand on Gerta's forearm.

"Gerta?" Amy asked quietly. "Are you all right?"

Gerta did not respond. She sat stiffly, pushed back in the chair, silent, stricken.

Amy moved out of her chair and crouched next to Gerta, whispering to her with sudden urgency.

"Gerta? What is it?"

"To on," she said, speaking Polish. *"Ten czlowiek."* This deepened Amy's concern, for Gerta reverted to her

1

native Polish rarely, and then only when extremely agitated. Amy wheeled around and moved quickly across the waiting area to the receptionist's desk.

"There's an emergency," Amy said, motioning toward Gerta.

The receptionist, accustomed to such occurrences in the cardiac gerontology unit, glanced over at Gerta, then summoned a nurse. The half dozen other patients in the waiting area watched as the nurse strode to Gerta and began an examination.

Gerta was uncommunicative. She shook her head no in answer to a number of diagnostic questions. All the while, Amy noticed, Gerta's gaze was fixed on something across the room. Amy glanced over and saw a man who appeared to be in his late sixties, early seventies. He watched the quiet drama unfold. He was a slim man and strikingly handsome, in spite of his years, with deep-set eyes and an aquiline nose. He possessed a full head of hair, gone gray now, but it remained thick and was neatly combed back.

A nurse appeared and spoke to him. He nodded and walked with her down the hallway. He moved slowly and with a noticeable limp that favored his right leg. He soon disappeared down a corridor where various cardiac tests were conducted. Amy watched as Gerta's gaze remained fixed on this man, following him until he was out of view.

"Gerta? What is it?" Amy asked.

The nurse, having determined that Gerta was in no immediate physical danger, stood back.

Gerta closed her eyes and shook her head in great sorrow.

"What?" Amy asked.

Gerta shook her head no. She would not speak. She was brought back in her mind to the makeshift wooden structure at the edge of the place, just inside the auxiliary gate to the left. She recalled it so clearly. She remembered the dust when the drought had come in summer and the ground had turned to a powder that blew in the slightest breeze and covered everything—the jeeps and trucks and staff cars, and the barracks, of course, and the wooden structure in which she worked. The wind would blow in from the east, from out of Poland somewhere, and whip the dust up so that everything was covered, sullied. Nothing stayed clean for long.

She thought of the photograph she had kept all these years. When the photograph had been taken it had been her responsibility to insure its distribution, and she had performed her task well. And she had managed to secrete away an extra copy for herself. The photo, in black and white, showed ten men together in the officers' dining area. She had accounted for nine of the ten men in the photograph. She knew what had become of them—knew who had died in the war, who had defected to the underground, who had been placed on trial. She knew who had served time in prison, who had since died of natural causes, who had been executed. She knew the fate of all except one: Friedrich Schillinghaussen.

Gerta suddenly noticed that Amy's face was only inches from her own. She was calling out to Gerta but Gerta had not heard. The nurse was there, as well, and someone else, a young man in a white jacket. The others moved aside for him, and he shined a light into her eyes. She turned and looked away. The doctor examined her further but found nothing. Suddenly, Gerta insisted upon going home. Her appointment with the cardiologist could be rescheduled. She had no energy for that now. She wanted to get home where she felt safe, where she could lock the door and draw the shades and keep the world away.

Amy guided Gerta through the hospital lobby and out to the parking garage. When finally they reached the car, Amy, by now exasperated with the old woman's behavior, turned to confront Gerta.

"What is it, Gerta?" she asked, her frustration obvious in her tone.

"*To on, ten czlowiek.*"

"Gerta!"

"It's him!" Gerta said. "It's him. The one from the picture. The last one."

And with that, Gerta Wahljak broke down and sobbed.

Gerald Wahljak was hunched over his desk preparing questions for a deposition when Amy called.

"Gerald, she is very upset," Amy said. "We just got home and I got her into bed. She's distraught, Gerald, because of a man she's seen. I don't know whether she is hallucinating or imagining things or what but she's very upset."

Gerald sat forward in his chair and placed an elbow on his desk. "What man? Is she all right?"

"She's upset," Amy said. "Very."

"Physically, Amy, is she OK physically?" Gerald asked.

"Yes," Amy said, "she's just very worn out by it."

"Begin at the beginning. What happened?"

"We were at Mass General, waiting for her test, and there were a number of people sitting around and, suddenly, out of the blue, she became very upset, as though she was in shock in a way. She insisted that we leave, and after a physician looked her over, we did leave."

"And she was OK?" Gerald interrupted. "The doctor thought so?"

"Yes," Amy said. "Then we got into the car and she started speaking Polish, and then she said in English, 'It's him. The one from the picture. The last one.' And then she cried and cried."

Gerald took a deep breath and rubbed his eyes with his hand. He stood up behind his desk and drew another breath.

"And when you got home?"

"She was worn out. She's lying down now."

"I'll be there shortly. Just stay with her. Stay right with her."

"Absolutely, Gerald," Amy said.

"And call me in the car if there's any problem," he said.

"Will do," she said.

Gerald Wahljak hung up the telephone and sat back down in his chair. The last man. Was it even remotely possible that Gerta had seen him? Could it really be Schillinghaussen? he wondered. Alive? Here in Boston? After all these years?

Whenever it came to his mother, Gerald Wahljak was the most careful and thorough of men. Gerald was forty years old and the managing partner of one of Boston's most prestigious law firms. He was active in a variety of civic affairs and was widely respected throughout the city. He was over six feet tall, thin, fit, an accomplished amateur tennis player. He was single, had never married, and though he dated now and again, the focus of his personal life was his mother. Gerald's father had died when he was two, and Gerald had long believed that because of the trauma and loss in his mother's life, she needed him. Gerald arranged for an associate to fill in for him at the deposition and drove home.

For as long as Gerald could remember, his mother had spoken of this man Schillinghaussen. As time had passed the importance of accounting for Schillinghaussen had grown in his mother's mind. Somehow Schillinghaussen had become a symbol of the entire experience. Gerta had believed for some time that if she were able to learn of Schillinghaussen's fate she would achieve a measure of peace. That that would end it somehow. It had been years, perhaps as many as twenty since the second-last man in the photograph had been accounted for. For two decades the only face not crossed out was that of Schillinghaussen. Was it really possible she had seen him?

Gerald pulled into the driveway next to his sprawling Victorian home on a street not far from Brookline High School, a quiet neighborhood of doctors, lawyers, businessmen and -women.

"She's calmer now," Amy said, greeting Gerald at the back door. "But she's wiped out."

Gerald placed his suit jacket over the back of a kitchen chair and ascended the rear stairs to the second floor, where his mother's bedroom was located. It was in the southeastern corner of the house, a large room with high ceilings, brightly colored draperies, and a fireplace. Gerta lay on her bed, propped on pillows.

He walked quickly across the room and sat on the

edge of the bed. He reached out and held her hand, squeezing it reassuringly as he smiled at her.

"Are you OK?" he asked in a soft voice.

She nodded. But as she did so, her eyes closed and her mouth tightened, and she began to cry, then caught herself.

"I'm all right," she said, gently nudging him away. "You did not need to be coming home."

He looked closely at her. She looked tired and older than she normally appeared. Though seventy-eight, Gerta was a vital, energetic woman who took a long walk every morning, worked in her garden, and volunteered two afternoons a week at the library. But now, as she lay there, she seemed frail.

"You know you're safe here, don't you, Mom?" he asked. "Safe here with me. You know that."

She nodded vigorously. "Of course, Gerry," she said. "Oh, God, I know this."

Gerald smiled. "So why don't you tell me what happened?"

She nodded. She pushed herself up on the bed to a sitting position. She reached for a tissue and blew her nose.

"Well, we are at hospital for appointment, in waiting room and just sitting, Amy next to me and, well—" She shrugged. "I see him. Sitting that close," she said, pointing to a sofa on the opposite wall of her room.

"Him?"

"Schillinghaussen," she said.

Gerald nodded. "How can you be sure?" Gerald asked.

She looked at him with surprise, and with a slight look of hurt in her eyes. "It is him," she said, and looked away.

"I'm sorry, Mom," Gerald said, "but it seems so unlikely. Here in Boston, all of a sudden. Of all places."

She nodded. "So, crazy old woman she sees things now, is this what?" she said.

"No," he said softly. "But sometimes we see things that, you know, aren't exactly what they seem."

She turned her head to the side and gazed out the window at the red maple in the yard. "Are you knowing me to be hysterical woman?" she asked.

"Of course not," her son said, meaning it.

"Then look at me," she said. "Listen to what am I saying to you. I see Schillinghaussen today. With these two eyes. With these eyes I see him."

Soon, Gerta was asleep. Shortly after dozing off she had cried out for Gerald. He had gone to her room and comforted her and given her a sleeping pill. She was now in a deep sleep.

For a time as she slept, Gerald sat on the sofa in her bedroom, ready in case she should wake again in fear. After a while, Gerald went to the desk in the corner of her room and began going through the drawers. And there, in the bottom drawer, in a large manila envelope with string wound around the clasp, was the photograph. Gerald removed the picture, went downstairs to the kitchen, and laid it on the table. He and Amy bent over to study it. The picture was cracked, but clear enough. Ten men, all thin and appearing fit. In the photo, three of the men wore the uniform of the Schutzstaffel, the SS, their tunics unbuttoned at the collar. Of the remaining seven men, three were in suits, their ties loosened or removed entirely. The men seemed tired. Two of the men in the picture were smiling, the remainder merely looked into the camera lens, their mouths set tightly, their eyes straight ahead. All of the men in the photograph, save one, had lines from a wax pencil drawn through them. On the back of the picture, in Gerta's tiny handwriting, was the name of each man. Through the years, Gerta had checked off each one as she had learned of his fate.

Gerald studied the picture now, gazing carefully at each of the faces, searching for the look of pure evil that these men embodied. He found the look in several of the faces. In three of the men there was a sneering arrogance, a look of condescension. The others, for the most part, appeared haughty, their heads raised a bit too high, their chins thrust forward too far.

Friedrich Schillinghaussen was in the back row, at the far left end. While the others stood shoulder to shoulder, Schillinghaussen stood slightly apart. He was taller than the others, a man who appeared to Gerald to have an air of the aristocracy about him. His jaw was square, prominent, and his nose, like the beak of an eagle, was flanked by eyes with an intense gaze. Gerald stared at him and wondered, What sort of man was this?

2

At 5:40 A.M. David Keegan closed yet another file folder and placed it on the stack to his right. Keegan reached to his left, took the next file from the stack, and laid it in front of where he sat. He opened the file and scanned the incident reports inside, replaced the papers, closed the file and slid it to the right, placing it on top of the folder he had just reviewed. Throughout the night Keegan had repeated the process how many times? Two hundred? Five hundred? He did not know. During the past seven months sitting at this same Steelcase table in this same dusty warehouse he had reviewed how many files containing how many pieces of paper? Ten thousand? Twenty thousand?

The files had been stashed here in the top floor of a red brick warehouse in South Boston; tens of thousands of files representing Boston Police Department incident reports from 1952 to 1963. The warehouse had been leased by the police department with the intention of turning it into a records center, but the capital budget that called for renovation had never been appropriated. And so the records had been delivered by the truckloads and stored haphazardly in boxes, file cabinets, and trunks that were strewn about the top floor. There was no pattern, no organization or even the pretense of one. Files containing millions of pieces of paper randomly strewn about.

This dusty old brick warehouse had become a second home of sorts. Keegan had spent countless hours here, searching. He had come to think of the warehouse as a kind of collective memory, this cluttered area that housed so much information, so many details of the past. It contained memories of the mundane, memories of heroism and heartbreak, of lives wasted, shattered, ruined and saved. It was all here, nobility and savagery, loss and redemption, all of those things in which we glory, and all of those things that we try to repress. It was all here buried away. He sought just one bit of information, just one sheet of paper, perhaps a photograph, a clue that would help him understand what had happened. He was oddly comfortable in this place. He had always been comfortable in libraries, in places where records were held, places where a certain amount of diligence enabled one to piece a story together.

Keegan got up from the table and stretched. He walked slowly to the far corner where he went into the bathroom and leaned over the sink and splashed cold water on his face. Keegan looked in the mirror and saw the overnight growth, the dishevelled black hair, the weary eyes with dark circles, heavy lids. David Keegan had a thin, angular face, with a slightly too-large nose, a prominent jaw, soft blue eyes, and thick black wavy hair. He was a nice-looking man, not particularly handsome, but pleasant enough. He was over six feet tall and physically fit. When he was well-rested, Keegan looked five years younger than he was, his eyes bright and lively.

Keegan saw that the paper towels had run out, and he was forced to dry his face and hands with toilet paper.

He walked across the fifth floor to the rear of the building and stopped just before entering the stairwell. He looked out the window down at a rotting tugboat listing in an oil-soaked channel. Beyond the channel lay Boston Harbor and beyond that, the open ocean. Keegan looked out across the harbor to the horizon. He wished he did not feel compelled to be in this building, to sit among the countless boxes and decades of accumulated grime. He wished he could walk out the door and forget it; go and concentrate on his work. He wanted to be able to turn his energy more to the task of becoming the next United States attorney for eastern Massachusetts. He knew he was qualified, knew he would do a good job, was certain that if he was given the chance he would shine. But he had been distracted of late, and he wondered whether his boss had noticed. Had Keegan lost a bit of his edge?

David wanted to be able to walk out the door and leave all the files behind, go see Diane and luxuriate in her presence. He wanted to be able to sit back and spend time with her without his mind being tugged at and his attention pulled back here to this place; this place that so jealously guarded its secrets. He wanted to be free of it so he could go to her, and say, "I love you, Diane, more than anything and I want to be with you. I want us to be together. To make a life together."

He imagined her in his mind. Diane was forty-three years old, five feet six inches tall with a slim, athletic build. Her hair was dark and thick and full, worn just off her shoulders. She was strikingly pretty with deep-set eyes, large and round, dark and alluring. She was an accomplished lawyer; a successful trial attorney with an enviable record in complex civil matters. And she was a well-respected professor of law at Boston College.

He cared a great deal for Diane, yet their relationship had cooled. She had grown impatient. He did not blame her. Initially, she had been supportive of his quest for the truth; of his search. But over time it had grown tiresome as it intruded into their lives. Many had been the evenings and weekends when he had been unavailable to her. There had been weeks when he had spent more hours in the warehouse than he had in either his home or his office.

They had talked about it; discussed the idea that the past had a place in one's life, but not a preeminent place. The past was surely a character in the drama of any person's life but to permit it to take center stage—Diane thought that a mistake. In theory, Keegan agreed. In theory he agreed with almost everything she said. He, too, wanted to spend more time with her. He, too, wanted to make it work. He, too, loved her, wanted to be with her.

But he could not help himself. He felt compelled to search.

He wanted to ask her to marry him, but he could not bring himself to do it. He knew she would say no. He knew that he would have to convince her that he was ready to move forward; ready to free himself from the past so that the ghosts could not come back and haunt him; haunt *them*. He was not sure whether he was ready to escape the past, but he did not want to lose Diane.

He looked at his watch and saw that it was nine minutes past eleven. He set noon as his deadline for the day. He would search until noon and then go home to sleep for six or seven hours before returning once again. His great fear, of course, was that the incident report for which he searched was not there; that it had been among those that had been lost or destroyed. He knew it was possible that he would search every file in this vast room and find nothing, not a shred of useful information. But he persisted nonetheless.

At a few minutes before noon, David Keegan opened a manila file folder and saw that his fingers, filthy from having sifted through so many dusty sheets of paper, left a smudge mark on the edge. When he opened the file and saw the name at the top of the incident report, saw that it was what he had been searching for so diligently, so desperately, his heart pounded in his chest, thumping so hard that, for a moment, it frightened him. His stomach seemed to contract in a sudden wave of nausea and his vision, for the moment, grew blurry.

Keegan pushed back from the table and took a deep breath. He pushed his hair back from his forehead and, for a moment, shut his eyes. Then he leaned over the table, his elbows spread to either side, and he looked down at the single sheet of paper. And he read:

INCIDENT REPORT: POLICE DEPARTMENT, CITY OF BOSTON
   July 29, 1954
   Patrolman Flaherty, Unit 3
   District Five
2203 hours unitt 3 responded to report of motor vehicle accident with PI, 600 block Belgrade Ave., Roslindale. Confirmmed upon arrival PI. Chevrolet sedan (vehicle #1), grayy, Mass. plate 017-311, struck utility pole. Travelling north, vehicle in question sideswiped by Oldsmobile (vehickle ##2), Mass. plate 497-662. Vehicle #1 out of control and stuck utility pole at in-

tersection of Newberg St. resulting in PI. Responses
from BCH and Boston Ambulance Squad. Passenger
Mrs. Jeanette Keegan transported by Boston Ambu-
lance Squad to Faulkner Hospital. Passenger Mr.
Richard Keegan transported by BCH unit to Faulkner
Hospital. Passenger Richard Keegan admitted to
Faulkner. Passenger Jeanette Keegan expired 2251
hours. Vehicle towed to city salvage lot, Frontage Road.,
South Boston.

David Keegan was perfectly still. The room was silent.
He rubbed the sweaty palms of his hands on his chinos.
For seven months he had searched and here it was. He
read the sheet of paper again. Then again. A jumbo jet on
approach to Logan roared nearby, but he did not hear it.
His breathing slowed down and his stomach eased. His
vision was clear.

He took the report, the flimsy sheet of onionskin on
which it had been typed, and carefully placed it in both
of his hands and set it to one side. When he did so, he
saw that beneath the report the file folder contained two
black-and-white photographs. One picture was of the
car from the front. It showed the windshield smashed, a
gaping hole, the steel of the hood crumpled like a dis-
carded milk carton. The second photograph was shot
from the back of the car and seemed to be designed to establish the angle at which the car struck the utility pole.
In the distance, thirty feet beyond the car, a police cruiser
was visible, the camera's flash reflecting brightly off of
something. Both pictures bore the stamp BPD PHOTO on
the back.

Keegan felt an extraordinary sense of calm. He sat in

the quiet and still of the moment, reflecting upon what he held in his hand. He believed it gave him a chance to learn the truth.

He placed the sheet of paper and the two photographs back into the file folder, then slumped back in his chair. He uttered a silent prayer. He sought only the truth. And he believed, as he clutched the file folder, that he would soon know the truth. He felt sure of it.

He bowed his head as his exhausted body experienced a feeling of calm, and he said aloud in a soft voice, "Thank you, God."

3

"The deterioration is more severe than we'd anticipated," said Carl Felz, chief of cardiology at Massachusetts General Hospital.

"Meaning what, exactly, Carl?" Sophie Naumann asked.

"Meaning we've got to go in and do some repairs," he said. "Two valves, possibly three, need replacing."

"But Carl, at Freddy's age . . ."

"Sophie, at Freddy's age the risk is heightened, but I have confidence we can handle this," Felz said. "There are some very nice new techniques that will reduce the trauma to his system. But I have to tell you it's not as though we have a lot of options."

"What about angioplasty?" she asked. "Didn't somebody mention something about that?"

"The issue then was opening up blocked arteries," Dr. Felz said. "The problem now is weakened valves. It's apples and oranges, Sophie."

She sighed and Dr. Felz sensed her distress.

"Sophie, I am confident that this is the right course," he said. "I really am." And he did believe that, though he also knew that Freddy's condition was such that if he did not have the surgery he faced the almost certain risk of a

17

heart attack in the near future. Carl Felz had known Sophie Naumann for twenty years. They had been on the
board together at the National Jewish Council, and for
five years Carl had been Freddy's cardiologist. As close
as he was to Sophie, however, Dr. Felz did not want to
put the terms as starkly as life or death unless he absolutely had to in order to persuade Sophie that the
surgery was necessary.

"He needs this, Sophie," Dr. Felz said. "He *needs* it."

"When?" Sophie asked.

"Next week," the doctor said. "Wednesday morning.
I want David Crage to do it and he has to work out a
scheduling conflict."

"Oh, Carl." Sophie sighed. "It's hard getting old, isn't
it? Anyway, I'll talk with Freddy tonight, but why don't
we plan on Wednesday."

"Fine," Dr. Felz said. "And Sophie? Have faith. He's a
strong man."

She managed a small smile as she nodded her agreement.
Yes, of course he was. A very strong man. Freddy Schiller
was, in fact, the strongest man she had ever known.

She placed the phone down and walked across her office,
a large, airy room flooded with sunlight, furnished in
shades of peach and a light green. Her desk was at the
head of the room, and next to it was an IBM personal
computer on which she did her writing. Adjacent to the
desk there was a small sitting area that included a love
seat and an easy chair separated by a coffee table. On
one wall was a fireplace that she kept lit most days
throughout the winter. Set in one wall of bookcases was
a sound system. Sophie went to it and placed a Bach CD
into the machine. Near the bookcase there was a round

table covered with chintz draped to the floor, a table crowded with a dozen photographs, most of them in simple, sterling silver frames. These photographs told the story of Sophie Naumann's life, at least the most recent decades. All of the photos, save two of her parents taken decades earlier, were in color, and the vast majority of them had been taken within the past ten years. There were numerous photographs of Sophie and Freddy's only child, Diane, and many pictures of Diane's two children, Christina, fifteen, and Jeffrey, thirteen.

These photographs brought a smile to Sophie's face. She picked up one taken on Cape Cod at a home they had rented for the summer. Diane and the children had spent nearly the entire time with them, for it had come on the heels of Diane's separation from her husband. It had been a difficult time for Diane. The photo showed Christina and Jeffrey on the beach, sitting side by side, half smiling.

Sophie put the photograph down and picked up another, a five-by-seven-inch picture that had been taken a few years earlier on her own wedding anniversary. They had celebrated with a quiet dinner at home with Diane and several close family friends. In the picture, taken by Diane, Sophie and Freddy were captured by the camera looking into one another's eyes. Their faces were creased and lined, the faces of handsome old people, but on those faces was, if not quite a look of wonder, then something close. A look of happiness and contentment. Of love. How fortunate I am to have you, to be with you, they both seemed to say.

Sophie gazed at the photo for a moment longer, then returned it to its place. She walked to the window of her office and looked out onto the rear of her property. The

house, a spacious stucco structure that resembled something out of the French countryside, was set in a secluded
part of South Brookline. She and Freddy had moved here
from New York just five years earlier to be near Diane
and the children. Both Sophie and Freddy had sensed
trouble in Diane's marriage then, and they had wanted to
be nearby to support her in any way they could.

They had purchased this particular house because it
afforded such privacy. While Sophie was a public person,
Freddy was an intensely private man. In New York, he
had been comforted by the city's cloak of anonymity. He
liked this house for the sanctuary it afforded. It was a
private space of an acre-plus, with no other homes visible from theirs. In the front of the house there were large
hedges and a grove of trees fronting a quiet street. The
property was surrounded by a mixture of pine, white
birch, and oak. Directly off the back of the house was a
flagstone terrace overlooking a garden and lawn.

Freddy Schiller spent many hours sitting on the terrace, an easel placed before him, painting various scenes
from the yard. As Sophie looked out, she saw him seated
at his easel, dabbing a brush in some paint, and then
carefully stroking it onto a sheet of textured paper. She
glanced back down at the anniversary photograph and
vividly remembered that evening. It was the year of his
first heart attack and she had been feeling particularly
vulnerable. The night of their anniversary they told old
stories about their life together in the early days. They
were careful not to go back too far, for Diane was there,
and the distant past was not something they discussed
with anyone. Not ever.

Sophie recalled that at the end of that night, she and
Freddy had gone up to bed, and there, in the quiet and the

darkness, they had embraced. She had spoken and tried to articulate her feelings, and it seemed that she had talked for a long time, yet she had not felt that she had succeeded at conveying what was in her heart. And then, when she had finished, there had been a long pause before he had said to her, "I have always loved you. I will always love you."

And he had said nothing more. She looked down at him now and felt a surge of emotion for him. She thought often of his words, of his love, for it was a love that had defined her life. She thought of the call from Dr. Felz and she sighed. Why, she wondered, when life seemed so complete in a way, so contented, did such realities have to intrude?

Frederick Schiller tried not to think of the past, but on this day, he was drawn to it. His eyesight was not what it once had been, but, still, it seemed to him that the woman in the hospital had been staring at him.

He looked out over the yard and tried to measure in his mind the late afternoon shadow so that he could get it right in his painting. He painted so slowly these days that he often found himself with lengthening shadows that threw his work out of balance. It annoyed him not to be able to get it right. His talent as a painter was modest, at best, yet working with paints and brush relaxed him as nothing else could. Painting focused his mind in the purest way and freed him from the distractions and intrusions of daily life. Whenever he painted he invariably finished up feeling refreshed and invigorated.

He gazed down toward the back of the yard and was unsure where the dark spaces between the trees ended and the shadows began. He set down his brush and got up from his chair. He walked slowly across the lawn, limping as he went, not terribly, but noticeably. There was not pain in his leg anymore so much as discomfort. It had been so long since the wound occurred that he was completely accustomed to this method of walking. He looked closely at the trees and saw where the shadows began. He walked back to his place and sat down.

"Freddy, that looks wonderful," said Sophie, who appeared on the terrace. She studied the picture and nodded. "Very calming," she said.

He frowned. "I don't know," he said. "The shadows aren't quite right."

"Oh, the shadows again," she said, needling him. "What's your preoccupation with the shadows? Nobody notices whether they're exact."

He shrugged. "I notice," he said.

She handed him a glass of iced tea and set a glass of white wine for herself down on a table. She took a seat in a lawn chair next to him.

"Shadows or not I like it," she said.

"Thank you," he said. "I guess I do, too."

Sophie's accent was all but gone. Every now and then there was a trace of guttural German, but in the years since she had left, the accent had steadily worked its way out of her speech. That was true to a lesser extent with Freddy.

"Carl called," she said.

There was a brief silence.

"Surgery?" he asked.

"How did you know?" she asked.

"I heard the residents talking," he said.

"Well, Carl says you need it and he has scheduled you for next Wednesday morning," she said. She looked at him as he frowned and then nodded.

He forced a smile. "If it has to be done, it has to be done," he said.

He smiled at her and reached out to hold her hand. "It'll be all right," he said. "I'm a tough old bird."

She was suddenly misty-eyed, and she wiped a tear away with the back of her hand. "I'm sorry," she said, feeling foolish. At a time when she should be supporting him it was the other way around.

He laughed. "No, no, this is good," he said. "This is wonderful. I'm glad you don't put up a false front for me. You pamper me too much."

She sipped her wine and looked out over the garden. It was still warm as late afternoon turned to early evening.

"Carl is lining up David Crage to do the procedure," she said. "He's supposed to be very good."

His look was serious now. "Darling, I'm fine about it," he said. "Truly, I am. I know that if Carl wants me to have it then I must need it. And if I need it, well?" He shrugged.

She studied him closely. "So then why do you seem troubled?" she asked.

He took a deep breath. "Oh, you know, I'm concerned about Diane."

"But she's seemed OK to me lately," Sophie said.

"I worry that she's lonely," Freddy said. "I'd like her to settle down and be with someone. She's been seeing quite a bit of David Keegan and I hope that works out."

Sophie frowned and pursed her lips. "I don't know," she said. "I'm not sure that's going very well."

"This obsession of his?" Freddy asked.

"After you went to bed the other night Diane said she thought he has really lost perspective," Sophie said. "That he was so preoccupied with this thing he was doing involving some sort of records search—I don't fully understand it, frankly—that she was wondering about his judgment."

Freddy shook his head. "That's too bad," he said, sounding genuinely sorry. "Those two are such a good match."

"If only they knew it," she said, smiling. "Really, though," Sophie continued, "Diane seems lonely to me some of the time. But lonely is better than tormented, as she was when the dreadful man was still in the picture. And I think she treasures the moments alone with the children so much." Diane's husband had been a cold, self-centered man. Early in the marriage he had been involved with another woman and Diane had been the last to know.

"I just want her to be happy," Freddy said, a mantra he had repeated thousands of times through the years. The truth was that Freddy worried far more about Diane than Sophie did. Sophie understood that Diane was a woman of considerable strength and determination. Like Freddy. Some daughters were inextricably bound to their mothers, others to their fathers. Diane and Freddy had been inseparable since she had been a little girl, since her stuttering had emerged. It had been so bad that through the early grades there were years when Diane refused to speak in class. When Diane did speak—privately to a teacher or in an after-school activity—it was so humiliating and difficult for her that she would come home more often than not exhausted, crying. But she had battled it, fought it, and over a period of decades she had conquered it.

"Let's call her and tell her about the operation," Freddy said. He knew how upset his daughter became when she did not receive family news promptly. Sophie fetched a portable phone from the kitchen and handed it to Freddy. Sophie watched him as he dialed Diane's number and saw his face brighten, saw his eyes widen with joy when Diane came on the line. Freddy was very direct: he told her about the operation and tried to calm Diane's concerns. After a moment, he rang off.

"She's on her way," Freddy said.

Sophie nodded. She knew that was precisely what Diane would do—drop whatever she was doing and rush to her father's side.

"Let's have dinner together," Freddy suggested.

"Let's," Sophie agreed. They sat quietly for a time as the shadows grew longer and the light softened into evening.

Freddy was sitting very still, gazing off, his mind's eye fixed on some point in the distance. As he gazed back out over the garden she continued to watch him closely, and it was plain to her that there was something else troubling him. After more than forty years together she had an uncanny knack for sensing his moods, for detecting even slight shifts in his emotions.

"What is it, Freddy?" she asked.

He shook his head. "Oh, it's strange," he said. "I had an odd experience yesterday at the hospital."

She cocked her head to one side, an expression of concern. "Oh?" she said.

"I was sitting in the waiting room before the stress test and there was this woman," he said. "I had just arrived, and they were preparing the machinery, and so for a couple of minutes I sat in the waiting area. And this woman, quite elderly, seemed to look at me very strangely across the room. Well, not really across the room but ten or fifteen feet away, far enough so that my eyes might have betrayed me. Anyway, she seemed to stare at me, very intensely. And then she seemed suddenly to fall ill."

Freddy Schiller stopped and knitted his brow. He turned to his wife with a look of concern.

"It frightened me," he said.

Sophie Naumann was taken aback by this for never before in his life had he ever acknowledged to her that he had been afraid of anything. Sophie could think of only two things that could possibly strike fear in Freddy's heart. One was if something were to happen to Sophie. She knew that their love was such, that his dependence on her and need for her—that his adoration of her—was such, that the prospect of losing her could terrify him. But there was no obvious possibility of that. Sophie was as fit as could be.

No, thought Sophie, the only thing that could scare Freddy like this was the past; the possibility that their secrets from long ago might be unearthed. Sophie feared it as well, of course. And she feared what it might do to them, for Sophie had long believed that the only real threat to the tranquility of their lives lay with the possibility of revelations from the past.

She tensed. She turned slightly away from Freddy, a shift that was almost involuntary, instinctive. Suddenly, she had a powerful sense of foreboding. She sensed what lay ahead and it was what she had feared for nearly a half century. For decades she had been past the point of believing that anything could seriously threaten what she and Freddy had together. But that had been hubris, she thought. She looked at her husband. For the moment, she said nothing.

4

David Keegan pushed open the door to his father's room and saw Dick Keegan propped up on the bed, gazing openmouthed at a boxing match on ESPN. Dick Keegan shifted his eyes from the screen and turned to face his son. He squinted and hunched forward in an effort to see who had entered his room.

"How are you feeling, Dad?" David asked.

"Davey!" the old man said, his tired eyes suddenly bright and wide, his spontaneous grin revealing his missing upper plate. Dick Keegan was seventy-four years old, a once beefy man whose bulk had been diminished by prostate cancer. With wisps of white hair going this way and that, he was an unkempt, unwell old man.

David stood by the bed. "So how's it going?" he asked.

The old man shrugged. "What the hell, kid, I'm still here," he said. "They came in today with that tube and that's not too much fun. New guy, colored doctor with an accent. He came in and looked me over with some others I'd seen before. But he was new. They didn't tell me anything, though."

"You look better than yesterday," David lied. "You've got some color back."

27

His father's face brightened. "Yeah," he said, "I do feel a little better as a matter of fact."

"Great," David said.

"So what are you waiting for?" the father said, nodding toward the book on the bedside table. This was part of their nightly ritual, a quiet time when David would read to his father, whose eyes were too weak to last more than a couple of pages. Some evenings David would read stories from the sports section, but usually he would read a chapter or two of a mystery or a western. On this night, they were halfway through an English mystery set at a racetrack. The reading soothed his father, David knew. One of the nurses, in fact, had discovered that it actually helped to lower his blood pressure.

"I think it's the stable boy, by the way," the father said.

"Could be," David said. "But my eye's on the jockey."

And so David Keegan sat in the chair next to his father's bed and read in a deliberate, animated voice. His father lay still, listening carefully, every now and then muttering to himself, or expressing surprise about some turn of events. After a chapter, David set the novel aside and his father switched on ESPN and the taped Mike Tyson fight.

"I'll tell you, that boy could punch when he first came up." He shook his head in amazement. "Jesus. But he was trained by Cus and Cus coulda trained a baboon to slip a punch." Dick Keegan snapped his head to the side and stared intently at his son. "Cus is dead and gone now," he said.

David nodded. "Some time ago," he said.

"Shit, I knew Cus," his father said, smiling. "I knew Cus on a personal basis." He smiled and nodded.

David smiled in response, knowing, of course, that his

father never knew Cus D'Amato, or half of the others he claimed to have known "on a personal basis" at some time in his turbulent life.

Dick Keegan motioned toward the fighter on TV, and said, "I think he's gone soft, to tell you the truth. I wouldn't want Cus hearing this but I think the high life has gotten to him."

"I don't know," David said, gazing up at the tube where Tyson was driving savage blows into the body of a soon-to-be-unconscious opponent. "Looks pretty sharp to me."

His father's eyes narrowed as the muscles in his face tightened. David knew this look, knew it better than any expression by any other human being. It was a look he had known since he was a child, for through the years it had preceded terrifying flashes of anger from his father.

"This is the fight game, though," Dick Keegan said, his jaw clenched. "This is the fight game, not some bull-shit law school. Right?"

David saw the intensity of his father's gaze, recognized with chilling familiarity where, under the worst cicum-stances, this might lead. He felt the anger rising in his chest, felt the urge to fight back. Yet as soon as he felt it he fought to repress it, struggled to remain calm, not to challenge his father in any way. David slowly nodded his agreement, and said in a calm voice, "You're right, Dad."

His father responded with a tight, curt nod. "You handle the book work and I'll cover the other, OK, chief?"

"Deal," David said.

Dick Keegan's life had been characterized by a con-frontational manner, by a temper that flared with fright-ening speed, by an inability to let any slight, real or perceived, pass without a response wholly out of proportion to the offense. As a child, David Keegan had seen his father in shouting matches with neighbors, in fistfights at Little League games, on subway platforms, at the grocery store checkout counter. Dick Keegan had always, somewhere deep within his angry heart, been something of a madman.

"Sure, Dad," David said good-naturedly, knowing that appeasement and retreat were the only chances—though hardly guarantees—for peace and calm. His father did not acknowledge David's response, but instead returned his attention to the boxing match, which was in its final stage, a round during which Tyson was charging straight ahead, not even bothering to bob or weave, for his opponent was now on queer street, rubber-legged. Tyson hammered the man with three quick left-handed jabs and then, suddenly, so quickly it was startling, he drove home a right uppercut that snapped the opponent's head back and the man crumpled to the canvas. Tyson stood over his prey momentarily before he was shoved to the neutral corner by the referee.

Dick Keegan smiled and looked at his son. "Kid's an animal," he said.

David expected a discourse now on Dick's fighting days, his Golden Glove championships in the middleweight division and his subsequent professional career of seven fights in a two-month period: four wins, two defeats, and one match that ended with a wild brawl that spilled out of the ring and involved the cornermen for both fighters as well as friends, relatives, and spectators. It had been initiated by Dick Keegan, naturally, and for his efforts he had been suspended by the Massachusetts Boxing Commission. After that, other promoters wanted nothing to do with him.

But, to David's surprise, there was no mention of Dick's pugilistic career. Instead, his father whispered, "Any smokes?"

David nodded as his father expressed an almost child-like glee. David got up and went over and opened the window, then took a single Marlboro Light from his shirt pocket and handed it to the old man.

"Oh, Jesus, that's great, Davey," Dick Keegan said, pushing himself up in bed, readying himself for what would be the most pleasurable two minutes of his day. The father placed the cigarette between his lips. David struck a match and held the flame steady while his father drew in the smoke, stoking the butt so that the tip glowed bright red and the ash lengthened. Dick Keegan inhaled deeply, shutting his eyes as the smoke descended into his lungs. Then, slowly, he exhaled, and as he did so he opened his eyes and smiled at his son.

"Thanks, kiddo," he said.

David nodded. "No problem," he said. "There's another where that came from tomorrow."

They had been caught once by a nurse and scolded, and it had been David's initial inclination to abide by the rules, but he'd seen how disappointed his father had been and so he had continued to conspire to violate hospital regulations.

"I saw that article in the Herald," Dick Keegan said. "You might get the big promotion, huh?"

David shook his head. "They'll decide sometime in the next couple of months," David said. "Could be me, but it could easily be Dunbar or somebody from outside our office."

"You got a good chance though, right?" Dick asked.

David was unsure how to answer. There had been no signals from the boss, no indication who he was inclined to anoint as a successor. David suspected Dunbar would be the choice. He had been an assistant longer, had worked higher-profile cases. But David had made a strong case for himself with his steadiness, his solid judgment. David had never remembered wanting something in his professional life so badly. And yet all he could do was do the best job he could. And hope.

"Decent chance," David said. "I'd say it's decent, not great."

Dick fell silent, smoking, and David watched him blow the smoke toward the ceiling. Dick made an oval with his mouth and tried to blow smoke rings the way he had done when David was a child, but they came out ragged, shapeless streams of acrid blue smoke. As his father neared the end of the cigarette, David put some water in a small paper cup on the nightstand next to the bed. He held out the cup for his father, who took a final drag so that there was nothing left except a tiny ring of tobacco up against the filter. Dick Keegan held it out so that he could see it was gone, then, reluctantly, dropped the butt into the cup proffered by his son. There was a brief sizzle as the burning tobacco settled in the water, and then David poured it down the toilet in the bathroom off his father's room. David took an aerosol spray can from the bathroom shelf and sprayed it around the room, a piney disinfectant odor now masking the smoke.

"There was something I wanted to tell you about, Dad," David said, sitting down in the chair close to his father's bed. "You remember Diane, right?"

"The girl you brought in here to visit?" Dick Keegan said.

"Right," David said. "Well, I wanted to tell you something before I tell anyone else. Before I even talk to her. I'm thinking of asking her to marry me, Dad."

Dick Keegan was clearly taken aback. "Jesus, kid, that's great, huh. Wow. I'm surprised."

David was surprised, as well. Why had he said this? Did he really plan to ask her? Why had this just come popping out of his mouth now? Under these circumstances? Was it that he wanted to hear the idea aloud? Was it more real when discussed openly? Was he pushing himself when he knew that a certain instinct within him wanted to go off and focus on the past, never thinking about or planning for the future?

"Well, yeah, we've been very careful about keeping things between us quiet. Technically, she's not divorced yet although she's been separated for two and a half years now. But I wanted to let you know first. Before anybody else. That this is something I'm thinking about in a serious way."

Dick Keegan seemed pleased by being accorded this special status, but he also appeared confused. "She's the lawyer, the professor, that one?"

"Right," David said. "She's in private practice and she teaches at BC Law School. She's accomplished some amazing things."

"She a Jewish girl?" Dick asked.

David, knowing his father as he did, had expected the question.

"She was raised Jewish, yes, Dad," David said.

"She looks Jewish," Dick Keegan said, without animation. "She's a pretty girl, David. Very pretty girl. Very nice, too, presented herself very good." Dick paused and reflected for a moment.

"I thought something might be up when you brought her in here. I mean, I just thought something might be up."

Dick fell silent again for a long moment. "So what about church?"

"I'll still go to church, Dad," David said. "She'll do her thing on religion and I'll do mine."

"Yeah, but the kids would be Jewish kids," Dick said. "That's how it works. The mother is Jewish, the kids are Jewish."

"At Diane's age, there probably won't be kids, Dad, but if there were, they would be *our* kids," David said. "What faith we would raise them in isn't something I've ever discussed with her. She doesn't go to temple really at all. She might be just as happy to have them raised Catholic. I don't know. But I guarantee you that whatever their faith I will do the best I can to raise them so you would be proud of them."

And even as he said this David felt a tug of regret, for implicit in the way he put it was that Dick Keegan would not be around to see his grandchildren. But if Dick picked up on this he did not let on. He clicked the TV remote control and turned up the sound. ESPN was now broadcasting a stock car race from Michigan. David sat observing his father watch the race briefly, then turn down the sound as he continued to look up at the cars silently whooshing around an oval track at nearly two hundred miles per hour. His father's green hospital johnny was askew, pulled down toward his left shoulder, the right side creased against his neck. The old man's mouth was opened slightly and his chest moved slowly, steadily, up and down. In minutes, David's father's eyes grew heavy and fell shut. His head tilted slightly to one side.

David watched his father sleep, feeling relieved, for David had learned during these long months of sitting at his bedside that the most peaceful moments came when his father dozed off. For when he slept there were no flashes of anger, menace, bitterness, no wistful recollections of celebrities he believed he once knew but never did—"Mayor Curley was a family friend. A *good* friend. I knew him myself on a personal basis."—no riffs of madness, no questions about people long dead.

Some of this, David knew, would come when his father woke, but which part or parts David could not know. He hoped for pleasantness, civility, for an absence of anger and malice, but he counted on nothing. As his father slid inexorably toward death, David was ready for anything, ready to absorb any aspect of his father's madness. Whatever came his way—whether a peaceful calm or venomous assault—David had vowed that he would do whatever he possibly could to soothe and comfort his troubled father. It had not always been this way. For some years David and his father had been estranged. David had reached a point where he could no longer tolerate his father's ways; a point where his own anger and resentment at his father's mistreatment and neglect of his family had grown to such an unmanageable proportion that carrying on any sort of relationship had become impossible.

So why had he felt so powerful a compulsion to tell his father that he was considering asking Diane to get married? He supposed it was his desire to have a *real* relationship with his father; a relationship where they shared things that mattered; a relationship based on the reality of their lives rather than on a desire to keep the peace at any cost. Rather than the acceptance of a relationship with a madman purely to have some contact; to have contact when to have none at all would be too painful.

David settled back into the chair and thought about Diane. Her patience with him was wearing thin. She had been understanding about his need to try and uncover the past, but his obsessiveness concerned her to the point of alarm. And she had told him this only a week earlier. She had been very direct: either he make a sincere effort to put it behind him or she would have to move on.

"I love you," she had said, "but I can't spend my life with someone who is mired in the mysteries of the past."

He understood. He understood perfectly. Why would she take any other view? Why would she want to be involved with someone who spent his nights, weekends, and vacations in a dirty warehouse?

He had thought long and hard, and he had decided that she was more important to him than anything. He knew the truth, and the truth was that he loved her. He needed her. They could be happy together. He believed this.

Asleep in the chair in his father's hospital room, David Keegan dreams of his mother. In the dream she walks into the room to visit his father. His father is seventy-four, his current age, but his mother, in the dream, is in her early thirties. His mother greets her husband cheerfully. She is loving and solicitous in her manner, while his father is gruff, coarse. She is dressed in a navy blue skirt, a sleeveless blouse that flatter her slim figure. She wears red lipstick and some rouge on her cheeks. Her auburn hair, thick and rich, is carefully combed.

Dinner arrives, and David's mother places the tray before her husband. Dick Keegan grows furious, picking up the tapioca pudding and flinging it across the room, splattering it on the wall.

She shakes her head slowly, frowning.

"Fuckin' tapioca!" he shouts. "You should know better."

"I'll see if they have custard," she says, amiably.

"I want butterscotch!" he bellows, and he reaches out for her but she deftly pulls back.

She says, "I'll check to see what they have."

She leaves the room and reappears a moment later with three containers of pudding: chocolate, vanilla, and lemon.

Again, he shouts angrily that there is no butterscotch.

"Fuckin' bitch," he says, the words hissing out of his mouth betraying a venomous anger, a bloodlust.

"Here's custard, too," she says, producing yet another option.

But this only increases his fury. "I told you no fuckin' custard." But when he says these words he does not merely utter them. He spits them out, biting them off, spittle forming on his chin. Butterscotch comes out with the harshest of Boston accents as "buttahskoch"; custard as "custid."

"Very well," she says in an oddly ethereal tone of voice, and she disappears again and, this time, is gone quite a while. When she returns she places a dish of butterscotch pudding in front of him. He says nothing, not thank you, not anything. He, in fact, does not acknowledge her. Instead, he picks up a spoon and begins eating the pudding. When he is halfway through he spoons too much into his mouth and it gets caught in his throat, jamming his windpipe, and he suddenly appears stricken, gasping for air. She stands by the side of the bed as he frantically gestures with his hands, pointing to the door, indicating that she should fetch the nurse or press the emergency button. She does neither, but merely watches as he chokes.

"I'm kinda cold," the father said, waking David with a start. David was slouched in the chair, and when he straightened, he felt a twinge in his neck, a pain where he had slept with his head heavily to one side.

He stood slowly and felt a chill. He went to his father's bed and saw that he was covered by a single sheet. David pulled the blanket up from the foot of the bed and spread it over his father's body. Dick Keegan seemed to wake at that moment and David realized that he had been murmuring in his sleep.

"Chilly in here," David said. His father's eyes quickly surveyed the room in an effort to get his bearings. Dick Keegan pulled his head forward and squinted at his son.

"Where's your mother?" he asked.

David went to the panel by the window where the controls for the heating and air-conditioning were situated. "It's up on high," David said. "Where would you like it, on low for a while?"

"All right," his father said. "Tell me, though, where is she?"

5

Dunbar went out the back door of the Harvard Club of Boston and walked briskly across the parking lot. He turned right on Newbury Street and walked toward a large cement parking garage at the end of the block. Dunbar entered the garage and rode the elevator to the top floor, the fifth. He could see the black Toyota Camry all the way across the roof, no other vehicle around it, facing out over the Massachusetts Turnpike Extension where cars and trucks raced through the heart of the city at sixty-five miles an hour.

Hunter, an investigative reporter for the *Boston Globe*, was seated in the driver's seat of the Camry. Hunter felt full of good cheer on this day for he was about to meet with one of the very finest sources he had ever had. Dunbar was assistant United States attorney in Boston, a man with intimate inside knowledge on all federal cases in the region. Hunter watched as Dunbar strode across the pavement. As always, Dunbar looked crisp and put together. He wore a dark blue suit, well-tailored, and Hunter noticed as Dunbar approached that the lawyer's black dress shoes were polished to a high shine. Dunbar was a precise man, a man who took care with his appearance. He was of medium height and slim build and in his narrow face and dark eyes there was a feeling of intensity. A look of seriousness. Hunter, in contrast, was dressed in wrinkled chinos and a cotton golf shirt. His long hair, which he often pulled back into a ponytail, was loose and spilled over his shoulders. In recent years, the two men had developed a relationship of mutual benefit. Theirs was the kind of kinship that sometimes developed between reporters and prosecutors; relationships where each benefited by the association. The reporter got stories and the prosecutor got his view of each case particularly well-represented in news coverage.

As Dunbar approached, Hunter reached across and unlocked the passenger-side door. Dunbar slipped into the car and nodded, tight-lipped.

Hunter cocked his head to one side and returned a nod. There was a brief moment of silence and then Dunbar spoke.

"You'll have to do legwork on this," Dunbar said, "because all I have is a tip. What I'm hearing inside." He hesitated, and Hunter nodded as though to indicate that he had no problem doing some legwork.

"You know David Keegan?" Dunbar asked.

"Of course," Hunter said. "I mean, I know who he is. He's not someone I do business with."

"He hasn't helped you on . . ."

Hunter shook his head, dismissing the idea. "Never," Hunter said.

"I get word inside that he buried a case," Dunbar said. "Buried a case against a relative of his."

Hunter sat up straighter in the seat.

"That Keegan did?" Hunter said.

"That's what I'm hearing inside," Dunbar said.

"When he was an assistant DA in Suffolk. Just before he came to the U.S. Attorneys Office."

Hunter liked this. The idea of a senior assistant United States attorney burying a case—Hunter liked this very much. Corruption by the feds, within the Justice Department. Venal corruption. It was his stock-in-trade. He enjoyed nothing more than unearthing such stories.

"Buried a case . . ." Hunter said.

Dunbar nodded. "You'll have to do the checking, check the records, but there's a place down near Fenway, that Keegan's brother has an ownership interest in."

"A place?" Hunter asked.

"A club, gin mill–type place," Dunbar said with a note of distaste in his voice.

"So the brother may have a piece of it," Hunter prompted.

"The brother is involved in a place called the Leopard," Dunbar said.

"The Leopard," Hunter repeated.

Dunbar nodded.

"So he has a piece of this gin mill," Hunter said.

"And it seems as though there is a problem there, some things happening, less than savory characters, some events, and the place is cited for violations," Dunbar said. "And this happens more than once and the place is about to earn itself a suspension but somehow, the paperwork goes missing."

"Cited by the city, state?" Hunter asked.

"BPD," Dunbar said.

Hunter raised an eyebrow. This was good. Hunter was wired at the department.

"So the place is cited for violations and the license is gonna get pulled and then somehow the paperwork goes

missing and the license does not get pulled," Hunter
said. "But violations of what type?"

"You'll have to run that down," Dunbar said.

"Repeated, though," Hunter said.

"Would have to be to lose the license," Dunbar said.

"To get the ticket pulled, yeah," Hunter muttered.

Dunbar gazed out the front window of the car. He
looked down at the traffic moving past on the turnpike.
He turned and regarded Hunter.

"So this is interesting to you?" Dunbar asked.

Hunter nodded slowly, raising his eyebrows. It was quite
interesting indeed, but Hunter did not want to demon-
strate excessive enthusiasm. He could see quite clearly that
Dunbar was peddling the story out of pure self-interest.
Hunter was well aware that incumbent United States Attorney Stone planned to retire at the end of the year.
Speculation was he would soon recommend a successor.
Among the candidates were both Dunbar and Keegan.
Anything that would diminish Keegan's chances would
enhance Dunbar's. If Keegan were to be caught in a
scandal then he would be eliminated from competition.

"It's interesting, yeah," Hunter said. The possibilities
were obvious to Hunter. For an assistant United States
attorney to have intervened in such a case on behalf of a
brother would be a scandal. Corruption within law enforcement. A separate standard for the relative of a law
enforcement official. Hunter liked the story.

"But very risky," he said, frowning. "Not sure it's worth
the risk."

Dunbar's face could not conceal his disappointment.

"What risk?" he asked.

Hunter was posturing but Dunbar would never know
that. "I think it's kind of obvious in that if Keegan is the

next U.S. attorney and I write a piece that tries to kill him, you know, and he makes it anyway. I mean, what's the expression, if you're gonna try and kill the king you better succeed because . . ."

Dunbar had not considered this angle. He had expected Hunter to embrace the story with great enthusiasm, to dive right in.

"But, I mean, it's something you want to pursue, I assume," Dunbar said.

Hunter was pleased. He had Dunbar precisely where he wanted him.

"I would say at the moment no, it's not something I could really go after, given the possible downside," Hunter said. "Sorry about that."

Dunbar pursed his lips. His eyes narrowed and he looked out over the cars and trucks racing along the turnpike. There was silence for over a minute, broken, finally, by Dunbar.

"Is there a way to increase your interest?" Dunbar asked.

"Put yourself in my shoes," Hunter said. The reporter pushed his hair back with his right hand and shrugged. "I mean, I guess I'm always interested in a good hit. Something out of the ordinary. Something special. I mean . . ."

Dunbar regarded the reporter. "So if I were to bring you another story, in addition to this, then . . ."

"Certainly," Hunter said. "This is done. This is done. We could . . . yeah."

"Let me think about it," Dunbar said.

"Sure," Hunter said. "Think it through and if we can come to some sort of agreement, great, and if we can't, hey, no hard feelings."

6

When Gerald Wahljak finished telling his mother's story, a hush settled over the office of United States Attorney Walter Stone. Stone, along with his two top assistants, Theo Dunbar and David Keegan, sat silently, uncertain what to say. The grandfather clock in the corner of Stone's office, an elegant piece of polished walnut, ticked away the seconds, slowly, steadily. It was the loudest sound in the room.

"So the question," Gerald said, "is whether this is a case where a camp survivor saw a man who may be a war criminal right here in Boston. Or whether this is an elderly woman whose mind is playing a kind of trick on her. And I guess my answer is I don't know. But I know my mother well enough to take this seriously enough that I thought the right thing to do was to come here and lay this out for you. I thought you could do some sort of initial look into it and get a sense of whether there's something that needs to be pursued."

There was a tension in the air, a sense of reverence for even the possibility that the story might be true; that Gerta might have seen an official from a Nazi camp; that that official might be alive in the United States, possibly in Boston. Walter Stone shifted in his seat and glanced at

Dunbar and Keegan. Keegan had been mesmerized by the story throughout its telling, incredulous at how after all these years the horror of events a half century earlier and half a world away could come back in this time and place.

"This is very painful, I know, Gerry," Walter Stone said. "I want to say I am terribly sorry for the suffering your mother has endured. And I don't know how much it helps but I can assure you that we will do everything within the parameters of our authority to get to the bottom of this."

"Obviously, confidentiality is a top priority here," Gerald said. "Whether what my mother believes to be true is accurate or not, it really is essential that this be kept in the strictest of confidence. It would be deeply humiliating to her for this to get out in any way. You can understand that."

Stone nodded. "You have my assurance that this will be kept strictly and entirely confidential," Stone said, turning toward his assistants, who both nodded their agreement.

"I appreciate it," Gerald said. "One other point. I've asked O'Toole to look into it. Check with the hospital, try and see whether he can ID the man." O'Toole was a former FBI agent who worked as a private detective. Much of his work was performed for Gerald's firm in major civil litigation. O'Toole's work was widely respected. "So he may come up with something."

"This will be handled carefully and professionally," Stone said. "Obviously, we'll need to sit down and talk with her as soon as possible. David will handle that." Keegan was surprised, though Gerald was not. In private, before the meeting, he had specifically requested that Keegan be the one to talk with his mother. Gerald did not know David well, but he knew him enough to know that Keegan would handle the discussion with sensitivity.

"I'd like to get it over with," Gerald said. "Tomorrow or the next day?"

Stone nodded. "We'll make the time," he said, turning toward Keegan, who nodded in agreement.

"So I'll call you later today," Gerald said to Keegan.

"I'll be here," Keegan said. "But may I ask, Gerald, before you go, whether you have an instinctive sense one way or another? Do you think your mother saw what she believes she saw?"

Gerald took a deep breath and exhaled slowly. "My mother is very sharp mentally," Gerald said. "Her eyes are not perfect but her mind is very strong. At the same time, she can be quite emotional. She has kept this photograph for more than forty years! She has been meticulous about checking off each name. With one man left, is there a sense of desperation? A sense that she must get this completed before she dies?"

Gerald paused a moment and shut his eyes briefly. "She is an intelligent woman. She is aware that her generation will soon be gone. She knows that there are many people out there who suffered in camps who will go to their graves feeling unresolved in some way. She also realizes that, for all of the work done through the years, there remains who knows how many men out there who will never, ever be brought to justice. This she cannot fathom. She believes that whatever efforts exist today by various agencies and governments to bring persecutors to justice should be increased tenfold. For soon they will escape into death."

Gerald half turned his body in the chair and was facing

David Keegan. He seemed to want Keegan to understand; to go to the session with his mother knowing what Gerald knew, or at least having some of Gerald's perspective.

"I guess I think the chances are that my mother is correct," Gerald said. "That's not to say that if you come away with a different impression I won't want to hear that. I very much do want to hear whatever your judgment is. But I think the chances are that she *did* see the last man in her photograph that day. I think the chances are that Schillinghaussen is a patient or was a patient at Mass General."

It was a chilling thought. Stone shook his head slowly, almost in disbelief. "So step one is hearing from you Gerald, which we have done here today. Step two is talking with your mother, which you will arrange for David to do in the next day or two. Step three is David comes back here, and he and Theo and I chat about what he has found, and we make a determination on whether to refer this to Washington. Either we'll think it's a serious matter and refer it, or we won't. We'll bend over backward, but you know that something we consider not serious will not get referred."

Gerald nodded his understanding.

"And if we determine it is worthy of referral?" Theo Dunbar said. "What of the man?"

Stone turned, and there was a cold look to his face as he said, "We will go out and track him down."

7

Freddy sat in the corner of the alcove, as was his custom each morning, with shafts of sunlight cutting in from behind his left shoulder and splashing across the kitchen table. Usually, Freddy could be counted on for a running commentary on world events as he read through the *Times*—how this leader had demonstrated courage, how that leader valued political posturing over all else. But not this morning, not lately. He sat silently, the only sound in the room the gentle rattle of the newspaper pages as Freddy turned them in his careful, deliberate fashion.

The fruit and English muffins he'd eaten each morning for as long as she could remember sat nearby, untouched again today, for the third morning running. Sophie stood near the kitchen counter, wearing a robe and slippers and sipping a cup of tea. She looked at the uneaten banana beside his plate, at the muffins and preserves, untouched.

"Can I get you an egg, Freddy?" she asked, cheerfully.

He cocked his head. "An egg?" he said, as though she had suggested something outlandish.

"Why don't I poach an egg and put it on a nice piece of wheat toast," she said.

He frowned, seeming half puzzled, half annoyed. "When was the last time I ate an egg?" he asked.

"Not in a while, but that doesn't mean you can't eat one today, Freddy," she said.

"The doctor says I should avoid eggs," he said, returning his gaze to the newspaper.

"Freddy, really," Sophie said, her tone light, "I don't think that an egg or two would kill you."

Freddy turned from the newspaper and glanced across the kitchen at his wife. His lips were pursed and she could see he was gripping the newspaper tightly.

"I don't want an egg, thank you," he said crisply.

"I was just trying . . ."

"I said I don't want an egg, thank you," he said, sharply. "Jesus . . ." she heard him mutter to himself.

Sophie was stung by his tone. Freddy so rarely snapped at her or anyone, so rarely evinced ill temper. As he had aged he had grown somewhat moodier, but not markedly so. And he had been so reasonable and calm through the years that she could summon from memory each incident of major discord between them.

Sophie glanced down into her cup of tea and stood very still. I should turn around now, she thought, and quietly walk up the stairs to my office. I should go there and close the door and focus on my writing, or I should catch up on my reading, or I should simply sit and meditate, clear my mind and permit it to relax. Perhaps, she thought, if I start to walk out of the room Freddy will call after me, stop me from going, offer an apology, an explanation. But, no, she thought, he would not do that, for his instinct now, she knew, was to retreat, to hide, to find a shell, a place he considered a safe haven and go there and barricade himself within.

"So tell me about this woman at the hospital," Sophie blurted.

Freddy stopped reading. Slowly, carefully, he closed the paper, folded it, placed the sections in the correct order, and set it down on the table. He then leaned forward, his elbows on the table, his chin resting on his hands. He did not look at Sophie, but, instead, stared straight ahead across the alcove, seeming to pick a spot on the wall and fixing his gaze on it for concentration.

"She was very old," he said, in a tone that sounded as though he was methodically reciting facts in a legal case. "She was accompanied by a young woman, a nurse, perhaps, or daughter. I was sitting idly, not really reading the book I had with me, not looking around much, but then, at one point, I looked across at her and, I don't know, I can't be sure, but I believe she was staring at me. Staring at me in a kind of intense way, as though she recognized me."

Freddy paused and turned his head to look at Sophie. She stood by the counter, still, listening.

"She might have spoken Polish," he said. "I'm not sure. Suddenly, a nurse was summoned and then a doctor and she was examined. And then my appointment time came and I left."

"And you didn't see her again?" Sophie asked.

He shook his head no.

"And you didn't recognize her at all," Sophie said.

"No," he said, shaking his head. "But, my eyes . . ."

She nodded.

She did not know what else to say. But she had a terrible sense that this could be the moment that they had feared and dreaded for so many years.

"Freddy, what . . ."

"Damn it!" he said, slamming his hand flat onto the table and startling Sophie. "I don't want to talk about it!"

"But we need to talk about it," Sophie said in a calm voice. "We need to be prepared for whatever eventualities . . ."

She paused and watched Freddy place his face in his hands, take a deep breath, and rub his eyes with a thorough massaging motion.

"And then if nothing happens," she continued, "then we will have prepared for no reason and so be it. But if . . . if there is something we must deal with, we will be better prepared."

"We should go," Freddy said wearily. "Leave. We could go to Europe."

"And hide?" Sophie said.

"And live," Freddy said defiantly. "And maintain our dignity and not be subjected to . . ."

Sophie shook her head. "No," she said. "It's too late for that, Freddy. Much too late for that."

8

The sunlight streamed in through the large windows in the Wahljaks' stately Victorian home. It was a minute before eight o'clock on a sunny summer morning, yet Gerta had already taken a walk, eaten breakfast, and looked through the newspaper.

David Keegan rang the doorbell at precisely 8 A.M. Gerta and Gerald were ready with coffee and breakfast pastry laid out on the kitchen table.

Gerald was tense, Keegan could see. They exchanged greetings inside the front door, and Gerald led Keegan back through the hallway into the kitchen. Sunlight poured in from the direction of the backyard.

"Mom, this is David Keegan, whom I've told you about," Gerald said.

Gerta forced a smile. "Good morning, Mr. Keegan," she said. David was surprised by how diminutive she was. She seemed barely over five feet tall. He was surprised, as well, by how sprightly she appeared. He had been expecting someone more stooped and elderly.

"Good morning, Mrs. Wahljak," Keegan said. "I want you to know that I appreciate your willingness to talk with me."

She nodded crisply. "Gerald says it's necessary, so . . ."

52

She shrugged as though to say she had to do it, so she would do it. "But I've just returned from my walk, so let me have one minute if you don't mind."

She disappeared for a minute or two and then quickly returned. "I go each morning first thing to the park," she said. "You know the lovely park down this street?"

"I saw it driving in," Keegan said.

"I walk, sometimes I read, I feed the swans and geese and ducks," she said. "It is a very pleasant, tranquil place."

"Would you like some coffee?" Gerald asked.

"Please," Keegan said.

"Cream?"

"Black's great, thanks."

Gerald placed the coffee on the table and they all sat down. Keegan had brought no briefcase, no papers, no legal briefs or documents of any kind. He was dressed informally in a pair of khaki pants and a plaid sport shirt. It was a morning visit, not a deposition. He wanted Mrs. Wahljak as comfortable, as unthreatened as possible. He paused a moment and looked across the table at Gerta, who sat up straight, her hands folded on her lap. She nodded her assent. Keegan sat back, half twisted around in the chair, his arm draped over the back.

"Why don't we begin by you telling me about the photograph," Keegan said.

She seemed puzzled. "Tell you . . ." she said, then hesitated. "What am I telling you?"

"Just, you know, if you could tell me about it, how you got it, what the circumstances were, that sort of thing," Keegan said.

"Well, it is picture in the summer of 1943 within the SS headquarters at Theresienstadt," she said.

"What is it called?" Keegan asked.

"Theresienstadt," she repeated. "A camp in Czechoslovakia. And I am responsible for distributing the copies. I give them out and then left over is one more picture. I put it away for myself."

"How did you happen to be in the SS headquarters?" Keegan asked.

"This is where I work," she said. "Where I am assigned to work."

"Office work?" he asked.

"Yes," she said.

"And so a photograph was taken. Who was in the photograph?" he asked.

"The officers," she said. "It is at a dinner when officers are all together. And there is a photograph and I am told to make copies and there is an extra one and I keep it all the years."

She got up and went out of the room, returning a minute later with the photograph. She laid it down on the table, and Keegan was struck by how old it appeared. It was on thick paper, cardboard almost. It was black-and-white, of course, sepia-like tones. Though it was worn at the edges it was in excellent condition.

"This is Spengler," she said, pointing to one of the men. "He is responsible for all of the work details. The prisoners must work, and he makes sure everyone works. The Jews are in charge, yes and no. In charge of some things and not other things. Not work.

"This is Berne," she continued, moving from left to right along the bottom row. "I don't really know his job but he does nothing anyway. Lazy. He is all the time smoking and making comments about the girls.

"This is Kreuger," she said, referring to an older man

in a Nazi uniform. "He does propaganda. He is always saying we are preparing for Red Cross to come visit. Show the world how Nazis take care of Jews.

"Kastner," she said. "Quiet, efficient man. He is in charge of buildings and getting jobs done. He does work, he bothers no one.

"And this," she said, looking down at the man farthest to the right in the front row, "this is Greutel." She paused, looking down at the man in the SS uniform, his posture erect. His brow was knitted, as though having his photograph taken annoyed him. His face was narrow, his nose beaklike.

"Greutel is evil man," she said. "Very cruel. Greutel is a man who never I don't think in his life lifted one of his fingers to spare someone pain or suffering. I remember that there is the search for food. At Theresienstadt always is the search for food. The SS, of course, are having special rations. Some of the Germans, I am saying, truthfully, most of them, if the food is being left over then they give it to people. Give it to the mothers for the children. Give it to the sick.

"Not Greutel. Greutel is making the show of discarding it, but always with the broken glass, sand, whatever, so it cannot be eaten."

She moved up to the top row, gazing down at the man farthest to the right. "This is Mansbach. He is the accountant. He is asking me now and again sometimes to double-check his work. Many many reports are required about how money is spent. Ah, so many details. Useless. Sometimes, he is up all of the night working on reports. In the morning, he is bleary-eyed." She paused. "He is not so bad. He is not at all political. I think he does what he must do without any interest. Without enthusiasm.

"Vogel," she said. "Comes down from Berlin. He makes many trips. He is visit for a couple of days, a week at a time and write his reports. Census broken down by nationality, population by age and sex and so on. What the purpose is, who is knowing."

She moved next to the middle man in the second row, to a man wearing an SS uniform.

"Heidler, of course," she said. "Heidler is . . ." She paused a moment looking down at Heidler. As she studied him her eyes softened. "There is something about Heidler," she said. "He is not always so bad. Though he is not a good man." Her voice trailed off as she recalled Heidler.

"And this is Froehlich," she said, referring to the man standing next to Heidler. "He is physician. In charge of all medical facilities, although Theresienstadt included something like three hundred doctors among the prisoner population. Imagine that," she said, marveling at the number. "So many fine doctors," she continued with pride. "I am sure many would have been far more competent and successful in normal circumstances than Froehlich, but he is the chosen man in charge."

She paused and looked up at Keegan. Then she looked back down at the picture. "And this is Friedrich Schillinghaussen," she said, quietly. "He comes from Berlin for some sort of meeting. For a meeting of some kind."

"And this is the man you saw at the hospital," Keegan said.

"Yes," she said. "I am in waiting room and I see him."

"And you saw him very clearly," Keegan said. "You had a good view of him."

She rose from the table and walked two thirds of the way across the room. She stopped and turned, looking at Keegan. "This close," she said.

"And you had a good long look at his face?"

"Yes."

"And he looks as he does in the picture?"

"Very similar," she said. "Just older."

"What did Schillinghaussen do there?" Keegan asked.

She thought for a moment. "He comes from Berlin, as I say, for a meeting of some kind. I am not exactly sure why."

"So his mission at Theresienstadt . . ."

She shook her head in the negative. "I didn't know, really," she said. "Someone said something about a meeting or interview, maybe."

"How long was he there?" Keegan asked.

She shook her head. "I am not knowing this for sure," she said.

"So he wasn't there on a regular basis?" Keegan asked.

"Not that I knew of," she said.

"And you had worked in administration for a while, for a year or more, so you would . . ."

She nodded her agreement. "I would likely know if he had been there before," she said. "The camp was a very large place. Very, very large. But the offices were small. It was administered by a small number of people."

"And you generally knew pretty well what was going on," he said.

"As much as any of the Jews," she said. "Except Heidler's office was at other end, far from us. I knew nothing of what happens there. No one knows. Separate everything."

Keegan nodded. "I understand," he said.

Keegan hesitated, then addressed Gerta. "Did you know or did anyone mention what Schillinghaussen's position was?" he asked.

She shook her head. "Just that he is government man from Berlin," she replied.

"But it was not clear to you exactly . . ."

She shook her head again. "Not exactly, no," she said.

"With a particular ministry?" he asked.

She shrugged again. She did not know.

"Did you have any dealings with Schillinghaussen at all?" Keegan asked.

She thought for a moment. "Once or twice, perhaps," she said. "Very briefly."

"Do you recall . . ."

She shook her head no even before he could complete the question.

"So you knew the others—the ones who had been there for some time—you knew them better than you knew Schillinghaussen," he said.

"Certainly," she replied.

"So, Mrs. Wahljak," Keegan said, his voice soft, his tone one that indicated he was seeking help, guidance. "I fully understand your interest through the years in Heidler and in Spengler and in Berne, for example. These were men you knew. You knew of their involvement in the camp, of their inhumanity, their cruelty. But . . . well, is Schillinghaussen not . . ."

"I see what you are thinking, Mr. Keegan," she said. "But, you see, he is there, right there among all of these other men," she said, pointing emphatically to Schillinghaussen in the photograph. "He is among these men. He is part of this. You see? Do you see that?"

Keegan listened.

"You see, he is part of it all, isn't he?" she continued. "If he is not part of it all, then why is he here, Mr. Keegan?" she asked. "Tell me why, please?

"I can see you look at me and think, 'Ah, crazy old lady obsessed with this photograph. Mad woman. She is having life only in the past. Demented woman.' "

"Mrs. Wahljak, I don't for a minute . . ."

"I am finishing, Mr. Keegan," she said. "This is something that matters to me very much so, Mr. Keegan. I want it to end. With finding Schillinghaussen, it ends."

9

"Hot out?" Dick Keegan asked his son.

"Ninety-something," David said. "Muggy."

Dick Keegan shook his head and half smiled. "This air-conditioning is great," he said. "I'll tell you, I always wanted an air-conditioner for the bedroom. Remember I got the used one and it broke right away. That bastard, what's-his-name, sold it to me from down in the Square.

"I didn't do well in the heat," Dick Keegan continued. "Those hot nights and I didn't get along. Didn't bring out the best in me, I'll admit." He frowned and shook his head. David was surprised by what was for his father an unusual level of self-deprecation. "I let the heat get the better of me, to be honest."

David recalled sweltering nights in the apartment, his father sitting in his T-shirt, watching the black-and-white atop the kitchen table, sitting sweating, holding a can of Carling's Black Label against his forehead and cursing the heat.

Growing up, David had always dreaded the summer, for in summer there was no school where he could go to escape his father and the confines of the apartment. In summer, Dick Keegan would grow more pugnacious. The heat seemed to exacerbate all his tendencies—he was quicker to anger than usual, slower to forgive. David's brother Billy had inherited their father's propensity to hold a grudge for an extended period. He barely spoke to their father now and had consented to visit the old man only occasionally and then only after David's incessant prodding.

Somehow, Billy, for all of his screwups, had not disappointed their father to nearly the extent that David had. David had managed to be a disappointment to his father for as far back as he could remember. He recalled that back in Little League—where David had been a good, but not great, player—his father was often deflated by David's performance in a game. And Dick Keegan had never made any effort to hide his feeling of disappointment in his son. As David grew older, he not only didn't hide it, he loudly trumpeted it.

Dick Keegan had been in the Marine Corps, was awarded a Silver Star in World War II. He had strongly urged David to join the Corps as well, but David went through ROTC and joined the Army, where he wasn't a combat soldier, like his father, but a member of the Advocacy Corps—an Army lawyer. When David was shipped off to Germany for an eighteen-month stint during the U.S. buildup in Vietnam, Dick was openly scornful. In Frankfurt David had spent his time shuffling papers while learning to read German. His spoken German was poor, but he was able to read the language quickly and well.

Dick Keegan had followed military service by joining the ranks of the Boston Police Department. He had long since retired, but back when he had still been on the force, Dick Keegan had wanted very badly for David to follow in his footsteps. Dick had loved being on the force; he had loved the camaraderie, loved being connected to something significant, something that mattered. And he had been deeply disappointed when his son became a prosecutor rather than a cop.

It had been more than a year since David had begun to try to patch up the relationship. It had taken persistence, but he had been able to make some progress after a few months. Then eleven months ago, when his father had been diagnosed, the old man had gotten scared and had welcomed David's attention. David had been with him every day in the hospital, before and after the surgery. He'd been at home in the apartment with him, as well. And during the seven months since Dick Keegan had been in the long-term care facility, David had visited every single day.

Theirs had been a turbulent, occasionally violent relationship. But now David was determined to do whatever he could to bring a measure of comfort to the end of his father's life. When David visited, there were often long silences, periods in which David would sit in the cool, semidarkness of his father's room and merely be with him. The silence was broken this time by Dick Keegan, who asked a question that startled David.

"Have I been a good father to you, son?" he asked.

When David heard the question, he was pushed suddenly back into his chair as though the question itself carried a physical force. David was truly stunned, for his father had never exhibited any tendency to self-examination in his life.

"I wanted to be able to ask you, you know," the father said.

"Dad, jeez . . ." David said.

"I mean I . . ."

". . . Jesus, Dad, yes, sure you have," David lied. "What a question." He laughed nervously.

There was a silence in the room.

"Because sometimes I think back . . ."

"Don't," David said, quickly cutting him off. "Please don't."

What does Keegan remember about her? He remembers that she was freckle-faced. Smiling. White teeth, straight white teeth, a toothy smile. Auburn hair, thick and shiny, always smelling of lemon.

He remembers that in the warm weather, on sultry summer nights, the smoke from her Parliament would hang in the air, thick and sweet, as it drifted ever so slowly across the kitchen, over the table, and out through the window overlooking the backyard. She would stand in the kitchen, leaning back against the counter by the refrigerator, sipping tea, smoking. She would cook for him and smile lovingly as she placed his meals before him. When she would lean over, to place his bowl before him or to wrap him in a warm embrace, she would smell of lemon soap.

"Are you happy?" he asked her one evening when he was eight. They were in the car, going out on an errand. She glanced down at him and saw how very serious his expression was.

"I'm always happy when I'm with you, Davey," she said. And he nodded his satisfaction.

"Are *you*?" she asked.

He nodded again. "Definitely," he said.

She watched him out of the corner of her eye, and

blurted, "You're a very serious little guy, aren't you, Davey?"

He'd been surprised, for he had never thought of himself as serious or not serious. He just was. And to be characterized in that way . . .

She smiled. "A lot of kids like to goof off or don't do what they're told."

David knew that, of course, but it was a matter of little interest to him. He had no desire to do anything except follow the rules. He wanted to do what was asked and expected of him. It comforted him to know the rules and boundaries and to make sure he stayed within them.

"Is it bad?" he asked her.

"Is what bad?" she asked.

"Being serious," he said.

"Oh, no, no, honey," she said, smiling. "It's fine. It's good, it's very good. It'll help you get ahead in life."

He remembers that her eye was swollen and pulpy one morning and she would not go out of the house. She sat at the kitchen table, holding her cigarette in her right hand, while she pressed ice wrapped in a dishtowel against her eye. The side of her face became swollen and the skin around her eye turned a nasty combination of black and purple. After a few days there were shades of yellow as the swelling began to subside.

His father disappeared for a time after that; perhaps four or five days, perhaps a couple of weeks, he couldn't be sure. When he came back David didn't talk to him for a while. Wouldn't respond to him in any way. David vowed he would never forgive him.

* * *

David Keegan sits thinking about her, just as he has at crucial junctures throughout his life. David is forty-one years old now, and he realizes, as he thinks back, counts his way back through the years, that she was thirty-three when she died. Thirty-three! This astounds him. She was so young. So very, very young.

He tries hard not to think about it; not to have questions about it, misgivings. But he cannot help it. The doubts are there in his mind, roiling about. They recede every now and then for periods of dormancy, but they always return, as his life progresses and he is reminded of her in some way. Occasions bring back memories of her, for he believes occasions work best when there is a wholeness to life. Occasions are for complete family units, not for fragmented families, lonely, angry people.

He sits watching his father sleep and he wonders, as he has—how many times? A thousand? Many more. Five thousand? Ten? He wonders what happened. Not generally. He knows generally what happened, of course. He wonders exactly what happened. He wants to know precisely what happened and how and why. Not so much the precise model of the Chevrolet or the color of the dress she was wearing or any of that. He wants to know what she said to him; what he said to her. What was she thinking at the time, in the final minutes? In the final moment? Did she think of him? Of his brother? He assumes that's what a mother's final thoughts would be.

What, exactly, happened back there? This is what he yearns to know. He raised it obliquely with his father, of course. He received the standard explanation. Sideswiped, out of control, spinning, a horrible thud, shattering glass. She wasn't that good a driver. And then sirens. Si-*reens*, his father called them. Many sirens coming from different directions. The EMTs, the firefighters, the police.

But there are other parts of the story that can be known, he believes. He does not know all that he should know; all that he needs to know. This must be raised with his father somehow. There must be closure here.

David Keegan looks at his father, at his openmouthed, rhythmic breathing, and he is struck by the realization that his father will soon be dead.

But before he is, David must know the truth.

10

O'Toole, the private detective, called Gerald Wahljak with his report: The man's name was Frederick Schiller. He was seventy years old, retired from a small New York law firm specializing in international matters. He currently lived in a large house in South Brookline. He had moved there five years before from New York. He had a daughter and two grandchildren, who also lived in Brookline. O'Toole delivered these rudimentary facts in a straightforward fashion.

"One more thing," O'Toole said. "He's married to Sophie Naumann."

Gerald heard the name but it did not immediately register. How could it? The notion that Schillinghaussen could be married to Sophie Naumann was preposterous; beyond the imagination.

"The woman from the National Jewish Council," O'Toole added helpfully.

"That can't be right," Gerald said reflexively.

O'Toole, having no idea why Gerald was interested in Schiller, didn't find this at all difficult to accept.

"Oh, it's definitely her," O'Toole said.

Gerald turned to the window of his study and looked

out at his neighbor's lawn. He took a deep breath and rubbed his forehead with the fingers of his right hand.

"Check it again, will you?" he asked.

O'Toole hesitated. "Yeah, I'll . . ."

"Check it right away, however you can," Gerald snapped. "Check it and get right back to me."

"But what's the . . ."

Gerald cut him off. "I'll wait for your call."

"It'll have to be tomorrow," O'Toole said.

"Morning," Gerald said. "I need it first thing."

By 6:30 on Friday morning, Gerald Wahljak had jogged five miles through the quiet streets of Brookline. By 7:15 he was in his office at International Place gazing out the window from his perch on the thirty-fourth floor. He could see out over the harbor and across the water to the south shore. He could see the jets taking off and landing at Logan. It had been misty and muggy in the early morning, but now thick storm clouds were moving in over the coast. There were faint rumbles of thunder in the distance, and Gerald thought that he saw the briefest flashes of lightning far off the coast.

Gerald had sent O'Toole back to double-check, more than anything to stall for time. Gerald knew that O'Toole would not make a mistake on such a matter. In the middle of the night, unable to sleep, Gerald had gotten out of bed and walked quietly down the hall and into his mother's bedroom. She, too, had been awake.

He had sat talking with her for a few minutes, asking her about the novel she was reading; about her garden; about the health of one of her friends. He had been unable to stop himself from pretending that life continued on its normal, tranquil path. Gerald Wahljak had worked hard to construct a life that sheltered his mother from any sort of unpleasantness. She had been so scarred by the events of long ago, the loss of her parents and her brother and her sister, that Gerald had taken it upon himself to build a moat around her; to provide her with whatever she needed. He had done so with the hope that she would be able to live happily, and he believed he had succeeded. He took a deep and abiding satisfaction from the fact that his mother was a vibrant woman at such an advanced age.

But now this. This intrusion. This violation. Gerald knew what lay ahead that day. He knew that O'Toole would soon call to report that yes, indeed, the man was Schillinghaussen, and yes, he was in fact married to Sophie Naumann.

But then what? Gerald wondered. Then, he feared, events would be out of his control. He paced back and forth in his office but he could not rid himself of the sense of foreboding he had about this. He wondered what effect this could possibly have on Sophie Naumann, a woman he had much admired. The idea that she was married to Schillinghaussen was madness. But when his telephone rang and it was O'Toole, Gerald knew it was true.

After meeting privately with Gerald Wahljak, United States Attorney Stone summoned Keegan to his office. He was grim-faced in breaking the news.

David Keegan had never been so shocked by a piece of news in his life. This was Diane's father Stone was talking about! Diane's father was the man Gerta Wahljak said she saw at Mass General; was the man Gerta said was in the photo; was the man Gerta said had been one of the Germans at the camp.

It was astounding.

Stone was talking, saying something, but David was not sure what, for he had suddenly lost his ability to listen, to pay attention. He had to get to Diane! He had to help her.

". . . So if you could check . . ." Stone was saying when David interrupted.

"Listen, Walter, I have a problem here," Keegan said. "A serious problem that forces me to recuse myself on this immediately."

Stone was visibly surprised. "What is the issue?" he asked.

"I am involved with Diane Schiller," Keegan said.

"With Diane!" Stone said. "I had no idea."

"We've been very discreet about it," Keegan said. "She's been separated for two years but she's still not gotten through the divorce process. We've been very careful."

Stone got up from his chair and walked to the window of his office overlooking the greenery of Post Office Square below. He stared out the window for a minute, perhaps longer. He turned back, returned to his desk and sat down.

"I think that's the wisest course," Stone said. "I'll turn it over to Theo. In the meantime, have you filed your report on your discussion with Mrs. Wahljak?"

"I e-mailed it to you last night," Keegan said.

"Good," Stone said, "so the matter is done from your perspective."

Stone hesitated, then spoke again. "There is another matter I wanted to discuss with you," Stone said. He rose from his seat once again and went to the window. He looked outside and then looked back at Keegan. "I want to let you know, in the strictest confidence, that next week

I will be in Washington and I intend to recommend to the Attorney General, the White House, and both our senators that you be nominated to serve as my successor."

It was as though some physical force—some energy source with immense power—suddenly pressed forward, driving Keegan back into his seat. It was as though he'd been suddenly struck by some massive g force.

"My God," Keegan whispered. "I am so very honored," he stammered. "I . . . I don't know what to say . . . I'm bowled over."

Stone rose from his chair and smiled, extending his hand. Keegan got up and shook his boss's hand.

"Congratulations, David!" Stone said. "You deserve it. You've earned it. There is no lawyer in the office with a better, more balanced sense of judgment. I have complete faith in you."

"Thank you, sir, I am deeply honored," Keegan said. "I truly am. This is . . . I don't know what to say."

"You'll do very well, David," Stone said. "You'll be as solid as a rock. And while you may certainly celebrate in your own mind, I would ask that this be kept strictly confidential until I get back. I've told no one here about my decision and, as you know, there are more than a few interested parties.

"I'm sure this is tempered somewhat by the other matter, David," Stone said. "We will certainly be discreet and we will act swiftly. We will now, obviously, have to interview her father. I am fond of Diane and respect her and, as a courtesy, I intend to call her myself to inform her of this immediately."

11

Theo Dunbar walked briskly out of the rear entrance of the Harvard Club of Boston. There was an energy to his step, a spring that came with the excitement of discovery. Dunbar had a plan he was convinced could work. Information, Dunbar thought, was power.

Dunbar went right on Newbury Street and walked to the parking garage at the end of the block. He went to the fifth floor and as he emerged from the elevator he spotted Hunter's black Camry on the far wall. It was, once again, facing out over the Massachusetts Turnpike Extension. The day was cloudy, overcast, with a slight chill in the air, though Dunbar felt comfortable as he strode purposefully across the pavement. He got into the passenger side of the car and was greeted by Hunter.

"What's up?" the reporter asked.

"You said that if I were to bring you another story in addition to the one we talked about the other day," Dunbar said, "then you would consider going more aggressively on that."

"Got something?" Hunter asked.

"That's what you said, correct?" Dunbar asked.

"Yeah, I said that if . . ."

"You said," Dunbar interrupted, "that if I brought

72

you something else good then you would consider going ahead on the tip about Keegan tanking the case for his brother. Right?"

Hunter nodded. "Right," he said.

"Okay," Dunbar said. "Here's what I propose. I have a story for you. It is a very good story. An unusual story. A local story that could be in the papers for months. I will give you a jump on that story—which absolutely nobody else has even a slight inkling of—if you move expeditiously on the Keegan matter. If you will move quickly to confront him with what you know."

"Confront him?"

Dunbar nodded.

"I'm not required to get it into the paper?"

"No," Dunbar said. "In fact, you should hold off on that until a signal from me." In truth, Dunbar wasn't at all sure he wanted the Keegan matter to get published. He was afraid that such a scandal might make Stone feel as though he had to stay on in the job for the sake of stability. Besides, Dunbar thought that Keegan could be so upset and rattled by an approach from Hunter that Keegan might remove himself from contention for the position, knowing the story would gain altitude if Keegan were to become U.S. attorney.

"Yeah," Hunter said. "That's no problem."

Dunbar looked out the window, watching the traffic move along the pike. He turned to Hunter. "Does the name Gerald Wahljak mean anything to you?" Dunbar asked.

"The lawyer," Hunter replied. "Of course. Everybody knows who he is. One of the biggest guys in town. Did that hundred million dollar liability case last year."

Dunbar nodded.

"Gerald Wahljak's mother is an elderly woman," Dunbar continued. "She lives with him . . ."

"Brookline?"

". . . in Brookline. Mrs. Wahljak is a concentration camp survivor from World War II. She lost her entire family in the camps, and she herself was in one for some years and narrowly escaped death. While she was in the camp, she somehow got a photograph of all the German officers who ran the place. Through the years she has followed the fate of each man. She has checked off every man in the photo except one. For some years now there has been only one man whose fate was unaccounted for."

Dunbar paused. "You with me?"

Hunter was listening intently. "Go ahead," Hunter said.

"Last week, Mrs. Wahljak was in Mass General for an appointment. While she was there she saw the man. She saw the last man in the photo. Right here in Boston."

Hunter's eyes widened and he pulled back involuntarily. "Are you serious?"

Dunbar nodded.

"But how can she be sure?" Hunter asked. "I mean, she's old and . . ."

"She is elderly but very sharp," Dunbar replied. "Also, Gerald came to the Justice Department and we've begun working on it. The chances are very high that this is the man."

"Who is he?" Hunter asked.

"I cannot tell you that," Dunbar said. "At least not yet."

Hunter frowned.

Dunbar did not like his look, and he spoke sharply. "If you don't like the story . . ."

"No, no . . . I just would like to know . . ."

"I am giving you information no one else has," Dunbar said. "I cannot at the moment do all of your work for you. You will have to actually get off your ass and do something. But what I am giving you is . . ."

"Understood, understood," Hunter interrupted. "Look, I appreciate it. Don't think I don't. Obviously it's an unbelievable story. I mean, Nazi war criminals loose in Boston coming face-to-face with camp survivor. It's fucking awesome, no question. Jesus!"

"So you like the story?" Dunbar said.

It was fantastic, Hunter thought. "I do," he said.

"So you want to do it?" Dunbar said.

"Yeah," Hunter said. "What are the conditions?"

"One," Dunbar said, "you must attribute your information—and I mean *must*—to Justice Department sources in Washington. You must specify Washington to deflect . . ."

"I get it," Hunter said. "Otherwise you're exposed."

"Two, you must, as I said, menace Keegan about the story. That's a necessity."

"No problem," Hunter said.

"Number three, you must assure me that if anyone asks ever, our discussions never took place. Ever."

"Fine," Hunter said. "Not a problem with any of them. No problem.

"So I go to Keegan and I say I'm working on a story about him tanking a case for his brother," Hunter said. "I tell him the details I've got and get his reaction. And that's it, I don't have to get anything in print?"

"Not for the moment," Dunbar said.

"So when that is done, then I proceed with the Wahljak article, right?"

"Correct."

Dunbar, in fact, half expected that after the approach from Hunter, Keegan would go to Stone and withdraw from consideration. That would be ideal for it would make Dunbar the only logical choice to succeed Stone. And it also gave Dunbar, once he took over, a perfect issue to use to fire Keegan.

There was a long moment of silence as the two men worked through their private thoughts. As Hunter reflected on this, he suddenly grew concerned. The truth was that Hunter was prone to moments of panic and anxiety.

"I want to go right away," Hunter said. "I'm worried about this leaking. It's too hot, it's too wild not to. It won't hold long. I mean there are, what, two or three or four people in your office who know and there are at least a couple people on the Wahljak side who know and then when it gets to Justice in Washington, Christ, Theo, you're talking a dozen or more people knowing and each one tells two or three people and suddenly you've got thirty or forty people who know about it and it *will* leak out, believe me! And you're holding back the guy's name and maybe somebody else gets that and they've got the whole story and I only have a piece . . . Jesus, Theo, you've got me in handcuffs here!"

Hunter had worked himself into a lather over the worst of all journalistic fears: losing an exclusive story.

"You're not going . . ."

"You've gotta give me the guy's name," Hunter said. "I have to have the name. It's a must."

Hunter's face was flushed and he was sitting forward, in a state of agitation.

Dunbar regarded him and was pleased. This was precisely where Dunbar wanted him.

"You move expeditiously on Keegan and you'll not only get your story, but I'll give you the identity of the man also," Dunbar said. "Not immediately. And in no way can the identity go in your first story. No way. The story must be about the Wahljaks and their complaint. Understood?"

"Absolutely," Hunter said as he picked up his car phone. "What's the main number at your place?" Hunter asked Dunbar. Dunbar told him and Hunter punched in the numbers.

"Expeditiously, huh," Hunter mumbled as he waited.

"Ah, yes, ah, connect me please with David Keegan," Hunter said. "Thank you."

He waited.

"Yes, I would like to speak with Mr. Keegan, please? Dan Hunter from the *Globe* calling."

Hunter held a moment while a secretary came on the line and said Keegan was busy. "Tell him it's important. Tell him it's about his brother."

Half a minute later, Keegan was on the line.

"Yeah, listen, David, we've got to sit down and talk. There's a matter involving your brother and you and . . . well, I'll give you the details in person, but we need to sit down."

As he spoke with Keegan, Hunter glanced over at Dunbar and smiled.

12

Diane placed the telephone down and sat very still. Her heart was beating hard and fast and she was not sure of what to make of the call. Had she heard correctly? Had Stone said that someone was accusing her father of having been an administrator in a Nazi camp?

Diane sat behind her desk, her hand still on the cradled phone as though stuck to it; as though she was physically unable to let go. They wanted to talk with her father; to interview him. The United States Justice Department wanted to sit down and talk with him. Stone had been kind and sympathetic, but the message of the call was simple: Diane's father was suspected of being somehow involved with Theresienstadt and lawyers from the Justice Department wanted to interview him.

Someone is confused, Diane had told Stone. It was my mother, not my father, who was at Theresienstadt.

The accusation, Stone had said, was that her father had been there as well.

She picked the phone up and dialed her parents' home number. Sophie answered on the third ring.

"Mother," Diane said.

"Oh, dear, I'm glad you called, I wanted to . . ."

78

"Mother, I have something we need to discuss," Diane interrupted.

Sophie instantly sensed trouble. "Are the children all right?" she asked.

"They're fine, Mother," Diane said. "But I just received a phone call from Walter Stone, the United States attorney for eastern Massachusetts. Mother, the call was about Dad."

"About your father?" Sophie asked.

"Mother, an elderly woman who is a survivor of Theresienstadt has come to the Justice Department and told them that she remembers Dad as an administrator . . ." Diane's throat constricted and she had trouble getting the words out of her mouth. "I can't even say it, but she said she remembers Daddy as an administrator in this camp. Mother, she has accused Dad of being a Nazi."

"My God, Diane!" Sophie said. She said nothing more for she was working madly to try to control her breathing. She suddenly felt light-headed, as though she might pass out.

"Mother, I'm on my way," Diane said. "You and Daddy and I can sit down and talk about what we should say back to them to stop this in its tracks."

Sophie moved swiftly through the kitchen and up the back stairs to Freddy's study. He was seated at his desk, writing on a legal pad. When he looked up and saw the expression on his beloved wife's face, he knew what had happened.

Diane drove west out of Boston along Storrow Drive headed to her parents' home in Brookline. Diane was a cerebral woman, a woman well known and respected for her legal ability; for her acumen as a lawyer and law professor. She was a woman who possessed a powerful, well-ordered mind. As she drove, she willed herself to concentrate. She ignored the tranquil scene on the Charles River to her right; did not see the sailboats gliding smoothly along the water's surface. She saw only the road ahead as she worked to get her mind engaged.

Let's be rational, she thought. Yes, it was true, that a woman characterized by Walter Stone as "a credible individual" had made an accusation about her father. Yes, it was true that the United States Attorney's Office took it seriously enough so that they wished to sit down and talk with Freddy. But it was madness, Diane thought. Her father was literally the kindest, most gentle man she had ever met. He was the finest man she knew. The most compassionate, the most loving, the most decent. It was surely a case of mistaken identity. The woman was elderly and she had seen Freddy and thought he was someone else. She was mistaken, and the mistake would be recognized right away. Her father, in fact, had been a lawyer in Berlin during the war. This she knew. Surely this could be proven. He had been in Berlin, far away from any camps. Far, far away.

Diane parked in the driveway and walked into the kitchen, which was empty. She looked out the window and saw her parents sitting on the terrace. She went out the back and walked quickly across the lawn.

Both her parents rose from their seats and greeted her as she approached. She went directly to her father and embraced him, holding him tightly for a long moment. "I love you, Dad," she said softly. She repeated the gestures with her mother, then they all sat down.

She was impressed with the calmness both her parents displayed.

"Don't worry," her mother said. "We will deal with it. We will get through it. Obviously this woman is mistaken."

Sophie's words sent a feeling of wonderful relief through Diane. Of course, she thought. It was really quite simple: this was a case of mistaken identity. What could be simpler? An elderly woman believes she sees someone a half century after the fact and recognizes him? It was nutty.

"My, God, Mother, Theresienstadt!" Diane exclaimed. "This was the camp the woman was in. That's where you were. Obviously Dad wasn't there or you would have known it."

"It's madness, Diane," Sophie said.

"Craziness," Diane said. "Obviously she is simply mistaken. And that will all be clear soon enough. But to clear it up the Justice Department will send one of its lawyers here to talk with you, Dad. In essence, he will be looking to see what information discredits what this woman has to say."

"What will they ask me?" Freddy wondered aloud.

"They will essentially tell you what they have heard from this person," Diane said. "They'll say that she says she recently saw you at Mass General and that she recognized you from the early 1940s from a camp." Diane looked at her father expectantly.

"And I will say," Freddy said, speaking in a deliberate voice, " 'I am afraid this person has made an error.' I will say that I was in Berlin where I was an attorney practicing civil litigation and had nothing to do with any camp or any Nazis." He shrugged his shoulders as though to say, "and that is the story." It was a story with which

Diane was familiar. She knew all about her father's routine, humdrum life practicing law in Berlin. She knew all
about the extraordinary drama of her mother's life back
then. She knew it all. And she knew that this elderly
woman, whoever she was, had made a mistake.

Diane called David Keegan, who was waiting by the
phone.

"I assume you know about it," Diane said.

"Yes, and I have recused myself, obviously," Keegan
said.

"It's bizarre," Diane said.

"This must be very hard for them," David said. "And
for you."

"It's unsettling," Diane said. "Obviously this is something that is so contrary to everything my mother has
ever stood for, is known for. I mean . . . my God . . ."

"I can't imagine," David said.

"But you have a situation where you have an elderly
woman," Diane said, "a woman, apparently, who is quite
elderly who thinks she sees something."

"Look," David said, "if there's anything I can do . . ."

"I mean, you have a basic case of a mistaken identity,"
Diane said. "Plain and simple. These things happen. Unfortunately, in this case, there are difficult implications.
A process has been begun, unfortunately. A process that
is, I would say excessive—I mean, for God's sake, this is
something an elderly woman has *imagined*."

13

Hunter pulled into the parking lot at Castle Island in South Boston. He parked the black Camry in the far corner and walked to a bench near where Keegan was seated. Hunter pushed the hair back off of his face. He wore gray corduroy pants that hung down over his shoes, falling all the way to his heel in the back, and a brown Harris tweed sport jacket, blue shirt, and striped brown tie. His complexion was pasty.

Hunter sat down, breathing heavily. He immediately lit a cigarette. "So I wanted to get at this tip I got, you know, with you," he said. "See if . . ." he shrugged. "See where it goes."

Hunter regarded Keegan, who was sitting with his legs crossed, his right arm draped over the back of the bench. Hunter was surprised at how calm Keegan appeared. Internally, of course, Keegan was in turmoil. He could feel a dampness under his armpits.

"So I've got a tip that kind of fell into my lap, to be honest," Hunter said. "About you, as I mentioned on the phone, and your brother, also. Anyway, this tip has you looking the other way on a complaint against a gin mill your brother has a piece of."

Hunter paused, then, "Ring any bells?"

Keegan said nothing. He merely shook his head no.

"It's a tip I got," Hunter said, almost apologetically. "I've got to follow it up, man, I mean . . ." He was trying to sound as though he did not want to do this but felt he had no choice.

"It's about the Leopard and your brother Billy," Hunter said. "It's about some violations against the Leopard. About how one was handled. You recall anything like this?"

Billy had shown up at David's house late on a steamy August night. It had come during David's final month as an assistant district attorney in Suffolk County, just before he had become an assistant United States attorney. Billy had arrived without warning, accompanied by their Uncle Leo, their father's brother. Neither Billy nor Leo had worked steadily in their lives, that is, until they had gotten involved with a bar in the Fens area called the Leopard. It tended to attract a certain clientele. Soon enough it was cited by police for violations involving drug dealing, prostitution, gambling. As the violations mounted, the police issued a warning: an additional citation would mean suspension of the Leopard's liquor license. It would have to shut down for a time.

"We're asking for some consideration, Davey," Uncle Leo said.

"Give us another chance, Davey," Billy implored his brother. "Give us another shot and there'll be no problems."

Leo took his handkerchief and wiped it across his forehead, mopping up beads of sweat. The night air had brought no relief from the day's intense heat and humidity. David Keegan, in gym shorts and a T-shirt, was damp with sweat. And he was now irritated by the pleas. They wanted him to violate his oath, to jeopardize his position because they had been unwilling to abide by some basic laws. The citation triggering a suspension of the Leopard had just been written up that day. It was sitting somewhere in the DA's office. All David had to do was go and remove the piece of paper from among so many other pieces of paper and dispose of it. In the infinitely sloppy world of code enforcement, where there were two staffers to do the work of ten, there would never be any follow-up.

David regarded his brother. Billy Keegan was as tall as David, but he was rail thin, with black hair to his shoulders. He wore tight blue jeans and a black Aerosmith T-shirt. Leo was shorter, a barrel-chested, muscular man like his brother. A man less angry than Dick Keegan, however.

David looked away and shook his head as though he could not believe what was happening.

"What?" Billy said. "What the fuck's that, Davey? You can't help your own flesh and blood? What the fuck, Davey? All I'm asking is that you take it out of the pile and lose it. That's all. This one time. Never again. I swear on Ma's grave."

David Keegan was silent for a while.

"Billy, do you know what you're asking me to do?" David said.

Billy nodded slowly. "I do, Davey," he said. "I'm asking you to save my ass."

Billy had paused. "It's all on the line here, Davey," Billy said. "This is everything. I've been over the numbers. We're gone if we lose the Leopard."

Billy used his handkerchief to wipe his brow once

again, then he wiped the back of his neck, as well. His thinning black hair was damp and clung to the top of his forehead.

"The Leopard's everything," Billy said.

Billy lit a Marlboro and cupped it in his hand. He took a drag and shifted from one foot to the other. Billy was a nervous, jumpy man whose eyes darted about quickly, warily regarding the circumstances around him. He had had trouble through the years with both drugs and alcohol, but since getting involved with the Leopard, he seemed to have settled down. He had an apartment and a girlfriend, and his life, for once, seemed reasonably stable.

"It's done all the time," Billy said softly. "Guys in the business have it done all the time. It's common. Favors are done all the time. It's part of the business."

"I have to sleep on it," David said.

"Sleep on it?" Billy said.

Billy stared at his older brother, a look of disbelief on his face. "Sleep on it?" he said. "What the fuck, sleep on it?"

"I need to think it through."

"What's there to think about?" Billy asked. "All you've got to do is pull a piece of paper out of a stack and lose it. One fuckin' piece of paper. Big fuckin' deal, man."

"It's not that simple, Billy," David said.

"Oh, no," Billy had said, his voice defiant. "If you don't pull that piece of paper out of the stack then you might as well take a gun and shoot me in the head."

On the morning after his visit from Billy, David Keegan had gone into work, calmly thumbed through the file of complaints referred to the office from the Boston Police

Department for prosecution, and removed citation number BX171553 charging the owners of the Leopard Lounge with violating the state entertainment laws. He had taken the single sheet of onionskin and walked to the men's room where he had torn it into tiny pieces.

"So do you?" Hunter asked.

"What?"

"Have any recollection?"

"Of what, exactly?" Keegan asked.

Hunter hesitated, then eyed Keegan. "Of disposing of a complaint against the Leopard. On behalf of your brother."

Keegan had decided that it was unlikely Hunter could have the facts of the story; or, rather, unlikely that Hunter could *prove* the facts of the story. No one had seen Keegan do it. No one knew for certain that he had done it. No one except himself and Billy and Leo. Keegan also knew that if this were to appear in the newspaper he would be ruined. His chances of becoming United States attorney would be destroyed. He likely would be dismissed from his job and investigated by the Board of Bar Overseers. He would likely lose his license to practice law for some period of time, and it was possible he would be indicted, charged with a felony. He would be the center of a scandal. Disgraced.

"It never happened," Keegan said.

"Never happened," Hunter repeated.

Keegan shook his head dismissively.

"Never anything like that," Hunter said.

Keegan appeared surprised. "Anything *like* that?" Keegan asked. "You mean was I asked by people through the years, people I knew, had grown up with, gone to school with, whatever—was I ever *asked* for a favor? All the time. Did I willfully subvert the law?" Keegan shook his head.

"Never happened," Hunter said.

"Never happened," Keegan repeated.

Hunter nodded and looked out to sea. A small jet came in overhead en route to a landing at Logan.

"My guy says it did," Hunter said casually.

Keegan was slightly jarred by this.

"Your guy?"

"My source," Hunter said. "I've got a guy inside. He says it happened. He says you pulled the citation. Made it go away."

14

In his mind, Keegan thought that this could have been the night when it all came together. This was the night he had been pointing toward. The night when they would go downtown to the fancy restaurant, when he would sit down across the table from her, tucked away in a discreet romantic corner of the bistro; when he would look across the starched white tablecloth and tell her he loved her and that he would always love her and ask her if she would marry him. This was to have been the night, this late June evening when the temperature was in the middle seventies without even a hint of humidity; one of those glorious summer evenings in Boston when the air is clear and the purplish light of dusk seems to backlight the city and create an aura of romance.

He had gone through it in his mind a number of times. They would settle in at the restaurant and as they enjoyed a good bottle of wine, David would speak to Diane from the heart. You are the best thing that has ever happened to me, he would say, and I want us to be together. I want us to explore together and to experience all the joys and difficulties life has to offer together. I know that I am sometimes stuck in the past and that this worries you, but I am ready to move forward. I want a life together. I want to be with you and to grow old with you and to care for you when you need me. I love you very much, and I will always love you, and I would like to know whether you are willing to marry me?

This was his vision, but reality was different. Reality intruded in an unpleasant, unromantic fashion. The reality was that not only weren't things settled, they were quite unsettled. Somehow they got off on the wrong track right away, talking about David's father. This was perilous territory, for Diane feared at times that David's desire to go back and delve into the past was so obsessive that it prevented him from moving forward; from focusing on his own life; from planning a future.

She wondered about his archaeological digging into what was clearly a troubled family past. Had he become so obsessed with delving into the past that he could not think about the future? Take joy from the present? They had been over this. She had always maintained that time was precious, that spending one's time digging through the past was profligate, or, at the very least, self-indulgent. She believed in moving on, forging ahead. What was done was done.

But David carried the hurts of his past around with him like a great weight, a weight that Diane believed had sometimes robbed him of energy and perspective. He could not let go; he could not take his eyes off the past. He was like a man in a speedboat racing through life, sitting in the stern, gazing only backward, unwilling to take his eyes off where he had already been.

"Amazing, isn't it, how we're bound to our fathers," Diane said. "I mean the bond to mothers is I guess so obvious and so much a given but the bond to fathers is an incredibly powerful thing."

"Your Dad okay?" David asked.

She frowned. "I mean, on the surface, yeah he's okay," Diane said. "But I know him pretty well and I can sense the anxiety within him. There's something going on, something he hasn't told me about. He's holding something back and that concerns me. I get frightened by the idea that he won't share his concerns and fears with me."

"He's a strong man, though, Di," David said. "The way you've always talked about him it's clear he's got a great quiet strength."

"And what *is* coming?" Diane asked. "I mean, I know that Walter will sit down and talk with him and Dad will answer questions, but where does it go after that? How is this settled? One person says this man was at such-and-such a place forty-some odd years ago and the accused says, well, that isn't actually true, I was somewhere else. How does that get settled nearly a half century later?"

"I don't know," David said. "I suppose they try to go back and see if there is any documentary proof of what either person is saying. There may be lists of some kind that can be checked. Records somewhere."

"I have to help him," Diane said. "I have to help get him through this. David, this man has done everything for me! He has been there for me ever since I can remember. When I was in gymnastics as a six-year-old, for God's sake, he was there, not just at the recitals, he'd come to the practices, Tuesday and Thursday afternoons! There were no other fathers there. When I was growing up in New York he'd walk me to school every morning. And most days when I got out he was there at the bottom of the steps to greet me and walk me home. I used to think it was so weird my friends didn't have their fathers to drop them off and pick them up.

"Mom traveled a lot. And every time she did he would create something special, some trip we would take to a museum or the circus or whatever, but he would plan it all out, and he didn't do it out of a sense of duty, he did it because he loved to. He loved being with me and teaching me and that's the way he's always been."

She paused and looked at Keegan, a look of pained sadness on her face. "And you know about the stuttering," she said. "The exercises from the speech therapist would take me an hour, two hours a day for the first few years. When I was eight, nine years old. And he moved his office home, to the back of our apartment so he could be there with me.

" 'Control your rate, honey,' he would say over and over again. His voice was so patient and kind. 'Slow down, honey, give the air a chance to work its way through so the words can ride along on the air.'

"He talked about prolongation and stacatto when nobody else knew what those terms meant," she continued. "He studied it. He'd go up to Columbia and meet with doctors, and I'd hear him and my mother discussing it. And later, I discovered that he had a shelf in our library dedicated exclusively to literature on the topic. Scholarly papers! He read it all. When I'd get stuck in the middle of a word, others would finish the word for me, thinking it was helpful. He never did it! He knew instinctively that that was embarassing.

"And nobody could sustain eye contact. Nobody! Except Dad. He would look me right in the eye and never look away. Sometimes we'd be alone together and discussing something and he would say to me, 'Do you realize that you just spoke for ten minutes and barely got stuck at all?' And he would tell me how much better I was getting and how proud he was of me.

"When I went through the divorce, he was incredible. When I needed a break, he made sure I got it. I mean, there are people who will do whatever you ask them to do, but a lot of times in life it's nice not to have to ask. Times when having to ask sort of ruins it. My father always knew—always!—when I needed something, time or money or help or whatever it was. He knew without being asked."

15

He remembered the frigid January morning when he and his mother had driven the interstate north out of Massachusetts, up through New Hampshire, northwest on into Vermont, and straight up through to Quebec. Most of the other boys on the team went in groups of three or four to a station wagon, but she saw this as an opportunity for them to be alone, for her to calm him and reassure him, to convince him that all would be well.

She had left his brother Billy, still only a baby, back with her sister in Roslindale. She had packed Davey's hockey gear in the back seat rather than the trunk so it would stay warm. She had been through his equipment bag three times to make sure that he had everything. She had laid it all out—helmet, shoulder pads, elbow pads, hockey gloves, pants, socks, shin guards, skates, game jersey, practice jersey, and a cup and athletic supporter. Though only eight David had made the Mite A team, and not only made the team, he now centered the second line. He had proven to be faster on his skates, quicker by a step than anyone else on his team. He would pick up a loose puck at center ice and streak into the other team's zone, faking a defenseman one way, faking another the other way, and then driving in on the goaltender, more often than not finding an opening to slide the puck into the net.

He had quickly grown to love being on the team. He particularly liked the camaraderie, the acceptance by the older, bigger boys who admired his talent but, more importantly, respected his desire and intensity. When he was on the ice he never let up. He played hard, with energy and exuberance both on offense and defense. Sometimes he would be sent sprawling by a bigger opposing player, but he would invariably pop right back up and jump back into the flow of the game.

"Dad's not coming at all?" David asked, as they drove north on I-89, north of Burlington, headed for Quebec.

"He can't make it," she said.

"At all?"

She shook her head. "He has to work," she said. "But if you make the finals maybe you could call him."

He wasn't sure. He wanted his Dad there to see him play—it was the biggest tournament of the year, after all—but he didn't want any trouble for his mother. He didn't want to feel nervous and scared for what might happen.

"Is Dad coming back home?" he asked.

She held her hands on the steering wheel at ten and two o'clock. They drove steadily north, the highway a ribbon of black through the thick layers of snow that blanketed the countryside around them. She glanced over at him. He was sitting up straight in the front passenger seat, barely able to see out the windows. His brown hair hung over the edge of his forehead. Sometimes she was struck by how young he looked. There were moments, in certain light at a certain angle, when he looked no older than six.

"Remember what I told you the other night?" she said.

"About him sleeping at work?"

"Right," she said.

"How come he has to do that?" David asked.

"Sometimes policemen have to do that because they have to protect people at night, also," she said.

"But he'll be sleeping," David said.

"But when something happens he'll be right there at the police station ready to go," she said.

This had been the story she had told him, the reason for the separation.

He nodded his head, accepting the explanation.

"You OK?" she asked.

"I'm fine," he said.

He was quiet for a few miles, then asked, "Are you mad at Dad?"

She hesitated, then said, "Sometimes moms and dads disagree about things. Sometimes, when they disagree, they argue."

"But are you mad at him?" David persisted.

"I was angry with him," she said. Then, to reassure him, she lied. "But not anymore."

"How come?" he asked.

"How come what?"

"You're not mad?" he asked.

"Because when I get angry it's usually only for a short time and then I'm over it," she said.

"Like when you get mad at me," he said.

"But I hardly ever get mad at you," she said.

"I know," he said. "But when you do it's short."

"It's kind of like that, I guess," she said.

"When is he coming home?"

She shook her head. "I'm not sure," she said.

"How come?"

"His schedule isn't done yet," she said. Another lie.

"How come he hurt you?" David asked.

She was taken aback. She knew David had sometimes heard her cries, but he had never seen anything. She affected a puzzled look as she glanced over at him.

"How come what?" she said, a lilt of surprise in her voice.

"He hurt you?"

"Daddy?" she asked.

He nodded.

"Daddy didn't hurt me," she said.

She glanced over and saw the look of confusion on his face.

"I heard you," he said.

"You heard . . ."

"You cried," he said.

"Sometimes people get upset, Davey," she said. "And cry."

They rode in silence up across the border and wound their way to Sherbrooke, where the tournament was being held with a dozen teams from the northeastern United States and eastern Canada. They checked into the Howard Johnson Motel and were assigned a spacious room with two king-size beds. He was giddy with excitement and immediately made for the hotel's indoor pool, his mother walking swiftly along the hallway in pursuit.

Throughout the weekend he thought on and off about his father. Most of the other boys had come with their dads, some with both parents. He watched the others with their fathers at the pool. Some of the fathers, wearing their huge swimming trunks below their bulging bellies, would dive into the water and fool around with their

sons and their sons' friends. Others would sit by,
watching, smiling. At the rink some of the fathers would
yell at their boys. Mostly, though, they encouraged them.
In the locker room everyone else's father, except one
other boy, tied their skates for them. David's skates were
tightened and tied by one of the coaches.

He missed his father. He had a feeling he wouldn't be
coming home soon. He just had a feeling.

And, though he missed him, that wasn't such a bad
thing. He liked being here in a way with just his mother.
He liked having a big room all to themselves. He didn't
want her hurt anymore. He didn't want her crying or
scared. If his father wasn't coming back anymore, maybe
that was all right.

Two days after requesting the records from the Boston
Ambulance Squad, Keegan received a fax.

BOSTON AMBULANCE SQUAD RESPONSE
REPORT 032914
     DATE: 7/29/54
     TIME: 10:07 P.M.
     TYPE: MV accident
     LOCATION: Belgrade and Newberg, Roslindale
     DISPOSITION: Patient identified as Jeanette Kee-
     gan transported to Faulkner. Massive trauma.

Keegan drove to the Boston City Hospital Annex where
a record-keeping facility was housed in the subbasement.
Keegan had learned during his research that back in the
1960s the city council had been looking for ways to increase the public payroll. In an effort to create new
public jobs the council created the Health and Hospitals

Records Division where the task of placing all BCH records on microfiche was undertaken. This led to the hiring of countless workers for a task of dubious merit. Keegan was grateful for it, however, since it made his research task a simple one.

He rode the elevator to the basement, went to the counter, and filled out a form identifying precisely what he wished to see. Fifteen minutes later a clerk handed him a roll of microfiche. He went to one of the half dozen machines near the counter and placed the roll on the spool. He flipped through the records and found that they were chronological. He moved swiftly through the months until he found records from July. He spun them by on the screen, finding the records for the final week of the month. He located a report for July 29: A stabbing in East Boston. A fight in Allston. A motor vehicle accident in Grove Hall. Another car accident in Brighton. A heart attack in Charlestown. Heat prostration in Dorchester. An accident in Hyde Park. An accident in Roslindale. Here it was. He fiddled with the focus knob so the words on the screen were as clear as possible.

BCH AMBULANCE
    July 29, 1954 . . . . 10:09 P.M. . . . . . MV
    Roslindale, Belgrade at Newberg
    NT

Keegan was puzzled. He went through the rest of the reports from the night of July 29 and found nothing else in Roslindale even remotely like the accident. Clearly, this was the incident report, but it carried no details.

Keegan got up from the carrel and went to the counter.

"Excuse me," he said to one of the clerks. "May I ask you a question?"

"Shoot," the young man said.

"On an ambulance report, when it says 'NT,' just the initials, what does that mean?"

"No transport," the man said.

Keegan was taken aback. "No transport?" he repeated.

"Meaning they didn't transport anyone from that scene," the young man said. "You know, they get there and the person's gone, or they're OK, or whatever."

Keegan didn't understand. He want back to the carrel and rewound the fiche. He placed it back into its box and returned it to the counter.

"All set?" the young clerk said.

"On the NT," he said. "Do they ever write it for another reason?"

"I wouldn't think so," the clerk said.

"Or maybe make a mistake?"

"Anything's possible," the young man said. "But what could be simpler. You show up. Nobody needs a lift to the hospital. You jot down NT and you're off. Hard to screw that up."

Keegan drove back to his office unable to get his mind off of the NT notation. His father had insisted that he had been transported to the hospital in a BCH ambulance. There was no question in his mind. But if that was not true, if he had not been taken from the scene by a BCH ambulance, then what had happened? Where had he gone? And why?

16

"**T**his is very difficult for me," Hunter said on the phone to Gerald. "This is not the pleasant part of my job. But it's a part that has to be done."

Gerald Wahljak was in his office at International Place, looking out over the harbor. He stood in stunned disbelief. He simply could not believe that the *Boston Globe* had the story. Hunter was sitting at his desk, his feet up, the keyboard to his computer resting on his lap.

"I wanted to let you know that we're running the story and to see whether you might have any comment or whether your mother might have any comment," Hunter said.

"Look," Gerald said. "You're presenting this to me as an accomplished fact, as though the story is done. Can't we talk about it?"

"About what?" Hunter asked.

"About whether this story should be published," Gerald said. "We're talking here about an elderly woman. This is not something—this whole experience—is not something she wants dragged through the public press, frankly. I think you can understand that."

There was an awkward pause. "I'm sorry," Hunter said. "This is a legitimate story."

"So what will this story say?" Gerald asked.

"You know, that the feds are investigating a report by your mother that she saw this Nazi from the camp."

"I can't believe this," Gerald said, his voice suddenly thick with emotion.

"What is that man's name again, Mr. Wahljak?" Hunter asked. "The man your mother saw?"

Gerald was silent. Finally he spoke. "I see," he said. "So the story talks about my mother but not about the man she saw."

"Sure it does," Hunter said.

"But not by name, correct?" Gerald asked.

"Well . . ."

"Do you know his name?" Gerald asked. "Do you know who he is?"

"Ah, not really," Hunter said.

Hunter could hear Gerald whisper "Jesus Christ." Then, suddenly, Gerald was furious. "How did you get this information?" he demanded of Hunter.

"That's not something I'm at liberty to reveal," Hunter replied.

Gerald nodded, disgusted. He had known that would be Hunter's reply.

"Does it matter to you that this will cause pain to a seventy-eight-year-old woman?" Gerald asked.

Hunter said nothing. "Does it matter to you?" Gerald demanded. "Don't you take such things into consideration?"

"I'm sorry, Mr. Wahljak," Hunter said. "I take it you have no comment?"

Gerald paused. "No, I have a comment," he said.

"Here is my comment: Shame on you."

*   *   *

Lou Betts pulled his 1988 Oldsmobile Cutlass Supreme over, two hundred feet shy of the Wahljaks' driveway on the opposite side of the street. After positioning himself so that he had a clear view of anyone emerging from the house, Betts set three cameras on the passenger seat of his car, two Minoltas and a Nikon. He screwed a tele-photo lens onto the Nikon, snapped the film into place, removed the lens cap and was ready.

Lou Betts was forty-seven years old, five feet eight inches tall, two hundred pounds. He had spent the past twenty-three years of his life riding around town moni-toring police scanners and shooting photographs of crimes and fires. Once in a while, when the picture in-volved a stakeout, the *Globe* photo department sent the assignment Betts's way. Most photographers were un-comfortable on stakeouts, finding the prospect of sitting at the end of a driveway waiting for a subject to show rather humiliating and below their journalistic dignity. Not Betts. He liked stakeouts. He liked confrontations with indignant subjects and their family members. He liked to wait until someone threw a fit, complaining about an invasion of privacy, and then he would raise the camera, aim, and fire. Bang, a humiliating picture, the subject out of control.

Betts shut off the Cutlass engine and reached into his shirt pocket for a package of Camel Filters. He tapped one out of the box, placed it between his lips, and snapped a Bic lighter. Betts inhaled slowly and let the smoke and nicotine wash around his lungs before ex-haling. Lou Betts had done this with forty or more ciga-rettes a day every day since he'd been old enough to drive a car. Betts rolled down his window and rested his left arm on the door. Betts was dressed, as was his custom, in tight blue jeans, black high-top Converse sneakers, and a short-sleeve Banlon shirt, black. His sideburns were long and he combed his dark hair straight back.

He sat waiting and watching. He had a general physical description of Gerta Wahljak, but he also knew that only one elderly woman lived at the house he was watching. He waited for better than three hours until, shortly after lunchtime, Gerta emerged from the front door. She was neatly dressed in slacks and a shirt, and she walked with purpose.

Betts flicked a butt out the window of the Cutlass and raised the Minolta. He looked up the street and trained the zoom on Gerta. She, of course, had no idea she was being photographed. Betts ripped off a series of shots, then set the Minolta down. He considered pulling away, but then he decided to get closer. There was no one around to bother him, shoo him away.

Betts got out of the car and crossed the street with the Nikon in hand. He dropped to one knee on the sidewalk. Gerta was approaching from perhaps eighty feet. Betts shot several horizontals, then several verticals. He did not move from his position on the sidewalk. As Gerta approached she saw that he was holding a camera. She stopped and turned to see what was behind her. Nothing. Then she continued on, a puzzled look on her face. Then, suddenly, it seemed to occur to her that he was taking her photograph.

She stopped. "Why are you doing that?" she asked.

"My job, missus," Betts said cheerfully.

"You are doing this for whom?" she demanded.

"*Globe*," Betts said.

Gerta didn't get it right away. "The newspaper?" she asked.

"That's it, missus," Betts said.

"But why . . . you mustn't do that," Gerta said, suddenly frightened. She wheeled around and began hurrying back toward the house. "You mustn't do this," she called back over her shoulder as she began to cry. "You have no right to do this to me!"

There was a progression here, thought Hunter. He would write the piece about the federal investigation and, perhaps through Dunbar, perhaps through another source, he would follow with a story revealing the identity of the man. Hunter hoped it would be a well-known person in the community—someone with visibility. That would greatly increase the size of the scandal. Hunter had a sense that there was depth and complexity to this story. The thought of Gerta keeping the picture through all of those years thrilled him. There were secrets buried away in those years, secrets that Hunter wanted to reveal.

As much as anything, he wanted to make sure that he beat the *Record American*. He felt a sense of dread at the prospect that the *Record* might get onto the story before the *Globe*. For all Hunter knew, the news might already have leaked to the *Record* out of the United States Attorney's Office. He literally shuddered at the thought. For the truth was that for all the noble pronouncements made by journalists about their motivation, fear of being scooped by a rival news organization was the most potent motivator of all.

In the privacy of his shabby office, the door closed, Hunter phoned Theo Dunbar. Hunter read through the entire draft of the article as Dunbar listened silently. When Hunter was done, Dunbar smiled to himself.

"You're very good at this, Hunter," he said.

Hunter was surprised by the compliment.

"You think it's good?"

"I think it's perfect," Dunbar replied.

Moments later, Hunter handed the lead of the piece to Globe managing editor Robert Vincent.

The United States Justice Department is investigating an allegation by a Brookline woman that she recently sighted in Boston an official from a World War II Nazi camp in which she had been held prisoner.

Gerta Wahljak, 78, a Polish Jew who survived imprisonment in several camps, is said to have seen the Nazi official in Boston within recent weeks. Wahljak is the mother of Gerald Wahljak, a prominent Boston attorney.

According to Justice Department sources in Washington, Mrs. Wahljak has kept a photograph of senior officials from a camp called Theresienstadt, which was located in Czechoslovakia.

Federal investigators are probing whether the Nazi official, whose identity has not yet been determined, lives somewhere in the Boston area. Officials say they will attempt to determine whether the man has violated U.S. laws against Nazis emigrating to this country.

"Dynamite," Vincent said, as he read through the lead to Hunter's story.

"Runs with the pic of the old lady," Vincent said.

"Absolutely," Hunter said.

"Good stuff," Vincent said. "We'll put it on one for tomorrow."

"On one," of course, meant the front page. And Hunter never got tired of seeing his byline on the front page of the newspaper. It was what he lived for.

17

Sophie Naumann walked slowly through her garden in the late afternoon. She took no notice of the warmth of the sun, the fragrance of the rich earth, and the newly-mown lawn. She stood still on the edge of the garden looking off to the rear of the property into a grove of fir trees and permitted her mind to wander.

For many years there had existed within Sophie and Freddy the fear that one day the truth of the past might emerge, that they would have to confront the distant reality they had determinedly sought to forget. In the early years of their marriage the fear of discovery had been a real danger, but as time had passed, after they had emigrated to the United States and built a new life, the odds of the past being recalled had diminished.

Sophie walked slowly from the garden to the terrace, passing from the sunlight into the shade. Suddenly she felt chilled, and she folded her arms across her chest. Freddy sat bundled in a heavy wool sweater, staring off into space, not noticing Sophie. The *Boston Globe* lay on the chaise lounge next to Freddy.

"Are you chilled, Freddy?" she asked, as she went to him, and placed a hand on his shoulder. He seemed startled by her presence.

"I didn't see you," he said.

She forced a smile. "I was in the garden," she said.

He nodded. There was a moment of silence between them.

Sophie sat down opposite Freddy and reached for his hand, holding it, squeezing it, surprised by how cold it felt. She looked at his face, his handsome but weathered face. His eyes were clouded and he seemed so very tired.

Sophie picked up the newspaper and looked at the photograph of Gerta Wahljak. It was a somewhat grainy photo, and her expression seemed odd, as though she'd been surprised at that moment. When they had seen the paper in the morning Freddy had said he was not sure. Sophie suspected that was denial.

"We have to assume that this is the woman you saw, Freddy," Sophie said.

Freddy nodded slowly. "It must be," he said.

"So we have to assume that since the article says they have a photograph of you that, inevitably, they will identify you," she said.

She waited for a response from him but none was forthcoming.

"Freddy, we have to be ready," she said. "What will we do? What will we say?"

He shook his head. "We will say nothing," he said. "We have chosen to live in the way that we have lived. This has been our choice and we are accountable to ourselves and only ourselves for our actions."

He paused and took a deep breath. He seemed defeated by all of this already, Sophie thought. He seemed to have no fight left in him.

"Life is untidy," he said. "Sometimes very untidy. We

have done the best that we can. The best we know how. What else can be expected of us?"

"But the newspapers will continue to . . ."

"The newspapers be damned," he said angrily. "What are the newspapers? We are accountable to ourselves. I will be judged by myself and by you. I shall not submit myself for judgment to the newspapers or any other self-appointed guardians of what is claimed to be righteous."

Sophie shut her eyes and worked to compose herself. She fought the frustration and fear she felt rising within her.

"So what is it that you propose we do?" she asked coolly.

"I've thought about this," he said, "and I don't expect you to agree right away, but I believe it's for the best. I'm convinced it's for the best."

He looked at her, fixed his gaze on her eyes. "I want to go back to Cleggan," he said.

Her eyes widened as though in disbelief. Cleggan was an all but unpopulated village on the west coast of Ireland, a wild, remote place where they had lived for two years in the forties.

"We can once again find peace there," he said. "We can be happy there without the intrusions of the world."

She shook her head, dismissing the idea. "No," she said. "I will not run and hide. We hid once when we needed to hide, when hiding was all that we could do, when it was what we had to do. But I will not now at the end of my life run and hide. No, Freddy. No."

On the day the story ran, Hunter received dozens of calls from readers wanting to know the identity of the man.

This delighted Hunter for it was clear the story had caused a stir in the city. There was something about it—some element of mystery, of history, of the verboten—that drew readers. Civic and religious officials, Christians as well as Jews, rallied in a strong show of public support for Gerta Wahljak. But Gerta preferred to remain at home, closeted with her son, as far away from the media spotlight as she could get.

Gerta, in truth, was sickened by the story, stunned that something so private, something she had held so closely, so solemnly through the years, was now a matter for public discussion. Gerald, for his part, was furious with the *Globe* for running the story. He had called the editor, Dave Johnson, and argued heatedly that the story should not be run, but Johnson had not budged.

His next call had been to Walter Stone.

"All I can say is that I apologize," Stone said. "I feel terrible about it."

"But where did it come from, Walter?" Gerald asked. "Only a handful of people knew."

"Well, I'll tell you where it didn't come from," Stone said. "It didn't come out of this office. Only three of us knew about it, and I trust Dunbar and Keegan. Unfortunately we gave a heads-up to Washington and it obviously came out of there. The article says according to sources in Washington."

"It's an outrage, Walter, and I am formally asking you to do something about tracking down the leak. I want to know who it came from and how, and I believe that person should be prosecuted. It's a felony, Walter, and you know it."

Stone, himself, was furious about it. He mistrusted and disliked dealing with the press, and hated it when preliminary investigations had to be done under the snooping eye of the media.

"We will investigate it beginning immediately," Stone said. "I'm putting Theo Dunbar on it today. We'll have him look into it and report back to me, and I'll keep you fully informed."

After getting the word from Stone about his new assignment, Theo Dunbar was thrilled.

Dunbar wanted to do it right. He wanted to convey the information in a way that would solidify his hold on Hunter; that would ensure Hunter would feel a deep and enduring gratitude. Dunbar wanted to make Hunter feel as though he carried an immense debt to Dunbar.

And so it was that Dunbar drove across town from his office and turned onto Massachusetts Avenue from Commonwealth. Dunbar drove up a block and went right on Newbury Street, traveling the length of the block before turning in to the large cement parking garage at the end of the block. Dunbar found a space on the first floor. He rode the elevator to the roof, where he quickly spotted the black Camry in the customary place. Dunbar walked slowly across the pavement, moving with a deliberate pace, a pace suggesting the confidence he carried. This information would electrify Hunter; Dunbar knew this as surely as he knew anything. For he knew that this story would be one that they would talk about in Boston for many years to come.

Hunter had fulfilled his end of the bargain: he had menaced Keegan with the story. He had unsettled Keegan. Dunbar sat in the passenger seat, regarding Hunter, and spoke in a soft voice. He wanted to understate; understate to increase the impact, the power of the information. When he told Hunter who the man was—and who the man was married to—Hunter sat stunned. Speechless.

Within hours, back at the *Globe*, Hunter had pulled an extensive amount of research on Sophie Naumann and her husband, Frederick Schiller. Hunter knew this was a once-in-a-lifetime story. How absolutely incredible that this man—this Nazi official whom Gerta Wahljak remembered from a half century before—was now married to one of the most prominent Jewish women in America.

"Have you read any of her books?" Hunter asked his research assistant, Hewlett. Hunter was seated at his desk, slouched deeply in his chair with his legs propped on his desk. Hewlett was seated in a wooden chair across the office, his legs up on a small conference table.

"*Midnight on Kurfurstendamm*," Hewlett replied. "I guess everybody has."

"Just about," Hunter said. "Says here it was on the bestseller list for three and a half years."

Midnight on Kurfurstendamm had been Sophie Naumann's first novel, published in 1951. It was the story of a Jewish family living in Berlin during the 1930s. The story centered on two members of the family, a brilliant young girl who aspired to become a musician and her father, a well-to-do merchant. The conflict in the story centered on the desire of the girl, when she reached college age, for the family to emigrate. The father, a stubborn man, saw the Nazi threat as a passing political fad and refused to budge from Berlin. The novel had been met with worldwide critical acclaim.

Sophie Naumann had written a dozen novels since then, most quite successful, though none with the impact of *Midnight on Kurfurstendamm*. None contained the raw emotional power and few had had such perfect timing. For *Midnight* had been one of the first works of Holocaust literature at a time when the world was still coping with the dimensions of the Nazi genocide.

Midnight on Kurfurstendamm had established an international reputation for Sophie Naumann. The book was widely thought to be autobiographical, though she had been reluctant during interviews through the years to reveal a great deal about the specifics of her family situation in Berlin. But it was clear that she had grown up in Berlin the daughter of a wealthy businessman and the family had chosen to remain there under Nazi rule, eventually being forced to give up their home and possessions and travel east to Czechoslovakia where they were placed in Theresienstadt, a ghetto specifically for holding prominent German Jews.

"The earliest mention I see is in fifty-one, when the book was published," Hewlett said. "She was living in London or Ireland then, apparently, but some of these articles have her in New York soon after that. By the midfifties."

"Here's a *Newsweek* piece," Hunter said. "Says she was born in 1917 in Berlin. Says she taught at Columbia for a while. Writing seminars. Written a number of pieces for the *New York Review of Books* through the years, articles, reviews, that sort of thing. Made a ton of money from her books. Most of them bestsellers, at least as paperbacks. Books translated into sixteen languages, published throughout the world."

Both men continued to read, sometimes stopping to make a notation, then proceeding on.

"Jesus, the honorary degrees are unbelievable," Hunter

said, reading from a list in one article. "Stanford, NYU, Chicago, BC, Wellesley, Harvard, Michigan, and on and on."

"Lots of humanitarian-type awards, too," Hewlett said. "From lots of different organizations, mostly Jewish."

"Says here," Hunter said, "that she's donated more than five million dollars to various causes, one million in one shot to the Holocaust Museum."

"She went on the board of the National Jewish Council in '72 and became chairman in '75," Hewlett said. "It's a four-year term. We should get reaction from some of her fellow board members."

Hunter pondered this, then shook his head, dismissing the idea. "Not yet," he said. "I want our first shot to be clean, no reaction from anybody. We talk with anybody outside the principles we risk getting beat on the story." Hunter turned and glared at Hewlett. "We can't have that happen," he said.

"It's strange, don't you think, that there's barely a mention of her husband in all of this?" Hewlett observed. "I've come across his name once only from a piece in the early sixties."

"I haven't seen him mentioned at all so far," Hunter said.

Hewlett put down the pages he was reading from and shook his head in amazement. "How could he have kept this secret all these years?" Hewlett asked.

Hunter shrugged. "Hey, it happens. People live with deep, dark secrets all the time."

"How is he?" Diane asked her mother on the telephone.

"Not well," Sophie said.

Her father had always been such a rock. He had never been anything but strong and cheerful.

"How so?" Diane asked.

"He is shaken," Sophie said. "He is very badly shaken, Diane."

"Look, Mother, I am leaving work now," Diane said. "I'll come right over."

"Yes, please, dear," Sophie said.

Diane moved swiftly from her law office, riding the elevator all the way down to the basement garage. As she got off the elevator, she came face-to-face with a man whom she did not know. He had shoulder-length brown hair and wore baggy corduroy pants. He wore a button-down plaid shirt and no tie. He smiled an obsequious smile and stepped directly into Diane's path.

"You're Diane Schiller," he said.

"Yes," she replied.

"I wonder if I could just get a minute . . ." he said.

"I'm sorry, do I know you?"

"I'm Dan Hunter with the *Globe*, Miss Schiller," Hunter said. "I wonder if I could just ask you a few questions?"

Diane was so stunned by this that she did not speak, did not move.

"I'm working on a follow-up article to the story I had in today," Hunter said. "And I don't want to run the story without giving your father and mother an opportunity to say something. Give their side. Balance out the story. Otherwise, you know . . ."

Hunter shrugged.

"I don't know, Mr. Hunter," she said. "What exactly do you want?"

"I'm working on an article saying that your father is

the man Mrs. Wahljak saw at Mass General; the man she remembered from the camp."

A powerful surge of panic rose within Diane. "You're writing an article about it?" she said, incredulous. "What are you talking about. Why would you say my father is the man she has accused?"

"I received the information from an unimpeachable source, Miss Schiller," Hunter said.

This isn't happening, she thought to herself. This is a nightmare from which I will now awake. This is not real.

Diane suddenly felt light-headed, physically ill. She needed to sit down. To take a deep breath.

"I have nothing to say to you," she heard herself saying. She felt herself walking away from Hunter toward her car.

"I know how you must feel," she heard the man say as he fell in step beside her.

"I can see that you are upset," Hunter said. "I'll give you a call a little later, how about that? Maybe after you've had a chance to talk it over with your parents you'll all see that it's really in their interest to sit down with me. Otherwise they get a one-sided story that doesn't really project your point of view."

They came to Diane's car, and she got in and started the engine. She pulled out, and as she drove toward her parents' home she could feel her entire body shaking. She had never in her life felt such a profound sense of fear. As she drove she worked to settle her breathing; to calm herself. But the truth was that she was terrified. And she was confused. She picked up her car phone and dialed David. He answered on the second ring. "I need you," she blurted out.

18

"He just was kind of *there* all of a sudden, this man from the *Globe*," Diane said to Keegan. He had just arrived at her parents' house. Keegan and Diane were in a small library tucked into a far corner of the house. The room was done in wood and a deep hunter green. The walls were lined with books, and there was a comfortable sofa as well as an easy chair. "He just kind of stood in front of me as I was about to go to my car and he said he was writing an article saying that Dad is the man from the camp." Diane stopped talking and stared across at Keegan. "He said he was the Nazi in the picture," Diane said, her voice soft.

"What was his name?" Keegan asked.

"Hunter," Diane replied.

"You know him?" she asked.

"We've met," David said.

"How can he . . ." Diane began, but then caught herself. "He said he wanted to write the article in the next couple of days, possibly for tomorrow.

"I mean, my God, David, Mom and Dad are elderly people," Diane said, "they've been through *so* much in their lives, so much they've had to endure. And now some crazy woman makes a wild accusation and the Justice

117

Department looks into it and the newspapers get ahold of it and it's all of a sudden going to be a big deal. And they're right in the middle of it, helpless, defenseless. Their reputations at stake. My God, David, my mother is one of the most respected Jewish activists in America. She is known throughout the world for what she has been through and accomplished, and now the story will go throughout the world that she is married to a man accused of administering a Nazi concentration camp!"

She began to sob softly, but quickly composed herself.

"And think of my poor father, David, who has *always* been there for her and I mean *always!* For my mother and for me. And now he has to endure this disgraceful, absolutely disgraceful assault on his reputation. And he has to do it at a time when his health is far from great and when he is on the verge of going in for surgery. And worst of all—and believe me for him this *will be* the worst of all—he is in a position where he is reflecting badly on my mother and her reputation. That will hurt him most. Humiliate him. Because he has always taken the greatest pride in being the quiet one, the one no one knew, but the one who supported her always through everything and loved her in such a pure way."

Again, Diane began to sob. This time, though, she did not catch herself so quickly.

David knew what he had to do. He knew that Diane needed him. That this was one of those moments where the course is clear and certain. She needed him, and he would be there for her, and what happened would happen. But he would not look back and say that he had fallen short; he would not look back and say that he had done anything less than everything he could for her. He loved her. She needed him. That was all that he needed to know.

"I'll deal with the reporter for you," David said. "Don't worry about him. I'll do the best I can and bring any decisions that need to be made to you. You shouldn't have to worry about dealing with him directly."

Diane was taken aback. "You can't get involved, David, given your position," she said.

"I'm going to take some time off," he said. "It won't be a problem. I need a break. And this is the perfect time." He shrugged. "Why don't I go pay Hunter a visit and see what he's up to. Then you and your parents make whatever decisions need to be made."

"Look, Walter, unfortunately the indications are that we've found the leaker." Dunbar hesitated. "You're not going to like this, Walter, not one bit.

"The evidence points to Keegan."

Stone frowned and sat forward in his seat. "That's ridiculous," Stone said. "These are leaks about Diane's parents. He's involved with her."

Dunbar nodded. "Who knows what the reasons are, maybe subconsciously he wants to step in as her savior, her champion. But I won't speculate on that. What I can tell you is," and here Dunbar glanced down at his notes, "is that on four occasions in recent weeks outgoing calls from Keegan's office line have gone to the *Globe*, not just to the *Globe* in general, but specifically to the private line assigned to Daniel Hunter, the reporter who wrote the article. And one of the calls comes two days before the publication of the article and another comes the day before.

"Also, within a few days before, three faxes went from Keegan's office fax machine to a fax machine located in the city room of the *Globe*."

Dunbar affected a pained expression. "I think we've got our leaker," Dunbar said.

Stone shook his head. "He hasn't seemed himself lately," he mused. "Let me think about this, Theo. Let me sleep on it."

"We need to meet," Keegan said to Hunter on the telephone.

"What's up?" Hunter asked.

"You asked me about something recently," Keegan replied. "Something from a few years back."

"Yeah."

"Still interested in that?" Keegan asked.

"Definitely," Hunter said.

"Then meet me at Castle Island in half an hour," Keegan said.

"I'll see you there."

A British Airways jumbo jet roared low over Dorchester Bay, past the Kennedy Library and directly above Castle Island in South Boston. Keegan stood at the far end of the parking lot watching the plane on its final approach to Logan. The late afternoon was humid and he was uncomfortable in the hot wind that blew out of the west, stirring little whirlwinds of dust around the parking lot.

Keegan had been waiting for fifteen minutes and he was becoming concerned that perhaps Hunter might not show. He watched as cars pulled in and out of the parking lot. People strolled along the walkway that led out around the island with its panoramic view of Boston Harbor and Dorchester Bay. People gathered around the parking lots in small groups, leaning against their cars, drinking cans of Coke.

Keegan peered down the boulevard at the oncoming cars, watching those that turned into the parking lot by the island, hoping that the next one would be Hunter. Storm clouds moved in from the west, bulging, dark cumulus that settled in over the coast while, in the distance, the faint rumble of thunder could be heard. A group of elderly men gathered around a picnic table not far from where Keegan stood waiting, began looking up at the sky, gesturing and talking. The men moved toward the parking lot and drove off in their cars.

Soon enough, most of the people fled as the rain came. It began as a gentle shower, a halting summer rain that appeared as though it would be over before it started, the sort of shower that barely dampens the grass, leaving the pavement glistening and the air steamy.

Keegan stood waiting, oblivious to the rain, uncaring that it matted down his hair, soaked his shirt and suit pants. As he waited, Keegan thought that he should have stood up to his brother back then. He should not have given in to sentiment. He was angry with himself for his weakness; for his inability to stay on course. One mistake. Literally, one mistake. He had always been so careful, so correct. One mistake.

A black Toyota Camry pulled into the lot, stopping near Keegan. Hunter got out of the car and glanced at Keegan, frowning, his eyes looking toward the clouds. Keegan began walking away from the lot toward a grove of trees that provided some shelter from the shower. There were benches and picnic tables under the trees, but they were all wet. Keegan stood, waiting for Hunter to walk from his car. The reporter did not look happy. He was wearing brown corduroy pants and his necktie was pushed to one side, the top button of his shirt unbuttoned. He wore a gray corduroy sports jacket, and as he walked toward Keegan he pushed the long, stringy hair from his face. Keegan noticed beads of sweat on his neck and face.

"What's up?" Hunter asked.

"I want to propose a deal," Keegan said.

"A deal," Hunter repeated.

"I am close to the Schiller family," Keegan said. "I am aware that you approached Diane regarding a story about her parents."

Hunter cocked his head to one side, unable to conceal his surprise.

"I was doing my job," Hunter said defensively.

"Here's my proposal," Keegan continued. "You leave them alone. Let them deal with this privately, the way it should be done. In return, you will get confirmation of the tip you got about me."

Hunter was not sure he had heard correctly. He hesitated a moment, and then said, "So I do nothing on the Schillers and Sophie Naumann, and I get confirmation on the story about you tanking a case for your brother. Is that . . ."

"Correct," Keegan said.

Hunter looked closely at Keegan, studying him carefully to see if this was some sort of joke or prank.

"Why are you doing this?" Hunter asked.

"Personal reasons," Keegan replied.

"Personal reasons," Hunter said.

Hunter had been involved with many stories through the years, had dealt with all sorts of different people. He had seen men and women, some quite powerful, at their most vulnerable. He had been involved in many stories that had destroyed careers—wasn't that the ultimate for a reporter? to bring someone down?—but he had never experienced anything like this. Ever. Many times he had encountered subjects of stories who offered information on others. Never had he had someone offer up himself.

"I don't get it," Hunter said.

Keegan said nothing.

"I mean . . ." Hunter said.

"There are personal reasons that aren't important to what you're doing," Keegan said. "The more important issue is that there's a proposal on the table. And it's a good one. You've already broken the story about Mrs. Wahljak and caused a big stir. Now, rather than advancing that story, you have an opportunity to write a piece that brings down a senior assistant United States attorney. One of the main candidates to succeed the incumbent. And for corruption. It's a big story."

"It would destroy you," Hunter said.

Keegan nodded. "Yes," he agreed.

Hunter was perplexed. He did not know what to do. "I need time to think about it," he said.

"Fine," Keegan said.

"Lemme think about it overnight," he said.

"We'll talk tomorrow," Keegan said.

In the distance, perhaps three hundred and fifty feet away, a man was crouched on the edge of the shore taking photographs with a telephoto lens. From a distance, he appeared to be any other tourist. In reality, it was Theo Dunbar, who had been alerted to this meeting by Hunter. Dunbar turned at one point and trained his camera on Keegan and Hunter, capturing on film the two men standing, face-to-face and talking.

19

In the early morning light, David Keegan walked toward the park. He carried the *New York Times* and a cup of coffee from Dunkin' Donuts. He sat on a bench and set his coffee down. Keegan let the newspaper rest on his lap for a moment as he surveyed the park. It was oval-shaped, with a small pond at the center and a walkway all around. There were beds of roses, well cared for, at regular intervals around the oval. Beyond the park were large houses, set back from the street, houses that had been built in the early part of the century. This was a neighborhood populated by professional people—doctors and lawyers and businessmen and -women. It was a largely, though not exclusively, Jewish neighborhood. More to the point for David Keegan, it was the neighborhood in which Gerta Wahljak lived. Keegan sipped his coffee and set it back down on the bench. He picked up his paper and began skimming the news articles, but his attention was not on the news but rather on the pathway that led down from the Wahljaks'. In the clean, whitish-yellow light of morning, Keegan watched for Gerta. This was the route of her morning walk—she had told him so when they had met.

He read and he glanced from the paper, his eyes shifting

back and forth and back and forth. Several people walked through with dogs on leashes. A young mother came along pushing a baby carriage.

Soon enough, he saw her. She was a tiny figure in the distance, but Keegan was sure it was Gerta. She moved steadily along, with a determined gait. She was very small, indeed, but she moved well enough and he could see that she was dressed as she had been on the day he had interviewed her: in a dark gray frock with black slacks, white Reeboks, and a clip that held in place her silvery hair. Again, as he had done when he had met her the first time, he took note of her sprightly manner; of the energy that came from her diminutive frame.

As she approached, Keegan set the paper aside. He picked up his coffee, sipped it, and then set that back down, as well.

She was about thirty feet away when he rose.

"Mrs. Wahljak," he said, smiling. "How are you?"

She stopped and stared at him for a long moment, squinting and shading her eyes against the sunlight.

"Oh, it's you," she said. "Mr. Keegan."

"How are you?" he repeated.

"Are you here for talking to me?" she asked.

Keegan hesitated. "Yes," he said softly. "I am not officially working on this at all any more. I have removed myself from the case because I know the Schiller family."

He waited for her reaction, but there was none. She remained silent. Finally, she said, "So you know this man?"

"I know his daughter," Keegan said.

Gerta nodded.

"And you are in love with her, no?"

Keegan could not hide his surprise. "Yes," he stammered. "I am."

"Which is why you want to ask me the questions again, to tell her, 'no, it is all right, your father was not a bad man.' "

Keegan was silent. He merely nodded.

She sat down on one end of the bench, her posture that of an aging ballerina, and fixed her gaze on Keegan. "So," she said. "Ask me those questions."

And so he did. He asked many of the questions he had asked the first time they had talked. He wanted to hear how specific she was in her memory of the man in the photograph. Her responses were virtually identical to what she had said before. And when it was clear that he was through with his questions, Gerta stiffened.

"So I cannot remember every detail, this is true, but what is this got to do with anything, Mr. Keegan?" she demanded. "Mr. Keegan, I tell you now that I am as sure as I am sure that these are tulips," she said, gesturing, "as I am sure that this is a pond, that these all are trees. Mr. Keegan, as sure as I am of these things then I tell you this: I am sure that this man I see in hospital was there. He was in the camp. He is in the photograph. And what exactly he does, how his job is, I do not know. But do I know was he there? I know this. And I ask you this question, Mr. Keegan. Why was he there? What can he be doing there, a man in this picture, dinner with officers at this camp? He must account for himself, Mr. Keegan. What he did was not right. Why was he there? Why was he there?"

"Listen, ahhh, I don't think that deal will work," Hunter said. "It doesn't really work from my end. I'm sorry, I know . . . aaahh."

Keegan shut his eyes for a long moment. "It's a good deal for you," Keegan said, weakly.

"Well," Hunter said. "I mean, actually, it's not. No disrespect intended, but there's something about this story that gives it a little more altitude than just another scandal in law enforcement."

There was silence.

"With all due respect," Hunter hastily added.

Keegan had suspected this would happen. He had hoped otherwise, but he had suspected it would come to this.

"Listen, for what it's worth," Hunter blurted. "I admire your courage. I really do. Nobody I've ever dealt with has put themselves on the line like that."

"Do me a favor," Keegan asked. "Hold off on running the story until Monday. Give them time to figure out what to do, how to respond."

"Oh, jeez, I don't . . ."

"They're not going to deal with anyone else on this, believe me," Keegan said. "If they talk to anyone—and I am not saying they will—but if they do, it'll be you. No one else."

"Can you get them to talk?"

"Can you hold it till Monday?"

"Yeah, till Monday," Hunter said.

"I'll do my best," Keegan said.

Whatever the truth, she will need me, Keegan thought. He did not believe it was a case of mistaken identity. There was something about Gerta's clarity of mind, about her sharpness and certainty that impressed him. And if it was not that, not a case of mistaken identity, then what was it? If Diane's father had been at the camp, what had been his responsibility? His assignment? Had people suffered and died at his hand?

Whatever the truth, Keegan thought again, she will need me. He had to be there for her. He wanted to be there for her. For this was about to become a nightmare. Keegan could feel it. He could see it coming. He needed to free himself to be able to help her. And there was only one way to accomplish that. He entered the office of United States Attorney Walter Stone for what Stone expected would be a routine meeting.

"Walter, I've got news that will be disappointing to you, I'm sorry to say," Keegan began. They sat in Stone's office, just the two of them, the door closed. "I have to withdraw my name for consideration for the position of United States attorney. I need to take a leave of absence to sort through some things . . ."

Keegan paused. "You may want me to resign, in which case I will do so without hesitation," he said.

"What the hell . . ." Stone interrupted.

Keegan told him the story. He explained the entire matter: how his brother had come to him; how he had removed the complaint; how the case never went any further. Walter Stone sat silently and listened. When Keegan was done he took a deep breath. "I'm really surprised, first of all," Stone said. "I am really very surprised. It's not like you. And I'm disappointed, naturally. I'm sad, because you would have been so good in the job."

Stone shook his head and frowned. He looked at Keegan as though he couldn't quite believe it. "Why?" Stone asked plaintively.

David Keegan did not respond right away. Instead, an image of his brother Bill flashed into his head. Keegan thought of his father.

"My brother would have been ruined," Keegan said.

Stone stared at him. Both men fell silent for a long while. Stone got up and went to the window and looked down upon Post Office Square. He turned from the window and faced Keegan.

"Lemme ask you something," Stone said. "Did you give the information about the Wahljak matter to a reporter at the *Globe?*"

"Of course not," Keegan said.

"You're sure?"

"I've never been surer of anything in my life, Walter," Keegan said.

Stone nodded.

"So you are requesting a leave of absence, correct?" Stone asked.

"Yes," Keegan said.

"Granted," Stone said. "It will be of undetermined length. Unpaid. I need to think about what to do here. What my obligations are. How I report this, to whom, whether I need to go to the Board of Bar Overseers. You understand."

Keegan nodded.

"So I guess that's it for now," Stone said.

"I'm sorry," Keegan said. "I'm sorry I've let you down."

Stone nodded. He did not move to shake Keegan's hand.

20

This was a weird one, thought Lou Betts. They wanted a pic of some old guy but they wouldn't say why. Very unusual. In fact, Betts never recalled it happening before.

Betts turned down the volume on his scanner and sat back in his seat. He'd been warned that he might have to wait all day for the guy to come out. Schiller. Frederick Schiller. Betts was ready. If a car appeared in the driveway, Betts would quickly hop out of his car and aim his camera. He would train it on the vehicle and hope Schiller was inside. Ideally, the window would be open when Schiller went by, giving Betts a clean shot. But he wasn't counting on that. He only hoped the glare off the window wouldn't destroy the shot.

As the day wore on, a number of neighbors who lived in the stately homes tucked away in the neighborhood took note of Betts parked on the side of the road. Some, driving by in their Mercedes, slowed down to get a better look. When they peered suspiciously in Betts's direction, he cheerfully waved. In midafternoon, Betts noticed a shiny new Crown Victoria moving slowly along the road. He noticed the driver wearing a necktie and blue blazer, and he recognized the car as one of the fleet from Boston Coach, a livery service catering to the city's well-to-do. It appeared to Betts that the coach driver was looking for a particular address. Betts got out of his car and hailed the coach.

"Can I help out?" he said with a smile.

"Schiller?" the driver asked.

Betts nodded. "That driveway," he said. "He's some kind of celeb, huh?"

The coach driver appeared surprised. "Yeah?"

"The old dude, yeah," Betts said. "Some bigwig."

The driver seemed impressed.

Betts leaned closer and spoke to the driver in a confidential tone. "Listen, I'm from the *Globe* and I'm supposed to take a picture of this old bird, but no luck," Betts said. "I'm here all day, nothing. You follow? And I get no shot, I get no pay," he lied.

"You're here all day?" the driver asked.

"All day and I got the doughnut," Betts said, removing his wallet from his back pocket and taking out a twenty dollar bill. "Listen," he said, "when you come out with the old bird, would you mind going by me on the slow side? So I can get a good pic?"

The driver frowned and hesitated. He glanced at the twenty, then looked up and down the street. "I guess I could," he said.

Betts broke into a wide grin. "Super," he said. "And do me a favor, roll down the rear windows, just till you get past me, OK?"

The driver nodded. Betts handed over the twenty, and the driver went in to pick up Frederick Schiller and Sophie Naumann to take them to Mass General for an appointment with Dr. Felz.

Minutes later, the driver exited the Naumann driveway and drove slowly past Lou Betts, the rear windows down.

Betts had time to focus his camera on the elderly man in
the backseat. As Betts did so, Frederick Schiller turned
and faced the camera, his brow knitted, eyes narrowed,
mouth pursed. Frederick Schiller was confused, wondering why this stranger standing on the side of the road
was taking his photograph, a photograph that would
soon run in newspapers and magazines throughout the
world.

Late Thursday afternoon Ridley, the *Globe* reporter assigned to the paper's bureau at the federal courthouse,
called Hunter.

"A head's-up," he said. "The wrecking crew was in to
see Stone." The "wrecking crew" was the derisive term
Globe editors and reporters used to describe the triumvirate of editors who were in charge of their hated rival,
the *Record American*. Hunter had been slouching in his
seat, his feet up on his desk, when he had taken the call,
but this news caused him to swivel in his seat, place his
feet on the floor, and sit straight up.

"When?" Hunter asked.

"Just now," Ridley said. "They just left."

"All three of them?" Hunter asked, clearly puzzled.

"All three," Ridley said.

"That's weird," Hunter muttered, struggling to think
of a reason for such a meeting. That the meeting had
been scheduled more than a month in advance, neither
Ridley nor Hunter knew.

"Ever seen all of them in there together before?"
Hunter asked.

"No," Ridley said.

"So you don't know the purpose of the meeting?"
Hunter asked.

"Nope," Ridley said.

"OK," Hunter said. "Keep me posted if you hear anything at all."

Hunter summoned Hewlett to his office and shut the door. He told Hewlett about the meeting between the *Record* brass and the U.S. attorney.

Hewlett shrugged. "Could be any number of things," he said. "Could be anything."

"All three of them," Hunter said, pacing back and forth in the office, running his hand through his hair. "All three of them. Why all three? I mean a routine thing, you've got one or two people. But all three?"

He paced, he kicked a metal file cabinet. He swore.

"If those bastards . . ." he said through clenched teeth.

He sat back down at his desk and was lost in thought for a minute. He was imagining the worst, of course. He was imagining that the *Record* triumvirate had somehow gotten a piece of the story and gone in to pressure Stone into confirming it.

He snatched the telephone and dialed Stone's number. He was not available at the moment, and Hunter left a message for him to call back. He got off the phone and banged his fist down hard on the desktop, startling Hewlett.

"Jesus, Dan," Hewlett said.

"The prick won't take my call," Hunter said, getting up and resuming his pacing. "The little fuck is ducking me. Goddamn it!" he shouted, bringing startled reactions from reporters in the newsroom outside his glass-walled office. Hunter was red-faced, furious. He was panicking, terrified that this story, which he believed could change his life, might slip away. Hunter had convinced himself that breaking this story could earn him the Pulitzer Prize, and with the Pulitzer would come a book contract, money. With this story would come a certain prestige that had stubbornly elluded him through the years.

He glanced toward Hewlett.

"We've got to go tomorrow," Hunter said. "We can't wait."

Hewlett was surprised. "Tomorrow?"

Hunter nodded. "We can't let the *Record* jump us on this," said Hunter.

"I thought you gave the family till Monday," Hewlett said.

"I said unless the competition had the story," Hunter said. "I think the three *Record* rats going into Stone's office is an indication they might have the story. I can't hold this back. It's too big. It's too important a story for this newspaper."

He banged the palm of his hand on his desk. "Jesus," he said. "We've got a responsibility to get this news out there. I never should have agreed to delaying it. What was I thinking about? This is too much, too huge to fuck with."

"But, Danny," Hewlett said. "You made a deal. A deal's a deal. You can't just dump it in the paper on them tomorrow. We can't do that to them. It'll probably give Schiller a heart attack."

Hunter forced a laugh.

"I'm serious," Hewlett said. "Call Stone back and find out if he spilled the beans. I doubt it."

"I have a call in to him, I'll call him again, but I'm at the point now where, to tell you the truth, I don't trust anybody on this and I wouldn't put it past Stone to fuckin' lie about it."

Hewlett looked at him as though he was off his rocker.

Hunter grew indignant. "Let's not forget the point here," he said. "The point is that we're in the business of breaking news, not supressing it. Our job is to get the stuff out there in the hands of the readers and let them make judgments. 'Sunlight is the best disinfectant' and all that. The point is that there are competing interests here—the public's right to know versus the desire of Naumann and her husband for anonymity. Now which right wins out, Jimmy?" Hunter was glaring at Hewlett now.

"What about a reaction from Naumann or Schiller?" Hewlett asked.

Hunter shrugged. "Up to them," he said. "I'll give them an opportunity, I'll call Keegan and tell them there's a change of plans at our end . . ."

"He'll freak," Hewlett said.

"I don't give a shit," Hunter said. "Look, Jimmy, we've got the story. If they want to react, fine. If they don't want to react, fine. Either way, we've got the story. It's there, confirmed, written. I mean, it's not like this comes out of the blue, some preposterous allegation by a crackpot. Gerry Wahljak is one of the most respected attorneys in this town. This is a very prominent, well-thought-of guy. He's got a living eyewitness, he's got a fucking photograph for Chrissakes!"

Spittle came from Hunter's mouth and his eyes were wide. Hunter went to his desk and held up the picture. "Jimmy, you've done the research, huh?" Hunter pointed to one uniformed officer of the SS. "What's his name?"

"Spengler," Hewlett said.

"Spengler, right," said Hunter. "Convicted at Nuremberg of crimes against humanity. Executed. Who's this?"

Hunter asked, indicating a gray-suited man, seated in the front row.

"Berne," Hewlett said. "Convicted of some such at a Czech trial. Imprisoned."

"And this?" Hunter asked, indicating another uniformed SS officer.

"Stefan Kastner," said Hewlett. "Convicted by the Czechs, imprisoned."

Hunter held the photo up for another moment, then slowly put it down. His tone shifted from indignation to a quieter rage.

"Schiller, Schillinghaussen, was there," Hunter said. "Gerta Wahljak remembers him. She has his picture. There's no question in my mind it's the same man. No question. He turns up years later in the U.S., his name changed. Why? Why change your name? He has no tracks in the snow. You went through the clips with me. She's all over the place. Him? Nothing. Is there any question there was a deliberate effort on their part to keep him in the deep background? No question. You saw the clips. What was there on him? Nothing, barely a shred."

Hunter picked up the picture and pointed at Frederick Schiller. "There he is," Hunter said. "There he is. What was he doing there? In the officer's mess of the camp? Has he denied that it's him? No. If it wasn't, if there was some terrible mistake, we would have heard a roar of protest out of them by now. I mean, if you're accused of being a Nazi, of having a hand in a death camp and there's any explanation, you cough it up pretty fast.

"Was he a dissident? Did he act to stop the slaughter? They were butchering people, Jimmy. Children. Old people. Did he intervene? We know he couldn't have because if he had he'd be dead. The Nazis would have killed him. Or if somehow he had survived, he would tell his story. If he's Schindler, then he'd tell us, wouldn't he? He'd tell the world."

Keegan ran to his car and drove through the rainy streets of Chestnut Hill to the home of Sophie Naumann and Frederick Schiller. When he arrived, he was greeted by Diane and they went right to the library where they were joined by Sophie.

"Bad news," Keegan said. "The *Globe* is going to run the story tomorrow."

Sophie drew back, her eyes wide, horrified. Her mouth hung open and she was momentarily speechless.

"Tomorrow!" Diane said. "But we have an agreement."

"Hunter called and said he felt the story may be in the hands of some other paper, and he said he has no choice but to run it tomorrow," Keegan said.

"Oh, God," Diane whispered.

Sophie sat on the sofa and straightened her back, stretching her neck to one side, then another. She took a deep breath and used both hands to smooth her slacks on her lap. She then placed her hands together as though she were going to pray and pressed them against her lips.

"All right," she said. "I've got to focus."

"Let's talk about several immediate concerns," Keegan said. "When Hunter called he pushed for a response, some kind of quote from you, Diane, or one of your parents. Do you want to say something?"

Sophie rose from the sofa and walked to the window overlooking her rear terrace and garden. The rich earth around the plantings was dark and moist in the rain, and the leaves and grass glistened. Sophie gazed out for a moment, then turned back to David and nodded her head.

"Yes," she said, folding her arms across her chest and walking back to sit opposite Keegan. "Yes, I believe I do."

Keegan nodded and handed her an index card with Hunter's phone number on it.

"Must I do it right away?" she asked. "I'd prefer to wait an hour or two if possible."

"That's fine," Keegan said. "You have until 9:30."

"Mother, don't you think you should contact certain friends so that they hear about this from you rather than through the media?" Diane asked.

Sophie nodded. "I'll make those calls tonight," she said. "There are definitely people who should hear it from me and no one else."

She scratched a number of names on a sheet of paper.

"The newspaper will be printed and available at the *Globe* at midnight, maybe a few minutes before," David Keegan said. "I'm planning on being there to get one of the first copies. Then I'll come directly here so you can know precisely what you're dealing with."

"Thank you, David," Sophie said. And then she sighed heavily. She turned to Diane. "Now I must go wake Freddy and tell him this is coming." Diane nodded.

"I'll come with you," Diane said.

"I must do this alone," her mother said.

"Are you . . ." Diane began.

"I'm sure," Sophie replied.

"Thank you, David, for your help," Sophie said. Keegan started to leave. As he did so he asked, "Is there anything else I can do?"

"Yes, David," Sophie Naumann said. "You can pray for us."

* * *

Sophie went down the hallway to Freddy's room. She found him sitting on a sofa by the window, dressed in a robe and pajamas, glasses perched on his nose. He was reading a law book.

"I'm sorry to say I have bad news," she said. "The newspaper is publishing the story tomorrow."

"Tomorrow!" he said. "But they said they would wait." He closed the book and set it down.

Sophie was shaking her head. "A meaningless agreement," she said. "David spoke with the reporter, and he said there were indications that the story might be published elsewhere . . ."

"Why are these people doing this?" Freddy cried in an anguished tone.

Sophie shook her head.

"Why?" he demanded of her. "Why are they doing this?"

"David asked the reporter that," Sophie said. "And he said they had an obligation to get the truth out."

Freddy's eyes widened in disbelief. "The truth . . ." he sputtered.

"I'm just telling you what he said, Freddy," she said. "Please don't get . . ."

"What in Christ's name would they know about the truth?" he said derisively. "My God," he said, shaking his head, "they know nothing of the truth. They do not care . . ."

"That's right," Sophie said. "They do not care about us or anyone else. If they have their sensational story they are happy. That is all that matters to them. But we now have to confront it, Freddy. We have to deal with it."

He shook his head. "No," he said. "We must go!"

He limped across the room to his closet in the corner

and brought out a suitcase. He tossed it onto the end of his bed and went to the dresser and began dumping boxer shorts and socks into the bag. Then he placed a row of shirts in on top of the underwear and socks. Then he charged toward the closet. Sophie watched in disbelief as he stormed around the room loading clothes into the suitcase. This was surreal, she thought. She watched the strongest of men behave as though he was unhinged. In all of the years they had been together she had never before seen him lose his composure.

"Stop!" Sophie said, holding up her hands. "Stop this madness now." He halted in midstride and gazed at his wife, a look of desperation in his eyes. He was breathing heavily, on the verge of hyperventilating. She went to him, and grasped his elbow, and led him to the sofa. She sat down and tugged on him to do the same.

"Freddy," she said, leaning forward and holding his hands, looking steadily into his eyes. "Let's pull ourselves together," she said.

Her tone was sufficiently reproachful that he sat silently and listened. "We must compose ourselves and determine what the best course of action is in the days and weeks ahead. We can get through this, Freddy, but we must summon all of the strength we have to do it."

He shook his head, slowly at first, then more forcefully. "No," he muttered. "No."

"No, what?" she asked.

"I don't think we can get through this," he said. "I don't think I can."

She stood up and walked away from him, turning her back on him, shutting her eyes and rubbing them with her fingers. She turned and went back to face him.

"Damn it, Freddy, don't do this now," she said. "Don't

do this. Don't suddenly become someone else, someone you've never been. Not now."

"We must get away from this," he said. "It is too late in our lives to have to face this now." He paused and thought for a moment. "Years ago, when we were younger, yes. We were strong then. But not anymore."

She frowned. "And so we go off to Cleggan," she said. "We flee and go there and then what? And then what, Freddy?"

"Then we live our lives," he said. "We live in peace. We live out our days in peace."

"But our lives are here," she said, speaking more calmly now. "We have built a life for ourselves here, in the United States. Freddy, we have been here for most of our lives, and we can't simply pick up and run away. We would not live in peace. We would be haunted by our having turned and fled."

"But here we will face nothing but ridicule and condemnation," Freddy said. "It would be unceasing. You know the American press. You know the sorts of people who would fuel it." He shook his head. "They cannot be placated."

"We will explain what we . . ."

"Explain?" Freddy said, angrily. "Explain? If we explain what was done they will demonize us even more. What was done was done. We cannot explain it now. Who would understand? Only those who faced what we faced and no others. And how many others faced what we did? We would be destroyed."

She sat silently, with no rebuttal.

"And, worse," he continued. "Once they start on us they will not stop. They will dig and dig and dig some more. They will dig until everything that is buried under all of those years that have gone by, until all that happened back there is exhumed. They will not rest until it all comes out. Until it is all revealed." He leaned forward in his seat slightly and fixed his eyes on hers. Then he nodded ever so slowly as though to say, yes, Sophie, you know of what I speak.

"The records," he said, speaking in a voice barely above a whisper. "What exactly is in the records? And if they look hard enough, they will find whatever records exist. There can be no denying it."

David Keegan had said that Hunter's deadline was 9:30; that she had to call with her comment by then. At 9:25 P.M. she dialed Hunter's number.

"Dan Hunter."

"Mr. Hunter, this is Sophie Naumann calling."

There was the slightest hesitation. "Yes, Mrs. Naumann, I'm sorry . . . you know, about all of this. But I wondered whether you might have something to say . . ."

"Mr. Hunter . . ."

"Mrs. Naumann, I know this must come as just as big a shock to you as it does to everyone else, and I wonder whether you could tell me what your reaction was when you learned the truth about your husband?"

Sophie Naumann was amazed by the question.

"The truth?" she said.

"Yes, when you found out about him," Hunter said.

"Mr. Hunter, I thought you wanted a comment from me for your article," she said.

"I do," he said. "But I was hoping to ask you some questions as well."

"As I'm sure you can understand, this is not a time when I have any inclination to respond to questions, Mr. Hunter."

"Well, Mrs. Naumann, is there something you would like to say for this story?" Hunter asked. "I know you know pretty much where it's coming from."

"Mr. Hunter, you spoke a moment ago of the truth about my husband. The truth is that I love my husband, Mr. Hunter. That is my comment. I love him very much."

Hunter stood in his office at 11:45 P.M. reviewing the first copy of the *Globe* printed that night. It had just been rushed upstairs to him, and he looked at the paper and saw his name on the top of page one as the author of a story that he was certain—there was no doubt of it— would be carried throughout the world in the hours and days and weeks to come. It was a story that would be talked about and debated for months or longer. It would make him famous in journalistic circles. A broad smile broke onto Hunter's face and he felt a sense of pure, unadulterated elation.

Suddenly his telephone rang.

It was the *Globe* intern Hunter had sent to get an early copy of the *Record*, to see whether they had the story.

"Nothing," the intern said, when Hunter answered.

"Nothing at all?" Hunter said.

"Not a word," the intern said.

David Keegan's heart pounded when he saw the newspaper, when he looked across the top half of the *Boston Globe* and saw the harsh reality of the article, in black and white.

*   *   *

FEDS PROBE LOCAL MAN AS DEATH CAMP OFFICIAL read the headline, across the top of the page. "Naumann's husband is target of inquiry" read the subhead. The lead to the story read:

The United States Justice Department is investigating an allegation that the husband of Sophie Naumann, the prominent Jewish author and activist, was an official at a Nazi-run camp in Czechoslovakia called Theresienstadt.

Senior Justice Department officials confirmed that the investigation was initiated this week after Gerta Wahljak of Brookline, a Theresienstadt survivor and the mother of Boston attorney Gerald Wahljak, reported a sighting of a man she said was a camp official, Friedrich Schillinghaussen. Investigators believe that Schillinghaussen is Frederick Schiller, Naumann's husband.

Naumann is the author of numerous novels, including *Midnight on Kurfurstendamm*, the story of a Jewish family in Berlin that passes up an opportunity to flee the country and is eventually sent away to a death camp, where most family members perish.

Little is known of Naumann's husband, who has maintained a low profile through the years that the couple lived in London and, then, for many years, in New York. Five years ago they moved to Brookline, where their daughter, Diane, and her two children reside.

Gerta Wahljak, who was conscripted to work in an administrative capacity in the camp, secured a group photograph of various camp officials in 1942 and has kept it through the years. Last night, during a brief telephone interview with the *Globe*, Naumann refused to answer questions concerning whether her husband had witheld information from her about his past.

"I love my husband very much," she said.

Keegan placed the paper on the passenger seat of his car and drove quickly through the rain-slicked streets of Roxbury, Jamaica Plain, and into Brookline. He presented the paper to Diane, who was seated with her mother in the library. The reality of it horrified them.

Freddy came into the room in his bathrobe, read the first paragraph, and began shaking. He looked away and could read no more. He began shaking his head, his eyes shut.

Sophie could not get past the first paragraph either. But what attracted her attention was the photograph of Freddy, taken earlier that day in front of their house. She gasped when she saw it, saw how terrible Freddy looked. He had been confused and off balance when the photographer had trained the lens on him. But what was confusion and surprise came out in the photograph looking angry, his brow furrowed, his eyes hooded. He appeared to be glaring, arrogant, disdainful. The picture made her husband appear menacing.

21

Walter Stone laid the photographs on the conference table in front of Keegan.

"Who took these?" Keegan asked.

"FBI," Stone said, who believed what Dunbar had told him.

Keegan looked at Stone and saw the hard stare.

"It's not what you think, Walter," Keegan said.

"No?"

"No."

"So what is it?" Stone asked.

"I was meeting with him to try and help Diane. To maybe head off a story."

"I'm very disappointed in you, David. I accept your resignation."

David Keegan drove out along the Jamaicaway past Jamaica Pond and on toward Centre Street. He followed Centre Street and turned off at Faulkner Hospital. The Faulkner was set atop the Moss Hill neighborhood, overlooking the sprawling Arnold Arboretum, hundreds of wooded acres bearing a wide array of flora and fauna from around the world. As he drove, Keegan felt a sense of growing anxiety.

He had exchanged a series of letters with the counsel for the hospital. Finally, he had been granted permission to review certain hospital records. He had provided the hospital with a description of the information he sought—namely, any files or records relating to his parents, but specifically information relating to them in connection with the accident on July 29, 1954.

Keegan's appointment was with Madeline Ryan, the head of the Records Division, a woman in her late fifties. She brought Keegan into a small conference room and asked to see his identification.

He reacted with surprise.

"I'm sure you are who you say you are but we must be circumspect about showing private records," Mrs. Ryan said.

"Of course," he said, hastily taking his driver's license out of his wallet and handing it to her. She studied it for a moment, holding it in both her hands. She looked up from the photograph, studied his face, then glanced back down at the picture.

"All right, Mr. Keegan," she said. "And you stated in your letter that this search is not conducted for law enforcement purposes?"

"Correct," he said.

"Because if it is we require an entirely different procedure," she said. "You understand?"

"It's purely personal, Mrs. Ryan," he said.

She looked down at the file. "Yes, your father sent us a letter granting permission to review his file."

David had written the letter and forged his father's signature.

"The only trouble is," she said, "that he has no file

here." She handed Keegan a manila file folder, which he laid out on the table in front of him.

"As you can see, there is a file on your late mother," she said. "You have everything on her, however brief it is. But there is no record of your father ever having been admitted to Faulkner Hospital."

Keegan was taken aback. "You're certain?"

Her eyes widened slightly in surprise. "Certainly I am sure, Mr. Keegan," she replied. "We pride ourselves on thoroughness and efficiency here. A comprehensive search was conducted, then repeated. There is no file on your father. He was never admitted to this institution."

Keegan frowned. "But I believe, Mrs. Ryan, that he was admitted the night that my mother was brought here, on July 29, 1954. I believe that . . ."

"So you stated in your letter," Mrs. Ryan said. "But we have looked very carefully, Mr. Keegan. I received clear instructions from higher-ups here to make sure that we cooperated fully with you and we have done so."

"Perhaps there was an error made . . ."

She shook her head dismissively. "An admission to the hospital is an event of consequence, Mr. Keegan," she said. "It is not something we overlook or fail to record. Admissions are our source of revenue. They are recorded with the utmost care and always have been. Is it possible an error was made? Anything is possible. Is it likely? It is extremely unlikely."

Mrs. Ryan rose from her chair. Keegan rose as well. "If there is any other way we can be of service, Mr. Keegan . . ." she said.

"Thank you," he said.

Keegan left the hospital and walked slowly to his car, which had been sitting in the hot sun, the windows rolled up, doors locked. When he got into the driver's seat, the heat was stifling. Sweat poured down his brow, his shirt stuck to his back. He tried to take a deep breath, but could not catch enough air. He sat in his car holding the file folder with his mother's name on it. He waited a moment before opening it. He read over the three pages very quickly. They provided detailed information about her condition when she was brought to the hospital on the night of the accident. Much of the report involved details about efforts to revive her. Keegan could not stand looking at it and closed the folder.

But he had to think. He sat in the car for a half hour trying to think this through. There was a possibility that the records at both the BCH and Faulkner were faulty. It could be that the BCH records were wrong and that the BCH ambulance had, in fact, transported Dick Keegan to Faulkner. It was possible that Dick Keegan was admitted to Faulkner but that the records had been lost. It had, after all, been a long time.

But was it likely that records at both places were wrong? These were hospitals. Records mattered. Records were cared for, watched closely. So if the records were correct, that meant that Dick Keegan was not transported from the scene of the accident by BCH ambulance. And it meant that he had not been admitted to Faulkner Hospital. If that was so, the question was, what had happened to him on that night? If it was so, that meant that Dick Keegan had lied to his son about the events of that night. For there was no doubt that Dick Keegan had told his son on several occasions through the years that his mother had been taken to Faulkner by a Boston Ambulance Squad crew and that he had followed in a BCH ambulance. That Dick had been admitted and spent "a few days" there.

But if that was not true, then why had David's father lied?

22

Freddy looked at the front page of the newspaper again. He read the first two paragraphs, but could get no further. He limped from the kitchen, up the back stairs and down the hall to his room. His suitcase, now fully packed, stood in the middle of his room waiting to be carried off. He swallowed the pills Sophie had given him, including a new one that she said would help calm him down. Freddy went to the easy chair near the window and picked up the telephone on the table next to it. He called Aer Lingus.

When Sophie walked into his room he was sitting forward in the chair reading the account number from his American Express card into the phone. Sophie walked across the room and saw the notes he had scratched on a pad of paper: "Flight 321, Bos/Shan, noon."

She stood silently as he provided the full name on his card and the expiration date. Soon, he hung up the telephone. He sat silently, without moving, his hand still grasping the receiver as it sat in its cradle.

"Are you mad, Freddy?" she asked.

"Mad?" he asked, the disbelief obvious in his voice. "I think I'm as sane as can be," he said.

"To simply up and run away . . ."

"You may call it that if you wish, but I view it as self-protection. Tomorrow at noon . . ."

"Tomorrow?" she said, astonished. "Freddy, you can't . . . What about the surgery?"

"Dublin," he said. He paused. "I have purchased five tickets. Us, Diane, and the children. I assume they'll want to join us."

"Freddy, I've never seen you behave this way," she said. "I love you, darling, you know that. But I must tell you that you appear to me to be unraveling."

"Because I want to avoid being destroyed, that is un-raveling?" he asked.

Sophie was exasperated. "No, this running away to hide in Cleggan, this is crazy, Freddy. This is our home, this is where we belong."

He paused for a long moment.

"Do you know what scares me?" he asked. "Spending the rest of my life as a symbol of something hideous. That scares me. This newspaper article is but the beginning. This article, this is but blood in the water. This will bring other sharks, they will see the blood, not so much the bodies being ripped and savaged. They will see the blood and begin to move more quickly. They will smell the blood. Many others will smell the blood. The other newspapers and magazines and the television programs and as they all rush in for their piece, their sense of ex-citement will build and then they will go into a frenzy. They will want to taste our flesh in their teeth; savor our blood in their mouths."

She turned away, revulsed by the metaphor.

"And they will," he said. "They will, if we let them."

He sighed heavily.

"And the result will be that for the final years of our lives we will be known for this and nothing else," he said.

Sophie spoke softly. "But we will fight back," she said. "We have to."

"Fight back how?" he asked.

"With the truth," she said.

"The truth," he repeated. "The truth," he said again, drawing out the words as though they were some linguistic oddity. "The truth or a portion of the truth? A version of the truth? We will tell them this, but not that? Proudly trumpet certain things and hope they do not find out about other things? This you call the truth?"

She averted her eyes when he looked at her. She gazed down at her hands, folded on her lap. "The truth is far too messy," he said. "Much too untidy to be used in our defense."

She could see that the new medication was taking effect and she wanted to get him into bed before he fell asleep.

"Here, lie down and rest a moment before Diane comes," Sophie said.

He nodded.

Sophie tugged gently on his hands and Freddy rose shakily. It took him a moment to steady himself. Sophie tightened her grip on his hands and reached with her right arm around his back to hold him.

"OK?" she asked.

For a moment she feared he would lose his balance and pitch forward, his weight far too much for her to handle, and she tried to position herself so that she could push him back toward the chair, where his landing would be softer than on the floor. But Freddy caught himself and stood steadily.

"I think so," he said.

He held on to her and she walked him slowly to the bed. Sophie undid his robe and removed it, laying it on a chair. Sophie then turned down the bed and Freddy sat gingerly on the edge of the mattress, then brought his legs up and lay down. Sophie pulled the covers over him, tugging them up under his chin, smoothing them. She patted him gently on the shoulder and turned out the lamp on his night table. The light from the hallway illuminated his face, and Sophie stood by the bed, her hand gently stroking his hair. After a minute or so she stopped. Freddy's breathing became more rhythmic. He was sound asleep. She stood watching him and, finally, she left the room and shut the door.

Sophie reached out to Diane and hugged her tightly.

"Is he asleep?" Diane asked.

"Yes," Sophie said. "I gave him a tranquilizer. Let's talk upstairs."

Sophie carried two mugs of tea and led Diane up the stairs and down the hallway into her office. She closed the door. She handed one mug to Diane, who placed it on the end table next to the love seat and sat down. Sophie went to her chair. Her tea was on the table next to her. She sipped it and found it only lukewarm. She set it down and sat straight up in her chair, her hands folded on her lap.

"Diane, I want you to know some things, to understand some things about him—and about us—that are quite difficult for me to talk about. And for your father as well."

"About?"

"The past," Sophie said softly. "About things that happened back forty and more years ago. We have not been entirely truthful with you through the years. We have tried to protect you from certain things . . ."

"Mother!"

Diane was suddenly red-faced. Distressed. Confused.

"Your father is a good man, Diane," Sophie said. "No matter what the newspaper might say or what people might believe, I know he is a good man." Sophie rubbed her eyes and tilted her head, looking into her daughter's eyes. "Perhaps we should have told you certain things years ago and, really, we nearly did. But it never seemed to be the right time. Those were very difficult times, Diane. Nothing was easy or clear-cut. It was hard to know what was right, it was hard to know what to do."

Sophie took a deep breath. She watched her daughter's expression of puzzlement turn to concern.

"He's a good man, honey," she said. "You as well as anyone know that. He did what he did so that we could have a life together, Diane."

"Please, Mom," Diane said. "Tell me . . ."

Sophie nodded. "Of course," she said. "Of course I will. I want you to know some things, so that you can begin to absorb them and understand them."

Sophie rose from her seat and went around to the window. A crescent moon hung in the sky—a fragile sliver of light. She looked back at her daughter and returned to her seat, sitting forward in her chair, leaning toward Diane.

"We did not meet in London after we'd gotten out," Sophie said. "We first met in Berlin before the war. In '37."

Diane drew back, a look of utter astonishment on her face. "Mom . . ."

Sophie nodded. Yes, she acknowledged with her nod and her glance down at her lap, yes she had lied about it.

Diane was stunned. "You mean that the whole story about you and Daddy meeting at that pub in Soho is not true?" she asked, clearly incredulous. "That he did not propose to you in the park by the Thames? That's all fiction?"

Her voice betrayed total disbelief.

"Most of what we have told you of our life in London is true, Diane," Sophie said. "But there are some things that are not entirely accurate. Some things that we've hidden from you."

Diane shook her head ever so slightly as though she was trying to see more clearly.

"So when did you meet?" she asked.

"We met in 1937," Sophie said.

"Where?" Diane asked.

"We met in Berlin," Sophie said quietly.

"But why, Mom," Diane asked imploringly. "Why would you tell me . . ."

Diane pushed the hair back off her face. She appeared pale, with circles under her eyes.

"I'll explain why, Diane," Sophie said. "But I want to talk about your father's position during that time."

"He was a lawyer," Diane stated.

"Yes, he was a lawyer," Sophie said.

"And he was in private practice, specializing in property and tax law, correct?" Diane asked, for this is what she had been told.

Sophie hesitated. "He did specialize in property law, but not in private practice," she said. "He worked for the government." Sophie said it softly, letting the sentence hang in the air, waiting a moment so Diane could begin to take it in, to grasp what it meant.

"The government," Diane repeated, dropping her

chin and staring intently at her mother. "The German government."

Sophie nodded.

"The Nazi-controlled government," Diane said.

Sophie nodded again.

"And what did he do for the government?" Diane asked.

"He was employed at the Reich Ministry of Justice," Sophie said.

"The Reich Ministry of Justice?" Diane asked, incredulous. "Mother, is this some sort of horrid . . . I don't understand . . ."

"This is what happened a long time ago," Sophie said. "And I want you . . ."

"Mom, did you not escape from the camp during a prisoner transfer?" Diane asked, visibly stunned. "Did you not then flee to England, to London, where you met Daddy? Did those things not happen as you have told me they did?"

"Not as I have told you," Sophie said.

"Mom, you have told me and Dad has told me that he left Berlin in 1939," Diane said, struggling to maintain her composure. "That he went to Austria and then on to England where he stayed with friends in London, found work as a law clerk, and met you. Is this not right?"

Diane cocked her head to one side as she asked this question. Her hair seemed slightly disheveled now and several strands hung down by her left eye. She put her hands together, as though in prayer, and placed her fingertips against her chin as she awaited her mother's reply.

Sophie shook her head. "No, Diane," Sophie said. "Your father did not leave in '39. He stayed."

"And he worked for the Third Reich," Diane said, her statement flat.

Sophie glanced away, then looked back at her daughter.

"Where is the article, Mother?" Diane asked. "Do you have it here?"

"In the kitchen," Sophie said.

"Tell me it's all wrong, Mom," Diane said, her voice weak. "Tell me that it's not Daddy in the picture."

Sophie went across the room to her daughter and embraced her, holding her for a moment.

"Come sit down," Sophie said. "We're both very tired." She led Diane to the love seat and they sat, side by side, as Sophie held her daughter's hand.

"I want you to know everything," Sophie said, knowing at that moment in her own mind that she would never tell Diane everything; that she could never know everything, absolutely must not ever know everything. But Sophie would tell her a great deal more than she ever had before.

"Diane . . ." Sophie said, and she stopped abruptly, cocking her head, listening, thinking she had heard a noise.

Freddy woke with discomfort in his upper body, not precisely sure where. He sat halfway up, trying to prop himself against the pillows. Suddenly, involuntarily, his right hand jerked up and clutched at his chest. He winced in pain and tried to sit up, but could not. His right hand pressed against the smooth cotton of his pajamas. He pressed hard with his hand, reflexively, to combat the pain, but there was a tightness within his chest that would not let go. It was as though some kind of claw had grabbed his insides and was squeezing harder and harder.

"Soph . . ."

He struggled to say her name, to call out to her to come to him, to help him, but he did not have the strength even to say her name in anything more than a whisper.

And so he whispered, as though he could impart a message to the air that would sit out there somewhere in the universe and somehow reach her.

"Sophie," he whispered. "I love you."

He cried out in pain and willed himself to throw a foot over the side of the bed, but even as he did so, Freddy clutched harder at the pain that felt as though it would sear through the wall of his chest, through his wrinkled skin, through the cotton of his pajamas. And it was at that moment that he felt himself out of control. He felt as though he were atop some perch, and he could feel as he raised his trunk up off the bed that he was pitching forward, in free-fall. And he believed that he was taking his last breath, and as he did so he thought of Sophie and he hoped his final words would reach her.

"Did you hear something?" Sophie asked Diane.

Diane shook her head no.

"I thought I heard . . ." Sophie said, rising from the love seat and walking out of the office. She went down the hallway to the bedroom. She slowly opened the door. And then she saw Freddy sprawled on the floor, his arms spread in either direction, his face on its side, his mouth open, fibers of the carpet pushing up at his mouth.

"Freddy!"

23

Diane heard her mother's scream and raced down the hall.

"Oh my God!" Diane said, seeing her father's lifeless form sprawled on the floor, his face gray, the color of ash. Sophie knelt by his side and felt for a pulse, pressing her fingers in at his carotid artery, searching, and she thought she felt something but could not be sure.

The EMTs arrived and ministered to Freddy briefly on the bedroom floor, then whisked him down the stairs and into the ambulance. Sophie and Diane rode in the back, and when they reached Massachusetts General Hospital, several doctors began working on Freddy right away.

Soon, he was moved from the emergency room upstairs to the intensive care unit. Hours passed. Various doctors held brief huddles with them. It was not until the early morning that a coronary specialist sat down and explained to them that Freddy had had a heart attack and possibly a stroke, as well. They would not yet be permitted to be by his side, but that would come in a few hours, the doctor said. In the meantime, the physician urged them to rest. But rest did not interest them. They had so much to discuss.

They were given use of a small, rarely-used consult

room with a panoramic view. They stood together, mother and daughter, arm in arm, gazing out the window. The sky was lightening, the darkness lifting, slowly, almost imperceptibly. Shafts of sunlight were soon striking the upper reaches of the Hancock Tower. This terrible day was dawning.

But it was on this day that Sophie Naumann began to tell her daughter the story of those days so long ago. The room was small, with just enough space for a love seat, two easy chairs, a coffee table, and a small bookshelf. It was done in muted shades of green and beige with prints of the New England countryside hung on the walls. It was a corner room with a view out over Beacon Hill and the Back Bay, as well as along the Charles River and over to Cambridge.

Sophie and Diane stood looking out at the river below. Two sailboats, their white sails luffing in the breeze, moved lazily across the water. Looking upriver, they could see a number of scullers slicing through the water, their oars dipping into the Charles and creating pools of white, foamy water. They could see out across the MIT campus to Kendall Square and, farther upriver, they could see the spires of Harvard. The Esplanade lay beneath them, running along the Boston bank of the river in front of the Hatch Shell, where the Pops played each Fourth of July.

"You OK?" Diane asked.

Sophie nodded. "Scared," she said. Diane nodded. Diane took her mother in her arms and hugged her tightly.

Sophie felt a profound sense of uncertainty. She did not know where this was going, where exactly it would lead, what the result of it all would be. Her greatest fear, of course, was that Freddy would die, but she feared, as well, the possibility of revelation. Through the years she had become expert at keeping her mind in the present, not permitting it to wander back beyond the recent past, forbidding it to travel back to the dangerous days so long ago.

"Come," Diane said, leading her mother to one of the chairs. "Sit down and take a deep breath."

What would she tell Diane? How would Diane react to what she would hear? For so long Sophie had sealed off that part of her memory that stored recollections of the past. But now she would open up that part of her memory, unseal it and permit some of what was inside to spill out. As she thought back, her mind open, she found herself remembering the night when everything changed, when any remaining illusions about their lives were forever shattered. She remembered her father racing from their house, running coatless into the cold November night. Sophie's knees and arms had pumped furiously as she had followed him out of the house and ran to catch him. And she remembered vividly that as she caught up to him she could hear his wheezing, his gasping for breath as he stumbled to a halt on the Tauberstrasse when he saw the men smash the plate glass windows of his market. There were others along the sidewalk smashing in the windows of other establishments—the tailor's and the butcher's, the delicatessen, the baker's, the stationer's, and the jeweler's. Sophie recalled one man in particular, squat and powerfully built, who stood before her father's store with an iron bar and systematically, patiently, smashed every bit of glass.

Suddenly her father had rushed forward and confronted the man. When he had done so, Karl Naumann had been struck across the face and sent crashing to the pavement, blood gushing from his nose, his spectacles shattered. Sophie remembered rushing to her father's aid as the store was set ablaze, flames rapidly climbing the walls, racing along the rivers of gasoline that had been tossed about.

"Dear God," Sophie whispered at the recollection.

Diane reached over and placed her hand on her mother's shoulder. "What is it?" she whispered.

Sophie blinked, trying to chase the memory from her mind.

"You're exhausted, Mom," Diane said. "Let's . . ."

"I want to talk," Sophie insisted. "For a while, anyway."

Sophie sat up in the chair and smoothed her dress across her lap.

"I wanted to . . ."

"I know this is hard for you, Mom," Diane said, taking the seat opposite Sophie. "But I have often wondered—and you and I have discussed this now and again—I have often wondered why your family didn't simply leave. Get out of there."

Sophie nodded. It was a good question, entirely reasonable, Sophie thought.

"It seems now, in retrospect, such madness to have stayed," Sophie said. "But things were not as easily seen back then. And leaving was not so easy. We were Germans, Diane. Like most Jews, we were very much assimilated. My father thought of himself as a German first, a Jew second. He loved Berlin. He loved Germany. It was where he had grown up, raised his family, built his business.

"Many of our friends did leave in '33 when the

National Socialists took over. But soon they realized that things were not so bad. The cataclysm some had feared never materialized. And so those who had left—many of them, anyway—returned.

"Nowadays, when people look back at that time, studying it in school, they see the anti-Semitism as larger than anything else," Sophie continued. "But the appeal of the Nazis to many Germans had to do much more with the fact that they stood up to the Communists, the Bolsheviks, and they promised economic growth and more jobs. To a nation that had suffered terribly since World War I, that sort of economic nationalism was very appealing.

"And we all believed—at least many of us believed—that the anti-Jewish program would pass. That the Nazis would focus on the Communists and the economy, and that the rhetoric about the Jews would drift away. I believed and most of my friends believed that it was a phase. No one really believed that the policies against the Jews would escalate to anything like what happened. No one foresaw that. Even as things grew more difficult with laws that made life more restrictive for us, my father would say, 'We are a resilient people. We have been through this before and we will go through it again.'

" 'We persevere,' he would say. 'We endure.'

"And so we persevered and we endured. And we made the best of what we had. The laws made it impossible for me to go to the university any longer and I began tutoring Jewish children who could not go to school. But even as I did so I continued studying literature on my own. I read a great deal and wrote, as well, and I would go to informal gatherings of students where Jews were welcome to discuss writers mostly."

Sophie was silent for a moment and then she smiled.

"That is how I met Freddy. At an outdoor cafe. In the summer of 1937. June. There was a group of students and professors who would gather informally to talk about literature, about the new American writers, about poetry and art.

"We had such a love," Sophie said. "It was as though we had reached across the universe and found each other."

Sophie wiped her eyes with Kleenex.

"We were like any young lovers—desperate to see one another, desperate to be together. But it was very hard. And quite dangerous. Denunciations had become commonplace. The government early on exhorted the people to spy on friends and aquaintances, even family members, and to report to the party the existence of any banned activities. People used them to get back at old enemies or even to harm the reputation of a professional or personal rival. Denunciations could be made anonymously to the party, and were commonly made against Aryan men and women involved romantically with Jews. Had Freddy been denounced and the fact of our relationship confirmed—he would have been destroyed professionally and probably prosecuted for violating the Law for the Protection of German Blood—the so-called Nuremberg Laws that deprived Jews of citizenship and civil rights."

Diane shut her eyes and slowly shook her head. She knew most of this, but the idea of all this affecting her parents seemed rather incredible.

"The laws prohibited marriage between Jews and Gentiles, and outlawed extramarital sex between Jews and Gentiles. Cases of 'race defilement'—sexual intercourse between Jew and non-Jew—could bring a sentence of ten years in prison, even execution. Marriages broke up as a result of the severity of these laws. Heinz Ruhmann, a popular actor married to a Jewish woman, divorced his wife to salvage his career."

Sophie folded her hands on her lap and studied her fingers for a moment. "But for me and Freddy none of this much mattered," she said. "We were committed to one another. We had agreed that we would be together no matter the cost."

Suddenly Sophie smiled broadly, a smile of such unexpected radiance that Diane was taken aback. "What?" Diane asked.

"So much about it was so wonderful," Sophie recalled. "We would sneak off together in the park where we would walk for hours on end, holding hands and talking about artists and writers. We talked about the music we liked, the American jazz. And we talked about our dreams for the future. To be free. To be in a place where there was no need to be afraid.

"On sunny days we would stroll in the park, and sometimes we would rent a rowboat and Freddy would row me around the pond, and we would simply be together. We would hold hands or he would put an arm around my shoulder, and we would be so very happy. Just being together. And we would go to certain cafes, there were certain places frequented by students where we could be together and have coffee and listen to music and all would be well.

"In a way, of course, Berlin was a terrible place to be. The worst place on earth to be in a way. But I did not pick that place. I did not choose that time to fall hopelessly in love. Those things just happened. I accepted them. I did the best I could with the circumstances. We did the best we could. We knew we would need to be patient. And careful. But mostly patient. What were we waiting for? A chance to be together. A change in the laws. A change in government. Something. Anything that would allow us to be together. But in the meantime, we agreed that we would wait and put ourselves in a position where nothing would jeopardize what we would have together. That became what rose above all else. We agreed that we would do whatever it took. Whatever it took. That we would wait out the Nazis, the war, whatever.

"And, soon enough, my family received notification that we were being sent away. And for Freddy and me, that was the ultimate test of our love."

24

Diane called in the very early morning.

"Dad's had a stroke," she told David. "We're at Mass General."

"How's he doing?" Keegan asked.

"Not too well," Diane replied.

"I'm on my way," David said.

At 6 A.M., two dozen doctors and nurses worked their way through the coffee line in the main Massachusetts General cafeteria. Two surgeons, an older man and a younger woman, stood conferring, arms folded across their chests, deep in conversation. Men and women in white or hospital green sat at tables throughout the cafeteria, having coffee and engaging in quiet conversation.

Keegan scanned the place and saw Diane in the corner, as far from the crowd as she could be. He strode down the center aisle and cut over toward the back, watching her all the while. Her elbows were propped on the table and her hands were folded in front of her mouth, fingers intertwined. She was staring straight ahead.

He approached from the side and stood still for a moment as she realized someone was standing there and turned her attention to him.

"I am so sorry," he said as she turned to face him.

"It's a stroke," she said. "We won't know until . . . maybe for a while."

"There's so much they can do," Keegan said. "The advances . . ."

"My mother and I were talking during the night," Diane said. "Somehow she thought she heard a noise and went to Dad's room. He was on the floor. He hasn't responded since then."

"They understand the brain so much better now," he said, groping. "More than ever before they . . ."

She paused and steadied herself. He reached down and took her hands and she stood up and they embraced and they felt, together, a sense of relief.

"I'm glad you're here," she whispered.

"Me, too," he said.

Keegan held her in his arms and looked down at her, her tired eyes, her pale face. Keegan marveled at her strength and steadiness. She had always been so focused and disciplined. She was not flashy or showy in any way, but she was strong and dependable. She had handled the raising of her children, her work as a litigator, even her divorce, with steady determination. Of late, she had had to deal with the uncertainty of their relationship, and now, on top of that, she was faced with her father's condition as well as the newspaper article.

"It's going to be OK," he whispered, "it's going to be OK. It is, Diane. It is."

He held her as tears welled in her eyes.

"Come on," he said, wrapping his arm around her shoulders and walking her through the back door of the cafeteria and out into a courtyard with gardens and footpaths and wooden benches set among the shrubs. They walked to the far end of the garden and found a bench tucked away in the corner. It was cool outside in the morning air. They sat side by side and he took her hands in his. He wrapped his arms around her and pulled her close. They held their embrace for several minutes, both of them silent.

"During the night, my mother started telling me about their lives," Diane said. "About what things were like for them long ago."

She paused and looked off toward the far end of the garden. Keegan had difficulty reading the expression on Diane's face, in her eyes. She seemed somewhat confused, frightened.

"There were things I was not aware of," she continued. "Facts and details I had not been told of. That had been kept from me."

She looked at Keegan, studying his expression, searching for a reaction, finding none. He sat impassively, listening closely. Diane watched him for a moment and then looked down at the ground.

"She's going to tell me everything, but I have a feeling it's going to take some time," she said. "And it won't be easy. For either of us."

Diane shook her head in amazement. "Imagine concealing facts and details about your life from your child. It really kind of blows my . . ."

She shook her head again as though trying to coax herself out of some fog.

"Anyway, we just started in the middle of the night, really."

Diane looked down at her lap, at her folded hands. "I had always thought what I told you, remember, about him . . ."

"That he was in private practice," Keegan said.

"Right," Diane said. "That's what I always believed. But that wasn't so. He was actually a government lawyer." She hesitated and glanced up at David, trying to judge his reaction. But she quickly glanced away.

"My father was Protestant. Lutheran. And I had always been told that they got together in London later, after they'd both emigrated. In the early forties. But, in fact, they met in Berlin in '37. By then Jews had lost basically all their legal rights. My mother had been a university student but, because she was Jewish, she was forced to leave school. She continued reading and writing and working hard, and whenever she got an opportunity to be among intellectuals to talk about literature, music, art, she took it. And that's how she met my father. He was a law student at the University of Berlin, and he would go to these informal gatherings in a cafe where this small group would talk about ideas, about writers. And they met at one of those sessions and they soon fell in love.

"But because of the situation at the time they had to keep their relationship secret," Diane continued. "So they did. They saw each other whenever and wherever they could. What was worse was that they could not talk about the relationship to anyone. Neither one told a soul for fear that they would be found out and prosecuted. My mother would have been charged with a crime and my father's career would have been ruined. So they kept it secret as they waited for the political climate to change.

"They decided the best thing to do was just to go on with their lives and to wait until they could be together. And so my mother taught in the homes of Jewish children who were not permitted to go to school. And she studied on her own."

She paused and looked squarely at Keegan. Her voice was softer now. "And my father went to work for the Reich Ministry of Justice."

She stopped and her gaze held his eyes. He struggled to remain impassive, but he found it impossible to conceal his surprise.

"Yes, I was shocked, too," she said quietly.

"I'm . . . I don't know . . ."

"I said to my mother, 'How could you deal with that? How could you get by that?'"

Keegan was at a loss for words. He reached over and took her hand, holding it firmly. He did not know what else to do or say.

"David, they've been concealing things from me for my whole life," Diane said. "They've been hiding things from me." She paused and looked away, shaking her head slowly and speaking softly, with a note of incredulity. "My own parents."

25

In Roslindale the heat rose up off the pavement in shimmering waves. The neighbors turned on their garden hoses and sprayed one another while teenagers down the block jimmied open a fire hydrant, sending a powerful stream of water cascading down the street.

At ten minutes before nine she had the car all packed: an old blanket to sit on, towels, a change of clothes for the boys, baseball gloves and ball, portable radio, a thermos of lemonade, sandwiches, cookies, and magazines. They had been on the verge of an argument about it, but he had pulled back.

"I want to do this as a family," she had said. "As a family."

Davey was eight years old, Billy just two. The thought of having a two-year-old at the beach was not a pleasant one for Dick Keegan. He had been back with his wife and sons for two months now. He had behaved. Dick Keegan hated the beach, but she had suggested this, she wanted this, and he would go along, as cheerfully as he was able.

They soon found, as they rode south through Quincy, that they had gotten out ahead of the traffic. They had expected a long, slow meander down to Nantasket Beach and found, instead, clear roads all the way. As they neared the shore the temperature dropped down to a pleasant eighty-five degrees, a full ten degrees cooler than at home. When they reached Nantasket they found a parking place and a prime spot on the sand.

Davey went racing toward the water, stopping short of going in until his parents sauntered down to the ocean's edge with Billy between them. Davey swam from one parent to the other, back and forth, in water up to his father's waist. Soon, Dick Keegan submerged and swam what seemed to Davey a truly vast distance underwater. Dick was a broad-shouldered man, well-muscled, and he swam with easy, powerful strokes.

There was space on the beach to throw a baseball, and Dick got the gloves and ball out of the beach bag. Dick went into a crouch on the sand, and Davey pretended to be a pitcher for the Red Sox.

"Two outs in the bottom of the ninth at the stadium, a runner in scoring position, and number seven Mantle comes to the plate. Davey Keegan steps to the mound, and studies the sign. Keegan shakes off the signal, shakes off the next signal, then nods. Keegan toes the rubber and goes into the stretch. He glances back at the runner on second, then turns and comes to the plate with a fast-ball low and away, and Mantle swings and misses! And the stadium crowd stirs. And young Davey Keegan, on in relief in the ninth with the game on the line for the Sox, the pennant on the line, the rookie out of Roslindale facing one of the greats. And Keegan looks in and goes into the stretch and he comes in with a change of pace and Mantle swings way ahead of the ball, missing it by a mile. Wow! What a pitch from the kid. And now the Bronx crowd is hushed as the hopes of these Yankee fans ride on the broad shoulders of the man in pinstripes. And young Davey Keegan, the rookie, goes to the resin bag, throws it down on the back of the mound. And he toes the rubber and shakes off a sign and he goes to the stretch and he rocks and deals and here he comes with a high fastball out over the plate and Mantle takes a mighty swing and misses! He struck him out! Davey Keegan struck out Mickey Mantle and the Red Sox win the pennant and the Red Sox are mobbing Davey Keegan!"

As the morning progressed the beach grew more crowded, but their spot down near the water was ideal— spacious enough, surrounded by families with young kids, not teenagers with radios blaring. In the late morning, Billy fell asleep on a corner of the blanket and she covered him with a towel to protect him from the sun. Dick Keegan stretched out next to Billy and thumbed through a magazine, while Davey and his mother walked down the beach, following the water line on the hard wet sand. They walked for a long time, reaching the far end of the beach where it became private. At that point they turned and started back, walking slowly, picking through shells every now and again, examining rocks, looking for sea glass.

They ate lunch on the blanket, sandwiches she had made, and drank Cokes in cold green bottles that his Dad bought at a stand across the causeway. After lunch, she rose and was about to go in swimming.

"Better to wait an hour," David's father said.

"Oh," she said, "it's . . ."

"It's safer, though," Dick Keegan said.

David could see his mother about to argue, but then

she glanced at him and paused. "You're right," she said. "Daddy's right, Davey. It's safer."

David marveled at this moment, this exchange, for he had tensed when they had begun the conversation, expecting trouble.

When she finally did go for a swim David and Billy and their dad lay back on the blanket watching her slow, deliberate strokes propel her through the water. She swam straight out for a while and then they could see her—see her bobbing yellow polka-dotted bathing cap—move ever so slowly through the blue-green water. They watched for a while and then Billy nagged his father for a story, and they settled down together as Dick Keegan read them *The Cat in the Hat*. After reading it once, he read it a second time.

"Very silly guy," Billy said.

"He is, isn't he?" Dick Keegan said.

"I like him," David said.

"But he's bad," Billy said, his eyes wide.

"Well, he's not really bad," David said. "He's kind of naughty."

"That's a good way to say it," Dick Keegan said.

"And funny, too," David said.

Suddenly, Dick Keegan grew tense. He sat up straining as he looked out over the water, his neck stretched, his head back, looking from left to right and back again. David looked at his face and saw him frown. David watched as his father jumped to his feet and stood with his hands on his hips looking back and forth, back and forth. Nothing.

"Davey, come here," Dick said. He scooped the boy up and put him on his shoulders. "You be the lookout, Davey," Dick Keegan said. "You spot Mommy."

David looked carefully across the water, letting his eyes move slowly from the left and then all the way to the right. He began to look back over the same terrain when his father said, "Do you see her?"

David hesitated.

"I asked you a question," Dick said, his voice tense, on the verge of anger.

"I . . . I don't, Dad," David said, suddenly tense and nervous himself.

In one swift move, his father placed him back on his feet and ran toward the water, his head now jerking to the left, the right, and back again, searching in vain for the yellow polka dots of her bathing cap. David ran after him, standing by his side, looking farther to the right and then farther to the left.

"There!" David said urgently. "There she is, Dad," David said, pointing to the far left. "Past those people. See?"

They could see her wave to them and they waved back. David could see his father trembling, could feel it as he brushed up against his father's leg.

"OK," Dick Keegan said, fighting to steady himself. "OK, then," he said, forcing a smile. He rubbed Davey's head affectionately.

"Good eyes," Dick said. "Good eyes, Davey." They walked back to the blanket and sat down. The father looked at his son and forced a smile. "Scared me," he said. "We wouldn't want to lose her, would we?"

By late afternoon, many of those who had crowded the beach throughout the day began drifting off, heading home. She lay on the blanket, with Davey asleep against her shoulder, watching her husband and other son play in the surf. She did not want to leave. She did not want this to end. This was what she wanted. This was everything. Peace and tranquility. Happiness. Was it too much to ask in life?

She watched Dick tickling Billy, watched as he chased him in the shallow water, watched them dodge the waves together, Billy laughing, giddy.

She regarded her husband, a ruggedly handsome man, and, for the thousandth time, she wondered what went on inside his head. What demons took hold of him? Prevented him from controlling himself? She would like to have understood, but she would settle for this. She would settle for not knowing, for never understanding; for having it go away and never return.

In the late afternoon they loaded everything into the car and walked down to the air-conditioned movie theater and saw *Journey to the Center of the Earth*. Billy cried, and she took him out to the lobby and waited until the picture was over.

As they walked back along the boulevard David asked whether they could go to Paragon Park, a vast amusement park across from the beach, just two blocks from where they were. Every time they had ever been to Nantasket he had asked to go to Paragon Park, but nine out of ten times they did not have the time or she did not have the money. The rides, the food, everything was maddeningly overpriced. But this time, when he asked, she looked at her husband, a hopeful look, and he nodded his assent.

"Wow!" Davey exclaimed.

"What?" Billy asked, sensing something good had just happened.

"We're going to Paragon Park!" Davey said. "We're going!"

"I want cotton candy," Billy said. "Can I have cotton . . ."

"It'll rot your teeth," the father said.

"Oh, Dick, I don't . . ." she started.

Dick Keegan smiled. "OK, OK," he said. "Cotton candy it is."

"Yaaayyy!" shouted Billy Keegan.

"Yaaayyy!" shouted David Keegan.

Yaaayyy! thought their mother.

On the Tilt-a-Whirl Davey felt sick to his stomach. On the Wild Mouse he felt dizzy. On the Ferris wheel he felt excited. Through all the rides and the hot dogs and Cokes and all the walking and waiting in line at Paragon Park, he thought not of the rides or the food or anything other than that this was how he wanted his life to be. As they walked along together, sauntering under the colorful lights and past the noisy rides and screaming children, as they walked by the vendors trying to entice them into the Haunted House and wanting them to throw baseballs at milk bottles, he felt a lightness of heart, a happiness, that he did not ever remember experiencing.

The very next night, one month exactly before she died, Davey was awakened sometime late, and he walked down the hallway from his bedroom and saw his father in the kitchen holding a small brownish bottle with a picture of four red roses on it. He poured from the bottle, his hand unsteady. He said something Davey did not understand, something in a low, gruff voice, something he said with a sneering look on his face. He could hear his mother in the bathroom, crying.

He dreamed that he fought with his father. He dreamed he was a grown man, his father's size, bigger even. He dreamed that they fought and that he was tougher and at the end of the fight his father lay still. He dreamed that he had killed his father and he was glad.

26

David Keegan hunched over the microfilm machine in the research room of the Boston Public Library. He spun through the spool searching for the *Boston Post* of July 30, 1954. He soon found it. The lead story that day involved President Eisenhower meeting with his cabinet, then issuing yet another in a series of warnings to the Red Chinese. Locally, the news focused on a water shortage due to a prolonged drought throughout New England. There was a photograph on the front of the local section of the paper picturing a group of children in Dorchester sitting curbside while a gush of water from a hydrant poured over them. There was a brief article about how people were coping with the prolonged heat wave. The article noted that on the previous day the temperature had climbed to ninety-seven, breaking a sixty-year-old record.

Keegan found the article about the accident, a three-paragraph story that didn't even mention the names of the people involved.

Then Keegan was struck with a thought. He opened his file folder and removed the photograph of the accident scene that showed the police cruiser. There was a very bright glare on the cruiser and Keegan studied it closely. What was it? He could not be sure.

Dunbar was aware of a low hum, aware of no other sound. Even the cleaning people who had come early in the evening and worked late into the night were long gone. Dunbar glanced at his watch and saw that it was 4:27 A.M. He gazed out the window of the National Archives II on the edge of the University of Maryland campus in College Park. This new building, a sleek, long, low glass-and-steel structure, was the most modern archive facility in the world. It had been Dunbar's home for nearly three straight days. For the better part of three days he had remained holed up in a modern conference room on the fourth floor with a pretty view out of the glass wall. He was in the reference branch of the archives in the department housing Captured German Records.

Dunbar stared at the greenish-tinted letters on the black screen. After all of those hours he had finally found Friedrich Schillinghaussen.

Dunbar heard the low humming sound and no other. He looked up at the wall and decided it had to be the air conditioning system. Perhaps it was part fatigue, part the rush of excitement he felt at having found Schillinghaussen. Dunbar's instinct at moments such as these was to slow down, slow way down so that he would think clearly and make the right judgments. He wanted to be careful and comprehensive. He wanted to take it all in, to understand it, to make sense of it. He had been painstaking in his research, and now he had been rewarded with Schillinghaussen's file before him on the screen. Suddenly, Dunbar rose from his seat and walked to the glass wall. He looked out into the blackness of the early

morning, at the street lamps that illuminated the walk-
ways around the archives building. He stood straight and
began to take a series of deep, rhythmic breaths. He
raised his arms above his head and stretched out the
muscles of his shoulders and back. The stretches, he
hoped, would chase away the fatigue he felt, help to en-
ergize him and sharpen his mind.

Though the Nazis had been extraordinarily orderly
about maintaining files, this collection was not organized in any discernible fashion. When the United States
had taken custody of copies of German records, there
had been an effort to make sense of them—an over-
whelming collection that included seventy thousand rolls
of microfilm. So massive was the task of seeking to make
sense out of this mountain of information that researchers
and scholars at the National Archives had written an astounding ninety-four volumes of "finding aids."

It was through some of these documents that Dunbar
discovered an identification number for Schillinghaussen, a lawyer's registration number. Once he had
that he was able to trace Schillinghaussen through a reg-
istry of government lawyers. And it was then that he discovered this personnel file that had been kept by the Nazi
Party.

Dunbar sat down before the computer and gazed at
the screen. The file stated that Friedrich Schillinghaussen
had been born on March 4, 1914, in Berlin. He was the
son of Ernst and Diedre (Schnellen). His father was a veteran of the First World War and had been a member of
the Nazi Party since 1929. The file noted that he took his
law degree from the University of Berlin in the spring of
1939, and that Schillinghaussen had begun work at the
Reich Ministry on December 12, 1939. He had worked

directly for Martin Koblenz, Chief of the Property Division of the Reich Ministry of Justice.

Dunbar struck the key on the right side of the keyboard that moved the file down. Under a notation for "Area of Responsibility," it read: "Property confiscation, Eastern Prussia: Ceding non-Aryan property to the government."

Dunbar was rocked by this. "Non-Aryan property." He felt his heart beat faster as he swiveled around in his chair and reached for one of the volumes of finding aids that had supplied definitions to various terms he had come across during his days and nights of research. He thumbed through it and found a reference in the index to "property confiscation." He selected another volume and thumbed through to the correct page.

"Holy Christ," he whispered as he read. The property confiscation program by the Reich Ministry of Justice had been a concerted effort by the Nazis to seize all property owned by Jewish families. It had commenced in the mid-1930s but had increased dramatically in 1939 and after. By the mid-1940s virtually all property owned by Jews had been seized by the government. This included residential as well as commercial property. The businesses had been transferred to Aryan ownership, while the residences had been given or sold to Aryans. Some of the grander residences, according to a notation, were taken over by prominent members of the Nazi Party.

The file noted that Friedrich Schillinghaussen held his post in the Reich Ministry until 1943.

Dunbar sat forward in his seat and rubbed his eyes. There could be no question about it: Friedrich Schillinghaussen's job had been to seize the property of thousands, perhaps tens of thousands, of Jewish families in Berlin, stripping them of their property before these people

were sent off to the camps. The husband of Sophie Naumann had not only been a member of the Nazi Party but
he had also been responsible for the seizure of property
from Jewish families. And he was now married to Sophie
Naumann!

Dunbar sat and read the file through again, and then a
third time. He hit the print button and two single-spaced
sheets of white paper emerged from the printer. He
folded the sheets of paper and placed them into the inside
pocket of his jacket. He shut off the microfilm machine
and put on his jacket. His necktie hung a couple of inches
below his unbuttoned shirt collar. And though his mouth
was dry and sour, and he felt dirty from having gone so
long without a shower, Dunbar felt a sense of exaltation.
He shut off the conference room light and strode down
the hallway, riding the elevator to the ground floor and
leaving by the rear entrance. He stopped to sign the night
log kept by the security guard and headed out into the
chilly predawn air.

Hunter dreamed that the telephone next to his bed
was ringing and ringing and ringing. He woke and
grabbed it.

"Hullo?" he said in a husky, whispered voice.

"There is some new information," Dunbar said.

"Hullo?" Hunter said, confused.

"Hunter, wake up," Dunbar ordered.

Hunter sat up in bed and realized he was awake, that
he was talking with Dunbar on the phone.

"What time is it?" Hunter asked.

"Time to get up and get to work," Dunbar said.

Hunter looked toward the clock, but it was obscured

by a large glass ashtray. He had been up late reading, smoking, and had left it there.

"Why are you . . . ?"

"Listen," Dunbar said. "There is some significant new information. Very significant. It raises the stakes."

"What is it?" Hunter asked.

"It is basically that Schiller was involved with running a program that confiscated the property of Jewish families," Dunbar said. "When the families would be sent away to the camps, the state would take custody of their real estate. This is the program he administered."

"Jesus," Hunter whispered.

"The United States Justice Department has uncovered this information and is actively investigating," Dunbar said. "The information comes from documentation held within the National Archives, Captured German Records. When I get back in town I will show you a document. You may not have it, but you may see it. That way you will know for certain that it is legitimate. And you may go from there.

"It appears," Dunbar said, "that Schiller was responsible for all confiscations in a section of Berlin, a large section at that. The indications are East Prussia."

"And East Prussia is what?" Hunter asked.

"Basically eastern Berlin," Dunbar said. "I've taken the liberty of doing a bit of research on my own so I could better understand this. I don't know whether you would want me to . . ."

"Please," Hunter said.

"Well, I was struck by something that I learned," Dunbar said. "The thing that struck me was that they would take the property, legally seize control of it, always careful to follow the law. Bizarre. Then they would send the family away to a camp and do whatever they pleased with the home. Sometimes, they would turn the home, especially if it was a particularly nice one, over to some Nazi official."

"Jesus Christ," Hunter whispered.

"Anyway," Dunbar said. "That's the story."

Hunter took a deep breath. "Look, man," he said, "I mean this sincerely. Thank you for this. It's . . . it's . . ."

"Yeah," Dunbar said, "I know."

27

Keegan saw the nameplate on the open door and looked into the office. A man who appeared to be in his mid-seventies was asleep in a chair. His wire-rimmed glasses were askew, his whitish hair sticking out in various directions.

"Professor Schoen?" Keegan asked.

The old man's head jerked up and he opened his eyes.

"It's me," he said cheerfully, rising from his chair and greeting Keegan. "Please forgive me. I come into the office very early in the morning so I sometimes find myself dozing off during the day."

Schoen directed Keegan to sit in a chair opposite his and they sat down.

"So you're Nazi hunting," the professor said.

Keegan shifted in his seat. "I'm not sure I'd say that, exactly," he said. "But, I guess, in a way I am."

Schoen nodded. He appeared quite tired to Keegan. His face was thin and elongated. He sat back in his office in an old stone building on the Boston College campus. Schoen was a German history scholar who had specialized on the Weimar years and the Third Reich. He had written a number of scholarly works on various groups within Germany—homosexuals, the retarded, Jews—who had been persecuted by the Nazis. He had also written several papers about Theresienstadt.

"What can I tell you that might be useful?" the professor asked.

"If you could give me some sense of what records might exist today, a broad overview," Keegan said.

"No problem," the professor said. "But I'm afraid that, as far as that goes, the good news is the bad news."

"Meaning?"

"Meaning that the Germans were and are the most remarkable record keepers," Schoen said. "To say they were fastidious about keeping track of things—people, events, schedules, et cetera, et cetera, would be to understate the reality. In truth, massive quantities of records were kept by every department of government at every level, by the Party itself at every level, by the various branches of the military at every level. There are federal records, state records, local city and town records for almost everything imaginable. That's the good news. It's also the bad news. Because attempting to navigate one's way through these mountains of information is daunting to say the least."

"There's a central repository?" Keegan asked.

"The Berlin Document Center," Schoen said. "But there are duplicates of most of the records there in our National Archives II in College Park. The originals are in Berlin and copies here on microfilm."

"And they're complicated?"

"There are somewhere between ninety and one hundred volumes that archivists there have compiled that are search aids—nearly one hundred volumes that do nothing but help you find your way through the maze."

"Jesus," Keegan muttered, overwhelmed by the task at hand.

"Indeed," Schoen said. "In the Captured German Records division there are seventy thousand rolls of microfilm. Seventy thousand rolls! It boggles the mind. Of course, the more information you start off with, the easier the search becomes. If you have birth dates, military identification numbers, addresses, that sort of thing, then your search can be entirely manageable. Otherwise, it can be a massive headache."

"I'm also interested in what other sources there might be on Theresienstadt specifically. Private archives, smaller collections, that sort of thing."

The professor's eyes widened and he held out his hands, palms up, as if to say, yes, of course. "Certainly, Mr. Keegan, there are many such sources, in general," Schoen said. "On Theresienstadt, specifically, there are also a number, but, really, there is one important one. In Berlin. Come on and we'll chat as we walk," Schoen said, as he led Keegan out of his office and down the hallway. The two men strolled across a quadrangle to a faculty lounge where they got cups of coffee.

"What do you know about Theresienstadt, Mr. Keegan?" Schoen asked as they walked slowly back toward his office.

"Not much," Keegan said. "Just that it was located in a little town called Terezin in Czechoslovakia. That it was mainly for Jews who were businesspeople, artists, educators. That's about it, really."

Schoen nodded. "Many Jewish families rejoiced upon hearing they would be going to Theresienstadt," Menke said. "Particularly early on when the full truth was not known. Remember now that the fear was of being deported to the east to one of the traditional concentration camps or the death camps, though it wasn't known to the Jews that the death camps existed. Not early on. Many Jewish families, when offered the opportunity, actually paid to go to Theresienstadt," the professor continued.

Keegan was startled. "Paid!"

"Theresienstadt was said to be the model community," Schoen said, as they arrived back at his building and returned to his office, settling into their chairs. "It was known as Hitler's gift to the Jews. And, remember, this sort of Nazi propaganda at the time was widely believed. So Jewish families, fearing deportation to the east and some wretched concentration camp would pay— sometimes very large sums of money—for a place at Theresienstadt."

"Expecting?"

"Expecting what was promised," Schoen said. "A home or an apartment where they could go with their family. This was one of the attractions, that you could go with your family and continue to be together. But there were other inducements as well. The talk was that Theresienstadt was a community where artists and musicians could pursue their work, a community run by Jews themselves with rules set by Jews. It was thought of as a place where self-determination could occur."

"But the reality was?" Keegan said.

"The reality was that Theresienstadt was a place that was unique in the world at the time," Schoen said. "It was schizophrenic. It was, in fact, a place where some of the finest Jewish minds in the arts and science and medicine were confined. Brilliant musicians performing original works. They had assembled an entire symphony orchestra. There were poets, novelists. Some of Germany's finest physicians. Talented writers and directors of stage plays. Again, original works were performed there. In some ways, for a period of a few years, it was the cultural center of Europe, as perverse as that sounds."

Schoen took a deep breath and exhaled slowly.

"But there was another side to Theresienstadt, as well," he said. "The truth was that it was a concentration camp. Different from others in that it housed so many from the elite classes, different in that families were allowed to be together, different in some other ways. But, in the end, it was a concentration camp where misery and squalor were the rule."

The professor shrugged. "It was a wretched existence," he said. "Many children and old people died of hunger and malnourishment. Many got sick and were without the medications they needed. And they died. Getting medications for certain ailments was all but impossible. And, as the war progressed, most of the inmates at Theresienstadt were shipped out to Auschwitz."

They sat in silence for a moment. Keegan waited for the professor to continue, but he seemed distracted.

"You know, Mr. Keegan, one of the prerogatives of age is that one is entitled to ramble on now and again offering sermons on this or that topic which just about no one listens to." Schoen smiled.

"But I have a pet fear that I want to convey to you in the hopes that it brings some added perspective. Would you mind?"

"Not at all, Professor," Keegan said.

"The truth is that most people—most people, certainly not all—did what they could back then," Schoen said. "Mostly what we study and read about and think about from that time involves stories of death. And that is as it should be for the scope of it, the scale of it—it is beyond the bounds of the human imagination. It was the work of demonic forces. Within humans, of course, but demonic forces nonetheless. Satan was at work then, Mr. Keegan. Satan himself."

Schoen cocked his head and studied Keegan.

"You may think me a crazy old man and perhaps I am, but I believe what I am telling you. Our retrospective view is so very clear. There are few, if any, blurred lines. Right is right and wrong is wrong, and we see it and we know it. It is certain and sure. There is great comfort in that. Think of how comforted we have been in our time by the certainty of our judgments. This or that was wrong and immoral, and we will not permit it to recur because we are right and just and moral people.

"But then, what, Mr. Keegan? Then Cambodia. Did we act to avert the slaughter? No. Why? Because the politics of the world are endlessly complex. Because reasonable people in civilized countries make what appear to be sound and reasonable judgments—we may not intervene in Cambodia—and, suddenly, millions of people are dead. In retrospect should we have intervened to prevent the slaughter? Of course!

"My point is that things are sometimes not so clear, not so easy at the time they are happening. The retrospective view always sharpens the eye's focus.

"So as you are going through your work, Mr. Keegan, consider that there were many people back then who made judgments they believed to be rational, defensible moral judgments that, in retrospect, seem inappropriate. You know, most of the time when we look back at that time we find stories of death, but think about the countless stories of struggle and survival. Good people fighting for their lives and the lives of their loved ones. People made compromises for what they believed to be the best of reasons. There were many Jews, for example, Mr. Keegan, who became members of the Judenrat. This was the council of Jewish elders who ran Jewish communities under the Nazis. They worked for the Nazis. It was their responsibility to carry out orders from the Nazis. Imagine a Jew executing the orders of an SS colonel. But these Jews did this for a reason, Mr. Keegan. They did it because they were compelled to do so or because they sought to protect loved ones or themselves. All of those stories of love and struggle and survival. Heroic stories, many of them. Consider those as you go along with your work. Consider that there were people back then like you and me, just normal people, terrified, confused, desperate, seeking only to survive. Seeking only to save those they loved."

Schoen looked away, lost in his own thoughts. Who knew what his family's story was, thought Keegan.

"You were mentioning earlier when I asked about informal records about something in Berlin," Keegan said.

"Yes, yes," Schoen said, reviving himself. "There is a man in Berlin who is quite elderly now, a Czech fellow who was at Theresienstadt. He was a professor of literature at the University of Prague. A man named Dieter Stegr. He had a very promising career, published a couple of works of criticism that were well received. And then the war came and he was sent to Theresienstadt. He's in his eighties now, of course.

"When he went to Theresienstadt he started a weekly newspaper reporting on events within the community there," the professor continued. "After a while the paper became quite influential and exposed the dark side of Theresienstadt. And the Nazis shut down his operation. He published underground for a time, but, eventually, he was forced to cease operations altogether. That's when he decided to become the biographer, in a sense, of the camp itself. He took it upon himself to go around gathering records and writing down the oral histories of various people there. Evidently he was a tireless worker and he assembled a huge store of information on people and events there. After the war he married a German woman and set about gathering even more information from Theresienstadt survivors, and the result is that he has built up, through the years, the central, definitive store of information on Theresienstadt anywhere in the world."

"Does he make the files available to anyone?" Keegan asked.

"Decidedly not," Schoen said. "But if you wished to go there, I would be willing to phone him on your behalf."

28

Late at night, with David by his side, the fear of what lay ahead gripped Dick Keegan in a merciless fashion, and he seemed on the verge of confession. Watching in the shadowy light of the hospital room, David could see that his father was a burdened man.

"There is something I have to tell you," his father blurted.

David Keegan gazed down at the old man and hesitated. "What is it, Dad?" David asked.

And in that moment, David could see his father catch himself. He could see the old man tighten and pull back, spooked by the prospect of crossing that imaginary line; frightened of the truth and its possible consequences. Dick Keegan rambled on and on, never quite getting to the point.

David felt angry that his father would not be straight, would not get to the point. But David held back. Was he doing so in order to comfort his father, or was it more subconsciously strategic? Did David want to do whatever was necessary to remain on speaking terms so that when his father was ready to talk, David would be there? For, clearly, there was something his father wanted to reveal to him. He had muttered incoherently at times, muttering words that were indecipherable, mumblings and sounds, but twice, when he did this, David had distinctly heard him say the name Leo. Leo Flaherty had been one of his father's friends back years ago.

On a humid summer day, shortly after noon, David Keegan drove from the Federal Courthouse in Post Office Square out Storrow Drive to the Jamaicaway and into Roslindale. Keegan followed Washington Street out through the square, up past the Pleasant Cafe. He turned left at the Beech Street project and wound his way over to Glendower Road. Keegan parked in front of a two-family house at number 37 Glendower and got out of his car. He looked up on to the front porch and saw Leo Flaherty sitting in a wicker rocking chair as though he had been waiting for Keegan.

"Mr. Flaherty," Keegan said, approaching the house.

Leo Flaherty looked up from his newspaper and squinted at David, uncertain who this man was. David walked up the stairs and smiled at the old man.

"Mr. Flaherty, it's David Keegan."

"Jesus, it is, too," Flaherty said. He smiled and shook David's hand.

"Look at you, hey," Flaherty said. He was a small man, compactly built, with silver hair combed neatly back. He wore a pair of chinos and a short-sleeved checked shirt.

"It's been so long, Davey," he said. "You were a law grad when I saw you back then."

"Wow," Keegan said. "It has been a long time. I've been out of law school seventeen years."

"Sit down here, boy," Flaherty said. "Sit down and tell me how's your Dad."

"Not that great to tell you the truth, Mr. Flaherty," Keegan said.

"Christ, I heard he had the cancer," Flaherty said, shaking his head. "So many of the guys we were with . . ."

"Yeah."

"Is he home?" Flaherty asked.

"Long-term-care place," Keegan said.

"Does he get the chemo?" Flaherty asked. " 'Cause them are poisons. They shoot you with so much god-damn poison, for Chrissaskes it's a wonder anyone ever comes out of it."

David turned and gazed down the street, silent for the moment.

"God bless us," Flaherty muttered under his breath.

"You look good, Mr. Flaherty," David said.

The old man brightened. "I feel good," he said. " 'Course I was different from so many of them smoking the cigarettes and drinking the booze. Jesus H. Christ that stuff'll kill you anyday. Plus I take a nice walk everyday and I don't eat all the fat they eat, Jesus, no." He sat looking off for a moment, nodding his head. "I'm seventy-eight now. But God is good."

Keegan nodded.

"So what brings you to the old neighborhood, Davey?"

"Ah, there's something I wanted to ask you about. From back some years ago."

The old man cocked his head. "Oh?"

"Something that happened a long time ago," Keegan said. "Back the night of the accident. I wanted . . ."

Flaherty hung his head, shaking it sorrowfully. Then, after a moment, he looked up at Keegan.

"You know, Davey, you look a hell of a lot like her,"

Flaherty said. "Honest and true you do." He shook his head again. "That was a terrible night, that was."

Flaherty sighed.

Keegan spoke more softly, more deliberately. "What do you remember?" Keegan asked.

"Jesus," Flaherty whispered.

There was a long pause while Keegan sat, waiting. Two teenagers ambled by, across the street, mimicking some television program. David Keegan felt pressure in his chest, a sense of anticipation.

"Just as I got there the ambulance pulled in, too," Flaherty said. "The car was on my right as I came down Belgrade Avenue. At first, I thought it was nothing, 'cause I saw the car she sideswiped on the left. Evidently she swerved into the oncoming lane of traffic and the guy reacted excellent, but couldn't get completely out of her way. She brushed him. Broke his left front headlight and left a scrape on the left side of his car. An Oldsmobile.

"So when I come down Belgrade all I know is I'm responding to a motor vehicle accident and the report says with PI, but as I'm coming I'm looking for an accident and I see the car on the left, stopped at an odd angle and the guy out looking a little dazed and checking out the damage, and I'm about to pull over because I think, 'Well, this is it.' But then I hear the sirens of the ambulance coming from out of the Square—evidently it was on Cummins Highway when it got the call—and it's then that I see the Chevy off to the right all smashed against the telephone pole.

"So I get up there as quick as I can and pull over," Flaherty continued. "And I run from my cruiser to where the car is against the pole. Well, really, you'd have to say the car was wrapped against the pole. The windshield was shattered. Gone. And I looked inside and I didn't see no one in there, and I thought, 'Oh, that's good. They got out.' But, hey, look, you don't think straight sometimes at a moment like that. I didn't stop to ask myself the question, how the hell did they get out. I was just kind of reacting.

"And then I looked up and I seen Jazz Mannering, waving like a maniac for the ambulance guys and when I saw that I looked down and there she was, on the ground and . . ."

Flaherty shook his head and looked away, down Glendower Road.

David Keegan sat with his hands folded on his lap. When Flaherty paused, Keegan waited, holding his breath.

"And?" Keegan said.

Flaherty would not turn around, would not now look at Keegan. Keegan clasped his hands together in front of his mouth, then rubbed his face and placed his hands on the arms of the chair, gripping the arms so he would remain still.

"And I could tell right away she was hurt real bad," Flaherty said.

"She was thrown?"

Flaherty nodded his head in the affirmative.

"Thrown from the car?"

"Yeah," the old man said.

Had Keegan heard this before? He was not sure. He guessed that he had known this, been informed of this fact at some point in his life. But when he tried to think of who might have told him this, he could not come up with anyone.

"This was near Newberg Street," Keegan said. "At the corner, right?"

"Right near the corner," Flaherty said. "Thirty, forty feet away."

Keegan stood up and walked to the porch railing. He gripped it with both hands and took a deep breath, exhaling slowly.

Thrown from the car?

He shut his eyes and tried to clear his mind of any images, but he could not erase the thought of her lying there, face down, on the pavement. Scraped? Cut? Bleeding? Bruised? Had any of her bones broken? Were her eyes open or closed? Did she feel pain? Did she feel anything when she hit the pavement? Did she, momentarily, feel a sense of loss? The loss of her sons? Of what was to come in life?

Keegan's knees buckled and he was forced to steady himself against the railing. He went to the chair and sat down.

"I'm sorry," Flaherty said.

Leo Flaherty disappeared into the house, leaving David alone on the porch. In a few minutes Flaherty returned with two glasses of iced tea and handed one to David.

"So the ambulance came?" David asked.

"It was there and she was transported to Faulkner by one of the crews, either the Boston Ambulance Squad or BCH. One or the other. Then he went in the other one."

David hesitated. "You saw him go in the ambulance?" David asked.

"Yeah," Leo said. "I was right there."

"You're sure?" David asked. "You saw him?"

Leo Flaherty appeared puzzled. He considered the matter.

"No, I guess I didn't, come to think of it," Leo Flaherty said. " 'Cause I led the ambulance to the hospital. I got in my cruiser and went like hell down Belgrade to the Square 'cause I wanted to seal off Washington inbound so the ambulance wouldn't even have to slow down. That's what I did."

"And after that?"

"After that I headed to Faulkner and, oh, I know, I got another call en route. Franklin Park somewheres."

"So you didn't go to Faulkner?" David asked.

"No," Leo said.

"So you didn't see my father in the ambulance? You didn't see him go to Faulkner?"

Leo considered this for a moment, then shook his head.

"No, I guess I must not have," he said. "I didn't."

Suddenly Leo perked up, as though remembering something. "And I was gonna go up and see him, but Jazzy put the word out not to," Leo Flaherty said. "Jazzy put the word out that your Dad was in rough shape and everybody should leave him alone for a couple days. So I didn't see him at all after the accident until the wake."

"Which was three days later," David said.

"Something like that," Leo said.

David sipped his iced tea and thought about this.

"So, going back to right after the accident happened," David said, "do you remember where my father was?"

"Jazzy's cruiser," he said. "I guess Jazzy musta put him there. I remember thinking Jazzy shouldn't have moved him. But then everything happened so fast."

"But you must have seen Jazz move him, right? Since you were the first officer on the scene."

"But I wasn't," Leo said.

"You were cruiser 27?" Keegan asked.

"That was Jazzy," Flaherty said. "Mine was 31."

Keegan considered this. The cruiser in the photograph, the one with its windows rolled up tight, was number 27. Jazz Mannering's cruiser.

David reacted with surprise.

"Are you sure?" David asked.

"Christ, I'm positive of that. I saw him when I pulled in. No question."

"But I thought the first response unit writes the incident report," David said.

"That's true," Leo said.

"So how come you wrote the report?" David asked.

"I didn't," Leo said.

David frowned. He reached inside his suit jacket pocket and removed a single sheet of paper, a copy of the incident report. He smoothed it out and handed it to Leo Flaherty. As Leo read it, he cocked his head and appeared incredulous. When he was done he looked at David, and said, "I never wrote this. It's not mine."

David hesitated. "So who . . ."

"Beats me," Leo said. "But I know it wasn't me. I'm sure I didn't write it because I would definitely remember it if I had done it. But what makes me doubly sure is this here," he said, showing the page to David and pointing to the name. "On every report I wrote during all my years on the force I used my full name. 'D. Leo Flaherty Jr.' Without exception. See here where it just says Leo Flaherty." He shook his head dismissively. "No way did I do that. No way."

He handed the sheet back to David, who folded it and put it back into his inside jacket pocket.

"Jazzy shoulda written the report as first response," Leo said. "You should definitely talk to him."

29

"Excuse me," Hunter said, "I wonder if we could have a word."

Diane stopped and looked at him, forgetting for an instant their previous encounter in the parking garage of her downtown office building. Then it struck her. She stood in the busy foyer of the Gray Building at Massachusetts General Hospital where, all around, doctors and nurses and patients' families moved in and out of the hospital.

"I have nothing to say to you," she said.

"Diane, you remember me, Dan Hunter from the *Globe*, and I just wanted to ask you a couple of questions."

Diane stepped back from him, a dark expression on her face.

"I have nothing to say," she repeated.

"I know how you must feel," he said, "but . . ."

She began walking down the hall toward the Phillips House elevators, but Hunter quickly fell in step beside her.

"It's important," he said, hurrying to keep up. "It's very important. I think you'll agree when you read this."

He handed her a single sheet of paper, with three typewritten paragraphs on it. She stopped walking.

"You should read this," he said.

"What is it?" Diane asked.

"It's the lead to a story we have going in tomorrow morning's paper," Hunter said. "I wanted you to know about it, to see if you or someone in the family might want to comment on it."

Diane cocked her head and looked at him in disbelief. She was suddenly jostled in a crowd of people, and she stepped to the side of the hallway, off to a small waiting area.

"I called a number of times earlier but nobody called back," Hunter said. "I figured I might catch you here."

She glanced down at the sheet of paper. When she read the first paragraph she felt faint and had to sit down on a chair nearby. She glanced up at Hunter who stared at her, grim-faced, and then she read all three paragraphs together.

Nazi records from World War II reveal that Frederick Schiller, the Brookline man recently identified by a former prisoner at a Nazi concentration camp, allegedly administered a program under which the property of German Jews was seized when they were sent away to death camps.

According to German records seized by the Allies at the end of World War II, records now on file at the National Archives in College Park, Maryland, Schiller allegedly oversaw the property seizure program for most of Berlin. Under that program the property of tens of thousands of Jewish families was seized and disposed of by the Nazi government. Some of the homes seized were turned over to prominent officials of the Nazi regime.

The records were discovered by Justice Department

officials whose investigation of Schiller commenced after Schiller was identified by Gerta Wahljak, also of Brookline. Wahljak had kept a photograph of ten officials at Theresienstadt, a Nazi-run concentration camp in Czechoslovakia, since she was an inmate there more than 40 years ago.

Diane looked up from the page and saw Hunter standing a few feet away. He was saying something but she did not get what it was. She saw people streaming past along the hallway behind where Hunter stood. Everything was somehow distorted, with people's faces elongated, some grotesquely so. Diane suddenly felt lightheaded and short of breath.

This could not be true, she thought. It was simply impossible. The idea that her father could have been involved with such a program was absurd.

"You can't publish this article," she said.

"Tomorrow," he said. "And if you wanted to comment, or maybe your mother . . ."

"Where did you get this information?" she asked.

"That's confidential," he said.

Diane suddenly stood up. She had to get to her mother. Diane started off down the hallway toward the Phillips House elevators.

"Did you want . . ." Hunter began.

"I have nothing to say," Diane said.

"Look, Diane," Hunter said. "What about this: How about we sit down and talk. You and me. I do a story about what it's like trying to deal with this from your end. A very empathetic piece. Your side of the story, basically. That way I could soften this piece here," he said, holding up the lead he had just shown her. "Tone it down quite a bit. Make sense?"

Diane started to walk away, but Hunter's words stopped her. "This isn't it," he said.

"Excuse me?" she said.

"This isn't all," he said. "This will keep going."

She stared back at him.

"You've got to talk at some point," he said. "You can't win against somebody who buys ink by the barrel."

"So where does this go?" she asked. "Where does it end?"

"I don't know where it ends or whether it ends," Hunter said. "But I'll tell you where it goes next. It goes back to Theresienstadt. What was his role at the camp? A hundred thousand people from Theresienstadt were sent to Auschwitz. Could he have stopped it? What did he do? What was his role? What were his obligations? What was his moral duty?"

Dunbar had read the story over carefully. He had asked Hunter to make a few changes, which Hunter made. Dunbar was uncomfortable that he was not mentioned. He thought that he should be credited with the discovery, but that the story should also say that he would not comment on the article. Dunbar picked up the telephone and called United States Attorney Walter Stone at home.

"Walter, bad news," Dunbar said. "I just got a phone call from a reporter at the *Globe*. I know we thought the leak was plugged, but this guy has an article he says he's running tomorrow concerning the archival information."

"Jesus!" Stone said. "What the hell . . ."

"Anyway, he asked me to comment and of course I said absolutely nothing, but I wanted to let you know I got the call. I also wanted to apologize for what was obviously a mistake. The other day I sent an electronic transmission regarding the archival material to our normal route here and I just double-checked and found out Keegan's still on that list. And the computer records show that he's been logging in to get his e-mail messages. I'm very sorry for that."

Sophie sat by the bed, holding Freddy's hand, stroking his hair, talking to him in a soft voice.

Diane entered the room and stood silently for a moment, watching her mother tend to her father. Sophie looked up and smiled at Diane, but Sophie knew from her daughter's expression that something was wrong. She stroked Freddy's hair once again and smiled down at him. Then she got up from the chair and faced Diane.

"What is it, dear?" she asked.

"The reporter from the newspaper was waiting for me downstairs," Diane said.

Sophie recoiled. "Here? In the hospital?"

"Yes," Diane said. "He handed me this. He said this is the beginning of a story they are running tomorrow morning." Diane handed the sheet of paper to Sophie.

Sophie took it and looked down at it. She read the first paragraph.

"Oh, dear God," she whispered. "Dear God."

She sat down in a chair and read all three paragraphs, then turned her head to the side and placed her knuckles against her chin. She seemed unable to look at her daughter. Finally, she did so, glancing up tentatively. "I'm sorry," she said softly to Diane. "I really am so sorry."

Diane stood in shock, literally speechless. Sophie could

see the look on her face, a look that pleaded for Sophie to say it was wrong, it was false, it was untrue.

Sophie rose wearily. She took Diane's hand and led her out into the hall, down to the end of the corridor to the consult room. Diane sat on one of the chairs, her heart pounding. Sophie glanced out the window, looking west along the river. She turned and faced her daughter, looked her in the eye, and said, "It's true."

Diane shut her eyes and rolled her head back and then, slowly, brought it forward so that her chin pressed down on her chest. She cocked her head to one side, a quizzical expression on her face. She regarded her mother, then began shaking her head slowly from side to side.

"No," she said. "It cannot be true."

"Diane, he . . ."

"It cannot be so," she said, cutting her mother off. "Please."

"Diane, this was assigned to him, he was instructed to do this, to administer a program involving Jewish property."

"Mother, the article says this was property seized from families being sent to extermination camps," Diane said.

"Freddy knew *nothing* of those camps," Sophie said. "Nothing. He administered a program, as he had been instructed to do. What were his choices? Really, Diane. Really, what were his choices? Not in the ideal world, in retrospect. But in the real world. What else could he have done except his job?"

Diane shook her head in disbelief. "I cannot believe you are saying this," Diane said.

Suddenly, Sophie covered her face with her hands and quietly began to cry. She trembled and shook as she sobbed, and Diane went to her, sat on the edge of her seat, and held her.

"I'm so afraid," Sophie said, through her heaving cries. "I am so afraid."

Diane patted her and held her but said nothing.

"You must hear from your father what happened and why," Sophie said. "He must survive so he can tell you about that time. So you will understand. You *must* understand."

"What else, Mother?" Diane asked, her voice low and firm, her gaze intense.

Sophie hesitated. "You mean . . ."

"What else will I learn from the newspapers in the days to come?" Diane asked. "What else have you with-held from me?"

Sophie shook her head. "Nothing," she said. "There is nothing else to learn. I am sorry, Diane. I should have told you long ago. Certainly you should not have learned about it in the way that you did."

"There is nothing else?" Diane asked.

Her mother shook her head, but, as she did so, Diane saw that she averted her eyes.

David Keegan was shocked when he heard the news from Diane. He read over the lead and handed it back to her.

"I'm sorry, Diane," he said. "This is so terrible. This is . . ."

"The reporter, Hunter, he's grotesque," Diane said. "He said something to me. It was frightening. He said, 'This isn't all. This will keep going.' "

Keegan said nothing.

"Did he mean what I think he meant?" Diane asked.

Keegan nodded. "This could go on and on and on. And who knows where they'll go with it next."

"He told me," Diane said.

"He did?"

"He told me that it goes back to Theresienstadt next," she said.

"How so?" Keegan asked.

"What his role there was. Whether he sent people to extermination camps. Whether he could have stopped it somehow. What his, as Hunter put it, 'moral obligations' were."

Keegan frowned. "So what . . ."

"The reporter asked me what his job was at the camp," Diane said. "He asked how many people he sent on transports to the east.

"But he could not have been an official of that camp," she said, driving the idea from her mind. "He could not have been. My mother said he was not. My mother would not lie to me."

Even as the words were coming out of her mouth Diane realized the absurdity of them. She shook her head, suddenly knocked back by the reality that her mother had, indeed, lied to her; that her father had done the same.

"But this is true," Diane said. "This I'm sure is right. He was there for some particular piece of business that we haven't gotten to. My mother hasn't gotten that far with me. But she assured me today, that there was nothing sinister about his mission. Nothing. He was not an official of that camp. He in no way participated in running that place. I just know my father and I believe that. He would not be capable of such a thing. He would not."

Keegan was slouched in his chair. He leveled his gaze at her.

"Can he prove it?" Keegan asked.

Diane drew back with surprise.

"Prove what?"

"That he wasn't an administrator there," Keegan said, "that he didn't send people away . . ."

Diane was suddenly red-faced. "So he must prove his innocence in the absence of an allegation?" she asked, clearly offended by the notion.

"But it sounds like there's likely to be an allegation," Keegan said. "And if there is, you can rebut it. And if there isn't, if you can disprove the allegation before it is made in the press, then you can head it off." He sat up in his seat, leaning forward. "Wouldn't it be better to be aggressive about this, to go and find out before anyone else? I mean, whatever the information, you should have it before anyone else has it. And if it is exculpatory, then all the more reason."

Diane stared intently at him, clearly considering the notion.

"The records are extensive," Keegan said. "Vast. And precise. There has got to be information buried away that would reveal who ran the place, who the administrators were. And that could prove . . ."

Diane shook her head. She had deep circles under her eyes and Keegan knew she was exhausted.

"I'm not myself," she said. "I'm not focusing very well. There's so much . . ."

Keegan took her hand.

"Stay at the hotel next door tonight," he said. "Try and rest. You'll be near your dad . . ."

"Will you . . ."

"And maybe I could stay with you if you'd like," he said.

Her shoulders slumped. She nodded slowly, looking at him carefully, searching for he knew not what.

Diane returned to her father's room and spent some time sitting with her mother, then she walked back across Blossom Street to the hotel where Keegan was waiting. They talked until Diane fell asleep. When she did so, he got up and went to the window. He looked outside, down Blossom Street at the hospital buildings. Suddenly, Diane was bolt upright in bed.

"Daddy!" she said urgently.

Keegan went to the bed and held her shoulders. She was trembling.

"Daddy!" she said.

"Everything's OK," Keegan whispered. "You're having a bad dream."

He sat in the chair next to the bed and watched Diane go back to sleep. This felt very good indeed to David Keegan. He felt a sense of comfort and security, and realized, as he sat in the hotel room, that he felt happy; happy to be with Diane.

Wearing a T-shirt and boxer shorts, Keegan sat with a pad of Holiday Inn stationery and began making notes. Whenever he was troubled or uncertain of what path to follow, he had a habit of jotting down his thoughts. From these fragmants or random thoughts Keegan could begin to put together a pattern to understand what it was that he should do. He thought back to his conversation with Professor Schoen at BC. Obviously Dunbar knew of the Captured German Records in College Park, for it had been Dunbar who had discovered Freddy Schiller's position as administrator of the property seizure program in

Prussia. But would Dunbar know of the private Theresienstadt archive that Schoen had talked about? What
was the man's name, the Czech professor who ran it?

Keegan fell asleep along toward 3:00 A.M. and he soon
began dreaming. He dreamed that he was standing on
the sidewalk along Belgrade Avenue near Newberg. On
his right shoulder he carried a television news camera,
and it was his responsibility to film an accident for the
news. He had been told by his assignment editor that an
accident would be happening at the corner of Belgrade
and Newberg at about this time. And so he had come
here, camera hoisted on his shoulder, ready to roll. In
fact he was rolling. He was filming already and he could
see in the frame the building that housed Western Auto
and Silver Welding. Both were on the ground floor, and
for three stories above the two businesses, there were
apartments.

Keegan was across Belgrade Avenue, and every now
and then a car or truck or bus would race through his
frame, traveling left to right or right to left. Keegan could
not see the car coming because he was doing his job: he
was focused on shooting the scene itself. Had he looked
off to his right he would have seen the car coming down
Belgrade Avenue from the direction of Holy Name circle.
He would have seen it leave the light at Howard Chevrolet
and then gun its engine, accelerating far too quickly, and
suddenly beginning to careen across the center line, and
then, very fast, swerving back to the right to avoid a
head-on collision with an MTA bus, and as it swerved to
the right it was out of control. When the car entered the
frame Keegan saw it hit the curb, and almost simultaneously, it struck a telephone pole. As it struck the pole

something came flying through the windshield, a mannequin, he thought, which rocketed forward, and seemed for the briefest moment to be flying through the air. It landed on the pavement, face-down, bouncing once and then coming to rest in a heap. Face-down. Keegan adjusted his camera lens and zoomed in as close as the technology would take him. His frame now was filled by just the mannequin's head and shoulders, and he could see a pool of blood rapidly forming on the pavement.

He woke with a start and quickly glanced around the room, at first uncertain where he was. The lamp next to his side of the bed was still on. Diane lay on her left side, facing away from him, breathing rhythmically.

His head throbbed. He sat up and rubbed his temples, but that made it worse. Each time his heart pumped blood to his head he could feel the pulsing ache. He felt as though he had some horrific hangover, but he had had nothing to drink the night before. Then he thought of the dream. He remembered he had been watching an accident on Belgrade Avenue.

Jesus, he thought. He got up quietly and turned the chair toward the window. He could see buildings mostly, but if he looked to his right down Blossom Street he could see some sky off to the northeast. He thought back to his conversation with Leo Flaherty. He thought of sitting on Leo's porch and listening to him talk about his mother and father. He thought of Jazz Mannering and he remembered that Leo had told him where Jazz lived, somewhere in Jamaica Plain. Keegan went to the desk and took out the telephone book. He thumbed through and found Roy F. X. Mannering, 17 Ignacia Terrace, Jamaica Plain. He picked up the telephone and was about to dial the number when he caught himself. Was he out of his mind? He looked at his watch. It was 4:40 A.M. He jotted the number down on a scrap of paper and stuck it in his wallet.

He sat back in the chair and soon dozed off again. When he woke, there was sunlight breaking in through the window. He looked at his watch—6:00 A.M. He felt suddenly as though he had overslept, as though he was behind schedule. He had a great deal to do, he knew, and the sooner he got moving, the better. He went into the bathroom and quickly showered, then dressed. Diane remained asleep. He went down to the lobby where he bought a cup of coffee and the *Boston Globe*. The story was on the front page above the fold on the left-hand side. A three-column headline read: NAUMANN'S HUSBAND DISPLACED JEWS, RECORDS SHOW.

Keegan sat down on a sofa in the lobby and read through the article. The first three paragraphs of the story were precisely as Hunter had given to Diane the night before. Most of the information after that was a rehash of the first article, although there were some critical quotations from leaders of various Jewish organizations. The article stated that the discovery of the information was made at the National Archives by Assistant United States Attorney Theodore O. Dunbar, but that Dunbar had declined to comment on the story.

Accompanying the article was the photograph of Diane's father that had appeared in the original story, the one in which he was riding in the backseat of the car, caught unaware; the one in which he appeared not confused and frightened, but dark and sinister.

Keegan read the story through and then found himself staring down at the photograph. What, exactly, had this man done? he wondered. What was the true story of what had occurred back there so many years before?

Keegan reached into his jacket pocket and dug out several slips of paper. He went through them and found the number for Professor Schoen at Boston College. He remembered that the professor had told him that he came into his office very early in the morning. Keegan went to a pay phone and dialed the number, and Menke answered on the first ring.

"Professor Schoen, it's David Keegan, I was in to see you the other day?"

"Oh, sure," Schoen said. "How are you, Mr. Keegan?"

"I'm well, thank you, professor. I wanted to call and see whether your offer to contact Mr. Stegr in Berlin on my behalf was still open?"

"You'd like to go through the Theresienstadt archive, then," Schoen said.

"Very much," Keegan said.

"I would be happy to call him for you, certainly," Schoen said. "I'll tell you, that's a popular spot these days."

Keegan thought that an odd comment. "How so?" he asked.

"Well, just yesterday I had another Justice Department lawyer in here asking me questions not unlike those you asked. He said the two of you used to work together, in fact."

Keegan's heart raced as he felt a sudden sense of dread.

"A Mr. Dunbar," Schoen said. "Bright young man. Asked good questions, listened well. He's interested in the Theresienstadt archive in Berlin, as well. He asked me to call over to Stegr."

Keegan struggled to maintain his composure. "Theo Dunbar, sure," Keegan said. "So did Theo say he was going over to Berlin?"

"He said he was eager to do some work in the archive on Mr. Schiller. He asked me to call Stegr today, in fact, because he said he intends to fly out tomorrow night."

Keegan could not allow Dunbar to do this. He could not allow Dunbar to get to the records first, to discover whatever was there before Keegan got to it.

"Tomorrow night," Keegan said absently.

"He's in quite a rush, no question about it," Schoen said. "Anyway when I call Stegr today I will happily mention your name, as well. When are you leaving, Mr. Keegan?"

Keegan considered the question.

"Tonight," he said. "I'm heading over tonight."

From the airport, Keegan reaches Walter Stone at home. He apologizes for the intrusion. Stone is chilly in his reception to Keegan. Yet there is enough history here, enough good will, that Keegan can make a personal plea. He has a hunch, he says. A theory. He makes a suggestion to Stone. He suggests that Stone confide a piece of fictional information to Dunbar about the Wahljak matter. Invent something. Tell no one else about what you have invented. Tell only Dunbar. Wait a few days and see what happens.

30

Sophie had fallen asleep in the chair next to Freddy's bed. When she woke she looked around the room, but nothing had changed. The oxygen hose still protruded from the wall behind the bed; the television was still suspended high up near the ceiling; the side table still stood stacked with magazines Sophie and Diane had tried to read. Sophie checked her watch and saw that she had been asleep for more than an hour. She rose from the chair, went into the bathroom and brushed her teeth. She studied her face in the mirror. She had always felt a secret sense of pride that her skin had remained smooth and youthful into old age. But, at the moment, she was struck by how wrinkled it was. She saw that her eyes were tired and her mouth and jaw were tight with tension. She took a damp washcloth and dabbed at her face, around her eyes particularly, but on her forehead and cheeks, as well. Then she applied lipstick and a small amount of makeup. Her hair, entirely gray, was pushed out of shape on one side and she took a brush and worked it back into position.

When Sophie came out of the bathroom, she found Diane sitting by the bed, gazing down at Freddy. Sophie went to her and took her hand, squeezing it in her own.

"No change?" Diane asked.

"No change," Sophie confirmed.

Diane took a deep breath and exhaled slowly.

"Let's talk," Sophie said quietly.

She led Diane by the hand, out of the room and down the hallway to the consult room. The two women sat down, facing one another.

"Let me tell the story in my own way," she said. "Please permit me that. I know you have questions in your mind, Diane. I understand. Very legitimate. But please permit me to do this my way. Will you do that for me?"

Diane regarded her mother. She could not refuse. "Of course," she said.

Sophie nodded.

"We received our notice that we were to be sent away from our home in Berlin," Sophie said. "Because my father was a prominent individual in the community and he knew many government officials, we were placed on a privileged list." Sophie smiled at the recollection. "The perversity of these terms . . .

"At any rate, we were destined for Theresienstadt in eastern Czechoslovakia. And we counted ourselves quite fortunate for Theresienstadt was a coveted destination. If one had to leave home it was thought to be the most desirable place to be.

"No one knew for certain what the destinations in the east meant," Sophie said. "But there was little doubt that misery waited at the end of the line. Theresienstadt was thought to be entirely different, vastly preferable to any destination. It was a place where many prominent German Jews—most from Berlin—had been relocated.

The word was that it was an exclusive mix of the most prominent businessmen, lawyers, doctors, scientists, professors, and artists.

"Theresienstadt had a reputation as a place where one could remain with one's family, where there was work available for those who wished to work. Those who wished to perform stage plays or sing in the choral group would be allowed to do so. There were said to be vegetable gardens and a library, well-trained chefs, freedom of speech even for Zionists. It was believed that families lived together in pleasant apartments. Some people actually paid substantial sums to local German officials to win a place at Theresienstadt.

"Shortly before we were to go my father was ordered to the southwestern part of the country, a farming area, where he was to advise the government on improving poultry production. It was shocking to learn that my father would be separated from my mother and me. This was devastating to my mother. She was a fragile woman. The thought of going off to an unknown place that held an unknown future was . . . it was quite terrifying for her."

Sophie paused. She took a deep breath and sighed before continuing. "What was Theresienstadt really?" she said. "It was the embodiment of schizophrenia. It was a haven, in its way, but also hellish."

Sophie shook her head at the recollection. "The crush of humanity. People sitting, standing, sleeping, eating side by side, fifty thousand people crammed into space for a tenth that number. There was an ever-present stench from the delousing facility, latrines, potato cellars. Dust billowed up and got into everything. We would be crammed into an attic to sleep in a windowless space, freezing in winter, sweltering in summer. There was no heat, no plumbing, little water. You were lucky to have a shower every other month. Your clothes would be laundered once every three to four months. Lice infested everything. The worst was the strict rationing of food. There were bits of bread, potatoes, and a watery soup. Hunger was a permanent condition."

Sophie suddenly fell silent for a long moment. Diane could see tears welling in her eyes. "My poor mother," Sophie whispered. "She was such a sweet, innocent woman. So fragile. So unable to cope with that place. She became ill periodically. We were not there long before I realized that I would have to take responsibility for her survival. I told her one night, one night when she cried for missing my father, cried for fear of what was to come, cried out of the sheer misery of the place, I told her that we would do whatever was necessary to survive."

Sophie felt very tired. She let her body relax as she fell into a pattern of slow, rhythmic breathing. Diane left briefly and returned with tea. Sophie sipped it and sat quietly.

"So you had no communication at all with Dad during this time?" Diane asked.

Sophie shook her head. "Nothing," she said. "I thought of him every day, but it was not an obsession, really. I was very busy. It required a great deal of energy merely to survive at Theresienstadt. So I was distracted much of the time by work, by efforts to find food, caring for my mother, particularly when she was sick.

"But I did try to find some time each day to think about him, to meditate on the future. The hardest thing was finding a place where I could be alone with my thoughts for a few minutes. I was fortunate to work in an administrative position where I would sometimes have access to an office where I could close the door and clear my mind and think about him. It was very important to me to be able to summon to my mind his laughter and his voice, the way he moved and looked at me. I would try to remember as vividly as I could any look or sound, the way he said certain words, anything that would make him seem real to me.

"It grew very difficult. As the months dragged on into a year and the year turned into two years and then three and beyond, as all of the time passed, it became very hard to remember certain things. I remembered certain looks particularly well, but I would sometimes get confused and frustrated when I tried to recall his voice."

Diane shook her head in amazement. "I don't know how you got through it," she said.

Sophie opened her eyes wide and shrugged. "I believed," she said. "I had faith. Unshakable faith that we would be together. I loved him with all of my heart and wanted only to be with him, to spend my life with him. And I knew he felt the same way. And I never wavered in my faith. Not for a moment, not for the blink of an eye."

Sophie stood at the window watching dozens of sailboats glide across the silvery waters of the Charles. It was early evening and the sun had begun a slow descent out over the buildings of MIT and Harvard. Sophie stood staring off into the distance, her tea cup in her hand.

"You mentioned an administrative position you held," Diane said.

Sophie stiffened momentarily. She turned and set the cup down on a side table.

"Most everyone at Theresienstadt worked in one way or another," Sophie said, striving for a matter-of-fact tone. "My job involved writing and editing reports." She shrugged. "Very mundane, routine work."

Diane frowned.

"But what . . ."

"Reports involving supplies and such matters," Sophie said, sitting down in the chair opposite Diane. Sophie raised her eyebrows and her shoulders simultaneously in a gesture that indicated there was nothing more to say.

"For whom did you work?" Diane asked.

"For the administration," Sophie said. "As everyone did. It was the sort of . . ."

"But who . . ."

". . . thing that you worked for the administration generally, whether you worked in an office, a bakery, the farm. Whatever."

"You had told me, I had always believed, you worked on the farm there," Diane said. She was about to say something more, but she caught herself.

"I did work on the farm," Sophie said. "For a time." A very brief time.

"And you worked in an office," Diane said.

Sophie nodded her head. "Yes," she said.

Diane cocked her head slightly. "You had never told me that," she said.

Sophie pursed her lips and glanced down at her hands, folded on her lap. "No," she said softly. "It's not . . ."

Diane waited, but Sophie said no more.

"So, you worked in an office," Diane said.

"Yes," Sophie said.

"What was done there?" Diane asked.

"Administrative functions," Sophie said. "There were two administrative operations, in a way. One involved the day-to-day running of the camp. The other, the one in which I worked, was involved in communication with . . . communication and reports with Berlin."

"Berlin?"

Sophie nodded.

"Did you work for the Nazis?" Diane asked.

Sophie drew back. "Everyone worked for the Nazis," she said. "I wrote reports for a camp administrator. Was he a Nazi? Yes, he was. I worked for him. Writing and editing. He ran the camp . . . Everyone worked for him, directly or indirectly."

Diane was momentarily lost in thought. "But there's a difference, isn't there?" Diane asked, "between working on the farm, producing food for people, and doing administrative work for the Nazi administrator. Isn't there?"

"Everyone worked." Sophie said. "I took the job I was told to take."

Sophie had expected Diane to react this way. She was clearly confused, off balance. She was fighting not to appear upset. She would need time to think this through. To process it.

"So you worked . . ."

"In an office," Sophie said.

"Was it directly for a Nazi?" Diane asked. "Did you work directly?"

"Yes," Sophie said.

Diane shut her eyes, then rubbed her temples. She sat forward in her seat.

"I'm having a little trouble with this," she said. "The idea of it . . . You know. The image in my mind . . . I mean, Mother, we're talking here about you having worked for the Nazis and Dad having confiscated the property of Jewish families sent away . . ."

"Please, bear with me, Diane," Sophie said. "Of course you should have been told everything years ago. I now realize that. We felt we were protecting you, in a way. But please let me continue on in my own clumsy way. What I am trying to convey to you is that we all worked for the Nazis, directly or indirectly. We all did what we had to do to survive. The highest principle of all was preserving life."

"What was his name?" Diane asked.

Sophie was caught off guard. "The . . ."

"The person you worked for," Diane said.

Sophie froze. She sat very still as she worked to control her emotions.

"I don't . . . let me think," she said. She hesitated. "I don't recall."

Diane twisted her head to the side and shot her mother a look of utter amazement. "You don't . . ."

"Heidler," Sophie said quickly. "Of course. Heinrich Heidler."

Sophie had not consciously thought of him in a while. She remembered when she first heard that he was the camp commandant—she had been en route to Theresienstadt—she had been encouraged. Heidler was a member of a prominent Berlin family with extensive real estate holdings and known as prominent patrons of the arts. The Heidlers were also known to many well-to-do Jews throughout Berlin, for many Jews had worked with the Heidlers on raising funds for the ballet, symphony, and art museum.

When Sophie had been at the university, Heidler had been a teaching assistant in the political science department. Sophie had never taken his class—she was forced out of school before she had a chance to do so—but she knew he had a reputation as a brilliant thinker. She had seen him speak on numerous occasions when she went to the many competitions sponsored by the university debating society. These events attracted hundreds of spectators.

Sophie thought back to the last time she had seen Heidler on stage, using humor and his charming manner along with a razor-sharp mind to outtalk his opponents.

Sophie went to the window. She looked out over the river as a purplish light cast its glow on the city. She tried to watch for the late scullers on the water, but her mind was filled with the image of Heidler. She remembered it all now as though it had happened the day before. She let her mind drift back over the decades, back to that place, back to Theresienstadt.

She had gone directly from the infirmary to his office, racing across the yard and up the stairs. He told her he could see her the following day.

"I must talk with you now," she had insisted. "I beg you. It is a matter of life and death."

He frowned. His bearing was erect, attentive. He was slim, tall with an air of confidence. He was a handsome man with soft eyes and a prominent jaw. He studied her closely, seeming somewhat annoyed by the comment. "There are matters of life and death here each and every day," he said. "It is very unpleasant duty, in that respect. There are forty-eight thousand Jews here, all of whom would prefer to be elsewhere."

She shifted in her chair, crossing, then recrossing, her legs.

He cocked his head to one side and narrowed his eyes. "Isn't there a certain arrogance to your coming here?" he asked. "A certain presumption?"

She took a breath and shut her eyes for the moment. "I don't know whether it is presumption or arrogance or what," she said. "My mother is gravely ill."

She thought perhaps that this pronouncement would shock him, jar him into a moment of pity or humanity, and that he would summon an assistant and the proper medicine would be found and delivered to her. But he sat still, his face impassive.

"I am sorry to hear that your mother is ill," he said, but his voice betrayed no such feeling.

They sat in silence, facing one another, neither moving, neither saying anything. Finally, she spoke again.

"I need medicine for my mother," she said. "I will do whatever is necessary to get it. Please. I beg you." She hesitated and gazed down at the floor. "I have seen how you look at me," she said, her voice soft, her tone confessional.

Heidler studied her as he thought for a moment. "You know that medicines are virtually impossible to get," he said.

"You can get it," she replied pleadingly.

He nodded, acknowledging the truth of what he said. He reflected for a moment.

"Beauty affords wide latitude, doesn't it?" he said. "It also causes a presumption not found in others. Because you are beautiful, you have the confidence to come here, to all but barge through the door, without the slightest hesitation or fear. Of all of the tens of thousands of Jews here, perhaps you are the only one about whom that could be said. The others would not do so for fear that they would be sent off on the next transport to the east. But you have no such fear."

"I don't fear anything at the moment," she said, "except the possibility of losing my mother."

He was struck by her candor.

"And if I am able to acquire the medicine . . ."

"I would be deeply grateful," she said, "eternally grateful. Truly grateful forever."

He nodded. Yes, he understood that. But he wanted more than that.

"I would want something in return," he said.

"I understand," she said. "Of course."

He hesitated, then said, "I would want you.

"I would want you to come here willingly," he said. "To show desire and passion. Not to come sullenly, against your will, to engage in an act you find vile and repulsive. But to come here willingly. To come here because you wish to come here."

Hadn't she expected something like this? She was surprised something like this had not occurred earlier. She knew of certain arrangements within the camp, knew of Jewish girls who were paid with food and clothes and other things for providing Nazis with sex.

But the way he put it; that was what surprised her. He would certainly be smart enough to know that she could not possibly come willingly, showing anything like genuine desire or passion. Or did he? Could he believe it was possible, or was he merely saying that she would have to act? To appear to be coming willingly, to appear to have passion?

"I want you not to be coerced into coming here, but to come willingly," he said.

She would do it once and then she would escape, run

away. She would do it once to get the medicine and then she would never do it again. She would refuse. And he would have her killed. So be it, she thought. She would do what she must.

"Perhaps you should think about it," he said. "I cannot accept an answer now from you. I am not a man to whom promiscuity appeals. I am not one to take advantage of certain opportunities in the camp, as others do. As I surely could. I want this to be a matter of free will.

"If you do not agree, there will be no penalty, no sanction of any kind," he said. "Of that, I can assure you." He rose from his chair. "Consider it," he said.

31

The cab moved swiftly along the Unter den Linden, traveling south, down through the center of the city. Keegan felt the sense of history here. This was where it had been centered. This was where genocide had been plotted. This was where Diane's parents had been born, grown up—where they'd met. While in the service, stationed near Frankfurt, Keegan had made one trip here, but he had not felt the aura of the past the way he did now.

Soon the glitter and beauty of central Berlin gave way to a sprawling warehouse district, block after block of vast stone buildings containing all manner of goods from furniture to office supplies. The cab driver turned left on to Klunbergstrasse and then right on Rhenberg and that was the point at which Keegan lost track of where they were. These streets wove through the area like catacombs, turning here and there and cutting back on each other to the point of utter confusion. But the cab driver moved with confidence through the maze. Only in the final few blocks did he pause at a couple of points to gaze up at the street signs and study the numbers on the block.

Keegan felt uneasy. Though he had checked with his father's doctor before making this trip and been told Dick Keegan was in no imminent danger of dying, he

231

worried that the old man would take a sudden turn for the worse. But the doctor had reassured him and so he had made the trip. He would be gone no more than four days, and he would attempt to be back in three. It all depended on how quickly he was able to search the records.

Soon, the driver pulled up to a gray cement building, a long, low structure that took up half a city block. Keegan paid the driver and got out into a light drizzle. There was little activity on the narrow street. A few trucks were backed into a loading dock across the way.

Keegan looked up at the entrance to 79 Schonholzer. He walked up three stairs to the door and turned the knob, but found the door locked. There was a buzzer, which Keegan pressed. As he did so, he noticed a small surveillance camera perched about twelve feet up on the side of the building, aimed directly at where he stood. He looked up at the camera and was startled by a voice coming through the intercom.

"You are?"

"I'm David Keegan," he said. "From the United States."

A buzzer sounded and Keegan opened the door and stepped into a small waiting area with two chairs and a small table. Keegan stood there, waiting, and within a minute an elderly woman entered the room. She was slightly stooped in the shoulders and neck, but she smiled and introduced herself as Helene Stegr. She guided Keegan along a narrow hallway that led to an office where she presented Keegan to Dieter Stegr. He was a short man, stout and quite bald, wearing a pressed flannel shirt, a dark necktie, and a gray cardigan sweater.

"You are Mr. Keegan," Stegr said.

"Yes, Mr. Stegr," Keegan said. "It is a pleasure to meet you."

"You don't mind showing some identification, please," Stegr said.

"Of course not," Keegan said. He removed his passport from his inside suit pocket and handed it to Stegr. The old man—Keegan guessed he was in his middle eighties—put on a pair of reading glasses and studied the passport. He leaned down and looked it over, then removed the glasses and glanced up at Keegan, then looked quickly back down at the picture. Finally, he nodded, and handed it back.

"Come in, Mr. Keegan, please," Stegr said, leading Keegan into his office. Keegan was struck by the neatness of the place. Stegr's desk was spotless, two small stacks of documents side by side in the center, precisely positioned. There were two chairs and a small round conference table in the office, as well as a map of some kind.

"My guide, my key, my roadmap through all of the terrain with which I have surrounded myself here," he said. He walked to the wall and pointed to a low spot. "Here we are," he said, "and here"—he ran his finger along a long, narrow corridor—"and here and here are the documents, arranged in a way that, well . . ." Here Stegr laughed, and said, "In a way that seemed sensible to me as I was doing it, but that now seems, well, I don't know what you'd say, Mr. Keegan, but the system works for me and I suppose that's all that matters at the moment."

Stegr moved away from the wall and shuffled over to one of the chairs. "Sit down, please, Mr. Keegan, and tell me why you've come, please."

"Well, first, thanks very much for your willingness to see me, I appreciate that," he said.

"Professor Menke urged me to do so and he is a very

fine man, so a recommendation from him . . ." Stegr smiled and held out his hands in a sign of welcome.

"My mission here is to see if I can find information about a man who was at Theresienstadt, a German official," Keegan said. "He was a lawyer at the Reich Ministry of Justice and he was involved somehow—I'm not sure exactly how—with the camp. That's what I'm trying to determine, precisely what his role there was."

"His name, please?"

"His name was Friedrich Schillinghaussen," Keegan said.

Stegr frowned and squinted his eyes. "Yes, that was the fellow in the news article I read recently from one of the American papers," he said. "He'd been with the Reich Ministry of Justice, gone to Theresienstadt, and now been identified by a survivor, is that correct?"

"Yes," Keegan said.

"Someone sent it to me. We have many survivors or heirs who send me whatever mention of Theresienstadt they encounter."

"And had you heard of him before that?" Keegan asked.

Stegr shook his head. "The name meant nothing to me. He certainly wasn't a prominent official at the camp, that is for certain. I know all of those names by now.

"That is not to say that he did not hold a minor post of some kind," Stegr continued. "Remember, we're talking here about a very large enterprise. People sometimes mistakenly think of Theresienstadt as a minor operation in a little village. It was no such thing. With a population at its peak of nearly fifty thousand people, all in all more than a quarter million Jews at one time or another were in residence at Theresienstadt. On top of that, of course, you have thousands of Germans—SS and, in some cases, regular army—who administered the place. We have something like eleven million pieces of paper in this building relating to every conceivable aspect of that operation."

Keegan was astonished. "Eleven million?" he said.

Stegr smiled. "Yes," he said, nodding. "People are always finding this difficult to imagine, but it is the case. There are some individuals alone about whom I have hundreds of pages, really, thousands in some cases. In the cases of the major leaders of the camp, both SS and Judenrat."

As Stegr was saying this, Keegan had the sinking feeling that attempting to wade through the mass of documents might prove all but impossible. The idea of this little old man and his wife—for there was no sign of any other life here that Keegan could tell—organizing all of that information into any coherent and usable system seemed unlikely.

It was as though Stegr could read Keegan's mind, for the old man sat back in his chair and explained the system on which his archive operated.

"You see, Mr. Keegan, we have devoted our lives to this resource," he said. "My wife and I have spent forty years working on this, gathering materials, organizing, cross-referencing. We were fortunate enough to benefit from the inheritance of some money, so we never had to concern ourselves with such matters. And we were not blessed with children for whatever reason. And so we have devoted our lives to creating this resource. And we feel a certain pride in what we have done. We believe we have made a contribution. This will stand as a resource, after we are gone, for scholars who wish to delve into a particular aspect of that time. Remember, Mr.

Keegan, some of the most prominent Jewish intellectuals of the time were sent to Theresienstadt.

"And, soon, there will be no one left alive on this earth who experienced that place." Stegr paused and looked off at the wall for a moment, shaking his head at the enormity and finality of what he was saying.

"Which, to me, is a very frightening thought," he said. "A profoundly frightening thought. Because then it is all a matter of history, of remembering through books and records, secondhand.

"That is why we have done this," he said, leaning forward, the intensity evident in his face. "So that when everyone has died there would still be an accounting."

After a pause, Stegr seemed to brighten. "So, what is the name again, please?"

"Schillinghaussen," Keegan said. "Friedrich."

"Middle initial, please?"

Keegan thought for a moment. "Sorry," he said, shaking his head. "I don't know it."

"Come, follow me, please. Let us see what there is to see."

Stegr led Keegan down a short hallway to a room with a thick metal door. "Catalogue room," Stegr said, removing a key from his pocket and unlocking the door. With some effort, the small man opened it and walked through. The room was square, with two long tables along opposite walls. In the middle of the room stood a series of filing cabinets with small drawers. These were all metal, and just above them were the heads of some sort of sprinkler system.

"I've become more diligent through the years about all kinds of security," Stegr said. "Years ago, when we had nothing more than stacks of boxes, documents organized in no sensible fashion at all, it did not seem so important to protect what we had. But as we have worked through the years to organize everything it has become paramount. A few years ago I would wake in the night sometimes, terrified by the possibility of theft or vandalism or a fire or flood or anything that would destroy the records."

Keegan was surprised. "Theft? Vandalism?"

"Oh, Mr. Keegan," Stegr said in a mildly scolding tone. "There are those here in our country and elsewhere who would very much like to wipe the collective memory clean. There are revisionists at work now striking the same themes over and over. It never happened, or it didn't happen the way we've been told, or it was on a much smaller scale, or it was a renegade element. All of these themes and, in the absence of this," he said, spreading his arms, "in the absence of the truth, those themes might well take hold one day. So many stories here. So many lives. The truth is here, Mr. Keegan. The truth is here all around us."

Stegr walked to the first file cabinet and opened a drawer. "You know, there are those out there who would also like to expunge particular records," he said. "Out of self-interest."

"Records that indicate . . ."

"All sorts of things, from grave misdeeds to mere presence in a certain place at a certain time. There are individuals who have grown old and who know that the historical record demonstrates a certain fact about their lives, and it is a fact that might cause them shame, or embarrassment, or humiliation, and they feel a compulsion, before they go to their grave, to clean the slate. This has been a terrible problem with all of the historical records here in Germany, whether it's the official archive, the Berlin Document Center, or one of any number of smaller, privately owned and run places such as mine. People coming in under the pretext of seeking to conduct research, and then finding a record that embarrasses themselves, or their parent or grandparent, and then stealing the document and seeking to destroy it. This has become a problem.

"You see here that we are little in demand these days," Stegr said, a hint of regret in his voice. "Once in a while there will be a scholar, particularly from Eastern Europe or Israel. They will be writing some aspect of their dissertation on Theresienstadt and they come here. And there is a young Czech student who is writing what she hopes will one day become the definitive history of Theresienstadt. She has completed the first of two sections and I must say it is an impressive piece of scholarship. Truly, it is."

"And so this is the master card file," Keegan said, glancing down at the drawer that was open next to where Stegr stood.

"Yes, this is the master file," he said. He glanced around the room, indicating sprinkler heads and alarm lights. "So," he said, turning to the open drawer. "Here we have Miss Stefanie Aaron," he said, flicking to the first card in the file. "And if you'll take a look here you will see that the card tells us that information about Miss Aaron may be found in four places. First, in the work files, that's what the 'W' designates. And that file will provide us with a history of her work assignments at Theresienstadt. Everyone there, you see, anyone able-bodied, at any rate, was required to work, and that file will or should give us a fairly comprehensive sense of what her work life was like there. Then, you see the 'M' is a medical file. There would only be a medical file if there was some sort of formal treatment that the person received. In other words the person would have to have gone to the clinic and seen a physician and had a medical file opened by the staff. So in the M section we could go and find out whatever there is to know about Miss Aaron's medical history at Theresienstadt.

"Under the D files we would find out in what way or ways Miss Aaron was disciplined," Stegr continued. "It may have been anything ranging from withholding of rations for stealing food—an extremely common offense—to some more major theft or act of violence or what have you. Theoretically, anyway, the full disciplinary file should reveal all of that.

"And, finally, for Miss Aaron, we see that she is cross-referenced in the T file, which stands for transport. That may not mean necessarily that she was sent on a transport to the east, but perhaps a family member was dispatched or perhaps she was originally listed to go, then removed for some reason."

Keegan nodded his head, amazed by the extent of the information available. "So you and your wife have done this yourselves?" he said, marveling.

"Of course we had help through the years, many students came to our aid and assisted with the cataloging. But yes, we organized it ourselves. From chaos, really."

Stegr smiled broadly, his wrinkled face showing his pleasure at this stranger from America's recognition of a lifetime's work.

"It's quite incredible," Keegan said. "Amazing."

Stegr bowed slightly. "Thank you, thank you," he said. "You are very kind, indeed. And now, on to Mr. Schillinghaussen." And he walked down to the far end of the cabinets checking the letters on the outside of the steel drawers and opening the one that read "Sc."

"Let us see what is recorded here concerning Mr. Schillinghaussen."

Stegr's fingers were bony and crooked, but he flicked quickly through the card file, nonetheless, and found three Schillinghaussens. The last of the three was Friedrich.

"Let us see," Stegr said, pulling the drawer out of the file cabinet and moving it onto a higher tray for easier viewing. Peering through his spectacles, Stegr moved close to the card.

"Mark this down, if you would, Mr. Keegan," Stegr said. "Mr. Schillinghaussen is cross-referenced here with a 'P,' meaning his personnel file."

"What's that likely to contain?" Keegan asked, hunched behind Stegr, peering over the old man's shoulder at the card.

"That would be the standard personnel file," Stegr said, "probably with a basic work and education history. A curriculum vitae, of sorts. If he is a German official, that would record his Party membership, as well."

"And the 'O'?" Keegan asked, looking at the card.

"Orders," Stegr said. "Obviously you would never have a Jew cross-indexed here. This would only be for officials assigned to the camp in some capacity, officers, usually. This would be a summary or, in some cases, an actual copy of their orders. They would come to Theresienstadt, present themselves to the commandant, and hand over their orders from the headquarters of whatever branch to which they were assigned, SS, regular army, whatever. That document—a summary of it—would be in the O file."

Stegr looked at the next entry and was clearly disappointed. It was marked "D (SS)."

"A disciplinary file," Stegr said. "An SS disciplinary file . . ."

"You mean he . . ."

". . . unfortunately the vast majority are missing," Stegr said. "The SS disciplined its own people and other German officials, and near the end, someone from the SS, no doubt, decided those files would be too revealing for Allied eyes. And they were destroyed. The SS had a giant bonfire before the camp was liberated. We had put away a huge store of information by then, of course, secreted throughout the camp, but there were certain files to which we simply did not have access.

"So I do not want to set you up for disappointment," Stegr continued. "I am virtually certain that there will be nothing there."

He looked at Keegan and shrugged.

"Can't hurt to look," Keegan said.

Stegr led Keegan along a short hallway to another, larger room containing scores of steel file cabinets. In the Disciplinary section he found a manila folder with the name Friedrich Schillinghaussen that contained a single sheet of paper. "Disciplinary proceedings commenced 11 April 1943 (in absentia)" was all it said. There were no other entries on the page.

"Ah, this is quite interesting," Stegr said. "Though it tells us nothing about the nature of the disciplinary proceedings against Mr. Schillinghaussen, it does seem to indicate that he was gone by the time those proceedings commenced."

"Meaning?" Keegan asked.

"Meaning I'm not sure, exactly," Stegr said. "But

what is odd here is that the rest of this is blank, meaning probably there was no further action against him. At least not while he was at Theresienstadt.

"It may be, in fact," Stegr continued, "that he was gone, permanently so, from the camp by then."

"What could they conceivably have disciplined him for?" Keegan asked.

Stegr sighed and shrugged. "It could mean any number of things," he said. "Any sort of breach of the codes of conduct. Anything."

"And there's no way of telling?" Keegan asked.

"This would be what would tell us," Stegr said, "but it is apparent that the record keepers were lax in the matter. Perhaps his personnel file will offer a clue."

Keegan followed Stegr into another room, similar to the one in which they had just been, though much larger and with many more file cabinets.

"This is our major source of information, here," Stegr said. "Basic, standard files on each individual. Or many individuals. There are two hundred seventy three thousand files in this room alone."

Stegr walked to the far end of the room to a cabinet that bore the letters "Sch." He went through toward the middle of the drawer, pulled out a manila folder, and walked to the plain wooden table in the center of the room. He placed the file on the table and indicated that Keegan should sit down. Stegr pulled a chair next to him and sat down, opening the file. The file was discolored around the edges, the portion most exposed to the air and light. The rest of the file, pressed in on both sides for decades, was remarkably well-kept, smooth and whitish in color. Keegan realized that this file had, in all likelihood, not been touched since the 1940s.

Stegr nodded. "A basic CV," he said. "Schilling-haussen was born in Berlin on March 4, 1914, the son of Ernst and Diedre Schnellen. His father was a veteran of the First World War. His mother deceased in 1920. He went to Graues Kloster, the most elite school in the city, so he was obviously a gifted student. And then on to the University of Berlin, where he took a law degree in 1939. Joined the Reich Ministry of Justice before that, probably while in training. Administered some sort of program for what appears to be a section of Prussia."

Stegr turned the sheet over. There was a single sheet of paper that indicated the date upon which Schilling-haussen arrived at Theresienstadt—March 27, 1943. Beneath that were a half dozen other sheets of paper. He read quickly through them, flipping each one over in turn. He shook his head, dismissively as he moved through.

"Nothing else of interest, really," he said. "All basic administrative information. Repetitive of the cover sheet."

"Except that with that date," Keegan said, "we now know that if he was gone by the time the disciplinary proceedings were commenced that he was at the camp for only a matter of weeks."

Stegr hesitated. "His arrival date was . . . ?"

"March 27," Keegan said.

"Ah, you are quite correct, Mr. Keegan," Stegr said. "I'm afraid my old tired brain didn't pick that up right away."

"And that means, as far as his being an officer of the camp somehow . . ." Keegan said.

"That he almost certainly was not," Stegr said. "For so brief a period of time, no, there is little chance he could have been someone within the camp administration. That is not to say that he did not play some role of consequence somehow in the life of Theresienstadt. He could have carried a message or an order of some kind from Berlin to the camp. One doesn't know. But certainly we will consult the master file of the camp administration shortly."

"Anything more about the program he administered?" Keegan asked.

Stegr flipped back to the first page. "Merely that it involved property of some sort. It simply says here it was within the Reich Ministry of Justice, Property Division."

Stegr considered that information for a moment. "I would suppose this would have involved, possibly, some sort of transactions involving Jewish property owners."

"So there's one more file," Keegan said.

"We'll review the orders file and then consult my master list of camp officials. That, more than any other document, will reveal whether he was an official within Theresienstadt."

They moved back along the hallway into a smaller room, again, with rows of metal file cabinets. Stegr went to a cabinet and looked through a series of identical folders, checking the names, until he came to Friedrich Schillinghaussen. He removed the folder and brought it to a plain steel table. He opened the file and revealed a single sheet of onionskin.

"Per order of the Fuhrer, Friedrich Schillinghaussen, Reich Ministry of Justice and so on and so on . . . to Theresienstadt in pursuit of assets rightfully belonging to the Reich."

Stegr shrugged. "That's all, I'm afraid," he said, clearly puzzled. "I must tell you in all honesty I am at a loss. I have never seen an order such as this and do not know what it could possibly have meant."

"What are the precise words again?" Keegan asked. "The 'in pursuit of assets' part?"

Stegr peered down at the page. "In pursuit of assets rightfully belonging to the Reich."

Keegan frowned. "Does the phrase mean anything to you?"

Stegr thought for a moment, then shook his head. "Nothing," he said.

"It's not some kind of legal idiom, perhaps?" Keegan asked.

"Ah, Mr. Keegan, you are asking the wrong man that question, I am afraid," Stegr said. "I am not, after all, a lawyer."

"Have you heard that phrase before, I wonder?" Keegan asked.

"Not that I can recall," Stegr said.

"So what do you suppose it means?" Keegan asked. "Just speculate, if you wouldn't mind."

Stegr drew a deep breath. "Well, let me consider this rationally. I suppose it must mean some kind of assets being held by someone at Theresienstadt. I would assume, if that were the case, that it would be held by a Jew."

Keegan nodded. "That would make some sense, wouldn't it? What were the laws then, generally speaking, governing Jewish wealth? Securities, that sort of thing?"

"Very strict," Stegr said. "Virtually everything was turned over to the Reich by families going to Theresienstadt. Some families, in fact, bought their way into Theresienstadt."

"I'd heard that," Keegan said.

"So, perhaps, someone agreed to turn over their assets to be permitted to go there . . ."

"Rather than to Treblinka, say . . ."

"Rather than to Treblinka or Auschwitz or Birkenau or wherever in the east, and perhaps it was later discovered that there were additional assets." Stegr shrugged. "Who knows."

They sat silently looking at each other for the moment, both mystified by what Schillinghaussen's mission might have been.

"Could we have a look at the list of administrators to see if he shows up there?" Keegan asked.

"Certainly," Stegr said, rising from the table. He placed the folder back in its proper place and they walked back along the hallway to Stegr's office, where he consulted a large, black leatherbound volume.

"This is my master reference book," he said, smiling. "Overall facts and statistics are compiled here."

He thumbed through the book and soon arrived at a page near the front that included a list of names. He sat running his finger down the page, then reviewed a second column of names and then a third.

He shook his head no as he finished reading. "Not here," he said, picking up the volume and handing it to Keegan. "See for yourself."

Keegan read carefully through the list of names once, then again to make sure.

"How confident are you that this list is comprehensive?" Keegan asked.

"I have culled that list from scores of other sources," he said. "I have taken the basic list that was in the SS files and added to it anyone whose other files indicated he played an administrative role of any consequence in any part of the camp. If, for example, a German officer was assigned to the farm and only to the farm, he would be included in this list. But if an officer worked on one transport and then was gone, then, no, Mr. Keegan, he would not be included."

"So, in your judgment, Mr. Stegr, with respect to Friedrich Schillinghaussen . . ."

"In my judgment Friedrich Schillinghaussen was clearly not an administrator at Theresienstadt," Stegr said.

"And you feel a certain confidence in that," Keegan said.

"I say that with an extremely high degree of confidence. Bordering on certainty."

"Mr. Stegr, if I draw up a document to that effect, would you be willing to sign it?" Keegan asked.

"Without hesitation," Stegr said. "Certainly. My only interest, Mr. Keegan, is the truth."

Keegan opened the file belonging to Diane's mother. The records indicated that she had worked on the farm briefly and then as a clerk for the camp administration, for Heinrich Heidler of the SS. Keegan read through and was about to turn to the second page in Sophie Naumann's file when he read the last line of the first page. It read: "Disciplinary proceedings commenced 11 April 1943 (in absentia)."

Keegan absently closed the file, ignoring for the moment the second page.

"Both of them had disciplinary proceedings initiated on the same day," Keegan said.

"In absentia," Stegr said. "Very odd. Let's check the file of Heinrich Heidler. I've learned that when you have any name in connection with any other, check it." Stegr went through other files and soon discovered something that jarred him. "It says here," Stegr said, "that disciplinary proceedings were also begun against Heidler on 11 April. Now that is very odd."

"Jesus," Keegan muttered under his breath.

Stegr sighed. "I am afraid I am at a loss," he said.

Keegan rode in a cab back to his hotel with two documents: one was a photocopy of the list of officers from Theresienstadt; the other a brief, typewritten statement that read: "Based on a search of historical records, it is my judgment that Friedrich Schillinghaussen, an official at the Reich Ministry of Justice, was not an officer or an administrator at Theresienstadt." It was signed by Stegr and witnessed and signed by his wife.

Keegan went to the concierge and arranged to have both documents sent by facsimile to Diane's home. After the documents were sent, Keegan went to his room and called her on the telephone. She was not at home, and Keegan realized that since it was evening in Berlin, it was midday in Boston. He left a message on her machine, and within an hour, she called him back from the hospital.

"I miss you," she said.

"I miss you, too," he said.

"But Dad had a good day. My mother thinks he responded to her twice, squeezing her hand. She's not absolutely sure, but she thinks so, and if true, the doctors say that's a very good step."

"That's great," Keegan said. "I have more good news."

"Really?"

When David told her that he had proof that her father had not been an official of the camp, Diane wept with joy.

32

Keegan was walking to his hotel restaurant when he was struck by an idea. He returned to his room and telephoned Stegr at home.

"I had a thought, Mr. Stegr, that I'd like to try out on you," Keegan said. "In a culture as hierarchical as Germany was in the 1940s, I wonder whether there was a prescribed process that was to be followed in any matter involving a disciplinary proceeding. In other words, if it was the first step in a legal process, even if that was under the guise of military law, there might be a process that would have been required."

Stegr considered this. "I am uncertain, Mr. Keegan," the old man said. "My familiarity with disciplinary matters was an interest more or less only in the outcomes. But if there was a precise procedure to be followed, that would be enunciated in the Military Code of Justice, a set of guidelines that, for all practical purposes, took precedence in a legal sense during that time."

"Is that available anywhere?" Keegan asked.

"Oh, in a number of the major libraries," Stegr said. "I will happily call around in the morning to try to find you an opportunity to look them over."

"What about tonight?" Keegan asked. "Would they be available anywhere now?"

Stegr was taken aback. "Tonight? Well, I suppose the main library at the university would have a set," he said. "Certainly, they would. If you go there I suspect they will be helpful to you. They are open quite late. And if you have trouble, using my name might prove helpful."

Keegan's ability to read German was quite strong. His spoken German was another matter. He struggled at the university library to explain precisely what it was he was interested in seeing. When, finally, he and the librarian were able to communicate, it was nearly 10 P.M. Keegan settled into a carrel in the upper reaches of the building, just two rows up from a collection of seventeen volumes of military legal rules and procedures from the 1940s. Keegan knew he had only until midnight, when the library closed, but he was unconcerned. Was there anywhere he was more comfortable than in a setting such as this, combing through remnants of the past, searching for clues, trying to make the pieces fit so that he could understand?

He read quickly, skimming through tables of contents and appendices until, finally, he found what he believed were the rules he needed. One particular set of procedures applied to camps and other facilities supervised by the German military. He was encouraged when he found that the term "disciplinary proceedings" was a formal term of law, clearly defined in the book, and he was further heartened when he discovered that there was a clear procedure required whenever disciplinary proceedings commenced. In such a case, the Reich Ministry of Justice was required to undertake an "immediate and comprehensive" investigation "to set forth the facts and conclusions in the matter."

The rain swept across Berlin in sheets, darkening the already gray hue of this city of massive granite structures. Keegan rode in a taxi through the downpour, following the twisting and turning route back to the Theresienstadt archive.

"Ah, good morning and welcome, Herr Keegan," Dieter Stegr said. "You went to the library last evening?"

"I did," Keegan said. "And I wonder whether you have any investigatory files or reports?"

"There is a voluminous set of reports that we have," Stegr said. "They are rarely consulted. I am not that familiar with them. The ones I have reviewed have tended to concern internal military or police matters. Very minor, mundane affairs. A soldier is tardy returning from leave. A fight between two guards. Generally that's the sort of thing one finds. Though, as I say, I do not have an intimate knowledge of the files. They are quite vast."

"May I see them?" Keegan asked.

"Of course," Stegr said. "Follow me." Stegr led Keegan along the main hallway and then into a series of small, connected rooms. Keegan stood by while Stegr consulted a thick, bound document. "Let us try over here," Stegr said, leading Keegan through one room and into another, larger area. Stegr spread his arms before a row of two dozen steel file drawers. "Any report would most likely be filed by the name of the individual, but it is possible there is another key," Stegr said. "I warn you that if what you are seeking is in these files—and it may not be—then it could be difficult to locate."

Keegan nodded. He understood. Throughout the

morning, Stegr and Keegan searched the files. They found
no reports under the names of Schillinghaussen or Naumann. They found nothing under Reich Ministry of Justice, nothing under the date in question. Nothing at all.
Until, that is, it occurred to David Keegan to look for the
files under the name of Heinrich Heidler.

INVESTIGATOR'S REPORT RE: CASE 4921776
REPORT TRANSMITTED 22 JUNE 1943
Investigation commenced 11 April 1943 by the Reich
Ministry of Justice into the matter concerning Hein-
rich Heidler, Sturmbannführer, SS; Friedrich Schilling-
haussen, the Reich Ministry of Justice; Josef Van
Strahlich, Luftwaffe; Elsa Naumann, Juden; Sophie
Naumann, Juden. Investigator: Josef Reist.

Investigation proceeded with review of existing files
re: Heidler, Schillinghaussen, J. Van Strahlich, E. Naumann, S. Naumann. Investigation proceeded with financial analysis of various accounts under the control
of F. Schillinghaussen in his position as administrator,
Property Confiscation Division/Prussia, the Reich Ministry of Justice.

Investigation proceeded with interviews with
various officials concerning the subjects of the investigation.

INVESTIGATOR'S FINDING OF FACT:
Heinrich Heidler was commandant of the Reich's se-
cure facility for Jews at Theresienstadt. Friedrich
Schillinghaussen was an attorney, the Reich Ministry
of Justice. Josef Van Strahlich was a Luftwaffe pilot. E.
Naumann and S. Naumann were Jews formerly re-

siding in the Grunewald, Berlin, who had been ordered to Theresienstadt 12 December 1938.

INTERVIEW WITH MARTIN KOBLENZ, CHIEF, REAL PROPERTY, THE REICH MINISTRY OF JUSTICE

Attorney Koblenz, who served as Schillinghaussen's superior, recounted the following conversation that took place on 10 March 1943:

Friedrich Schillinghaussen came to me on approximately 10 March 1943 and indicated to me he had information that suggested that significant assets held by Jewish families had not been disclosed as required by law. The problem of undisclosed assets held by Jews was thought to be a significant challenge. Recovering those assets was difficult and I believed an effort to try to do so was warranted.

In this case, you must understand that I was dealing with a man I considered to be of unimpeachable character. Friedrich Schillinghaussen had an exemplary record, perhaps the finest record of any young attorney I was aware of at the Reich Ministry. It was unblemished.

When he informed me that he thought he might have discovered undisclosed assets I asked him to place a value on the assets. He estimated somewhere in the range of fifteen to twenty million marks, possibly more. With that as the potential I gave him permission to proceed with his work and to try his theories on several test cases. I advised him that he could take two weeks to begin this process. I told him that on the basis of his initial work we would then decide whether to proceed on a broader basis.

He then indicated to me that he had identified three families he suspected of hiding assets and all three were located at Theresienstadt.

Question from Investigator Reif: So you did not order him to start at Theresienstadt or in any way suggest he begin there?

Response from M. Koblenz: No, I did not. He initiated the idea of his going to Theresienstadt.

Investigator Reif: So it was clear he wished to go to Theresienstadt.

M. Koblenz: Very clear. He wanted to go there.

BACKGROUND ON FRIEDRICH SCHILLINGHAUSSEN

As the investigation moved in the direction of F. Schillinghaussen's embezzlement, an effort was undertaken to determine the background of F. Schillinghaussen.

Investigator's Findings: F. Schillinghaussen was the son of Ernst and Diedre Schillinghaussen. Ernst Schillinghaussen worked as a foreman in a furniture manufacturing facility in Wannsee. He served in the German Army in World War I, with distinction. Upon return from the war Ernst Schillinghaussen worked odd jobs as a plumber's or carpenter's assistant.

Diedre Schillinghaussen died when Friedrich was six years old.

Ernst Schillinghaussen joined the National Socialist Party in 1929. He became an active Party member and has been recognized through the years as such.

Friedrich Schillinghaussen joined Hitler Youth at age thirteen. He was an honor student at Graues Kloster.

He led his class at the University of Berlin and received a law degree in 1939.

BACKGROUND ON HEINRICH HEIDLER

Commandant Heidler was the son of Heinrich and Ulrike Heidler Sr. H. Heidler Sr. was chairman of Heidler and Company, the largest holder of commercial property in Berlin. The Heidler family was widely known for its prominence in business and as generous patrons of the arts. H. Heidler Sr. served as chairman of the board of the Berlin Museum of Fine Art and of the University of Berlin Medical Center. Mrs. Heidler was a member of the board of the Berlin Symphony Orchestra and the Berlin Ballet.

Commandant Heidler joined Hitler Youth at age twelve. He took a doctorate in political philosophy from the University of Berlin. He won the university debating contest twice.

Commandant Heidler was commissioned in the SS in 1939. He became commandant at Theresienstadt in 1940. His record, previous to 11 April, had been exemplary.

It is apparent that H. Heidler and F. Schillinghaussen were aquainted prior to Schillinghaussen's arrival at Theresienstadt.

BACKGROUND ON JOSEF VAN STRAHLICH

Oberlieutenant Van Strahlich was raised in Munich, the son of Wilhelm and Sonia Van Strahlich. W. Van Strahlich served as administrator of the Munich air commission and the Munich airport. Oberlieutenant Van Strahlich learned to fly at a young age and was commissioned in the Luftwaffe at age eighteen. He flew numerous reconnaissance missions during 1939 through 1941. In 1942 he received a combat commission and was subsequently shot down over Czechoslovakia.

Oberlieutenant Van Strahlich was then assigned duty as pilot to various Reich officials traveling throughout the Reich and beyond.

It is believed that Oberlieutenant Van Strahlich and F. Schillinghaussen were known to one another prior to 11 April, and prior to Oberlieutenant Van Strahlich piloting the craft that brought Schillinghaussen to Theresienstadt.

BACKGROUND ON ELSA NAUMANN

Elsa Blumberg was born to a working-class Jewish family in 1883. She attended secondary school and then art school. She went to work as a teacher of art and music and married Karl Naumann in 1896. Elsa Naumann's husband, Karl, was the proprietor of three markets in various sections of Berlin. The Naumanns were a prosperous family residing in the Grunewald.

Elsa Naumann, acting on her own, made application in 1937 for a family visa to the United Kingdom. That application was denied for failure to make application by the head of household.

BACKGROUND ON SOPHIE NAUMANN

Sophie Naumann was born in 1917 in the Grunewald. She attended the first rank of public schools and scored at the highest levels in academic achievement. She played the piano to a certain level of achievement at a young age. She went to the University of Berlin, where she studied literature, but was required to leave after enactment of the Laws for German Purity. She tutored Jewish children living in and around the Grunewald.

INVESTIGATOR'S FINDING OF FACT (Continued)
Various bank accounts under the control of Friedrich Schillinghaussen were examined. Irregularities were found in all accounts.

Accounts involved property administration program and provided funds for taxation, utilities, maintenance, bank fees. Accounts also paid various vendors for services rendered concerning upkeep and maintenance on the numerous properties seized by the Reich.

Taken in total, the accounts were missing approximately 1.8 percent of the funds claimed to have been held. No account was out of balance by more than 3 percent.

It is clear from the auditing of these accounts that a great deal of time and attention went into the embezzlement of Reich funds. It would not be an overstatement to say that the accounts had been misappropriated in a painstaking fashion.

In one account a substantial discrepancy was uncovered. An account labeled "administrative expenses" was intended to fund a variety of administrative costs for the property confiscation program. A ledger, personally maintained by Schillinghaussen, was discovered in a safe in Schillinghaussen's office at the Reich Ministry of Justice. It indicated that the account balance, prior to Schillinghaussen's trip to Theresienstadt, stood at 5,337.00 marks. In reality, the account held 53,370.00 marks. Funds embezzled in small amounts from other accounts had accumulated in this amount in the administrative expenses account. Funds had been diverted on a systematic basis since March of 1939.

INVESTIGATOR'S FINDING OF FACT (Continued)
During the nine-day period prior to his arrival at Theresienstadt, financial records indicate that Friedrich Schillinghaussen cashed Reich Ministry of Justice checks at eleven banks throughout Berlin. In all, he received 51,311 marks. Every account from which he withdrew money was left open with small balances remaining.

Schillinghaussen arrived at Theresienstadt on 27 March 1943 under the apparent pretext of seeking to recover 'assets rightfully belonging to the Reich.' He was flown from Berlin to Terezin in a Junkers 52, piloted by Josef Van Strahlich.

INVESTIGATOR'S FINDING OF FACT (Continued)
A number of officers present at the time reported seeing Commandant Heidler and Friedrich Schillinghaussen enter the officer's club in the early evening and take a table near the far wall. There was no indication of conflict between the two men. Oberlieutenant Herbert Von Euw was standing at the bar when Commandant Heidler and Herr Schillinghaussen arrived. The commandant invited Von Euw to join them for a drink and Von Euw did so. The commandant introduced Oberlieutenant Von Euw to Schillinghaussen. Oberlieutenant Von Euw sat down at a table with Commandant Heidler and Herr Schillinghaussen near the far wall.

Oberlieutenant Von Euw recalled that Commandant Heidler explained to Schillinghaussen that certain of the young women at the club were made available to officers on an informal basis.

Schillinghaussen expressed surprise at this revelation, according to Oberlieutenant Von Euw. When he did so, Commandant Heidler, to the best of Oberlieutenant Von Euw's recollection, said, "You've been sheltered in Berlin too long, Friedrich. Here, we make do."

INVESTIGATOR'S FINDING OF FACT (Continued)
Commandant Heidler invited Schillinghaussen to a dinner at the officer's quarters on the evening of 7 April. Schillinghaussen was the last to arrive. He seemed, according to several of those present, reluctant to attend. After a dinner of rack of lamb, those present—ten men in all—sat around the table enjoying after dinner beverages and smoking cigars. There was much talk of the war, of comradeship. Commandant Heidler ordered that a photograph be taken to memorialize the occasion. An officer with photo equipment was summoned and the ten men shuffled around until they were instructed to line up. At that moment, Schillinghaussen began moving toward the door. Heidler called him back.

"Schillinghaussen, come and join us for our photograph," Heidler said. "I want to commemorate this evening. An enjoyable evening even as the Reich faces defeat in the war. Come."

Schillinghaussen turned and smiled. "I am very tired, Commandant, and I hope you will excuse me," Schillinghaussen said. "I don't photograph particularly well."

But Commandant Heidler walked across the room and patted Schillinghaussen on the back, placing his arm around his shoulder and walking him back to the group.

"Join us, Schillinghaussen," Heidler insisted. "It is an honor to have such an important lawyer from the Reich Ministry of Justice. Please. Line up with us."

Thus Friedrich Schillinghaussen moved to the back row, far left, and stood stock-still as the photographer snapped one picture after another. A few days later copies of the photograph were developed and distributed to all of the men pictured. The photo was distributed by a camp inmate, an office administrator, by the name of Gerta Wahljak.

See "Findings and Conclusions; Recorded: Reich Ministry of Justice, 1943"

Keegan saw that he had come to the end of the file. He quickly checked the files nearby but all concerned other matters. He hurried down the hall to Stegr and explained his predicament.

"Oh, yes," Stegr said. "I have noticed before that this will sometimes happen. They will have separated the findings from the rest of the report. Why, I do not know, but this will sometimes happen. Whether we would have the findings here, I am not certain."

"You don't have a separate section containing findings?" Keegan asked.

"I am afraid not," Stegr said.

Keegan winced.

"Any thoughts?" Keegan asked.

Stegr knitted his brow and considered the matter. "I would say the best hope is to search these files here. Perhaps it was misplaced at some point. If we have it here in our collection, I believe the likelihood is that it is in these files here."

Keegan nodded.

"May I pitch in?" Stegr asked.

"You don't need to," Keegan said.

Stegr smiled. "I'd like to," he said.

The two men went to work systematically opening every file drawer and moving along the rows reading the description on the tab of every file folder. They worked quickly and in silence, and there were several instances during the course of the day when they believed they had happened upon it. But in each instance they would open the file and find documents having nothing to do with the case. They worked throughout the afternoon and into the early evening as a feeling of desperation, and then disappointment, overtook Keegan.

By that night, after they had worked their way through every filing drawer in the section, they were empty-handed. Keegan felt the intense frustration that went with knowing he was so close to knowing so much.

"There is another place," Stegr said. "It is in the south of the city in a large basement facility. It is an adjunct of the Berlin Archives but managed by the Legal Association. It contains many judicial and quasi-judicial records for many different proceedings during that period. It has been proven to be of little use to scholars and sits quietly, rarely used anymore."

"Can we go there tonight?" Keegan asked.

Stegr shook his head. "I'm afraid not," he said. "It is very strictly controlled by the Legal Association. Few are admitted there. I have been on two occasions but it takes time to get approval. At least a few days, sometimes weeks."

"No, it can't . . ."

Stegr held up his hands to stop Keegan. "Believe me, Herr Keegan, if it could be done more quickly I would do it, but I know these people well enough to know their inflexibility. They make no exceptions."

"When is the soonest, realistically, I could get in there do you think?" Keegan asked.

"Next week," Stegr said. "Perhaps not that soon."

Keegan thought of his father's precarious health. "I have to get back in the next day or two at the latest," he said. "I . . ."

Stegr perked up. "I would happily go there for you," Stegr said. "I could go and search, and if I find the document I could forward it along to you."

"You could fax me a copy," Keegan said, suddenly excited by the idea.

"Certainly," Stegr said.

"That would be wonderful," Keegan said.

They walked along down the main hallway of the archive toward Stegr's office. At Stegr's office, Keegan put on his suit jacket and got his briefcase. He was about to bid Stegr and his wife farewell when he remembered something.

"There are a couple of files I meant to glance at," Keegan said. "I left them out. May I?"

"Of course," Stegr said. "You go ahead. I must be off to an appointment, but my wife will be here and she will see you out when you are through."

"Mr. Stegr, I cannot thank you enough for your help," Keegan said. "It's been a true pleasure to meet you."

"Ah, you are so kind, Herr Keegan," Stegr said. "The feeling is quite mutual, I assure you."

Keegan went back down the main hallway and turned off into one of the side rooms where he had left Sophie and Elsa Naumann's files laying on a table. Keegan thumbed quickly through Elsa's file, then turned to Sophie's. There was something nagging at his mind that he had neglected to do, yet he was not sure what. He went through Sophie's file and quickly reached the last page. That was it. When he had been through the file earlier he had not read the last page.

He removed the sheet of paper and saw that it was a medical record containing several entries. He was surprised for it appeared that she had suffered from some sort of illness. But then Keegan read the entries on the medical form and he saw that it was something else entirely.

He reread the entries and sat back in his seat, confused. But how could that be? he wondered. How could that have happened under the circumstances? There was no mistaking the language. *Schwanger.* Pregnant. Diane's mother had conceived while at Theresienstadt. The record indicated that the estimated date of conception had been January 15, 1943. Keegan realized that that date was nine weeks prior to Friedrich Schillinghaussen's arrival at Theresienstadt.

Keegan took the sheet of paper, folded it, and placed it in the inside pocket of his suit jacket. He returned the files to where they belonged, and he left, bidding Mrs. Stegr farewell and trying hard to understand what had happened back there.

33

Just as Keegan was checking out of his hotel he received a phone call from Stegr.

"I've been meaning to ask you about someone and I'm glad I caught you before you left. It's quite a coincidence, but there's a man coming tomorrow who is also from Boston and from the federal government of the United States," Stegr said. "A man named Dunbar. Do you know him?"

Keegan hesitated.

"Mr. Stegr, have you already arranged to see him?"

"I have, yes," Stegr said. "Tomorrow afternoon."

Keegan nodded. "Mr. Stegr, I am sorry to say that I am aware of this man who calls himself Dunbar. Did he use the first name Andrew, David, or Theo?"

Stegr was clearly perplexed. "Theo, I believe," Stegr said. "Yes, Theo."

Keegan nodded. "He's been using that and Andrew quite a bit lately. Before that it was often David. Usually the last name is Dunbar, but sometimes it's Collins, occasionally Farnsworth."

"I don't understand," Stegr said.

"He's an imposter, Mr. Stegr," Keegan said. "He is a man who evidently believes he is a lawyer for the United

264

States Justice Department, and he attempts to shadow our activities. He uses public information available to anyone—newspaper articles, case motions—and travels around pretending he is working on a particular case. He's harmless enough, but utterly delusional. He's neither a lawyer nor an employee of Justice. He is merely a wealthy man with too much time on his hands and an imagination run amok."

Stegr was amazed. "I am flabbergasted," the old man said. "Professor Schoen phoned me about him."

"That's how persuasive Dunbar is. Professor Schoen doesn't know the true story."

"So should I . . . Would you if you were me . . ."

"Would I permit him in there to the place you've spent your life working on?" Keegan asked. "I certainly would not. I would revoke the invitation without explanation."

"Yes," Stegr said. "Yes, that's precisely what I'll do. And thank you, Mr. Keegan, very much."

Keegan smiled. "My pleasure," he said.

Keegan rode to the airport knowing he needed to make a stop on the way home, a stop in Cleggan, Diane's birthplace, the place she had often spoken of going for a vacation, a place she wanted to visit with Keegan.

As his plane lifted off the runway in Berlin, Keegan settled back in his seat and thought about some of what he had just uncovered. He thought about the investigator's report, the portions about Friedrich Schillinghaussen's financial misdeeds, the painstaking embezzlement of government funds, and he was amazed by the precision of it, by the patience and discipline involved.

Keegan imagined Freddy in his office at the Reich Ministry of Justice, late at night, the door locked, a pool of yellow light spilling across the rows and columns of numbers in the account ledger, numbers that concealed painstaking years—literally years!—of preparation. It was clear that he had had a plan. But Keegan wondered for how long? How had he chosen when to act? What had caused him to move when he did?

The property had been on the list for some time, ever since Sophie and her family had been sent away. But Freddy had never dared go and see it. Yet now he was on his way. Now he had a reason to see it!

Freddy's heart raced as he pushed open the door and stepped inside to the foyer, slowly closing the door behind him. He stepped into the main hallway and stood still, looking around. No sound could be heard.

"Hello?" he called out.

There was no response. He stepped forward, walking slowly along the hallway, passing a large sitting room on the right and then a cozy library with an ornate fireplace.

"Is anyone here?" he shouted, more loudly this time. He was greeted only by silence.

He stepped into the library, walking across the Oriental carpet and stopping before a dark wood table, topped with a thick layer of dust and a decanter of sherry. There were three photographs atop the table, all in silver frames. One showed the Naumann family, Karl, Elsa, and a much younger Sophie—Freddy guessed she was twelve or thirteen at the time the picture was taken—standing together on what appeared to be the edge of a lake somewhere. Sophie was smiling broadly. The two other pictures were of Sophie alone. In one, she was, again, much younger. It appeared that she was at the lake as well, but this time she was swimming and only her head was sticking above water.

The third photograph was the one Freddy found most arresting, even unsettling. It was a formal portrait and appeared to have been taken quite recently. Her head was cocked slightly to one side and, from the photograph, she was staring directly into Freddy's eyes. She was wearing a simple sweater with a single strand of pearls. Her hair was pulled back, making her appear much older than she was. She stared at the camera with not even a hint of a smile on her face. Freddy was unable to take his eyes off the picture. The longer he stared at it the more fascinated he grew. Its black-and-white tones made her appear cooler, more aloof than she really was. And far older. It was as though, Freddy thought, he was getting a glimpse of Sophie ten years hence, as though he was seeing her in the future. She appeared serious and composed, quietly determined. And alone. He was chilled by the thought and forced himself to move away from the picture.

He stepped to the bookshelves and began examining the spines of various volumes. He was surprised to see so many in one particular section were written in Hebrew.

From the library, he walked through the hallway toward the back of the house, through a pantry area into a large kitchen, where he saw a set of stairs and followed them to the second floor. At the top of the stairs he followed the hallway, glancing into one room and then another. Both appeared to be spare bedrooms. The next room, he could see, was hers. He could feel it. He believed, as he stepped into the room, that he could feel her presence here. He smiled.

The room was done in muted shades of peach and plum. It was large, with two windows and light streaming through. He sat in the window seat in one of them and looked outside across the expansive lawn. He sat there for a few moments knowing that she must have spent countless hours in this very spot reading, thinking, writing.

He went to the closet and saw himself in her full-length mirror. He stopped and stared into the glass, disappointed that he could see only himself and not the reflection of her that must have been seen here thousands and thousands of times through the years. He stood staring into the mirror, transfixed by a vision in his mind's eye of Sophie, laughing, coming to him, putting her arms around his neck, kissing him . . .

The vision was so jarring that, at first, Freddy did not know what was happening, for there, directly in front of him, in the mirror in Sophie's room, was the image of a barrel-chested man in a freshly pressed SS uniform, looking quizzically at Freddy.

"Captured by your own image, Herr Schillinghaussen?" the man said, frowning at Freddy. "You are Schillinghaussen, are you not?"

"Oh, of course," Freddy said. "I'm sorry, I . . ."

"I called out for you downstairs, did you not hear me?" the SS man asked.

"I'm sorry, I was trying to be as still as possible," Freddy said, lying. "I thought I heard something in the eaves, a bird or squirrel, perhaps. You must be Sturmbannführer Rudel."

"I am," he said. "And I have no use for rodents in the attic. What have you heard?"

"Nothing, actually," Freddy said. "I listened intently

for some time and not a sound. I think what I originally heard was a bird landing on the edge of the windowsill outside."

Rudel nodded. "I want that checked out," he said. "I want the attic and the eaves examined." He glared at Freddy.

"I understand," he said.

Rudel nodded.

"My being here will remain confidential," he said. "I will not be living here full time. Just some of the time. You understand?"

Freddy nodded. Rudel would use it as a place to bring women, away from the watchful eye of his wife. Increasingly, of late, Freddy had been required to transfer properties to prominent Party and military officials. As they walked through the Naumann residence, Rudel grew increasingly enthused about taking stewardship of this home.

Rudel withdrew a flask from his pocket and drank from it. "Aghhhhh?" he grunted, offering it to Freddy.

"No, thank you," Freddy said.

They had reached the library, and Rudel spotted the decanter of sherry on the table. He went to the pantry and returned with two glasses, filling both with the dark, reddish liquid.

"Here you go then," he said. "Here's to my new home." He laughed heartily and drank.

He saw that Freddy had not drunk and he suddenly appeared insulted. "Drink up," he said. "Drink!"

Freddy brought the glass to his lips and sipped the sherry.

Rudel looked around the room and nodded with satisfaction, breaking into a wide smile. "Yes," he said, "yes, this will do nicely. I will strive to spend as much time as possible here. My family is outside Munich, but I am more and more frequently in Berlin. The logistics of our section . . ." He shook his head.

"And your section is?" Freddy asked.

"Transit," he said, glaring at Freddy as though looking for a sign of disdain or disrespect. "I would have preferred a more strategic position, but . . ." He shrugged his shoulders.

"We move the Reich," he said, grinning. "This is our motto. 'We move the Reich.' And it is true! The vehicles, civilian and military, surface and air, passenger and commercial—the number of vehicles over which we have jurisdiction boggles the mind. Tens of thousands of kilometers of roadways, airports, train stations, locomotives, aircraft . . . On and on."

He stood up from his chair, a touch unsteadily, and refilled his glass. Freddy had had but a single small sip of his drink. "Come on, Schillinghaussen," Rudel said. "Drink up! We may all be dead soon anyway. Enjoy yourself. Enjoy life while you can."

He sat back down and suddenly seemed to get an inspiration. "Schillinghaussen, you must know many girls from the university," he said. "Surely some would be interested in a good time with a major in the SS!"

"I really don't," Freddy said. "It's not something I'm very good at."

"Schillinghaussen, you don't mean to tell me there aren't girls at the university who are lovers of life? Girls with reputations, perhaps," he said, laughing. "Girls seeking a favor from the government. A man needs a diversion from all of the rest of what we must deal with.

And it will only worsen as time passes. Things are not going particularly well on either front, you know."

He seemed suddenly deflated, casting a disconsolate glance at Freddy. But, quickly, he brightened. He looked around the library. "This is such a beautiful house," he said. "Such a sin to have it wasted on Jews for all these years." He shook his head as a look of distaste crossed his face. He pulled the flask from his pocket and drank deeply from it. "Vodka," he said. "Very good. Here." He thrust it at Freddy, who sat impassively, looking at Rudel's flushed and sweating face, at the rolls of fat on his neck overhanging the starched collar of his uniform.

"Ah, no thank you," he said slowly.

Rudel shrugged and drank again.

You are a disgrace to Germany, Freddy thought. You are a disgusting man. Freddy was repulsed by the thought of Rudel living in Sophie's house. Looking at the man, at his thick neck and blunted features, Freddy was suddenly sickened.

Rudel looked across the room at a burgundy velvet sofa placed not far from the fireplace.

"Ah, you will arrange for firewood, perhaps, Schillinghaussen, for a delivery," Rudel said. "Then I shall have a roaring fire and a lovely girl and I would put her down on that sofa and have her there. I can almost see it now. She arrives and is dazzled by the splendor of the home, and she is eager. But I do not rush things. Rather, I serve some drinks and we chat. And soon she is flushed and warm and ready, but, ahhh!—and this is the trick—wait! Yes, wait, though it nearly kills you. Wait until she seems irked and unhappy. Wait until she needs it; until it is not a matter of pleasure but of need. Then she will do anything; anything that you wish, you will have. To fuck her from behind? Whatever you wish."

He paused, smiling at Freddy. "You have seen women in this condition of need, no?"

Freddy did not respond immediately. He looked at Rudel, working to mask his contempt.

"When you do this you must be careful not to damage the furniture," Freddy said, feeling foolish as soon as the words had escaped his mouth.

Rudel looked at him as though he'd lost his marbles, then he burst out laughing. "Ah, you are an amusing man, Schillinghaussen. For a moment there I thought you were serious."

Freddy forced a laugh.

"Actually, I wonder whether there might be any legal action by the owners when they come back," Freddy said.

"Ah, Schillinghaussen, you naive young man," Rudel said, shaking his head in mock sorrow. "You may be a sharp young lawyer but you know little of the ways of the world, do you?"

"Meaning what?" Freddy said.

"They're not coming back, Schillinghaussen," he said.

Freddy knitted his brow. "I know some won't be back, but . . ."

"None of them will be back," he barked. "Ever! Never. They'll never be back."

Freddy did not understand. "Some of them, certainly, will come back," he said, "if only to pick up possessions, put their affairs in order. But surely some will return to their homes, their businesses. At some point."

Rudel shook his head vigorously. "You are not listening to me, Schillinghaussen," he said, red-faced.

"Listen to what I am telling you. They will not be back, the Jews. None of them. I know this. I have come from a conference at Wannsee, an interminable meeting that was held of representatives of every major department within the government. I was one of those from Transport. A plan has been made. It will soon be put into place. It involves a final solution to the Jewish problem.

"They will never return," he continued, his voice softer. "Ever. They will be gassed, every last one of them."

Freddy heard the words but did not believe them.

"No," he said, shaking his head. "That is impossible."

"It is not only possible, it will happen," Rudel said. "We will get them to their destinations, to the camps, by rail. And then they will be gassed. Zyklon B, it is called. Hundreds at a time. And they won't even know that that is their fate until it is too late. It has already begun."

"Gassed?" Freddy said, the disbelief obvious in his voice.

"Every last one," Rudel said. "Millions and millions of them. Gone. The curse lifted."

Freddy was not in control of himself. He rose from his chair and walked unsteadily out of the room, his vision blurred, suddenly sweating heavily. He found his way to a bathroom and closed the door behind him, locking it. There, he fell to his knees in front of the toilet and began retching.

The plane hit a patch of turbulence and bounced around at 41,000 feet. The seat belt sign was back on.

Keegan thought of Diane. He summoned the image of her face to his mind. He missed her and had been away from her for only two days. He could not imagine what it must have been like for Freddy not to have seen Sophie for years; to have had no contact whatsoever. What must it have been like for Diane's father back then, sitting in his office alone at night trying to summon to his mind how she looked and sounded and smelled. Probably, he had been comforted by the knowledge that she was at Theresienstadt, for he would have known that it was the place where the important Jews were sent and where they were said to be well cared for.

What did he think of during those times? Keegan wondered. Merely being together? Did he think of simply holding her, talking with her, listening to her, as Keegan thought of Diane?

In midafternoon, Keegan's flight landed at Shannon, in the west of Ireland. He rented a car and drove through the lush, stunning greenery of Limerick up to Galway and on through Connemara to the sea. From Clifden, he wound along the coastline on a narrow seaside road up to the tiny seaside village of Cleggan. The sea was high and fierce off of this coast and even in the protected Cleggan harbor the fishing boats at berth rocked and swung in rhythm with the long powerful swells of the North Atlantic.

He had phoned ahead and the clerk of the village was in her office to meet him.

"Oh, yes, the American who wishes certain birth records, is it?"

"I was hoping you might have had a chance to find that record I mentioned to you," he said.

"Yes, actually," she said. "Took a while, but we have records in the basement going back a couple of hundred years."

She went to a desk and opened the bottom drawer.

She flipped through a file and removed a large manila envelope. She walked to the counter and handed it to Keegan.

"Thank you so much," he said. "I appreciate it."

"Happy to help," she said.

Keegan took the envelope outside where he sat down on a bench. He held the envelope in his hand as he looked out into the Cleggan harbor and watched a few boats rock on the water.

Do I want to see this? he asked himself. Do I want to know this? What purpose is served here? he wondered. But he needed to understand. He opened the envelope and removed the document.

Diane's birth certificate. It showed what he already knew: that she had been born in Cleggan on 20 October 1943—nine months and five days after conception at Theresienstadt.

34

Hunter is now tailed by George Barry, an agent of the FBI, a surveillance expert. More importantly, a friend of Keegan's. It is all quite informal and nothing on paper, but, yes, George Barry is willing to spend some of his own time on something that matters a great deal to Keegan. It is, like all surveillance work, tedious. Days pass when there is nothing to report. Then, George senses something is happening. He follows the black Camry through the Back Bay and all the way to the end of Newbury Street, where the Camry enters a concrete parking garage. Very tricky. But George likes this because it is a maneuver designed to detect surveillance. George smiles to himself, thinking that Hunter wouldn't recognize surveillance if it assaulted him.

George follows at a discreet distance as the black Camry climbs the ramp past the fifth level. George peels off here and parks. He moves quickly from his car with a black briefcase and ascends the stairs to the sixth level, the roof. He crosses to a far corner and wedges himself in between a cement wall and an electrical box. He has a clear view of the Camry and soon George Barry is astonished to see none other than assistant United States

Attorney Theodore Dunbar striding across the concrete and getting into the passenger side of the Camry.

George Barry flips the latches on his case and removes a small yet quite powerful device. He shifts his body position so that he is able to train a thin wire, no more than a filament, really, in the direction of the Camry. George puts on earphones, adjusts a dial, and soon he is listening to—and recording—the conversation in the Camry as though he were in the backseat.

And what he hears is Dunbar telling Hunter that the feds are on to another case virtually identical to the Wahljak matter. It has the potential to be a great story. The problem is, it is pure fiction. It is a fiction from the mind of Walter Stone. A fiction confided in Theo Dunbar and no one else in the world.

Keegan arrived as Diane was guiding her mother to a booth at the back of the small Italian restaurant on Charles Street, a couple of blocks down from the hospital.

"I want to thank you with all of my heart for what you have done for us, David," she said. "You have brought some much needed and welcome light to very dark days and we are grateful."

"I'm very glad that it has helped," he said.

"It has helped a great deal, our spirits as much as anything," Sophie said.

A waitress appeared and took drink orders, quickly returning with sherry for Sophie and wine for Diane and David.

"To Dad's health," Diane said, raising her glass in a toast.

"Diane tells me there are some encouraging signs," Keegan said.

"Small signs," Sophie said, "but, yes, definitely encouraging. The physicians all say that any indication of understanding—squeezing a hand or anything such as that—indicates brain function, so there are good signs.

"But, enough about the Schillers," she continued. "Tell me about the Keegans, David. I'm very sorry to hear that your father is not well."

"Well, thank you," Keegan said, looking down at the table, at its red tablecloth. "He, ahh . . ."

"His cancer has metastacized," Diane said softly to her mother. "So that it's only a matter of time now."

Sophie shook her head. "I'm sorry," she said.

There was an awkward pause.

Sophie sipped her sherry.

"I never cease to be amazed at the juxtapositions in life," Sophie said. "I could live to be one hundred and I would still be simply amazed at how cruel and painful life can be, and then, when you turn around and there is a new day, at how very beautiful it can be."

"Diane has told me that your father worked as a policeman," Sophie said. "That must have been very stressful work. Was it?"

Stressful? he thought. Stressful. "Yes, it was," Keegan said. "But my father really loved being a policeman. He, ahh, it was something he enjoyed. That gave him a certain satisfaction."

He paused, reflecting. "He actually did a lot of good as a policeman," Keegan said. "He was known in his area, when he was a patrolman and then as a detective, he was well known as a man who would not tolerate any sort of bullying. He protected the weak. I think there were a lot of people who felt safer—who *were* safer—because of him.

"There was a man I met not long ago, quite old now, but he told me a story going back some years when this man's son, who had a terrible alcohol problem, would come home and assault his father. And the old man tried everything until one day, very embarassed, he called the police, and my father showed up and dealt with the young man. Pretty soon the beatings stopped. And after a while when the man was trying to get the kid into rehab, my father put in a word and the kid made it into a clinic and cleaned up his act.

"So, I think . . ."

"That must make you feel very good about him," Sophie said. "Does it?"

"Oh, absolutely," Keegan said.

"Then you must grasp that so very tightly, David, and cling to that feeling, to that emotion, because relationships between parents and their children—their adult children—can be very complicated and difficult, can't they? Sometimes there is ambivalence; torment, even. So that when you have such feelings as you do, you must hold them within your heart for they are very precious— very precious, David."

She was leaning forward as she said this, her head tilted slightly, her brow knitted, her gaze intense. Her expression was a cross between pleasure and pain. She seemed to be pleading with him in a way.

Diane was slightly embarrassed by her mother's homily, but Keegan thought it touching. And appropriate. There was a prolonged silence at the table with no one quite sure what to say.

Keegan could see that the wine was having an impact on Sophie. She sat back in the booth and, for a moment, shut her eyes. She was clearly very tired.

"Mom, let's get you back, OK?" Diane said, noticing her mother's fatigue.

"I'm all right," she said, perking up and flagging down the waitress to order coffee.

"You've barely touched your food," Diane said.

"They give you so much," Sophie said, "and what I ate was plenty for me. I'm quite full. Really, this is wonderful. I am very happy to be here with you and David. All is well."

Diane smiled and reached over and took her mother's hand, squeezing it. "I'm really glad you feel that way," she said. "But I have to go and return a phone call. I'm sorry but it's a must. Will you both excuse me for five minutes?"

"Of course, dear," Sophie said.

David rose as she left the table and watched her walk away.

"You take great pleasure in being in Diane's company, it is obvious," Sophie said.

Keegan smiled.

"I'm very happy for Diane," Sophie said. "She's had a rocky time of it and I so want her to be happy. And she is clearly very happy with you. You have stood by her at a time when some friends have not done so. You did not have to do what you have done. I know that what you have done has placed you in professional jeopardy and I am sorry about that. But I hope you know inside that what you have done is a brave thing and a noble thing."

Sophie sipped her coffee and rearranged her napkin on her lap. "And I must say one more thing, ask one more question that is a difficult question to ask but I must," she said. "May I speak to you in confidence, David? May I do that?"

"Yes, of course," he said.

She leaned forward slightly, her head cocked, turned slightly sideways to hear what she anticipated to be a whispered reply.

"Were there other records that you found relating to me or my family?" she asked.

Keegan was stunned by the directness of her question. He said nothing, for at that moment Diane returned to the table, and as she did so Keegan noticed that Sophie pulled back, straightened up in the booth, retreating discreetly.

"We were just chatting," Sophie said, a slight defensiveness in her voice, as Diane sat down. And it was clear to Keegan that Sophie Naumann wanted Keegan to share information with her, but not with Diane.

"I had a message from Gerry Wahljak," Diane said.

Sophie seemed stunned.

"He said that he received the material I sent to him and found it very interesting," Diane said. "He thanked me for sending it and said he was willing to sit down and talk."

"So you are going to do that?" Sophie asked.

"I think it can only help," Diane said. "I want him to hear from me about Dad. If he hears about the human being, and not just a face in a photograph, it will make it much harder for him to believe that Dad is some sort of demon."

Diane paused. "You think I should talk with him, don't you?" she asked her mother.

"I do," Sophie said. "I do. I just worry that it is harder

for people these days to understand what happened and what people did back then to stay alive and to keep some semblance of hope." She looked down into her coffee cup. "There were compromises made." She glanced up at Keegan, and then at Diane, with a look that asked for understanding. "For survival."

When Keegan arrived home, all of the lights were out and the windows and doors were shut tight and locked. The house was oppressively hot.

Keegan went around opening windows and leaving open the front and back outer doors so some cool night air might circulate through the screen doors. He removed his shoes and hung up his suit and necktie, tossed his dress shirt into the corner, and put on a T-shirt and a clean pair of boxers. He got a can of Budweiser from the refrigerator, cracked it open, and took a long sip. He heard a car and went to the front of the house and looked out the screen door, thinking it would be Hunter. Instead, it was one of his neighbors. Keegan went outside and got a lawn chair from the back of the house and brought it around front. He sat down in the darkness and sipped his beer. He glanced up and down the sleepy little street at the modest, two-bedroom ranch houses, most of which were identical to his, though two had added garages. He had liked this neighborhood, a street where most of the residents worked for the police or fire departments or the Edison or gas companies. The people were pleasant, good neighbors.

In a moment, a Camry pulled up out front and Hunter got out. He walked slowly across the lawn, wearing wrinkled corduroy pants and a plaid shirt with the sleeves rolled up to his elbows. He walked over to Keegan and looked him up and down.

"No need to dress up for me," he said sarcastically.

"Here," Keegan said, getting out of his seat and indicating that Hunter should sit there. Keegan went around back and got another chair, this one with a large tear in the fabric. He brought it around front and sat down a few feet from Hunter.

Keegan studied Hunter, looked at the rolls of fat beneath his chin, the beads of sweat on his face and neck.

"You look like shit, Hunter," Keegan said.

Hunter nodded. "You, too."

"You want a beer?" Keegan asked.

Hunter's eyes widened. "That would be great," he said.

Keegan went inside and got two cold cans of Bud. He came back outside and handed one to Hunter. They sipped their beers in silence.

"So what's up, guy?" Hunter asked.

Keegan handed Hunter two sheets of paper. "Look at these," he said. "That first sheet is a list of the officers at Theresienstadt. Alphabetical. Notice that Schillinghaussen's name does not appear. I spoke personally with the head of the Theresienstadt archive in Berlin. He affirmed what everyone already knew—that the Germans were meticulous record keepers. Very precise. If he had been an administrator, in any way responsible for that camp, he would have been listed.

"Plus," Keegan continued, "that second sheet is effectively an affidavit, with the head of the archive swearing that to the best of his knowledge Schillinghaussen was not an officer of the camp, not an administrator in any way.

"What he was, you already know and have reported,"

Keegan continued. "He ran a program that seized the property of Jews. You know that, have written it."

Hunter nodded. "Yeah, so?"

"So the story's over," Keegan said. "There's no place to take it. It has no more legs. You know what there is to know about these people. A sad chapter draws to a close. That's it, Hunter. We're talking old people with not much longer to live. The decent thing is to leave them in peace. Let them be. Move on to something else. Find another story."

Hunter frowned. The idea of getting off a story such as this was unthinkable. But he had to admit he had been deeply disappointed learning that Freddy Schiller had not been an administrator at the camp. That would have taken the story to a new level.

"What's there to prosecute?" Keegan asked.

Hunter shrugged. "He's in the photograph," he said, as though the case was obvious. "He was at the camp. He was a lawyer with the Nazi government. He administered the property confiscation program."

"All true," Keegan said. "And none prosecutable under U.S. law. I mean, the property confiscation thing is the closest call and it's not a close call. He managed the program in a certain area, a portion of Berlin. There were scores of other similar programs all across the country. We should prosecute all of these people we can find? We should prosecute anyone who held any sort of administrative role in the government?"

"He was a Nazi," Hunter said.

Keegan nodded. "He was a member of the Nazi Party," he said. "No question about it. His father was a party member and he joined. Like tens of millions of other young Germans at the time who were ambitious and wanted to get ahead, he joined the party. Having been a member of the Nazi Party, however repulsive it is to us today, is not a crime in America.

"Let's be honest," Keegan said, finishing his beer, "this got blown up because you people wanted to blow it up. It was a great story, but after the story runs, and the second-day story and the reaction story and the mop-up story, what's left behind? Fragile old people who have been hurt in the process. Lives already immensely complex made more difficult. Anyone soothed or aided or enhanced by what you've done? No."

Hunter regarded him suspiciously. "It was an important story," he said. "People had a right to know about it."

They sat in silence for a moment, then Keegan went inside and got two more cans of beer.

"So he won't be prosecuted because there are no grounds," Hunter said, snapping his can open. "But there's still the issue of what his moral responsibility was, given the circumstances."

Keegan looked at him, and Hunter appeared serious. "The real question, more than whether there are grounds for deportation, is whether he did what he should have done under moral law. Could he have used his power to save any Jews? Even one Jew. One?" Hunter asked.

Hunter sought to stir some sense of moral indignation within himself, but his words came across hollow, his self-interest all too obvious.

"Plus, don't forget that Mrs. Wahljak may insist on some sort of action," Hunter said. "She has certain rights here. Let's not forget who the victim is here, Keegan."

Keegan considered this.

"And if she doesn't?" Keegan asked.

"Doesn't what?" Hunter asked.

"If Mrs. Wahljak does not press for any action," Keegan said. "If she pulls back, if she is unwilling to serve as a witness, unwilling to cooperate with the feds. What then, Hunter?"

"Well, then . . ."

"Then there would be nothing more," Keegan said. "The records prove Schillinghaussen was not an official at the camp, was in no way active at the camp. He was a bureaucrat. And now, if she were to pull back, then there'd be nothing left."

"That won't happen," Hunter said reflexively.

Keegan watched him carefully.

"What if it does, Dan?" Keegan asked in a quiet voice. "You talk about judging him on moral grounds. Isn't that Mrs. Wahljak's call? More than yours or anyone else's?"

Hunter was silent.

"If the Wahljaks leave it alone, would you be willing to do the same?" Keegan asked.

Hunter looked off down the street as though studying the lines of one of the houses across the way.

"I don't think she will," Hunter said. "She's out there already. Why quit now?"

"Maybe she wants peace."

Hunter considered this. "If she pulls back then . . . yeah," Hunter said. "Yeah, if the Wahljaks get off it, I'll get off it."

35

Freddy felt a hand on his head. He felt a slow, rhythmic motion of someone's hand smoothing his hair back. It was a gentle, careful touch. He felt it, his eyes closed, and he knew that it was Sophie. He opened his eyes, and even the dim light in the room seemed harsh and stung them. He was not sure, at first, where he was. When he opened his eyes all the way, he saw her smiling down on him.

"I knew you would be OK," she said softly. "I knew it all along."

He tried to talk but nothing came out. He forced some words out in a hoarse whisper. "Where am I?" he asked.

"Mass General," she said. "How do you feel?"

He glanced around the room. "Tired," he said.

She smiled and placed her hand on the side of his face. "You look wonderful," she said. For it was wonderful to see him conscious; to hear his voice.

"How long have I been here?" he asked.

"Thirteen days," she said.

"Unconscious?"

She nodded yes.

"You had a stroke, Freddy," she said.

"A stroke?" he said.

"But you're going to be OK," she said.

287

*   *   *

"My dad wants me to take him to Mass and I'm thinking of doing that tomorrow morning," Keegan said.

"Is he up to that?" Diane asked.

"Good question," Keegan said, as they walked along the banks of the Charles River watching the sun move lower in the western sky. "I told him I'd take him to the hospital chapel, which is just an elevator ride away, but he insists on going to this little church over in Roslindale, this little old stone place that he has these memories of. He knows the priest there. Some crazy old priest who was saying the Latin Mass for years after the switch to English."

"Is that wise?" Diane asked.

"Well . . ." Keegan had considered the wisdom of it, of course. Taking him out of the hospital, driving him across the city, going to a Mass and then coming back might demand more strength than he could muster. But Keegan had been struck by the intensity of his father's interest in doing this. When Keegan had suggested that they get an ambulance of some sort to take him there, the father had been vehement.

"I want to go with you, Davey," he had said. "Just me and you. Please, Davey." He had implored him.

Keegan spotted an empty bench, and they sat down and looked out over the Charles toward MIT.

"It's very important to him," said David. "He . . ."

Keegan shifted his position on the bench, draping his arm over the back and half turning in her direction.

"No, no, go on," Diane said. "What were you going to say?"

"Oh, just that, you know, his life has been . . . It's been hard."

Diane frowned momentarily and looked away.

"What?" he said.

"No," she said. "Nothing."

"Something," he said. "Come on . . ."

"You talk as though he was at the mercy of forces outside his control."

David considered this. "His real enemy has always been himself," he said. "His rage. I know that. But sometimes . . ." He looked off into the distance and shook his head. "I don't know. Sometimes I think that I should be humbled by how much adversity he's faced. Other times I'm really angry about the fact that he created most of that adversity. And that in the process he . . ."

David hesitated. He turned and looked at Diane, growing suddenly red-faced.

"Screwed up other people's lives," he said, his jaw tightening, his face flushed. "Fucked up other people's lives."

His eyes narrowed, and she saw the muscles in his face and neck tighten.

"Because that's what he did. That's just the truth. He fucked up my mother's life."

Diane looked into his eyes and spoke softly. "And yours, too," she said. "He screwed up your life, too, didn't he?"

David looked away.

"Didn't he, David?" she said, her voice still soft, but her tone insistent.

David bowed his head and covered his face with his hands. He was suddenly unable to speak. He merely nodded. She moved closer to him and put her arm around him, laying her head on his shoulder. She hugged him tightly and decided she would say no more. And they sat there, looking out across the river, watching as darkness began to fall, and as the boats all put into the dock and as the joggers and roller bladers and walkers disappeared; they sat looking out as darkness fell on the city.

David Keegan pulled over to the side of the street opposite the Cabot Estate condominiums on the Brookline side of Jamaica Pond. He got out and walked down the embankment to the paved walkway that circled about a mile and a half around the circumference of the pond. On this mild summer morning there were dozens of people in view. A number of mothers and baby-sitters walked around pushing baby carriages. Walkers moved briskly, arms pumping, some of them moving nearly as fast as the slower joggers who plodded along, heaving and gasping for breath. People walked their dogs, and some children and old people stood on the banks watching fishermen cast their lines. Wood ducks and Canada geese lazily paddled near the shore. And three magnificent swans trolled the waters about twenty feet offshore.

Keegan hung back watching the man he was sure was Jazz Mannering. Jazz wore khaki pants, a blue-and-yellow striped polo shirt, and a Red Sox cap—the wool, fitted type. Under his left arm was tucked the *Record American*, and in his left hand Jazz held a large bag of peanuts. He would shell the nuts, let the shells flutter to the ground near the edge of the water, then toss the nuts down the embankment for the geese, ducks, and pigeons. Though he was in his late seventies, Jazz looked quite fit. He was of medium build with a narrow face, a thick nose, and wide, brown eyes.

Keegan walked over and stood nearby, his hands in his pockets, watching Jazz toss the peanuts. A pigeon stood near Jazz and waited for the shells to drop, gobbling them up while letting the others fight over the peanuts.

"He eats the shells," Keegan said.

Jazz nodded. "He doesn't want to be in the scrum," Jazz said. "Some are like that."

Keegan watched him a while longer, until Jazz had no more peanuts. Jazz balled up the brown paper bag and tossed it into a trash can.

"You're Jazz Mannering, right?" Keegan said. "You were a cop."

Jazz regarded Keegan closely, studying him, but unable to identify him. "Do I know you?" Jazz asked.

"I'm Dick Keegan's son," he said. "I'm David."

Jazz Mannering shifted his feet and stood staring squarely at Keegan. He looked him over carefully, then nodded his head.

"Jesus, you remind me of your mother, though," he said. "Anybody tell you that? The old timers?"

"Sometimes," Keegan said.

"Same expression," Jazz said.

"I'd like to sit down and talk if you wouldn't mind," Keegan said.

Jazz looked at him and nodded slightly, then dropped his head and was silent. "Let's go across," he said. "Up over by the monument over there. We can talk there."

They crossed Francis Parkman Drive and walked across a broad expanse of lawn leading up toward the Hellenic College campus. There was a granite war memorial there, with a bench nearby shaded by the trees.

Jazz motioned to the monument, a large piece of granite with names engraved upon the face of the stone.

"Nobody pays any attention to these," Jazz said. "Nobody ever comes by here. Sits here. Well, some people bring their dogs. Shit on the grass, piss on the base of the granite. But nobody looks at the names. I come here and when people walk by I watch 'em to see if they stop to read the names, but nobody ever does. Nobody ever has. Not once that I've seen. They're just names in the stone that don't mean nuthin'. The past doesn't mean anything to anybody."

Jazz Mannering sat forward on the bench, rocking in a jerky, nervous way. He placed his hands on his knees and sat straight up.

"So you wanted to . . ."

"I wanted to come and just talk with you," Keegan said. "Just to find out some things."

"We're all gettin' old, is the thing," Jazz said. "No tellin' how much longer . . ."

He continued the jerky motion, his shoulders hunched, tensed. "I hear your dad's not doin' too good . . ."

"Not so hot," Keegan said.

Jazz shook his head. "All this cancer everywhere," Jazz whispered. "Christ Almighty . . ."

Jazz took a deep breath and exhaled loudly. "So it won't be too much longer, will it?" he asked.

"Pretty soon," Keegan said.

"Well, look," Jazz Mannering said, "what can I tell you?"

Keegan nodded slowly, calmly. Go easy, he told himself. Go slow. Always take it slow in these matters. Plodding is the way to do it, to investigate, to probe, to dig. There's no flash. Just slow, deliberate movement. Understand fact one, then move to fact two, and so on down the line. Jazz will volunteer nothing. But he will, Keegan felt, answer questions truthfully. He will not answer what he is not asked. Think clearly and ask the right questions. There will not be another chance.

"Leo Flaherty said you were the first on the scene of my parents' accident," Keegan said. "He says he remembers that because you wrote the report. You had responsibility for that."

"I coulda' sworn Leo's name was on that report," Jazz said.

"I'm not interested in whose name was on it," Keegan replied coolly. "I'm interested in who wrote it."

Jazz eyed him.

"You'd have to talk to Leo . . ."

"I already talked to Leo," Keegan said. "He says you were first on the scene. First arrival is responsible for the report."

Jazz shook his head. "Gee, I don't know," he said vaguely. "Leo's name is on the report."

Jazz paused. "When I pulled up to Ansonia, Leo was already there," Jazz said. David could tell he was lying. But even as he processed the lie he was struck by Jazz's mention of Ansonia.

"Belgrade and Ansonia," David said.

"Right," Jazz said.

"Leo thought it was Belgrade and Newberg," Keegan said.

He paused.

"Leo was pretty sure of it," Keegan said.

Jazz dismissed this. "Ansonia," Jazz said. He was sure of it. Then, suddenly, a thought struck Jazz. His eyes widened and he was still for a moment. He flashed an embarrassed grin, as though he had just revealed something inadvertently.

"What's the matter with me?" Jazz said, forcing a laugh. " 'Course it was Newberg. Right near the corner. It was Newberg."

Keegan was turned sideways, looking directly at Jazz. When Keegan looked Jazz in the eye, the old man turned away.

"So she was driving down Belgrade toward the Square . . ."

"Toward the Square," Jazz said, nodding. "And they swerved to the left into the other lane and right into the path of a car, a Grand Prix, and sideswiped him and he was OK, but they were pulling back to the right and it just went out of control . . ."

Jazz looked at Keegan, a pleading kind of look as though he was asking whether they could simply stop this conversation right there. "Just out of control," Jazz said.

"And hit the telephone pole," Keegan said, softly.

Jazz nodded, but said nothing.

"And she . . ."

"She was hurt very bad," Jazz said. "She was really hurt."

"She was thrown from the car," Keegan said.

"And I'm wavin' for the ambulance because when they came down Belgrade they thought at first the accident was the other guy, a couple blocks up, but . . . it wasn't . . ."

Keegan took this all in.

"And so you're standing there in the street and she's on the ground, and you're waving to get the attention of the ambulance, and . . ."

Jazz Mannering took a deep breath. "And the ambulance arrived . . ."

"Which one?" Keegan asked.

"Well, they both arrived about the same time, maybe a minute apart," Jazz said. "And the EMTs went to work, one on her and the other on him . . ."

"And he's where?"

"What?"

"My dad," Keegan said. "He was where at the time?"

Jazz hesitated. "On the ground. Sidewalk." Jazz was a bad liar.

Keegan nodded.

"And the EMTs worked on them both and got them off to the Faulkner as quick as possible," Jazz said.

"And my mother went in which ambulance?" Keegan asked.

Jazz squinted. "I don't recall at the moment," he said.

"But you're sure they both went in ambulances," Keegan said. "To Faulkner."

Jazz Mannering regarded David Keegan. "Yeah," he said weakly. "I'm sure."

Keegan nodded his head slowly.

They sat in silence for a while.

"It was hot that summer," Keegan said.

"Tell me about it," Jazz Mannering said. "Hottest summer on record. Six weeks over ninety every day. Six weeks."

"Was the cruiser air-conditioned?" David Keegan asked.

Jazz regarded him as though he was crazy. "Back then? Air-conditioned! 'Course not. 'Course not. No."

Keegan reached down and picked up the manila envelope he had laid on the bench next to him. He undid the metal clasp and withdrew a photograph. He glanced at it and handed it to Jazz Mannering.

"Your cruiser?" Keegan asked.

Jazz studied the picture closely. "Jesus," he said softly. "Where'd you get this?"

"Is it yours?" Keegan asked.

"That was mine, yeah," Jazz said.

"How come the windows are all rolled up?" Keegan asked. "How come when it's ninety degrees out, you have no air-conditioning and the windows are rolled up all the way. Why is that?"

Jazz Mannering shut his eyes tightly for a long moment. He said nothing.

David Keegan swiveled around on the bench so that he was facing Jazz Mannering. Keegan leaned forward and spoke in an urgent whisper to the retired cop. "I need to know," Keegan said. "I need to know the truth."

Mannering turned away.

"I made a promise," he said. "A long time ago. I promised him."

"Well it's time to break that promise," Keegan said. "You have to help me."

Jazz Mannering rubbed his face with his hands. "Don't do this . . ."

"How bad was it?" Keegan asked. "How drunk was he?"

"Oh, Jesus, Davey, he was bad," Jazz Mannering said. "He was real bad."

Keegan winced. He looked out over the pond, watching as two geese glided in and landed, softly, on the calm water.

Jazz Mannering turned his head and looked David Keegan directly in the eye. The two men stared for several seconds. Keegan did not blink.

"He was cut up, but not hurt real bad," Jazz said. "I put him in the back of the cruiser, laid him down and rolled up all the windows, locked the doors. I wasn't sure who'd show up. Not everybody would cover for him like me. I was tryin' to protect him.

"I knew I couldn't let him go to Faulkner. They'd of reported him. So when the ambulance left with your mother I took him over to Dr. Ford's on South Street. I knew Ford well, we kept an eye on his place, his office was downstairs from his house. He'd gotten ripped off once or twice and so we kept a close eye out and he appreciated that. He'd done some favors.

"But when I took your father over there, Ford didn't like it at all," Jazz continued. "I begged him to just look at him and forget about it. No records, no talk, nuthin'. I told him Dick was on suspension. Number two. That any blemish would mean the end, kicked off the force."

Jazz took his Red Sox hat off and ran his hand over his head. "Ford didn't like it, but he went along," Jazz said.

"Suspension?" Keegan asked.

Jazz nodded. "He'd been suspended once before for something, I forget what," Jazz said. "And then, like two years later, there was a fight in a bar . . . You don't want to know. Anyway, he was on duty and so they suspended him again and the message was clean up your act or you're gone. Another incident would mean the end."

Jazz looked at Keegan. "You know what that would of meant to him," Jazz said. "It would have been a death sentence. Pure and simple."

"So you covered for him," Keegan said.

Suddenly Jazz became highly agitated. "What was I supposed to do?" Jazz asked. "Here was a guy, he'd been my partner breaking in, and, Jesus, he'd covered my ass on more than one occasion, and he was there, laying there in the backseat, balled up, like he was a baby, like he was a fetus all curled up, covering up, and he was cryin' and cryin' and cryin' and just moanin' over and over again, just sayin', 'No, no, no, please, God, please, God.' And he says to me, 'Jimmy,' he says, 'Jimmy, please, Jimmy, you gotta help me . . .' And I did. But, afterward—" Jazz shook his head, hanging it now, sorrowful, and suddenly he began to cry.

"I'm sorry," he said. "I'm so sorry. I shoulda told the truth, but it was his life and he begged me and he was my friend. And he said to me, 'Jimmy, don't ever tell no one.' Afterward, he says to me, 'No one. Ever. Right?'

"And I says, 'Right,' and I never did tell a soul, ever."

Jazz sat shaking his head.

Keegan watched him and he felt for him, but Keegan needed the truth, he needed to know.

"What happened at Belgrade and Ansonia?" Keegan asked in a quiet voice.

Jazz cried harder, but he brought himself under control. "Jesus, Davey, he was so freakin' drunk, it was a terrible thing," Jazz said. "And she was drivin' and I guess he distracted her and she hit this kid in a Ford comin' out of Ansonia, and somebody called and I got dispatched and there was a hell of an argument with your old man and this kid, a teenager, 'cause he was dented, but it was a nothing of a dent and I give the kid twenty bucks and told him to get lost, and so he did, and I'm done with the kid and I turn around and she starts walkin' away, says she's gonna walk home. He's too drunk, she says, says she's sick of it, says he can stay at my place that night, and he goes up behind her and he grabs her and he drags her back into the car, and I say, 'Hey, whoa, Dick, you can't . . .' And he tells me go fuck myself, and he kind of shoves her into the car and closes the door and she sits there, angry and afraid, and then he goes around to the driver's side . . ."

"*He* goes to the driver's side?" Keegan said.

And Jazz nodded. "Yeah, he goes around and he gets in behind the wheel, and I come around the car and says to him, 'Dick, no way can I let you drive like this,' and he says nuthin', but then all of a sudden he takes off, floors it, and he's flyin' up the street and into the other lane and the Grand Prix swerves and he sideswipes him and swerves back and goes outta control and he hits the pole and there was a terrible noise and . . ."

David Keegan sat frozen, still, absorbing this information, knowing the truth now, finally, after all of these years. Knowing, at long last, what he had always suspected: his father had killed her.

36

"One day in April of 1943, I was instructed to go to a certain place within the camp," Sophie said. "The officer's club. I was told I would be interviewed by someone from Berlin concerning some financial matter. That was all I was told. So I went at the time I was instructed to go and I went into this large room, walking past an SS guard to do so."

Sophie stood at the window of the consult room looking out at the Charles River basin as she spoke. She paused and went over and sat in the chair opposite her daughter.

"When I entered the room I saw that all the way across, in the far corner, near a large bookcase, was a small round table. There was a man at the table, though I was unable to see his face. He was bent over the side, reaching down onto the floor, into a briefcase, something like that. He heard me come in and called for me to cross the room. His voice was muffled. I walked across to the table and stood there. There was a large glass pitcher of water and two glasses placed on the table.

" 'I'm Sophie Naumann,' I said, and as I said that, he turned and rose from the table and it was Freddy. I was shocked beyond measure, stunned, and I suddenly began to faint and, could not help it, I screamed and, as I did so—he anticipated this—he elbowed the pitcher of water onto the floor and it smashed into a thousand pieces. The noises brought the SS guard running into the room.

" 'A broken pitcher frightened her,' Freddy said very quickly. But the SS man did not move. He stood watching us, watching as I buried my face in my hands and began to weep uncontrollably.

" 'Why is she . . . ?'

" 'She will be fine,' Freddy said. 'She does not like the topic she is now forced to discuss.' Freddy nodded reassuringly to the SS man, who backed out of the room. But I could see that he listened and did not hear the guard descend the steps and knew that he was outside the door, eavesdropping.

"Freddy sat down at the table and quickly began writing on a sheet of paper. It said, 'Play along as best you can.'

" 'You are Miss Naumann,' he said, his words businesslike, clearly intended for the ears of the SS man.

" 'I am,' I said, as best I could.

" 'I am Friedrich Schillinghaussen,' he said, 'from the Reich Ministry of Justice, and I am here to investigate a suspected instance of hidden assets, assets that your family is suspected of concealing from the Reich. If this has been done, I advise you that you have an obligation under the law to declare this and to make restitution to the state. Otherwise, you are subject to prosecution. Do you understand what I am saying?'

" 'I do,' I said.

" 'All right, Miss Naumann,' he said, 'I want to ask you some questions concerning certain properties and businesses in the city of Berlin. Let us begin with

Naumann's Markets. This company is owned by your family, correct?'

" 'It was owned by my father,' I said. 'But no longer.'

" 'And there were four markets,' he said.

" 'Actually three,' I said.

" 'South Berlin, Unter den Linden, and . . .'

" 'Grunewald,' I said. 'There was one in the Grunewald.'

" 'And this particular property was at what address?' And as he posed this question, I could see Freddy listening and then we could hear the SS man descend the stairs.

"Freddy placed his finger in front of his lips, indicating quiet to me, and he crossed the room to the door. He opened the door and checked the stairway. The SS man had gone. Freddy crossed to the other side of the room where there was another door. He checked in that stairwell, but it, too, was empty.

"He came back across the room and looked at me and smiled, and he took me in his arms and held me and I was weak, I collapsed and cried and I was never so hurt or vulnerable; never so happy; for here I was after all of this time at my darkest hour and here, suddenly, from nowhere, was Freddy . . ."

Diane sat, utterly riveted by the story, by her mother's recollections. Sophie was forced to pause, overcome, momentarily, by the emotion evoked by the memory.

"He said to me, 'Dear God, Sophie, how I have missed you.' He held me, pulling me close so fiercely I thought he would hurt me. He said to me, 'I have thought of you every day, every single day, and I knew that this moment would come.' "

"And you . . ." Diane asked.

"I told him I loved him," Sophie said. "And I cried. I could not say much."

Sophie shut her eyes and took a deep breath. "I was in a state of . . . I don't know," she said. "My mother had just died two days before. She gave up. She couldn't fight any longer. She died peacefully enough . . . I've told you this part."

Diane nodded for, indeed, Sophie had told Diane on several occasions about the death of her mother.

"So, emotionally, it was almost too much to handle," Sophie said. "My mother, then, without even the slightest bit of warning, there is Freddy . . .

"He told me he had heard about the death of my mother and was very sorry. But he said that what was most important at that moment was that we gather ourselves together, summon our strength and concentrate on what lay ahead.

"He told me basically that it was very important that I follow through on the charade he was going through. He said he would ask a series of questions and that we would have a discussion about property and assets, and he told me that if they were to ask me later about it that I was to simply tell them what it was we talked about. And he told me to admit that my family had hidden assets and that we were willing to turn them in.

"He said, 'I know you have no such assets, but that does not matter.' And then he said something I have never forgotten, something I will never forget. He spoke in a whisper, yet with the greatest strength. He said to me, 'Trust me, Sophie. I have a plan.' "

Sophie did not tell Diane, would never tell Diane, the full truth. She remembered well the second time she went for an interview with Freddy. She recalled that they were alone in the lounge, at the table near the wall. It was there, in that place, that she told him her secret, there, in that place, that she saw the look on his face, the look as though he had been shot through the heart. He shook his head in disbelief over and over and over again until, finally, he slumped forward in his chair, unable to speak. She embraced him and held him and she believed, after she told him, that she would now lose him forever; that in trying to save what they had, she had killed it.

After his crying eased she whispered to him that she loved him, that she had always loved him and would always love him, no matter what.

"I did it because I believed I had to do it, for all of us," she had said. "So that Mama could live. So that I could live. So that you and I could be together, Freddy. I did it because I love you, Freddy."

37

The fax from Stegr arrived first thing in the morning. Keegan sat back with the stack of pages in his hands and began reading.

FINDINGS AND CONCLUSIONS:
INVESTIGATOR'S REPORT
RE: CASE 4921776
REPORT TRANSMITTED 22 JUNE 1943
In all, twenty-seven persons, most of them in residence at Theresienstadt and in the town of Terezin, were interviewed at length to determine the events of 11 April. Among those interviewed were: SS Corporal Alec Schvelen, telegraph operator Ernst Boberach, Dr. Hermann Strasser, the coroner for Terezin, Luftwaffe mechanic Otto Dietl, and others.

In determining the events of 11 April the investigator reviewed a variety of documents, chief among them the coroner's report from the town of Terezin.

On the morning of 11 April, Josef Van Strahlich worked on the Junkers 52 in a hangar at the Terezin airfield. As he worked, Van Strahlich engaged a mechanic at the facility in conversation. The mechanic, Otto Dietl, said he had been assigned to do major repair work on another Junkers and had yet to do scheduled routine maintenance on two other Luftwaffe planes used to defend Terezin from possible attack.

It was at this point in the conversation, according to Dietl, that Van Strahlich offered to conduct the routine maintenance on the two attack planes. Van Strahlich said he was not scheduled to fly out until later and had time on his hands. Dietl was very grateful to have the help, he said, and pleased that this would insure that the routine maintenance would be done on schedule. Dietl accepted Van Strahlich's offer.

Van Strahlich then went to work on the two planes. Later examination by Dietl and other Luftwaffe personnel, including two Luftwaffe pilots, revealed that both planes had been intentionally disabled by removal of spark plugs and intake valves.

In the late morning, Commandant Heidler's staff car was brought to the front of the administrative building. Sophie Naumann entered the backseat of the car. Friedrich Schillinghaussen took the front passenger seat in the car.

The chauffeur, SS Corporal Alec Schvelen, drove the passengers out of the Theresienstadt camp to a field where many who had died within the camp had been buried in mass, unmarked graves. It was here that the older Naumann woman, Elsa Naumann, had been buried. Records indicate that she had died in her sleep. After a brief stop at the burial ground Corporal Schvelen drove into the town center of Terezin, a distance of less than two miles. After a short drive into Terezin, the car came to a stop in front of the telegraph office. During the brief trip no words were exchanged in the car.

At the telegraph office, Schillinghaussen told the driver that he need not accompany them; that he could wait in the car. At that point, Schillinghaussen handed Schvelen a fresh pack of cigarettes. Schvelen said he remained in the vehicle.

According to Terezin telegraph operator Ernst Boberach, Schillinghaussen had visited the office two days before to discuss with Boberach what he intended to accomplish. Schillinghaussen said he would bring with him a series of account numbers at various Berlin banks and that he would need the telegraph operator's assistance in determining via wire whether the accounts remained active; that is to say, whether the accounts held assets.

Ernst Boberach, to the best of his ability, reconstructed the events that transpired in the telegraph office on the morning of 11 April.

Herr Boberach said that Schillinghaussen arrived and repeated for Boberach the type of financial information he sought. He handed Boberach a sheet of paper that listed various account numbers.

Subsequent investigation revealed that all of the account numbers listed on the sheet of paper Schillinghaussen gave to Boberach were, in fact, Reich Ministry of Justice accounts under Schillinghaussen's control. These were accounts from which Schillinghaussen had embezzled funds. They were accounts he knew contained funds, albeit modest amounts. Boberach's assignment was merely to determine whether an account was "active"; that is to say, whether it contained any funds whatsoever. An account, for example, containing a single mark would be revealed via wire as an active account though it would be impossible to determine, without further codes, the actual amount contained therein.

Herr Boberach sat down at his keypad and began tapping out various codes, first to establish contact with a particular bank. Then, once contact was established, he tapped in the account numbers. He would then move on to the next bank and so on, through five different institutions, seven different accounts.

After some time passed, confirmation came from two of the institutions that two accounts were, indeed, active. Herr Boberach, intending to convey this information to Schillinghaussen, walked from the back room of the telegraph station, where his keypad was located, along a narrow hallway leading to the larger front room. As he walked down the hallway he witnessed the following scene:

He saw Schillinghaussen and the Naumann woman embrace. At that moment the front door to the telegraph station opened and Commandant Heidler entered the room. Commandant Heidler appeared startled, though he maintained his composure. He stood quite still and clasped his hands behind his back. Schillinghaussen and the Naumann woman quickly separated. Schillinghaussen seemed quite embarrassed.

Heidler said nothing. He merely stood still, standing erect, his hands clasped behind his back. He glanced down at his feet and then looked up, first at Schillinghaussen and then at the woman. His face grew reddish. He frowned.

"An indiscretion," Herr Schillinghaussen said.

Heidler stood, stock-still, looking from one to the

other. Silently, he walked across the room and sat down in one of the chairs. He crossed his legs and propped his right elbow on the arm of the chair. He rested his chin atop his hand and gazed at the Naumann woman.

"So this began how long ago?" Heidler asked, his voice hushed.

There was no reply.

"How long?" Commandant Heidler prodded.

"I don't know what you are talking about," Schillinghaussen replied.

Heidler cocked his head to the side and regarded Schillinghaussen. "When did this begin?" he asked, his voice steady.

Schillinghaussen hesitated. "I am here to recover hidden assets for the Reich," he said. "The Naumann family is on my list of those suspected of having secreted assets away in violation of the law. That is why I have come. That is my mission."

Heidler nodded slowly. "I think that you are not telling me the truth," he said. "But I understand that. I think that you are perhaps quite clever. That there is something happening here that is rather brilliant in its way."

Schillinghaussen said nothing.

"Let me speculate that you intend to go from here to the airfield," Heidler said. "With Miss Naumann. Is that . . . ?"

Schillinghaussen waited a moment, then replied. "If there is confirmation that the accounts I have queried are open and contain any assets, then it is my responsibility to return Miss Naumann to Berlin where she will face a series of interrogations at the Reich Ministry of Justice."

Heidler took this in, nodding slightly.

"So these queries have gone out to a bank or a number of banks?" Heidler asked.

"Several banks," Freddy said.

"And if word comes back that the accounts contain assets, then you will have your confirmation that the Naumanns have illegally hidden assets. Correct?"

"Yes," Schillinghaussen said.

"And then?" Heidler asked.

"And then, with your permission, Miss Naumann will be taken to Berlin for a series of interviews, and a determination will be made concerning the property."

Herr Boberach said that it was at this point that he stepped forward. "I have . . ." he began, holding up a sheet of paper. "There is confirmation."

Herr Boberach said he handed the paper to Schillinghaussen, who quickly reviewed the document.

"Two accounts are active," he said.

Sophie flashed a look of indignance. "But that is ridiculous," she said. "My family has complied with all laws of . . ."

"And so now you seek my permission to transport Miss Naumann to Berlin, is that correct, Schillinghaussen?" Heidler asked crisply.

"Yes," Schillinghaussen said. "I do."

Heidler nodded. "Then you have it," he said emphatically. "I shall take you to the airfield myself."

Heidler walked out the front door. He was followed by Schillinghaussen and Miss Naumann.

Herr Boberach moved to the open doorway of the

telegraph station and watched the group depart. He saw Heidler hold open the rear door of the staff car. Miss Naumann stepped inside and sat down.

"Please," Heidler said. "Friedrich, you may join the lady in the back." Schillinghaussen got into the back of the car, as well. Heidler climbed into the front, and the car moved swiftly down the dirt road leading out of Terezin and looping down past the farm area and back around to the airfield beyond.

Luftwaffe mechanic Otto Dietl noticed Commandant Heidler's staff car pull up. He saw Schillinghaussen, the woman, and Heidler get out of the car and then he saw the car drive away. Dietl said during an interview with the investigator that they stood awkwardly on the tarmac just outside the hangar for a moment.

"You may go, Corporal," Heidler told Schvelen, according to Dietl's recollection. "Go back to the camp."

At this time, looking out a hangar window, Dietl saw Van Strahlich revving the engines of his Junkers though he did not taxi forward toward the hangar. It was Dietl's opinion that Van Strahlich was awaiting a signal from Schillinghaussen.

Then, through the open window, Dietl heard Heidler speak to Schillinghaussen.

"I would like a word with you inside," the commandant said.

Heidler walked into the hangar through a doorway and Schillinghaussen followed. Dietl was in the mechanic's loft, no more than thirty feet from the two men, raised on an enclosed platform above their heads. Neither man noticed him, and Dietl, for fear of incurring either man's wrath, remained still and silent.

Dietl recalls that the two men stood facing one another. Heidler squinted, a pained expression on his face,
as he regarded Schillinghaussen.

Dietl recalled the conversation to the best of his
ability:

"You may go," Commandant Heidler said. "You
may flee. I will not act to stop you. I do not know your
destination, but wherever it is, you may go. I will say
nothing, cause no pursuit, nothing."

He hesitated. "But she must stay."

Schillinghaussen did not respond.

"Has she told you of . . ." Heidler asked. "Has
she . . ."

Schillinghaussen nodded. He shut his eyes tightly
for a long moment.

Heidler nodded, a grim expression on his face. "She
must stay," the commandant said.

Schillinghaussen then spoke softly, in a deliberate
fashion. "She is coming with me," he said. "We are
leaving now." Schillinghaussen leveled his gaze, an intense, determined gaze, directly at Heidler.

Schillinghaussen then picked up his briefcase and
started toward the hangar door.

"Stop!" Heidler ordered. "You may not . . ."

"Do not try to stop us," Schillinghaussen said. "Do
not." His voice remained quiet. "There is decency somewhere within you," Schillinghaussen said. "I know it.
Do not try to stop us."

Schillinghaussen then proceeded toward the door,
but, as he did so, Commandant Heidler suddenly
withdrew his sidearm. Schillinghaussen stopped,
frozen.

Then, suddenly, without warning, Schillinghaussen

lunged forward toward the commandant. Instantly there was a deafening report from the commandant's weapon, an explosion that echoed sharply throughout the hangar.

Schillinghaussen grasped his leg just below the knee, grimacing in pain. He went down hard on the concrete hangar floor.

The sound of the gun brought Sophie Naumann into the hangar, and as she entered the commandant turned to her and started to say something.

"You will remain here," he said.

But then Dietl saw that Schillinghaussen, sprawled on the floor, was reaching into his briefcase and withdrawing a Walther. At that moment, Dietl shouted a warning to the commandant, who spun around, but as he did so, Schillinghaussen steadied his weapon and fired, and there was a thunderous report that echoed painfully throughout the hangar. And Dietl saw the commandant knocked back by the force of the round. He grasped at his chest and fell into a heap on the ground.

Dr. Hermann Strasser, the coroner for Terezin, stated that Commandant Heidler died instantly from massive trauma.

The Naumann woman aided Schillinghaussen in getting to his feet. He was in obvious pain and bleeding heavily. Dietl watched from the window as Van Strahlich taxied the Junkers to the hanger. The two passengers embarked quickly and the Junkers was soon racing down the runway.

Dietl sounded an alarm, but the pilots on duty were

unable to start their planes due to the disabling done by Van Strahlich earlier in the day.

The aircraft headed in a southerly direction and is believed to have flown across Austria possibly to the Swiss border, though that cannot be determined with certainty. There has been, as of this date, no reported sighting of Schillinghaussen, the Naumann woman, Van Strahlich, or the aircraft.

Those, in sum, are the investigator's findings concerning the events of 11 April.

38

Sophie stood alone in the consult room, soothed by the view she had of the river and its calm, protected waters. She was comforted by the scene, by the majesty of the massive, powerful MIT buildings; by the elegance of the Beacon Hill architecture; by the prettiness of the river and its esplanade.

Sophie thought back across the years and remembered Cleggan, a day when the wind gusted in off the Atlantic and she turned her face toward Freddy and pressed herself against him, hiding herself from the harshness of the wind and the chill. He wrapped his arms around her and held her there, and she pressed her face against his chest. She could smell the sea, and when she gently kissed his coat, she could taste the salt spray.

The wind continued its fierce assault coming in clear and unobstructed off the ocean that roiled and tossed whitecaps on swells several feet just offshore. The water was a deep bluish green, and as they walked back along the craggy coast they could see a fishing boat making its way back toward Cleggan Harbor, just a mile farther up the coast.

They walked carefully along the shore, up the rocky terrain and then, precipitously, down again, cautiously looking over the edge as the cliff fell away thirty feet to the sea. The wind and the cold made them hurry along the coast, then follow the perimeter of a small inlet, where the cottage was set on a bluff. It was a small, two-room place, primitive in its mortar-and-wood construction, but solid and well made. The large fireplace in the main room kept the cottage warm and the sturdy walls kept out the wind and cold. The furnishings were modest—a sofa, rocking chair, a wooden kitchen table and chair. But it suited them perfectly for it afforded complete privacy. There were no neighbors for several miles in any direction, save for cows that would occasionally wander across one of the vast grazing areas nearby.

"Ah, I'll get us some tea," Freddy said, as they arrived back at the cottage, welcoming the warmth of the fire and hanging their damp wool coats and hats just inside the door.

Sophie stood facing the fireplace, rubbing her hands together, then turning around and feeling the warmth against her back. She felt a kick inside and thought that her stomach seemed even larger since the day before, and she sat in the rocking chair, holding herself, moving her hands around to one spot, pressing, then moving to the next spot feeling for any kicks or movements.

Freddy brought the tea and presented it to her and they sat, gazing into the fire, sipping the hot, sweet liquid. They were calm now. They had gotten past the worst of times, the time of what felt like unending sorrow. Sorrow that, at times, Sophie had felt could not be endured.

They had made their way to London where they had been interviewed at some length by officials at the

International Committee for the Red Cross. Sophie provided many details about Theresienstadt, while Freddy reported on the property confiscation program. He told of what he had heard about the conference at Wannsee, about the logistics of extermination.

It had been in London, as well, that they had both received medical attention. Freddy's leg would heal reasonably well, according to the orthopedist, though he would have to endure a limp and some degree of pain for the rest of his life. For Sophie, the medical news was that she was simply too far along to do anything about the pregnancy.

In London, Freddy made arrangements to rent the cottage and they made their way to Ireland. It suited their needs, for they wished only to be left alone, to spend time with each other, and to be able, in solitude, to determine what to do with their lives. For three months, Freddy had feared for Sophie's emotional stability. She would cry for prolonged periods, sobbing for her parents.

Every now and again they would travel into town for supplies. The newspapers would bring word of the horror of the extermination camps, and Sophie would be devastated by such reports.

"Why has this happened to so many people, Freddy, and not to me?" she would ask. "Why were they all sent to such an unspeakable end and I am here, alive?"

Once when he fumbled for an explanation and he talked of humans not always understanding God's ways, she grew furious and ridiculed him for his faith.

"If there is a God then what do you think now of his benevolence?" she shouted at him, slamming the

International Herald Tribune report on Treblinka down
on the table.

There was nothing he could say or do at such a time.
He would seek only to support her and soothe her. He
did not know precisely what she had been through, but
there were times when he would sit and use his powers of
concentration to try to work through, in his mind, what
her life had been like from the time she and her parents
boarded the train at Anhalter Station to the time he arrived at Theresienstadt to take her away. He wanted to
understand her and to provide strength for her, and to do
so, he would have to have infinite patience. And so he
would try to imagine what her life had been like; what
she had been through with her mother, the indignities . . .
the compromises. And as mightily as he tried, using the
details she had told him about, he realized that it was impossible to understand the horror fully unless one had
lived through it. And so he stopped trying and altered his
tack. He worked and prayed for infinite patience and understanding. He prayed most, though, to be able to accept the child to be born.

Freddy discovered a tiny church three miles from the cottage where Mass was held several days per week. And
though it was a Catholic service, he did not care; it was a
service and he needed ritual; he needed the connection to
faith and to God that ritual helped to elicit within him. It
was a chapel not unlike the one in which they had married back in England, soon after arriving there. And so,
three days per week, Freddy would walk to the chapel
for morning Mass and he would remain in the back row
of the small, wooden structure, and listen to the wind
whistle through the cracks in the wall and to the

muttered Latin from the old priest who came to this out-post by horse and buggy. Freddy would see the same few people each time, all much older than he, farmers, he guessed, and sheep herders. And it did not matter that Freddy understood little of the Latin, and did not grasp some symbolic aspects of the ritual; what mattered to him was the ritual of praying, connecting with God.

And each time that he went, he prayed with all of the intensity he could muster, to be able to provide support and understanding for his wife. And he prayed to be able to accept the child.

When the first indications of labor were apparent, Freddy went to the home of the midwife three and a half miles away, and she rode swiftly back along the twisting roads in a horse-drawn carriage, Freddy at her side. It was late afternoon when she arrived, and Sophie's dis-comfort was just beginning. The midwife, Mrs. Daly, was in her late forties and had delivered hundreds of ba-bies. She took over the cottage in a quiet way, with a strength and confidence that could be felt. She seemed tireless. Throughout the night, as Sophie screamed in agony, terrifying Freddy in the process, a self-assured smile never left the face of Mrs. Daly.

She was calm and deliberate, and it was not until the early morning, in the darkness just before dawn, that she became intense, urging Sophie to push ever harder, and harder still, and then still more forcefully until, finally, just as the sun's rays appeared over the water, the baby was born.

There had been many nights when she had lain awake and felt not sorrow so much as fury, unmeasurable anger at the thing inside of her. She had despised it. She felt not just anger, but dread, as well, for she could not imagine this baby as a child, a child she would have to raise and who would remind her every moment of the past. She had wished, so often, that she could have destroyed it.

But that had changed in the instant of birth. When Mrs. Daly cleaned the baby and wrapped her in a soft cotton blanket and handed her to Sophie, Sophie held her and looked at her and, as shafts of sunlight broke into the room, she felt a great love for this child who had come from her own womb.

In the late morning, Mrs. Daly had gone home, but before she had done so, she had said what Sophie would hear hundreds of times in the years to come: "She looks so much like her mum."

One day, while the baby was napping, Sophie sat down at the wooden table and began writing in a thick, black-and-white notebook. When Freddy asked about it she told him that she had some ideas, some thoughts she wanted to try to work through. Late each morning and afternoon the baby would nap for two hours and Freddy would urge Sophie to do the same, but she said she wasn't at all tired and she would instead sit at the table and write in her notebook, hour after hour. Soon it was filled and a new notebook was purchased and then that, too, was filled and had to be replaced. By that point, Sophie said she had made all of the notes she wanted to and was engaged in writing a story that would, in time, become *Midnight on Kurfurstendamm*.

Where once she had felt terrible guilt, now she felt blessed. Sophie realized she could choose the past or the future; she could choose the darkness or the light; death or life.

She chose life. For she believed that she had a responsibility to get outside of the dark, ominous place within her that was memory, that was the past; she had a responsibility to the baby, to Freddy, and to herself, as well.

She was healing, she knew. She had come a long way. And Sophie had come to believe that their life together would be all right. That they would be able to provide the baby with comfort and protection. And they wished to do this, they decided, in America, for that was the place where freedom was all around you. It was a place of opportunity. A place where immigrants were welcome.

Sophie knew that their life would be all right when Freddy returned from Mass one morning and entered the cottage. The baby was sitting up, struggling to stand.

Freddy smiled down at her and reached his arms out, and the baby smiled and reached her arms up, and Freddy scooped her up and held her, and said, "My daughter."

39

When Sophie was finished speaking, the room fell silent. Diane glanced down at her wristwatch. Her mother had spoken without interruption for one hour and twenty-seven minutes. In that time Sophie had told her story—the story of her life in Berlin, of meeting Freddy, of their secret relationship. She talked of going to Theresienstadt, of struggling to keep herself and her mother alive. There were parts she left out, of course. She did not mention Heidler. She said little about the time she and Freddy spent in Cleggan. But she had told much of the story, most of the story, and when she was done she folded her hands on her lap and she sat staring down at the brown spots on her knuckles.

The grandfather clock in the Wahljaks' living room was the loudest sound that could be heard. On this warm summer evening the spacious living room in the Wahljaks' Victorian home was cool and pleasant. Sophie sat in an easy chair covered in green chintz. To her left sat Diane in a wing chair. To Sophie's right was Freddy, in a wheelchair. Across from Sophie on the sofa sat Gerald Wahljak and his mother. Though no one had spoken during Sophie's recounting, every now and then, as Sophie recalled some detail, Gerta Wahljak would shake her head in sorrow. When Sophie talked of the fate that befell her own parents Gerta wiped tears from her eyes.

"My mother and I want to thank you, Mrs. Naumann, for coming to our home and for taking the time to recount to us, as you have, what is a very moving . . ." Gerald took a deep breath, clearly affected by what Sophie had said. "Story," he said, clearing his throat.

"When Diane and I discussed the possibility of this meeting I told her that if we were to do this it would be important to me that I be able to pose certain questions to you, Mr. Schillinghaussen. If it's all right with you, I would like to do that now." As he said this Gerald looked from Freddy toward Diane, who nodded her assent. She and Gerald had had two lengthy conversations prior to this gathering in which they had worked out informal ground rules. Both sought to protect their parents. Diane, in particular, wanted to make sure her father would not be subjected to unduly harsh criticism.

But Diane believed even risking such criticism was worth it, for she held a strong conviction that her parents would forever be demonized by the Wahljaks unless they were to come face-to-face and tell their story. To speak truthfully about the past would help the Wahljaks see them in a more human dimension. When they had arrived and Gerta had turned away at the sight of Freddy, Diane had feared the whole thing would disintegrate. But Gerta had sat close to her son on the sofa and, as Sophie had talked, Gerta had grown calmer.

"May I ask, Mr. Schillinghaussen," Gerald said in a respectful tone, "why did you take the position at the Reich Ministry of Justice? When you learned of the assignment, why did you not seek another position?"

Freddy nodded his head. Yes, he understood the question. He'd known it was coming.

"I want to answer your question as honestly as I can," Freddy said, his voice betraying a residual weakness from his stroke. He spoke slowly, deliberately, choosing each word carefully, all the while looking directly at Gerald.

"But I want you to know that in my candor there may be part of my answer that is offensive to you. Perhaps to your mother and even to my wife and daughter, as well. And, it is something that, to me, is offensive. Now. In retrospect . . . well, in retrospect it is all so clear. But some of it was not so clear then."

Freddy paused briefly to catch his breath.

"When I was growing up, at home and in school it was believed and it was taught that the Jews had damaged Germany and needed to be . . . punished or contained, if you will. It was an article of faith in Germany that the Jews had had a negative impact on the country in many ways. That they had accumulated too much economic power, had too many coveted positions in academia, and that that should be controlled. Did I disagree with that prevailing thought?"

Freddy shook his head no. "I am sorry to say that I did not think about it very carefully. I did not take the time to examine it very closely, to subject it to any kind of scrutiny," he said. "Few did. And those that did tended to be Communists, and Communists were despised.

"The idea that the Jews were to be punished—this was not a radical concept. This was not something I found offensive. I feel a great sadness in saying this, in admitting it, but it is true."

Freddy paused again to take a deep breath.

"In time, of course, I saw the truth," he continued. "Through Sophie I learned that the Jewish people were like any others. I came to believe that what we had been taught about the Jews was a lie. But I learned that only after meeting Sophie. Only after I came to love her.

"But in answer to your question why I did not decline the assignment I was given at the Reich Ministry of Justice. I did not do so because I did not—and, again, I am sorry this is the case but it is the case—I did not see a compelling reason to do so. I believed it was wrong, but there were many wrongs at the time."

Gerald shifted uncomfortably in his chair, frowning at what he was hearing.

"Also, such things were not done," he said. "Some historians I've read say that dissent of that sort was not in the German character." Freddy shrugged. "Perhaps that is so. But more than that, I think, for so long we believed—I believed and my friends believed and I know many Jews believed—that what was happening in our country to the Jews would pass. That the backlash against them would go so far and no further, and then that would all calm down and we would return to normal life. I believed that for a very long time and I think most Germans believed that. The idea of a final solution . . ." He looked down at the floor and shook his head. "This was not known. It simply was not known. Not before 1942, not before the Wannsee Conference.

"But before that, before there was any general knowledge that Jews were being killed, I had only one mission and that was to put myself in a position where I could wait for Sophie. Wait for her to come back from the east. When I learned what was happening . . ."

There was a tightness in Gerald's voice when he spoke.

"You could have taken another position, though, sought another position," Gerald said.

Freddy nodded his agreement. "I could have," he said.

"Or you could have chosen to act against the regime," Gerald said.

"Yes," Freddy said. "I could have."

"Why didn't you?" Gerald asked.

Freddy knitted his brow and considered the question. "Because I suppose I believed that National Socialism would pass. And because I saw a colleague, another lawyer who sought to help a Jewish physician and his family. He altered records for the family and provided them with papers indicating they were of Aryan descent. And . . ."

Freddy had to pause for a moment to take a breath. "He was taken away by the SS."

Freddy looked across the room toward the windows.

"It was important to me to be beyond suspicion," Freddy said. "I make no pretension of bravery. Of any sort of heroism. Quite the contrary. I cared only about Sophie. And so I remained above suspicion. Had I not I would never have been permitted to travel to Terezin."

"You had power," Gerald said. "Power that you could have used to do good."

Gerald's eyes were hooded. He was plainly angry, working to control his anger.

"You could have used your position to save lives, possibly," Gerald continued. "Could you have saved five lives, or ten? Or fifty lives? Fifty Jews? I suspect you could have. Could one of them have been a child? A child who would grow up to become a scientist, a physician who finds a cure for cancer? A brilliant little Jewish child. Saved by you."

Gerald stared, his face tight and reddening. "Could that child have died because you failed to act?"

Freddy faced him, looked back at him, silent.

"And so in retrospect what I did was wrong," Freddy continued. "I abetted the government in its persecution of the Jewish people. It is true. And I am sorry." He looked at Gerta Wahljak, looked into her eyes, and said, "I am sorry, Mrs. Wahljak. I say to you as one human being to another, I am sorry for what I did. But I did it because I loved Sophie more than anything in the universe. I loved her more than life itself . . ." Freddy shut his eyes for a moment and, when he opened them, tears trickled down his cheeks. "I did it for love. And, in a way, I know it was wrong. But I must also say to you that I would do it all over again."

Gerald led his mother upstairs to her room, where she sat down to rest. He and Diane spoke in the hallway.

"I can tell when she's overdoing it," he said. "She's resting now, but she insisted that she be able to come back down in a little while. So if you don't mind waiting a few minutes."

"Of course," Diane said. "We'll just . . ."

"Just stay right where you are," he said, "or, if you'd prefer, perhaps you'd like some fresh air."

"That would be good," Diane said. Diane pushed her father's wheelchair across a flagstone terrace with Sophie walking alongside. They stopped at the end of the terrace where there were two lawn chairs. Diane and her mother sat down, and the three of them were silent for a long moment.

Diane looked at her father, who sat silently looking across the lawn. "You OK?" she asked him.

He nodded. "I'm OK," he said.

"You?" Diane asked, looking to her mother.

"Oh, yes," she said. "I think this is good." Sophie hesitated. "But I wonder how you are?" she asked. "Is there anything . . ."

Diane turned to her father. "I'd like to hear more about the man you worked with who was taken away," she said. "What was his name?"

Freddy seemed surprised. But he did not hesitate in responding, did not have to search his memory for the name. "Ernst Strasser," Freddy said. "He was in the office next to mine. He'd been out of the university maybe three years. I was not there the day they came for him, but I was told that two SS officers arrived and took him away. He had forged identity papers for a Jewish family—people who he'd known all his life. I think a doctor and his family. And when the papers were discovered to be false, they somehow learned that he had been involved."

Freddy stopped speaking and looked down at his feet, propped on the runners of the wheelchair.

"And so he was taken away," Diane said.

Freddy nodded.

"And killed," she said.

Freddy nodded again.

"What did you think of what he had done?" Diane asked.

Freddy looked at her and thought for a moment. "What do I think now, or what did I think then?" Freddy asked.

"Both," Diane said.

"Now, I think of it as a noble gesture," he said. "Then, I thought it was reckless."

Diane cocked her head and shot him a quizzical look. "Reckless?"

"I wanted to be above suspicion," he said. "To be above suspicion was to acquire the power to deceive. To be above suspicion I did my job as well as I could do it. In so doing, I was in a position to act as I did."

"But . . ."

"I cared only about being with your mother," he continued. "There was war. There were people dying and suffering everywhere. I did not want your mother and me to be among them. I wanted us to live, to have a life. For us to be together, this, to me, was a noble goal, Diane. This was something to fight for. I was willing to die for your mother. But for no one else."

Diane blinked at the naked candor of his statement.

"It would have been far nobler, I know, to be willing to die for an idea, or a cause, or for others, strangers to me," he said. "But that was not in my nature. It was not that I hated anyone. It was that I loved someone."

"Do you regret it?" Diane asked, the words escaping her mouth before she was sure she wanted to pose the question. "I know what you said inside, but . . . do you ever?"

Freddy looked across at the cluster of birch trees and studied them for a moment.

"Being sure is hard," he said. "Being absolutely certain—that is not an easy place to get to. When the questions are difficult ones, even profound, then certainty is elusive. There have certainly been moments of regret for me. Of doubt. But if I were faced with the same circumstances all over again . . ." He shrugged. "I would do it the same way."

* * *

"It's good that they are coming here," Gerta said, nodding for emphasis. "This is the good thing." She tilted her head to one side and looked at Sophie. "We are alike in some of the ways," she said. "We are Jews who wanted only to have life, to have in life our families and to be free and safe. What for we need anything else?"

Sophie nodded.

"I want to forgive," Gerta said, looking at Freddy. "This is not so easy to do. But I am happy you have come here and I am hoping that again next week you will come and visit us and we will talk some more. Is this possible?"

"Oh, yes," Sophie said, brightening. "We would be honored to do that."

"Forgiveness is not so easy sometimes," Gerald said. "But forgiveness is like peace in a way. You don't make peace with your friends."

In the end, there would be forgiveness, Diane saw. But it would not be easy and it would not come quickly. But come, it would. Diane knew this when, as they were leaving, Gerald took her aside and said he would be placing a call to the U.S. Attorney's Office to inform Stone that his mother would not go ahead as a willing witness in the investigation.

Keegan was not surprised when he received the message from Diane's mother. She had sounded hesitant on his answering machine, but he had known the call would come; that whatever reticence she felt would be overcome. He called her back and she invited him to her home.

Sophie made her way to the garden, her heart pounding.

"Ah, David, so nice to see you," she said. "I appreciate your willingness to come over."

"I'm happy to do it," he said.

She nodded and glanced down at her hands, folded on her lap.

"David, what you have done for us is a wonderful and generous thing," she said. "It's a noble act, I believe. And I know that you did not do it for us, really, but that you did it for Diane. It is clear to me that you must love her very much."

"I do," David said quietly.

"I know you do," Sophie said, "and I think she is very lucky indeed. Very lucky. To have someone love you like that . . . it is a very great thing."

She paused and looked Keegan in the eye. "I say that from experience," she said. "I have had someone who loved me beyond all else. We have been through a lot together, my Freddy and I. And he has shown a love for me and a devotion that most people would not understand, I don't think. And he has shown a love for Diane and a devotion to her that is . . . that it would be a crime to see affected in any way.

"Am I making sense?" she asked.

Keegan nodded.

"So I guess I wanted to talk with you in confidence here to see if there was anything that you might have discovered during your digging into the Theresienstadt archive that might in any way be something that could be hurtful or disruptive or . . ."

"Yes," Keegan said. He stared at her intently and nodded his head. "Yes, Mrs. Naumann," he said. "I found the documents you're talking about."

She froze. Her heart pounded.

Keegan removed two sheets of paper from his inside jacket pocket and handed them to her.

Sophie Naumann looked down at her medical record, then she looked at the birth record that showed Diane being born six months later.

"It's the original," he said. "I took it from the archive. No other copy exists."

Her eyes widened.

"You mean . . ."

"I have always intended to give it to you, but I wasn't quite sure how to do that," he said. "I have of course said nothing to Diane. Nor would I. Nor will I. Ever. If you wished to talk with her that is something you must decide. I assume you won't; that it is your desire that she never know."

Tears flowed slowly down Sophie's cheeks and she sniffled. She wiped one away with her hand.

"Thank you, David," she said. "Thank you for this. How can I ever thank you enough?"

40

Dick Keegan wore a green hospital johnny, tied loosely in the back. He sat up in his bed with some difficulty and winced at the pain that movement caused. David stood by the side of the bed, holding his father by the shoulders, helping him shift around.

"You OK?" David asked.

"Yuh, yuh," Dick said, his voice hoarse.

"You know, we can go down to the chapel," David said. "I mean, it's an elevator ride away. Easy."

Dick shook his head as vigorously as he could manage. "No, no," he said. "Leahy's. I want Leahy's."

By Leahy's Dick meant the small stone chapel where Father Edward Leahy presided. Leahy was a very old man, well into his eighties, who said the Latin Mass each day for a small but loyal flock. The Latin Mass had been outlawed in the church some years back, after Vatican II, but there were stubborn Catholics out there who refused to switch and Leahy was among them. Dick Keegan had known Leahy back in his days on the police department when Leahy had been the department chaplain.

"Then Leahy's it is," David said. He took a pair of boxer shorts and held them out, helping his father step into them. When his father did so, stepping onto the

333

floor, he grimaced in pain. David helped him get into a pair of pants, and then put a flannel shirt on him, doing all the buttons. He placed socks and shoes on his father's feet and helped him slide from the edge of his bed into a wheelchair a foot away.

Dick settled uneasily into the chair.

"You OK?" David asked.

"Good," Dick grunted.

"Here we go," David said, wheeling his father out of the room and down the hallway to the elevators. As they moved slowly along, Dick acknowledged several nurses and another patient.

They rode the elevator to the ground floor and David wheeled his father carefully through the crowded lobby out the main entrance. He opened the passenger door of his car, and he and a security guard standing nearby combined to ease Dick into the front seat. David folded the wheelchair and placed it in the trunk of his car, then went around and fastened his father's seat belt and closed his door. They set off through the city traffic under gray skies. Dense storm clouds had moved in over the city and rain had threatened. But now it seemed a storm was imminent. Thunder rumbled nearby and David could see flashes of lightning just to the west.

"Rain's coming," Dick said.

David glanced up at the sky. "I think you're right, Dad," he said.

They drove out the Jamaicaway, following it past the Pond and up Centre Street into Roslindale. As they drove the rain started to fall, gently enough at first, but then it seemed the clouds were turned on their sides and emptied, for a downpour came that was so severe that visibility was all but eliminated. David gripped the steering wheel tightly with both hands and leaned forward in his seat, peering hard through the driving rain, able to see the car directly in front of him and nothing more.

From Centre Street they cut over toward the arboretum and then down a side street to the chapel. When they pulled to a stop out front, the rain was pounding down loudly on the roof of the car. David shut off the engine and glanced at his father, who was clearly in pain. Dick Keegan had passed up his last two scheduled doses of painkiller so that he would be as lucid as possible at the Mass. But with his clear-mindedness had come terrible pain.

"We're here," Dick muttered.

"Nice and early," David said. "Mass doesn't start for fifteen minutes. Would you be more comfortable here or inside, Dad?"

"Inside," Dick said.

"Good," David said.

He got out of the car and retrieved an umbrella from the trunk. He held it over his head with one hand while he struggled with the other hand to unfold the wheelchair and lock it into place. He wheeled it around the side of the car and opened his father's door, holding the umbrella over the wheelchair at the same time. David held the umbrella up while reaching down to help his father out of the car, but, as he did so, David half knelt on one side of the wheelchair and heard a sudden snap. He looked down and saw that a metal bar supporting the chair on one side had broken. The thing sagged uselessly to the side.

"Whoa, hold on, Dad," David said. "I think this thing's broken." David squatted down, the rain driving

down soaking his back. "Yeah, this is gone, I'm afraid,"
David said.

He glanced at his father and saw a look of terrible disappointment in his eyes, a childlike disappointment as
though all of life had now been ruined.

"What'll we do?" Dick asked, a note of desperation in
his voice.

"Don't worry, Dad," David said. "We'll be fine."

David took the chair back around and placed it into
the trunk. He went back around to his father's side and
leaned into the car.

"Can you hold this?" David asked, showing his father
the umbrella.

Dick nodded. "I think so," he said.

"Good," David said. "OK, Dad. You've got a big strong
son here and this is what we'll do. I'll scoop you up, and
you'll hold the umbrella, and we'll walk right up the
walkway into the church. Sound OK to you?"

"Sure," Dick said, weakly.

"OK, ready, one, two, three," and with that, David
lifted his father off the seat, cradling him, David's left
arm under his father's neck and back, his right arm under
the back of his knees.

David stepped back out of the car and stood straight
up and, as he did so, a gust of wind tugged the umbrella
from Dick Keegan's frail hands and it was carried into
the air and then quickly crashed to the pavement.

"Ooh," Dick said.

"Don't worry, Dad," David said, as they were pelted
by the downpour. "It's OK."

David moved as swiftly as he was able up the walkway
leading to the chapel, but they were exposed long
enough to get soaked through their clothes. David had

difficulty getting the church door open, but he was finally able to do so and he stepped inside, standing still as he waited for his eyes to begin to adjust to the near darkness of the chapel. It was a small room with no more than twenty rows of pews, a small altar, and a row of votive candles to the right of the altar, down toward the first row of pews.

Once his eyes had adjusted some, David walked carefully down the aisle and chose a pew halfway back on the right.

"This OK?" he asked his father.

"Good," the old man said.

David stepped into the pew and leaned over, placing his father gently down on the bench. Dick settled down and David could see him wincing. David slid him down to the end of the bench and wedged him into the corner so that Dick was leaning against the wood in back and on the side. That way he could sit up without being held by David.

David smelled incense and thought back to when he was a child in Catholic school, when he was forced to go to church and when that smell was sure to make him feel nauseated. But now it comforted him because it was the smell of ritual, of coming together to pray. Others began gathering in the church as time for Mass drew near. Most were elderly men and women for whom the change to an English Mass was too jarring, who needed the familiar Latin Mass to feel as though they were participating in a true sacrament.

David looked up to the front of the church and watched the rows of candles in squat red holders cast their soft light. Each time the door opened and the wind blew in, the flames of some of the candles would dance up the cool, smooth stone walls of the church, giving the place an eerily medieval feel.

David glanced down at his father and noticed he was shivering.

"I've got a sweater in the car," David said. "Be right back, Dad."

Dick Keegan nodded. David quickly retrieved the sweater. He placed it over his father's head and then worked his father's arms into the sleeves.

Dick Keegan then said something that David could not quite hear. Something about a handle, David thought.

"Candle," Dick said, more emphatically this time. "I want to light . . ."

"You want to light a candle?" David said.

Dick nodded his head.

"Sure," he said. David slid his arms underneath his father's back and knees and lifted him, walking slowly down the aisle to the front of the chapel. The others in the church, perhaps a dozen or fifteen people, were kneeling and praying and took little notice of this strange sight.

The candles could not be reached from the front bench, so David knelt down, holding his father in his arms, as Dick reached out and took hold of the long wax stick and held it in one flame, waiting for it to ignite, and then slid it to the side, his hand trembling, and attempted to light another candle. He was unable to hold his hand still enough to get it to ignite, however. David could not help because he needed both hands to hold his father. At that moment an old woman stepped forward and gently took hold of Dick's hand and steadied it over a particular candle, and it was lit. She smiled at both the men.

"Thank you," David said. She nodded and returned to her seat.

Dick closed his eyes and made a sign of the cross and prayed. Soon, he opened his eyes and looked at his son and nodded.

David walked slowly back to the pew and placed his father back down on the bench.

At that moment, Father Leahy appeared on the altar and began the Mass. He moved swiftly through the prayers, the blessings, the liturgy. When he moved to the altar to distribute communion, Dick nudged David and nodded to him. He wished to receive the Eucharist.

"Me, too," David said, smiling at his father. Once again he carried him in his arms and walked slowly down the aisle, getting in line behind eight or ten others. When they shuffled to the head of the line, Fr. Leahy paused before placing the host on Dick's tongue. The old priest winked at Dick, though David was not sure he noticed it, then gave communion to the son.

When the Mass was ended, the others were quickly gone, but Dick Keegan wanted to remain seated in the pew for a few minutes. David sat patiently next to him, pressed against his father's side, wedging him in so he would not fall over.

"You don't look like yourself, Dick," said a voice from the front of the church. Fr. Leahy, having removed his vestments and wearing black with his Roman collar, walked down the aisle toward where they sat.

He moved into the pew to get a closer look. He extended his hand to Dick, who reached out tentatively and shook weakly.

"No, Padre," Dick Keegan said, "I don't feel that good."

Dick nodded toward David. "My son," he said. "Big shot lawyer."

Leahy extended his hand and shook with David Keegan. "I've read about you," he said. "Your father must be very proud of you."

Dick nodded. "I am," he whispered. "I am."

"Well, God bless you for making the effort to come here today," the priest said. "He will bless you for that. You have sacrificed to come here. He can see that, and He appreciates it. He will bless you for it."

The priest nodded. "You see any of the old gang?" the priest asked, meaning fellow cops.

Dick shrugged. "Not so much," Dick Keegan said.

"Jazz comes by sometimes," the priest said. "You remember Jazz Mannering."

"Sure," Dick said, nodding.

"How long have you two known each other?" David asked the priest.

"Oh, jeez, quite a number of years back," Leahy said. "Well, of course, I married your mother and father, so since before then."

David felt stricken. He had not known that.

"I didn't know," he said weakly.

"Oh, sure," Leahy said. He shook his head. "She's with God now, of course."

Dick nodded. David looked away, focused on the shadows of flames climbing the stone wall.

"Padre, I wonder if you would hear my confession?" Dick asked.

"Certainly," Leahy said. "Now?"

Dick nodded.

"I'll wait in the back," David said.

"Fine," the priest said. "I'll get my stole." He went to

the sacristy and got his stole and returned to the pew and said a brief prayer. Then he leaned down so his ear was within a foot and a half of Dick Keegan's mouth.

David could hear the sound of whispering, but no words. What was he saying? David wondered. What were the sins he was confessing? What could he be saying at this stage of his life that might lead to redemption? David was not one who recalled much that he had read through the years, but he had always remembered the poignance of Sophocles' remark that "the greatest griefs are those we cause ourselves." Of course it was true. And that was why Dick Keegan's life had been so hard, so difficult. But David did not wish now to add to his father's grief; he wished to comfort him; to soothe him and lessen his pain.

David watched as his father whispered to the priest. Father Leahy listened intently, saying nothing for a long time. Finally, the priest spoke. Then he straightened up and made the sign of the cross over Dick Keegan.

David walked back to their pew.

"Well, then, bless you both," Leahy said. "Take good care of your father now, David."

David sat down next to Dick and began sliding his hands in behind him, but Dick held up his hand, asking his son to hold off.

"I want to tell you something, Davey," the father said. He looked down at his hands, then glanced up and looked into the eyes of his son. His brow was knitted and he was in obvious pain. He looked pleadingly at his son.

"Davey, I have done so much wrong . . ." he began, then struggled for breath. "People who say they have no regrets . . ." He shook his head in disbelief. "I don't know how . . . I have so many."

He winced from the pain. ". . . So many," he said, shaking his head. "But no one is to blame but me, Davey," he continued. "Only me. But there is one regret, son, that I . . ." And at this point the mere thought of it was too much for Dick Keegan, too heavy a weight for his fragile psyche.

"Son, I . . ." the father said, struggling to compose himself, struggling unsuccessfully, as he was overcome by emotion, crying like an inconsolable child. He wept and then he struggled to control himself enough to be able to say to his son, "There is something I have to tell you, Davey, something terrible that I did . . ." and he cried some more.

And so David Keegan now knew the truth. And in knowing the truth he felt now that he understood his father. Dick Keegan had covered up the truth of the accident all these years and it had destroyed him. He had deprived his sons of their mother when they were children. He had done it. No one else. It had been his fault. And afterward he could not live with himself. He had grown to so despise himself, to so hate what he had done, that he had destroyed himself, his own life. The poison that was his anger had killed him.

David gently rubbed his father's back and spoke in a soft tone. "I know, Dad," he said. "I know about it."

Suddenly, the father's eyes widened and he sat stunned, gazing in disbelief at his son. He shook his head, not understanding.

"How . . . ?"

"I've been talking with people," David said. "I needed to find out. To know. I needed to know while you were alive so that I could tell you how sad it makes me. How much it hurts me. But I want to also tell you that I forgive you, Dad. And I love you."

Dick Keegan closed his eyes upon hearing his son's words and he nodded very slowly and deliberately, and he placed his hands on his face, and said in a whisper, "Thank you. Thank you."

And David Keegan took his father in his arms and brought him to his chest and held him tightly. Dick Keegan gazed up at his son. The old man was openmouthed, grayish in color. He tried to say something, but was unable. And it was then, in his son's arms, that he died.

41

David Keegan followed the West Roxbury Parkway down through Holy Name Circle and across the railroad tracks. He turned left off the parkway on to Belgrade Avenue. He drove slowly along Belgrade, past Clay Chevrolet on his left, several blocks down past Silver Welding nearly to the corner of Newberg. He pulled over to the side of the street and parked.

He knew from studying the pictures precisely where it had happened and he walked slowly to that point on the sidewalk. He stood there, hands in his pants pockets, and looked down Belgrade Avenue. The traffic was light in either direction. There were kids on the sidewalks, residents of the two- and three-family homes and apartment houses along the street. There was a little boy—Keegan guessed he was about seven—pedaling toward him, watching him.

"Watcha doin'?" the kid asked. He stood half straddling his bike, one foot on the pavement, the other on a pedal.

"Oh, me? I'm just looking around," Keegan said. He looked at the little boy, a pasty-faced kid with a few freckles and fiery red hair.

"You don't look so happy," the boy said.

Keegan was startled by this, jarred by it. "No?" he said. The kid shook his head no.

Keegan smiled. "How about now?" he asked.

"Better," the boy said. "I like it when people are happy."

"Yeah, me, too," Keegan said. "We sure agree on that."

"What's your name?" Keegan asked.

"David," the boy said. "What's yours?"

Keegan laughed. "Mine's David, too," he said.

"Yeah," the boy said, "I know two other Davids. One on Tindale and one on Guernsey.

"Well, I'm not really supposed to be talkin' to strangers," the boy said. "But my sister's over there. She's older. So I guess it's OK."

"I'm sure she won't mind this once," Keegan said. "Besides, you were just being nice."

The kid thought about it for a second. "Yeah, I guess," he said. "Well, see ya."

"Yeah," Keegan said. "It was nice meeting you, David. You take care, OK?"

"I will," the boy said, and rode off.

Keegan watched him as he rode slowly down the block and turned onto Newberg Street. Keegan walked slowly along until he reached the corner. He stood near a telephone pole and looked up the street, imagining the car coming down, careening out of control, crashing. Was this the pole, or had it been replaced at some point through the years?

He did not know for sure, but he suspected this was the pole. He reached out and touched it with his fingers, then he placed his palm on it. It was odd. He felt a strange sensation. It had happened so very long ago. So much had gone on since then. And now he had to get on with his life. Knowing what had happened gave him a feeling of freedom. It would allow him to forge ahead, to live his life.

He thought of what the little boy had said—that he did not look happy. He had not been happy for he did not know how long. But he believed that would change. He believed that the years that lay ahead would be good ones; years spent with Diane in which they built a life together. Would he find the happiness that his mother had never had? Would he find the peace that had eluded his father until he was near death? He had a chance. He had a chance.

He suddenly realized he had forgotten something. He went back to his car and reached in the backseat. He took out a large bouquet of flowers. He walked back to the intersection of Belgrade and Newberg and squatted down next to the telephone pole. He laid the flowers on the pavement a few feet from the pole at a spot that he judged to be where she had lain on that night in 1954. He stood up and looked at the flowers, at the spot, and said a silent prayer.

Keegan turned to go knowing that his search was over. That his new life had begun.

Don't miss this riveting novel
by Charles Kenney

THE SON OF JOHN DEVLIN

"The dirty cop will inevitably reveal himself.
He'll always give off a sign, an indication."
Tough words to hear for detective Jack Devlin,
whose father apparently committed suicide
after being tied to the biggest scandal in
Boston's history. Now, more than twenty years
later, a letter from his dad surfaces, pushing
Devlin to reopen old wounds. Through con-
flicting emotions of anger and devotion, he
searches for truth, hoping to uncover the
secrets behind his father's infamous fall from
grace and tragic death. But what he finds
could bring the Boston police force to its
knees—and there are some who would kill to
keep history silent. . . .

"STUNNING . . . POWERFUL . . .
[A] well-plotted, moving thriller . . . filled
with tough, poignant portraits, disappearing
evidence, suspenseful stakeouts, and
unexpected plot twists."
—*Publishers Weekly* (starred review)